Blackbirds Sing

(A Ruadhán Sidhe Origin Story)

By Aiki Flinthart

2019

Thank you to the readers who have enjoyed my other books enough to leave nice reviews and to let me know. Because of you, I keep writing.

Thank you to my amazing beta readers who give me such fantastic ideas for how to improve – Rob, Darren, Caitlyn, Caroline, Neen.

Thankyou to Caitlyn for devoting so much time and love to the illustrations and making these women come to life.

To Traci Harding and Pamela Freeman –who were gracious enough to advance read for me – and to cry in all the right places.

And…as always…thanks to my husband for his patience and encouragement. Seriously. Patient. Unbelievably patient.

BLACKBIRDS SING

Cover artwork by Rosi Helms
Cover design by Lou Harper
Internal illustrations by Caitlyn McPherson
Copyright © 2019 Aiki Flinthart

> *All rights reserved. No part of this publication may be reproduced, stored in a retrieval system, or transmitted in any form or by any means, by any person or entity (including Google, Amazon or similar organisations) without the prior permission in writing of the copyright holder concerned, nor be otherwise circulated in any form of binding or cover other than that in which it is published and without a similar condition, including this condition, being imposed on the subsequent purchaser.*

A Cataloging-in-Publications entry for this title is available from the National Library of Australia.

ISBN-13: 978-0-9945928-6-6 (Trade Paperback)
ISBN-13: 978-0-9945928-5-9 (e-book)
Cat Press
PO Box 3388, Darra
QLD 4076, Australia

Contents

1486 London Map 6
1. Sing a Song for Sixpence 11
2. A Pocketful of Rye 29
3. Four and Twenty Blackbirds 45
4. Baked in a Pie 61
5. When the Pie was Opened 77
6. The Birds Began to Sing 93
7. Wasn't that a Dainty Dish 111
8. To Set Before the King? 127
9. The King was in His Counting-House 143
10. Counting Out His Money 163
11. The Queen was in the Parlour 179
12. Eating Bread and Honey 193
13. The Maid was in the Garden 205
14. Hanging out the Clothes 221
15. Along Came a Little Dog 233
16. And Nibbled Off Her Toes 249
17. And the Blackbird Still is Waiting 267
18. And Her Eyes Have All the Seeming 283
19. Of a Demon that is Dreaming 299
20. And the Lamplight O'er Her Streaming 315
21. Throws Her Shadow on the Floor 331
22. And My Soul, From Out that Shadow 351
23. That Lies Floating on the Floor 367
24. Shall be Lifted…Nevermore 387
25. Two and Twenty Blackbirds 409
Story Extras 433
Other books by Aiki Flinthart 443

1486 London Map

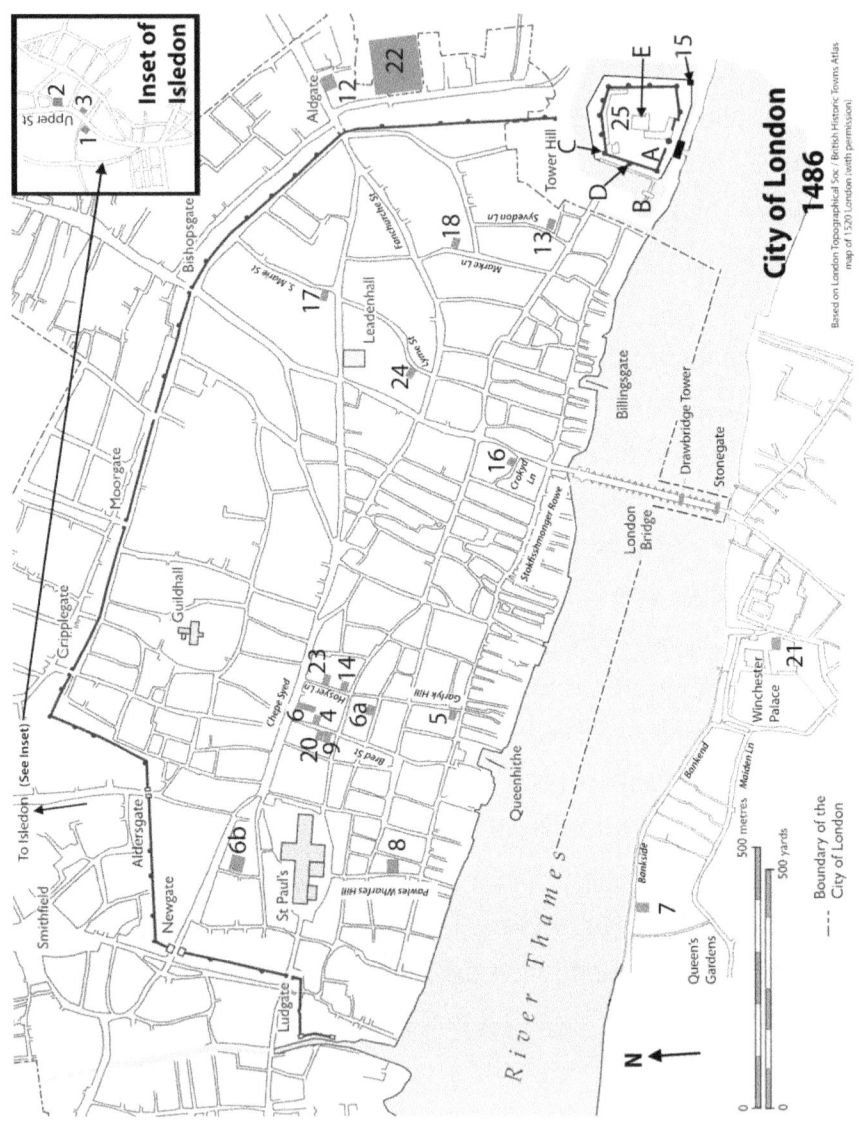

Key to London Map

Numbers also correlate to story number

Isledon Inset Map
1. King's Head, Isledon (Islington)
2. St Mary's Church, Isledon
3. House of Lizzie Brewster

London and Southbank Map

4. House/Bakery of Catherine Miller
5. Rundown boardinghouse/thieves haunt run by M ama Rolfe
6. The Broken Seld.
6a: Fellowship of Minstrel's Hall.
6b: Lovell's Inn (London residence of Lovell family – houses of the wealthy were often called 'Inn')
7. The Cygnet, stewhouse/bawd-house run by Eliza Parry
8. Derby House (London Residence of Lord Stanley, Earl of Derby)
9. House/Cahorsin shop (pawnbroker) owned by Cecily Hayward
10. (See #9, #6, and #20)
11. (See #6 The Broken Seld)
12. Emma Turner's honey farm
13. St Anna's Chapel (fictional name, real chapel) where Flora Leon meets Lovell and Edmund finds them together.
14. House/Laundry of Griselda Moor, laundress
15. Tower Leading to the Iron Gate (later named Develin Tower)
16. House of Thomasine Smithe, barber-surgeon
17. House of Scientia Wilson, student

18. House of Nicola Willoughby's parents: Christopher, 10th Baron Willoughby de Eresby and Margaret Jenney
19. (See #6 – the Broken Seld)
20. House/Candlemaker shop of Dorothy and Nick Jacobson
21. The Clink – Men's and women's prison attached to Winchester Palace (Bishop of Winchester's)
22. Abbey of St Clare without Aldgate (Franciscan)
23. House/Workshop of Olivia Grey, seamstress
24. House of Laura Kennet, midwife
25. The Tower of London
25. A: Queen's House   B: Barbican/menagerie/Lion Tower (Main entrance) C: Robin-the-Devil's tower (later named Devereaux Tower) D: Beauchamp's Tower   E: White Tower

Blackbirds Sing

Aiki Flinthart 2019

NOTE:
This book is written with AUSTRALIAN
SPELLING/ENGLISH,
not USA spelling/English.
Don't panic.

Some historical details have been deliberately changed in this alternate-world historical fantasy. Detailed notes at the end.

1. Sing a Song for Sixpence

Amsel Mór-Ríoghain, 432
Travelling minstrel
Village of Isledon (Islington),

Monday (afternoon), 18ᵗʰ September, 1486

In mid-September, the year of their Lord 1486, an old promise to a human carried me back to London when wisdom should have kept me away.

My mare plodded up the last rise, her head low, hooves scraping the dust. I shaded my eyes against the midday sun's cloud-hazed heat. Far in the distance, huddled up against the Thames, London's misery of buildings squatted beneath a miasma of smoke and hid behind the old Roman wall. Outside the barrier, a few buildings clung to the walls like poor relatives, begging for entry.

I paused on the ridge. Did I want to see the town again; to walk with Cormac's ghost through the same streets we'd lived in so happily? Not really.

What *did* I want there?

Perhaps a way to ensure lasting peace for my people. Perhaps to find redemption for failing to save Anne de Mortimer. Perhaps I was simply drifting—as I often did—following the vague premonitions that plagued my dreams.

Six bells in the church nearby tolled their delightful cadence. Dozens of churchbells in London joined in, their clashing clamour rolling around the valley, calling the faithful into churches and cathedrals in the city.

But still, I hesitated, letting their music cascade through me; flush out old memories. It had been decades since my last visit to London. But, with the Lancasters and Yorks settling their differences, I'd reluctantly come out of self-imposed exile and rejoined the world.

Partly to fulfil my promise to a dead woman, partly to see what progress had been made. Or not. Humans tended to do the same stupid things, just in new and creative ways.

I continued along the main street of Isledon, the certainty that had carried me this far fading. Reluctantly, I stopped at the King's Head, a neat timber-and-thatch hostelry. At least the green leaves hanging on the sign outside indicated a fresh batch of ale. The one thing I did miss about London was the variety of ales. Though I didn't want to know what went into some of them to produce their…unique flavours.

An urchin scurried out from the stables as I dismounted, and I threw him a farthing to care for my mare for the evening. A bone-crackling stretch eased the worst kinks in my back. Nearby woodland provided enough of the *sianfath's* cool green background energy to heal the saddle-bruises on my backside. I drew power, savouring the taste of cut grass and the ice-chill sensation prickling across my skin. It left me more refreshed than after a night's sleep.

That was the worst part about coming to London—the distance from the forests that provided my people with healing energy. I would need to find accommodation near one of the large private gardens.

I settled sword and dagger on my hips, collected my bow, saddlebags and gittern. Time to assume the guise of Alastair Morrigan, minstrel. To present my true self—Amsel, daughter of Mór-Ríoghain the Eire goddess and *sidhe* warrior—would be…unwise in these still-unrestful days.

I sauntered into the hostelry. The low-ceilinged room was lit by a dozen flickering oil lanterns and tallow candles. My sensitive eyes found comfort in the semi-gloom. The *sidhe* were of the forest, our eyes adapted to low light. The humans thought us fae and of the wyrd. We thought them plodding, oblivious to the world's needs, their lives brief and brutal.

And yet, here I was, trying to help them. Many of my kind would hate me for doing so. Even I wasn't certain I had chosen the right course. But a promise was a promise.

Inside the small room, five rough-hewn tables and benches crowded close around the central peat-fire. Smoke drifted up to the peaked, thatched roof and a cauldron of pottage bubbled over the low heat. The air was warm with the smell of cooking onions.

I nodded amicably to the few people scattered about the small room. They watched me with surly suspicion; a motley assemblage of farmers and tradesmen by the looks of their rough tunics and hands.

Under their scrutiny, I suppressed the urge to check my attire. It had been long since I'd donned male gear to purposefully deceive humans. My tunic, hose, and doublet were old-fashioned and plain. Not fine enough to tempt thieves, and cleverly tailored to hide my slight female attributes. With my hair cut to the collar and the few well-earned lines of four hundred years creasing my eyes, I appeared to be around thirty human years. Old enough to earn me respect. Young enough to make thieves think twice before attacking an armed man.

Perhaps the signature sharp features and dark-gold skin of my people caused a few of the townsfolk's narrow looks, but not enough to warrant the effort of maintaining a *glamour*. Cormac used to tell me I was lazy. He was probably right. But I'd always found simple lies were easier to remember, and casting a *glamour* was a complex lie, indeed.

So, I ignored the stares and approached the hearth-fire. Food and a place to sit was higher on my list than placating suspicious locals, anyway.

Something stirred the rushes strewn on the floor. A mongrel flop-eared dog emerged from under a table to snuffle at my boots. The bitch whined and pushed her nose into my palm. I patted her and the room's tension eased.

Interesting.

I collected a mug of ale from the innkeeper and paid for pottage and a room. After declining the offer of a heavy slab of dark rye bread, I took my bowl to one of the corner tables. Half-forgotten habits made me sit with my back to the wall and the entrances in sight. I smiled and sipped the thick ale. Cormac would be proud.

In the opposite corner, deep in shadow, three men glanced furtively at me and whispered amongst themselves. Two brothers—maybe in their late forties or fifties; I found it difficult to tell with humans. Both squat, surly, and dark-haired. Plus, a much younger lad with a riot of mouse-brown curls and a sullen, girlish face. Notably, the dog avoided them.

If I wanted, I could hear what they said, for my hearing was more acute than a human's. But I had no interest and they made no move to approach, so I ignored them. Strangers in a village were always the subject of gossip.

The door opened, pushing back the gloom, and three more men entered. One willow-lean with dark hair, one like a birch: pale, strong, with white-blond hair. The last was an oak: so tall and broad-shouldered he had to stoop and turn sideways to get through the low doorway. He paused and surveyed the room. His dark-rimmed grey eyes caught mine and he stilled. Recognition shocked through me leaving the faint taste of grass on my tongue and a chill of foreboding goosepimpling my skin.

Another *sidhe*. A complication I hadn't anticipated. Our people were scattered; driven far into the wildlands these days. London was the last place I expected to find another full-blood.

But was he Dark or Light *sidhe*? And what was he doing here?

He broke eye contact and followed his companions to join the three men whispering in the corner. More and more interesting. What was a *sidhe* doing in such company? The five humans were better-dressed than most in the room. Though their clothing was nothing more than basic tunic, hose and plain doublet, they were well-made and of fine cloth. Rich men playing at being poor? Or rich men hiding their meeting here in this tiny village. Why?

No. None of my business. I knew better than to get involved. I took a deep draught of ale. I was here to do a job. Then I could go home again and ignore humanity some more—hopefully until wisdom dawned in the species. Which could be a while. I was content to wait. Humans meant nothing to me.

Not anymore.

One of the men raised his voice in protest. Another shushed him and glanced nervously around. They smelled of trouble.

Reluctantly, I watched sidelong and extended my senses, listening with more than my ears. Their *sidhe* companion had strong mental shields in the form of a forbidding stone fortress. I left his mind well alone. He would feel any attempt to read his thoughts. Instead, I slid into the surface thoughts of the small, dark-haired man next to him. The others all looked to him as he spoke in earnest, low tones. His hands were white and slim, a massive garnet glinting on his little finger. And the sword at his hip bore rubies in the pommel. At a guess, he was the money behind whatever little venture they planned. Perhaps a minor nobleman, by the way the others bowed and scraped to him.

Ah, there. He actually thought of himself using his full title: Lord Francis Lovell. That changed the game, somewhat. Fortuitously, perhaps. Only time would tell.

I frowned, unable to dig beyond a few ghostly, superficial

thoughts. I checked the others. Surprisingly, every man in the group had basic mental shields in the shape of a plain, square house with no windows. But strong. Each one the same. The work of the *sidhe*? But why? Had he erected them because of my presence, or had he done it before?

I withdrew. What was I thinking? Surely I'd learned my lesson after Cormac's death. I downed half my ale in three long gulps, seeking to fill the hole left by the severance of my intimate connection with Cormac. Even after thirty years, I ached.

But I had given Anne de Mortimer my oath.

When I lowered the mug the big *sidhe* stood over me. He appeared to be about twenty human years—a tenth his real age, no doubt—his countenance handsome and open. I'd felt his approach, but he moved with remarkable silence. Clearly, he'd spent time in the forests, even if he lived amongst humans, now.

On closer inspection I revised my initial estimate of his age down to around one hundred years. He bore an air of intense certainty common amongst the younger, more idealistic of our people. Those who still thought they could save our world from the human tide of destruction. I had too, until wisdom prevailed. And hurt.

'Greetings,' I said. 'May I help you?'

He inclined his head and indicated a stool nearby. 'May I sit?'

I shrugged. 'Could I stop you? As you will. Tis of no matter to me.'

He pulled up the stool and placed his elbows on the table. 'You're of the Dark. Why are you here?'

I grabbed instinctively for my dagger. He held out a large hand, palm down.

'Nay. Draw not in here.' He indicated his table. 'My companions are a mite jumpy. I simply wish to know your intentions. Art here to stir trouble?' His words were slightly old-fashioned and faintly Eire-accented, his voice a mellifluous baritone.

Releasing my dagger, I studied him from beneath half-lowered eyelids. A strong jaw that spoke of determination. Hands calloused from sword practice. But eyes that held more wariness and pain than I expected.

'Why does it matter what I am and why I'm here?'

He raised one shoulder and looked south, as though he could see through the plastered wall toward London. 'I keep an eye on these folk.'

'Well, I'm only half-Dark *sidhe*,' I said, mildly. 'And I'd be interested to know how you could tell. Rest assured, as yet I've felt none of the Dark's urge to subjugate the world or crush thrones beneath my heels. I'm here merely to visit the Masters at the Fellowship of Minstrels. Learn some new music. Visit my half-brother, who's a clockmaker here. Perhaps purchase a few gifts for friends at home. Then I'll be on my way.' I glanced pointedly at his companions. 'So, your little conspiracy has naught to fear from me.'

He started and his fingers curled into a fist on the table. 'How…?'

'How have you lived so long amongst humans without clearly seeing the tells that betray their emotions?'

For a long moment his body held the tension, like a bear poised to fight or flee. Then he relaxed, deliberately, and bared his teeth in a smile. I signalled to the innkeeper for two drinks. My guest waited until they were brought before speaking again.

'I'm called Calain…Gilmore,' he said. 'My thanks for the drink—and the warning. I shall speak to my compatriots about being more discreet.'

'You're welcome. I'm Amsel Mór-Ríoghain.' I lifted my mug in toast. 'But call me Alistair Morrigan, an you please.' There was no point in trying to hide my sex from another *sidhe*.

Calain lifted his brows. 'Mór-Ríoghain? As in…?'

I cocked my head at him. 'Dost thou always pry into people's families when first you meet?'

He flushed. 'Forgive me. Tis only that I'm of the Eire as well and I find myself too much amongst these boorish folk of England. And I'd oft wondered if The Morrigan was *sidhe* or just a folk tale.'

I grimaced. 'Aye. The Morrigan's real enough. Or was. She was my mother. Cúchulainn, my father. She gave me the Dark side of my nature.' With a fingertip I drew doodles in spilled ale on the tabletop. A crude image of a bird. 'She styled herself as the protector of the people of Eire. Her favourite glamour was the seeming of a crow. A bird of death. Because of her I saw so much war as a child that I swore never to partake. You have naught to fear from me.'

His mouth twisted. 'How have you fared these last years, then? With the Lancasters and Yorks at each other's throats and ripping up the country. And the wars with France before that.'

'How have any of us fared?' I shrugged. 'I've stayed home a lot. Hence my trip now, when it's finally peaceful. I'd be pleased to see it stay that way, actually.'

His glance slid to his fellows. 'Were you for the Yorks or the Lancasters?'

I sipped my ale. My reply could shape my destiny—and his—and I wasn't yet certain what I wanted my destiny to be. 'Who were you for?'

'Do you always answer a question with a question?' Calain frowned.

I laughed. 'I find I waste less time that way. Oft as not people don't want to hear my answers, only their own. Very well. I care not which king's arse warms the throne. I've outlived a dozen kings already. I'm for anyone who'll make peace and pay me. As long as the fighting stops.' Old grief, softened by familiarity, stabbed through my chest.

'Aye. Point well made.'

'And well-taken?' I forebore to look at his tablemates.

Calain grimaced. 'My compatriots await me. I came only to ensure…'

I nodded. 'But you'd best give a better reason when you return to them.' I picked up my gittern and twanged the strings. The first pair of C strings were out of tune. I turned the pegs and plucked a few jaunty little notes. 'Perhaps, if you pay me, I can sing a song and cover your conversation.'

He hesitated, then his eyes twinkled. 'Thus making peace and getting paid. You have my gratitude.' He withdrew a purse and laid sixpence on the table. 'And my coin.'

I pushed the coins back. ''Tis too much for a mere song.'

'Consider it a downpayment.'

'For what, exactly?' I sent him an amused look.

He had the grace to blush and shifted in his seat. 'I didn't mean…' He cleared his throat. 'Just for more music, my good wom…sir.'

Having successfully discomfited him, I pocketed the coins and said loudly. 'Very well, sir. Merry songs you shall have. My thanks and a good e'en to you.'

He rose, bowed, and returned to his table with only a single backward glance. I retuned the slipping C strings and plucked out a quick little dance tune while I mulled our conversation over. The other patrons smiled and nodded, feet tapping mostly in time with the rhythm. The stableboy appeared from nowhere, tabor in hand, and drummed the dance beat on the skin. I lifted my voice in song.

Across the room, movement on the stairs caught my eye. A

woman of twenty-five or so glided down and wended her way to the fire. She dropped something into the pottage, stirred the cauldron, then returned to the stairs, ignoring calls from several men to join them.

I began a fresh song, old and sweet. She paused halfway up the steps, her head bowed. She sat gracefully on the risers and leaned her cheek against the railing, her eyes distant and haunted. Red-gold hair rippled down the back of her grey woollen kirtle and she absently wiped reddened hands on a clean apron. The memory of loss shadowed her plain face.

When I finished that song, her dusk-dark blue eyes met mine and—for the second time—a frisson of connection coursed through me. Fainter than before, though. Another *sidhe*, but only half or quarter-caste. Perhaps unaware of her heritage for her only reaction to seeing me was a faint flush to her pale cheeks and a shy, flickering look beneath long lashes.

I smiled. She pursed her lips, wiped her eyes, and vanished back upstairs. For some reason, my heart urged me to follow her; to comfort her pain. But I had given my word to Calain, so I continued to sing and play.

Another ale appeared on my table, courtesy of Calain, and the crowd thickened as more goodmen arrived to slake their thirst. The afternoon promised to be a merry one. Yet, still Calain and his fellows huddled in their corner, a picture of gloom and potential trouble.

My voice roughened and gave out long before my listeners' enthusiasm. Luckily a recorder player—another young lad—joined the drummer and I was able to rest while they played.

In Calain's corner, the small lordling scowled at one of his companions—the thickset man with a shock of white-blond hair. The conversation did not appear to be going well. I placed the gittern high on a shelf and tucked my saddlebags and bow well beneath the table.

A shout erupted from the white-haired man. He leapt to his feet and overturned their small table. Calain and his companions rose, two trying to soothe him, two holding back the smaller man. The dog jumped up, barking at all of them.

The music died away and carried conversation with it. The innkeeper emerged, wringing his hands and blustering, settling the bitch. The lordling waved him away peremptorily and the innkeeper hesitated. Over half the patrons quaffed or abandoned their ale and sidled out the door.

I relaxed back, watching. But my feet were firmly planted, my sword and dagger close by. I had no intention of interfering, but I would defend myself if needs be. How would Calain handle this? His *sidhe* speed and strength was greater than any human's, but would he reveal that?

'Damn you, Lovell,' the white-haired man yelled, his bass voice rough with emotion. He snatched out his dagger and stabbed wildly at the smaller man. Calain made no move. Lovell blocked the man's arm, holding it back with surprising strength. His mouth stretched into a grimace. He shifted and drew his own dagger. The white-haired man pulled back and the two stared at each other, panting.

'Taverner, think this through,' Lovell said, low and hard. 'I'm a man of my word.'

'That's what I'm afeared of,' Taverner growled. 'You damn us all.' He lunged again.

Lovell sidestepped and plunged the blade beneath Taverner's ribs and up, precisely through the heart. He withdrew the dagger and wiped it on Taverner's arm. The dying man staggered a half-step, clutched at Calain with a pleading look, and folded to the filthy floor.

The red-haired woman appeared at the top of the stairs and hurried down. She knelt beside the victim, pressed on the wound, and felt for the pulse on his neck. Everyone stilled, waiting. I could sense his life-force had gone. I'd felt the shift in power as his *enath*—his soul—joined the *sianfath* energies that bound all living things into one. Across the room, Calain grimaced.

The woman rose and wiped her hands, leaving blood on her apron. She glared at Lovell, who still held the dagger in one fist.

'You'll be brought before the King's Court for this, sirrah,' she said. 'We don't allow murder here. Dick?' She addressed the innkeeper. 'Gather the other men in your tithings group. Raise the hue-and-cry and take this man into custody.'

Lovell turned amusement on the innkeeper, who lowered his gaze. Lovell switched his attention back to the woman and inspected her in a leisurely, sneering fashion. My blood quickened and I gathered myself.

Perhaps this was the opportunity I needed. I sought for clarity in my dream-visions and found none, so I waited.

'My good woman,' Lovell drawled, his light tenor thin and flat to the ear, 'This was my sworn man and he attacked me. The King's Court will never try me, for it was clearly self-defence.' He levelled the tip of his dagger at her. 'Who are you to presume to lecture me?'

She hesitated and glanced at the men backing him up. Her chin rose. 'I'm Helen O'Reilly and my husband—'

'I don't care a whit who your husband is,' Lovell sneered. 'He won't stand in my way and nor will any female.' His charming smile appeared and he looked her full figure up and down with deliberate appreciation. 'Unless she wants to, that is?'

Her jaw clenched into mulishness. Idiot woman was going to get herself killed. I hesitated. Would stepping in now gain or lose trust? I opened myself to truths, but my seersight had always been fragmented, weak; best in dreams. No help. I'd have to decide for myself and hope I chose well.

The woman lashed out with a slap. Lovell caught it and chuckled. She whimpered.

I sighed. The path was clear, now. Tied to hers, as though her action had crystallised mine. But the route was a maze, the end obscured by blood and fire. And death. Why was it always death?

No point in trying to avoid it. I'd learned that lesson the hard way.

I rose and strolled across the room, weaving between tables until I stood at her side. I bowed with a flourish.

'My lord,' I said—more the make her aware she was dealing with nobility than to make obeisance to him. He released her arm. She gasped, touched slender fingers to her throat and bobbed a curtsey.

'My lord,' I repeated, weathering his cool stare unmoved, 'allow me to offer my assistance.' I indicated the fallen man. 'Clearly you're short a man. I'm new to town and have no fixed plans. Allow me to step in.'

Lovell's wolf-brown eyes swept over me. 'And you are? Apart from insolent, that is?'

'Forgive my intrusion, my lord,' I bowed again. 'Alistair Morrigan, at your service.'

There followed a tense silence while Lovell studied me and I looked back as inoffensively as possible. He let the uncomfortable silence stretch, heavy eyelids drooping, lip curled. He held a kerchief to his nose and a naggingly familiar, sweet-woody scent reached me. Ah. He wore *eau de chypre*. Expensive tastes.

A quick knock made itself felt on my mental shields. I opened a window and allowed Calain's mental presence inside mine.

-*Prithee, Amsel, what are you doing?*-

In honesty, my thought was to protect the woman from harm. What service did your fallen man provide for Lovell?

There was a long pause, then a reply heavy with reluctance. *-He was an expert archer. Accurate up to 200 yards-*

Tell Lovell I can do better. You know I can't lie speaking mind-to-mind.

Calain stepped forward and laid a hand on my shoulder. 'I'll vouch for him, my lord.'

Surprising. I'd expected him to question me further. He continued, his fingers tightening, 'He can shoot as well as Taverner, if not better. Our families are…kin.'

Lovell switched his attention to Calain. 'Very well.' He pointed to his companions. 'Humphrey and Thomas Stafford. Richard Clinton.' His eyes flicked to the body at our feet and he sighed. 'Tis a pity about Taverner, though. He was a good man, if hot-headed. Calain, take Humphrey and Thomas and remove his body to the sexton. Richard?' He nodded at the curly-haired lad. 'Give the innkeeper some coin to silence his complaints. You.' He pointed to me. 'Get that woman out of my sight then return. There is much to acquaint you with and little time to spare.'

Calain nodded and gestured to the surly, darkhaired brothers, who each grabbed an arm on the corpse. The three of them hauled the body out the door. Villagers trickled back in, whispering and eyeing Lovell uneasily. The innkeeper, apparently mollified by Lovell's openhandedness, tossed straw on the blood and shouted everyone a half mug of ale. A cheer went up and the remaining villagers settled back to their chairs as though nothing had happened.

I bowed and turned to the red-haired woman, still standing behind me. I gripped her elbow and hustled her up the steep stairs, into a low-pitched room in the second storey—the bedroom the innkeeper had assigned me.

Closing the warped timber door, I rounded on her. 'Are you mad, woman? What made you provoke him in that manner?'

Helen shrank from me, then seemed to regather her courage. 'How dare you speak to me thus? My husband is the lord's reeve…was…' Her soft alto voice faded and she turned aside.

'Your husband is dead?' I said bluntly, not enjoying her flinch and paling cheek. 'And so will you be if you don't learn to guard that unruly tongue around men like Lovell. He's the sort to think all women fools and useless for aught but a tumble in the hay. Now I'm committed to helping the dogbotherer.'

Her dark blue eyes flew to mine. 'You…you stepped in to protect me? Why?' Her cheeks flushed delicately pink.

I scrubbed at my face, feeling the weight of years and expectations, and the tug of bittersweet emotions I'd thought left behind thirty years ago. No. There was no place for such here. She was still endangered, as was I, now. And so were many more. I needed to keep my task in mind.

'Because,' I finally replied, 'protecting others is what I'm called to do. A few more words and you'd have joined Taverner on the floor.'

Helen's eyes widened. She stroked at her throat; a nervous gesture.

'Well, I thank you for your assistance.' She brushed absently at the front of her kirtle. 'I must return home, now. I…I wish you luck with your new companions.'

I bowed and held the door for her. 'My thanks, madam. Tread with care when you pass Lovell.' Unable to resist, I added, 'I'm sure we'll meet again, soon.'

The colour in her cheek deepened.

An image flashed to mind and my heart stuttered. Now to find a way through the tangled web ahead. I laid a gentle hand on her arm and she started.

'When you come to London, leave a message for Alistair Morrigan with the Minstrel's Guildhall, that I may find you.'

'London? But I'm not…' She sent me a quick, confused look, and vanished down the stairs.

The window-shutters lay open and warm afternoon light streamed into the little room, dust dancing like tiny fireflies in the beam. I moved to the window and watched the street below. Helen emerged, tying a white coif over her bright hair. She threw a quick glance over her shoulder and I withdrew from view.

I laughed softly. Quite possibly, I was the mad one. Now I was committed to far more than I'd ever bargained for on this trip.

But I couldn't bring myself to regret it. Nor to regret meeting her.

Not yet, anyway.

2. A Pocketful of Rye

Helen O'Reilly, 28
Healer
Village of Isledon,

Monday (late afternoon), 18th September, 1486

I rushed from the King's Head Inn so blindly that I was halfway home before I remembered my healer's bag. I stopped with one foot on the stile, cursed then glanced around guiltily. I'd have to go back. My bag of tinctures, herbs, and ointments was too valuable to be left in that pigsty inn full of thieves and murderers.

With a sigh I turned back and trudged up High Street. The last thing I wanted was to confront that horrid Lord Lovell. I shuddered. Men and their violence. It was like a sickness with them, this need to hurt and destroy. How easily he'd killed his sworn servant. And why had that woman—I had no doubt it was a woman, for all she wore men's clothing—deflected his anger? And when would I learn to hold my tongue, as she'd said? John always warned me—

I cut the thought off, grief strangling words in my throat. My husband was no longer here to warn me of anything. I had failed him and little Robert. What did it matter if my tongue ran loose and got me killed? I had nothing left. No-one to love or to love me in return.

Tears swelled and blurred ragged the lines of the street. What was the point of going back for my healer's bag? I sagged and my steps slowed. The blanket of pain had lifted for a few minutes when that Alistair man-woman had saved me; cared for me. Made me feel as though a future could be possible again. Where had that come from, that glimmer of sunlight through the dark cage I'd lived in these last few weeks?

But hope was a fickle mistress. I knew that, well.

Now grief returned tenfold and suffocated my thoughts in darkness.

'Mistress Helen, Mistress Helen,' a shrill voice called from one of the upper windows along the street.

Lizzie Brewster hung half-out of the window, haggard; brown hair thin and limp. She beckoned me closer.

'It's my William, Mistress. He's poorly.' She pointed across the street at the King's Head. 'Like young James you were tendin' this mornin'.'

I froze, my feet sinking into the street's muck. 'The same?

'Just the same. Vomitin' and thrashin' about like the Devil's in 'im.' Lizzie shivered and clutched a tattered grey shawl about her thin shoulders. 'Moanin' and talkin' 'bout hearin' the colour green.' She dropped her voice to a penetrating whisper and hissed. 'Mebbe I should call Father Vaughan. Mebbe it *is* the Devil.'

'Don't be a gudgeon,' I said staunchly, though the words came out strangled. 'He's sick, not possessed. I'll get my bag and be right in.' I picked up my skirts and hurried into the King's Head. Oh, dear God, not again. Please?

Dick Fuller, the innkeeper, waited for me, his florid face anxious, pudgy hands wringing the filthy apron tied at his thick waist. I peeked quickly around the room, relieved to see the lord gone.

'James is no better, Mistress.' Dick followed me upstairs. I collected my bag and felt the boy's damp forehead. He wasn't fevered, but his dark hair lay plastered against his skin and he moaned and muttered in his sleep. His hands were cold and puffy.

'I know, Dick,' I said. 'But I've done all I can. I have to go see Lizzie's boy. They're friends, aren't they? Maybe they both caught the same thing.'

Dick cast a horrified look at his young son. 'Y'don't think it's the plague, do ya Mistress?'

'No. As John always say—' I stopped myself then continued. 'The symptoms are wrong.' I patted his wrist. 'Let me go see William.'

His shoulders slumped. He was a good man. He'd lost his wife and daughter only two years before to the flux. James was his only family. The tears that were never far away these days, smudged the room. I dashed them aside and ran downstairs then across the street.

Upstairs in William's dark attic bedroom, he fared no better. The stink of sweat and vomit was stifling. I flung open the window shutters to let in some cool air and Lizzie shrieked.

'Fresh air never harmed anyone, Lizzie,' I admonished, sitting on the bed. I felt William's pulse. Too fast, just like James. The boy thrashed in the bed, muttering wild, incomprehensible words. 'How long has he been this way?'

Lizzie shifted from foot to foot. 'Dunno exactly. He came in late yesterday. Had his supper. Found him all sick-like this mornin'. What is it?'

'Not the plague,' I said drily. She gave an audible sigh.

William's body stiffened. His face twisted into a rictus of pain and his body shuddered, twitching.

'Elf-shot,' Lizzie whispered, crossing herself.

'No' I said. 'James was like this, too. Hold him. Put something in his mouth to stop him biting his tongue.' She jammed a piece of cloth between his teeth and we held him until his body softened. I felt his pulse, still racing. But he wasn't feverish, either. His fingers were icy cold.

I couldn't risk invoking my healing energy with Lizzie standing over my shoulder. Besides, it was more difficult to find the power here in town. Much easier in the outlying houses, close to fields and trees.

Why, I had no idea. And the energy—which always left the taste of fresh hay in my mouth—had only worked for a short time on John and Robert. They'd improved to the point where they could again eat a little bread and milk. But then they'd relapsed and worsened.

I turned aside to stare out the window. Now it was happening again. First John and little Robert, then five other of our neighbours all within a week. Now these two boys. And, if my healing power didn't work, I could do nothing. None of my herbs had cured the others. I dug through my bag, seeking inspiration. I couldn't lose another patient. Lizzie didn't deserve to lose her son. Nor did Dick Fuller. No-one did.

The peppermint and some of my carefully-grown ginger might help William's nausea. Had I tried mistletoe on John for the seizures? Yes, I was sure I had. It had helped a little. But nothing had stopped the visions or the fast heartbeat. And nothing woke him up when he fell into a final, unwaking sleep, or healed his blackened fingers and toes. I placed the clay jars back into my bag and stroked my throat, scowling. There had to be something.

'Mistress Helen?' Lizzie's tentative question broke into my thoughts.

I had to show confidence where I felt none. Perhaps if I tried something new. 'Clearly the four humours are unbalanced,' I said, rising and brushing at my kirtle. 'He has not enough fire in him. See how cold and white his fingers and toes are? Make a hot soup of ginger, garlic, rosemary, peppermint, buttercup root, and mistletoe. Oh—and hawthorn to stimulate bloodflow.' I pulled the more difficult ingredients to find out of my bag. Ginger was horribly expensive, but I was desperate.

Lizzie screwed up her nose. 'That'll taste awful, that will.'

'I know. Add a spoonful of honey. Make sure it's warm when you feed it to him.' I concentrated. What could I do differently here? 'No bread or meats, either. Nor any milk. Nothing heavy. We must help his blood flow to his fingers and his stomach has to work too hard to digest those things. Is anyone else in the house sick?'

'Nay, Mistress.'

'Have the boys eaten anything you haven't? Or been anywhere they might have caught a sickness? The marshes, perhaps?'

Lizzie grimaced. 'Who knows, Mistress. They're off a-runnin' about like wild things half the time. A-huntin' with Matilda, my niece, sometimes. Will's to be 'prenticed to the cordwainer next month so I don't mind him havin' a bit a fun now.' She sniffed. 'Better'n bein' dragged off to another war like my poor George.'

I sighed. She, like most of the village womenfolk, had lost men to Richard and Henry's battles for the crown. Thank Heaven it was over, and peace restored.

'Well, if he speaks any words of sense, ask him what he ate yesterday. Maybe they found something poisonous from the hedgerows or the northern forest. I'm going to the church to pray for them and speak with Father Vaughan. He'll know if any more have been taken poorly in the parish. Then I'll be going home. Send one of the children if Will takes a turn for the worse.'

She bobbed a curtsey and nodded. 'Thankee Mistress. I got naught to pay you with, though. For the treatment.' She studied the scrap of ginger dubiously. 'Not sure I can afford this, Mistress. Less you'll take a bag o rye to make your bread. Not milled yet, though.'

I nodded.

'Good,' she said. 'I'll go get it and show you out.'

I waited for her to leave, then touched Will's forehead and sang the lullaby I'd sung to Robert. The same my mother had sung to me.

Hush, pretty baby, don't say a word.

Mama's gone and called you a sweet blackbird.
When that little blackbird does come,
Mama's gonna buy you a big war drum.

William sighed in his sleep. I could *feel* the sickness in him—just as in John and Robert. I had to try healing him. Focussing, I drew in energy from the little garden behind Lizzie's house. Filled with golden light and the taste of hay, I poured some of it into Will and muttered, 'Lord, guide my power to do your bidding.'

Afterward I sagged, drained. Will seemed no different. He still tossed and turned, moaning and sweat-soaked. Pointless. Why did the Lord give me this gift if it did no good? With a sigh, I descended the narrow stairs and met Lizzie at the front door.

She held out a sack.

'Where did you get this from?' I said. 'I thought the grain merchant wasn't due until next week?'

'Seems the boys did a favour for a farmer from up north. He was bringin' his cart o grain to mill before going on to Lunnon to sell. Got stuck in a ditch. Ooh—I think he had some herbs, too, if you want to catch him. He's stayin' at the inn. Anyway, Will and James and my niece, Matilda, helped him get the cart out and he gave them each two sacks.' She admired the sack. 'I call that right kindly, don't you?'

'I do. And good of the boys to help. I can't carry it and my bag, though. Can you send it over to my house?'

'I'll send Matilda. She's headin' your way to check her rabbit traps, anyway. Tilda?'

At Lizzie's call, a skinny girl of around fifteen emerged from the back room. She dusted her hands on her tunic and gave me a wide, crooked-toothed grin. Her broad, freckled face was open and healthy in the way of someone who spent a lot of time outdoors. Lizzie gave her the bag with instructions to take it to my cottage.

'Tilda? Goodness,' I said weakly. Her straw-blonde hair was cut unwomanly-short, and she wore a man's hose and tunic. 'You've grown. I haven't seen you for an age. I'm sorry for your loss. Your mother was one of my dearest friends. I miss her. Are you living here, now your parents are…gone?'

A shadow swept across her cheerful countenance. She made a fuss of adjusting the bow she carried over one shoulder. A cloth quiver full of arrows hung on her narrow hips. 'Nay, Mistress. Just deliverin rabbits to Aunty Lizzie. Gotta get home.'

'But that's miles the other way from my house.'

Tilda shrugged easily. 'I'm used to it, Mistress.'

I was too astonished to protest the girl's unconventional appearance. Perhaps even a little envious of her freedom. So, I nodded, trying to hide my confusion. Tilda dashed out the door like a jackrabbit.

When I moved to leave, Lizzie laid a sympathetic hand on my arm. 'Are you doin' alright? With Master John gone, I mean?'

I swallowed convulsively as the despair welled up from deep within again. 'I'm fine, thankyou Lizzie. It's only been three weeks. These things take time.'

With a knowing little smile, she stood aside. 'Well, don't you take too long, Mistress. There's Dick Fuller lookin' sideways at you these last couple of days. He's a fine man. A good catch. Everyone in Isledon says so. Not right you livin' all on your own so far out of town. Not safe. No one to work your land, either.' She nodded firmly as though the argument was won and closed the front door behind me.

I stood in the street, fists clenched. As I marched toward St Mary's church on Upper Street, it was all I could do to hold my head up. Every eye seemed to be upon me. Were they all planning my next marriage? Already? With John not even a month under the ground. I shuddered.

At the iron-studded timber church door, I paused. Father Vaughan didn't much like me. The Church taught that only men should be healers. When John was alive, his position as the manor's reeve made it hard for Father Vaughan to speak against me. What would he say now?

Girding myself, I pushed the door open and stepped into the gloomy interior of the new stone building. I lit a tallow candle and placed it beside the others, knelt, crossed myself and muttered a quick prayer. Then I entered the confessional and settled onto the seat.

'Bless-me-Father-for-I-have-sinned,' I rattled off. 'It's been a week since my last confession.'

'And?' Father Vaughan's reedy, impatient voice sounded from the other side of the screen.

I hesitated. If I told him of my thoughts of suicide, what would he say? The truth was, I could hardly bear life without John and Robert. I should have saved them. Every day their faces, their cries, their agonies haunted my waking and sleeping hours. I wanted nothing more than to join them, but death by my own hand was a dreadful sin. As was the anger—no, rage—I felt at God for taking them. I wanted little Robert's sweet-scented skin soft against my breast. Was that greed? I wanted John's hands on my body at night. Was that lust?

I wanted to rail against Father Vaughan and the Church for taking the two people I loved most in the world so cruelly from me. And now God was doing it again. Taking more people in my village. Was it punishment for being a female healer? Would that be Father Vaughan's reply to my questions?

'Mistress?' Father Vaughan prompted me.

Clearing my throat, I named a few inconsequential sins and listened half-heartedly when he gave me penance. I felt no different for having held back the worst of myself. Surely, I could tell God myself, at night, when I prayed to Him for the strength to make it through to the next morning in an empty, cold bed?

I emerged from the confessional and hurried toward the door, suddenly loath to speak to Father Vaughan about other illnesses in the village.

'Mistress O'Reilly,' Father Vaughan called me back.

I kissed his outstretched fingers. 'Yes, Father?'

'I hear two more are sick in town.' His eyes blazed dark with the Lord's fire and purpose. 'Just like your husband and son and those other pour souls last month.'

'Yes, Father,' I said.

'And that you've not been able to heal them, either.' There was no mistaking the smugness of his tone now. How had he gathered the news so fast? I kept my expression calm but ground my teeth to stop hot words. Undoubtedly someone ran the news here on feet fleeter than mine. Busybodies, all of them.

'No, Father,' I replied.

'Leave them to the Lord's blessing, child,' he intoned, sketching the sign of the cross. 'Pray for them, but do not try your woman's spells on them lest someone gets the wrong idea.'

His smile was condescending, but his dark eyes were hot. 'After all, we don't want you being accused of witchcraft, do we? Leave doctoring to men, who are better suited to such things. Tis unseemly for a woman to see unclad men and boys not of her own family. We all know how lustful—how sinful—a woman can be.' His gaze drifted down my body until I felt too lightly clothed. 'Best get yourself a husband and hie you to town where your fellow goodwives can watch out for you.'

I wanted to spit in his sneering face, to slap his sallow cheek and claw at his plucked-chicken neck with my nails. Instead, I curtseyed and gathered my bag.

'Yes, Father.' I practically ran from the church, holding back tears.

By the time I reached my lonely little farmhouse the long late-summer's day was nigh over and soft dusk raced shadows across the fields. Lizzie's large sack of rye lay neatly against my door and I smiled, grateful for the reminder of kindness. Inside the two-room cottage I dropped my bag and the rye on the rough table and lit the fire against the cool seeping in. Then I rushed through neglected chores—feeding and locking up the chickens and geese, feeding the pigs and bringing Berta in to her stable. She lowed at me, contentedly munching on hay and shifting her big body in the stall.

I looked out the door at the neatly tended toft, where my vegetables and herbs grew. But beyond that stood the five unharvested acres where the year's wheat would wither and die soon. I leaned on Berta's flank and let her brown hide soak up my tears. Lizzie was right. Managing even such a little farm on my own was nigh on impossible. But that left me only two choices: leaving and paying a fine to the manor house, or marrying a man I didn't care for who would manage it for me. Get me with child. Expect me to wait on him hand and foot as John never had. Maybe even forbid me from practicing my healing.

Perhaps that was the lesson God was trying to teach me: that I should give up healing folk and settle down.

With a sigh, I shut Berta in and returned to the house. Cooking supper was beyond my strength. Instead, I lit two tallow candles, tipped out the rye grains and began methodically separating the ugly black grains from the brown ones. My mother used to laugh at my obsession. John did, too.

I tossed the black nubs into the fire, where they sizzled and popped like wet wood.

The week before John died, he and Robert had come home complaining that the Widow Smith's bread tasted better than mine; swearing that the dull taste of my bread must be because I threw away the best bits. He'd brought two loaves home and I'd been angry and jealous.

Tears formed again, and the candlelight smeared. I stopped and lowered my head to my forearms, letting the pain of missing him flow out and splash to the tabletop. I'd thought myself lucky when he came back from the wars alive. But I'd only had him back for a year and now he would never return. No amount of tears would fill the hole left by his absence.

A loud thudding woke me. I stared around the darkened room blearily. The fire had long since guttered to ash and the tallow candles had burnt to nothing. The faintest, grey light crept in around the window shutters.

The thudding came again, rattling on the door.

'Mistress Helen! Art awake?' A woman's voice. Lizzie's.

I straightened, my body stiff with cold and discomfort. I brushed hair and rye chaff away, tidied my skirt and hurried to the door.

'Lizzie?' I fumbled with the slide bar. 'What's the matter? Is it William?'

'No, Mistress.' She held a shielded oil lantern high. Matilda stood by her side, anxious. 'It's James at the inn,' Lizzie said. 'He's worse. And some of Dick's guests at the inn are sick. One woman's lost her unborn babe. Come quick. Tilda's here because her young brothers are sick, too. She brought them to my house so you could see them.'

'So many?' I took a step back, hand to throat, breathless. What if I couldn't help them, either? John's agonised face swam before me, with Robert's pale, still form in his arms.

'Please, Mistress?' Lizzie's watery brown eyes fixed on me.

I snatched up my healer's bag but my heart was heavier than any carry-all.

When we reached the King's Head, the sun's first rosy fingers stroked the treetops and a cold mist rolled across the fields. I shivered and followed Lizzie through the stout timber door. A small crowd was gathered in the front room. Local townsfolk, all. They stared at us when we entered, conversations dying away to a mixture of curiosity and hostility. The musician from last night was missing and I wasn't sure whether to be relieved or frightened by her absence. Was she one of the sick?

Father Vaughan pushed to the front and stood over me, an imposing figure in black, dark frown marring his harsh features.

'Mistress O'Reilly, I told you to stay out of this. Healing is men's work. I've sent for a doctor.'

I stared at the bag in my arms. 'I know, Father.'

He gestured expansively at the gathered crowd. 'I've heard you were here yesterday. That you put something into the pottage the sick folk ate. Is that true?'

'Yes, but it was only—'

'Enough!' Father Vaughan hardened. 'I warned you, woman.' The crowd muttered, their voices rising in accusation. Beside me, Lizzie stirred and whimpered.

I glared. 'I'm only trying to hel—'

'Don't interrupt me.' Father Vaughan's cheeks reddened. 'You're treading on very dangerous ground. Your husband and son died under your care. Five of your neighbours died. Now young James and half a dozen of this good innkeeper's guests are sick of the same thing. You put something in their food and you want us to believe you're helping? I think not!'

My heart beat a drumroll so loud in my ears I could hardly hear his words. The crowd pressed close, venomous, darkness waiting to kill in revenge for death, needing a scapegoat.

I backed away. Maybe it was true. Maybe I was a witch. These healing powers I had. Perhaps they were from the Devil and I didn't know I was being used. I muttered an apology. The crowd glowered silently at me. Father Vaughan's lip curled.

I fled into the street, then stood there, bathed in morning light, trembling. I was lost. Cast out by God and my neighbours. Had I killed my own husband and son? My knees weakened and a sob escaped my lips.

'Mistress?' Lizzie approached hesitantly. Tilda stood beside her, glancing back at the inn.

'You shouldn't be seen with me, Lizzie,' I said, holding out my hands to fend her off. 'They might come after you, too. It's true, after all. Maybe I am doing more harm than good.' I bit my lip, trying to hold back the cry of anguish.

'No, Mistress,' Lizzie said. 'I told you. Will's fine this mornin'. I fed him the soup and didn't let him eat anythin' else, as you said.' She shrugged. 'I mean, he's still weak and all, but he's not havin' fits and he's talkin' sense again.'

I turned on her, a bud of hope blossoming. 'And Tilda's brothers?'

Tilda nodded, eager. 'Aunty Lizzie gave them the same soup last night and they're gettin' better this mornin'.'

'I need to talk to Will,' I said. 'Is he awake?'

Lizzie nodded and led the way to her home.

Upstairs, I sat on Will's bed. His cheeks were rosier today and his eyes brighter. But the hand he gave me in greeting was frighteningly weak and still puffy. Just like John and Robert when they had made their small recovery. Would Will relapse as well? How could I stop it?

'Good morrow, Will,' I said. 'I'm glad you're feeling better. Do you remember if you and James went anywhere different or ate anything different the other day?'

'No, Missus. We jus' went a-huntin' with cousin Tilda. Caught some rabbits. And she shot a deer.' He stopped with a quick, terrified look at Tilda. I patted his arm.

'It's alright. I'm not the reeve's wife anymore.' I managed a tight smile. 'I won't tell on her for poaching deer. We'll have to hope she doesn't get caught by the new reeve, Mr Cooper. But was there anything else? Anything you and James did or saw or ate. Please? It's important.'

'Only that grain-merchant, missus,' he said, doubtfully.

I nodded. 'You helped him get his cart free and he gave you the sacks of rye.'

'Aye, and some bread to eat on the way home.' A gap-toothed grin split his face. 'Tasty it was, too, missus. We et it all.'

Lizzie made a huffing noise and glared at him. I shushed her and stared blankly at his honest expression.

'Tilda?' I looked at her.

She shrugged. 'I took my loaf home for the little-uns.' Her eyes widened.

'And the merchant was stopping at the inn for the night, wasn't he?'

'Aye, so he said, missus. Then goin' on to Lunnon today to sell his bags.'

I rose so fast Lizzie started. 'I have to go back.'

Her mouth fell agape. 'To the inn, Mistress? You mustn't! That crowd will tear you apart.'

I tugged at my kirtle. 'I must. I know what's causing this. If they kill me…then that's the Lord's will. I have to try. For young James's sake. I was too late to save John and Robert, but maybe I can save him.'

Lizzie's throat worked and her cheeks turned ashen. She glanced at Will and rose as well. 'I'm comin' with you, then.'

'Me too,' Tilda said stoutly. Her knuckles were white where she gripped her bow.

'You can't, either of you.' I confronted Tilda. 'I'm called to it. But you both have family that needs you. I…' I drew a deep breath. 'I have nothing left to lose. I thought I had nothing left to give, either. But I now know I *can* help. I must. And I'm ready to stand up to Father Vaughan to help the people of Isledon.'

Lizzie cocked her head. 'Aye, Mistress. And, in the stories, it sounds all mighty fine to sacrifice yourself to save people. Truth is, you need to live in order to save people, don't you? You can't do nothin' if you're dead. We're comin' an that's that. We'll tell em how you helped our young-uns.'

I gave a weak chuckle and hugged her. She was right, of course. I did need to live. People needed me. Not just John and Robert. My gifts were God-given and I must help wherever I could.

I straightened my spine and lifted my chin. It would be a long day.

3. Four and Twenty Blackbirds

Matilda Barrowman, 15
Poacher
Village of Isledon,

Tuesday (morning) 19th September, 1486

'Tilda Barrowman,' hissed Aunty Lizzie, 'where do you think you're goin'?'

I grinned at her and sidled along the inn wall, holdin' my bow close and watchin' the crowd. Lucky they were all lookin' at Helen and Aunty Lizzie, not me. Most of the villagers jammed into the King's Head hardly saw me these days. Not since I took to wearin' Pa's clothes instead of Ma's. Fine with me.

Most girls my age were married with a brat or two squallin' at their feet already. I got two little brothers, Bertie and Joe and they were enough. Well, they were twelve and eleven, so not really little. But why would I need more? Or some great lummox of a man thinkin' he owned me.

Then I'd *never* leave this place.

When I got to the back corner of the inn, I climbed onto a bench to see what was happenin'. Helen and Lizzie were standin' off against Father Vaughan. A pair of angry mother geese backin' a cowardly mongrel cur into a corner. Good on 'em. Father Vaughan was one of the handsy ones. Like that high and mighty lordling who'd been here last night when I dropped off a brace of rabbits to the cook. Lucky I had my dagger on me. And lucky for the lordling his big servant called him off me.

What was it with important men? Before I stopped goin' to church regular-like, Father Vaughan'd put those big, skinny hands in all sorts of places. Even Ma'd complained and told me to stay away from him. And away from Jeff Cooper, the new reeve. He was just as bad. I wanted to be left alone and they all wanted to own me. Or sard me.

Seemed it was all they thought I was good for. Maybe it was.

Risin' up tall, I studied the villagers in the room. Cooper was there, alright. Standin' in the middle, arms folded and a glare on his sweaty red face like a wild dog that's smelled another pack's piss-mark in his territory. At least I could see him and he couldn't see me.

With Master O'Reilly dead, the lord of the manor had set up Cooper as the new reeve. I'd have to be extra careful out at night, now. With the two boys to feed I couldn't get caught huntin' again. O'Reilly had let me go. Cooper wouldn't. Not without a price.

I shuddered.

I didn't mind sex. It was how I paid the rent to Squire Nash, after all. But that was more of a bargain we'd worked out. At least, after the first time when he made me and I couldn't see any other choice. But I was used to it now. And the pennyroyal and bishop's lace herbs stopped me gettin' with child.

It was a good deal for both of us. I didn't have money and Squire Nash didn't get anythin' tasty at home. His wife was a nasty piece with a devil's tongue and a face like a pig's arse. Ed Nash was a lonely man who cried into my shoulder more often than played nug-a-nug between the sheets.

Reeve Cooper, though. He was a levereter. All about power and who he could hurt to get it.

Cooper glanced around and I ducked behind Widow Clarke. When I peeked around again, he was watchin' Mistress Helen with a hunger that made me want to put an arrow through his brain. Not that I ever would. But I wanted to.

Mistress Helen seemed to have overtalked Father Vaughan 'cause the priest was lookin' fair gobsmacked. She and Lizzie bustled around, orderin' the menfolk to get home and stop interferin'. I almost laughed out loud at that—and at the gape-faced sheep-stupid look on the men. Helen told 'em not to eat the bread or grain the farmer had sold 'em yesterday. A few of the townsfolk grumbled and complained they'd go hungry. Mistress Helen glared and gave 'em a choice between hungry for a few days 'til the next cart came through, or dead. That shut 'em up.

I tucked away the slingshot I'd had ready in case the room got a mite frisky. Seemed like I wouldn't be needin' it. For all her book-learnin' and lady-like ways, Mistress Helen was a good-un. Smart. Tougher than she thought.

She started talkin' about havin' to go to Lunnon to find the farmer and stop him from sellin' the grain. My ears pricked up. Could I maybe go with her? I sighed. Not with Bertie and Joe still sick. Probably not 'til they were grown up. One day, I'd get there, too. There and a hundred other places. Scotland, maybe. France, even. Anywhere but Isledon.

Not today, though.

The crowd began to melt away. With a nod to Mistress Helen, I slipped out behind the last menfolk and headed up the north road. Lunnon was south, but food was north, in the woodlands. The deer I'd brought down yesterday was already a-hangin' up and bein' smoked. The hide was sittin' in salt gettin' cured.

But that deer was already bespoke. Sold to John, the blacksmith. I needed another. Kids will eat and I couldn't leave them with Aunty Lizzie for too long. She had three of her own to look after and the lazy lard-arse new husband she took after her first died with a Lancaster sword in his guts. I'd promised a deer for her larder as payment for takin' Bertie and Joe in while they were sick. It was a big risk. I usually only took a deer every three months or so. Just enough to feed me and the boys. But fair was fair.

Time to go a-huntin'. Good thing Pa taught me a few things

before he went off and got himself killed in that war for the king. Whichever king it was. I wasn't even sure who sat on the throne, now. Richard? Henry? Who cared, really. Some prick who thought only nobles should eat deer.

I grinned savagely and trotted along High Street toward the big stretch of woodlands north of town, over the ridge. There was a nice little herd in there, last time I'd been that way. I'd have to watch for the farmers lettin' their pigs root 'round in the forest. And Cooper, of course. But he'd be busy in town with this fuss over the sickness.

I had to pass by St Mary's. Father Vaughan was back in the inn, so I snuck into the graveyard to pay my respects to Ma and Pa. Their gravestones were way back in the corner. I sat and leaned my back on the sun-warmed stone wall nearby. I traced the writin' on the gravestones. Aunty Lizzie said Pa's said *Died 1485 givin' his life for his country and king.* Like he had a choice when King Richard's men had forced him to march off to some battle or other.

And Ma's said *Died 1485.* I guess they couldn't write *Died protectin' her children from King Richard's food-thievin' bastard soldiers.* I shook off the useless memories and said good-bye.

I was about to get up when Reeve Cooper's growly voice cut through the air.

'There's no-one nearby, my lord.'

I froze, huddled against the stone.

'Yes, yes.' It was the voice of that slimy lordling from last night at the inn. Lovell, the innkeeper said his name was. 'Now go wait over there. Out of earshot.' There was a pause, the sound of retreating footsteps, then he said. 'There's something about you, Morrigan. I'm not sure I trust you.'

A third man replied, 'And why should you, my lord? We've only just met and trust is earned.' That was the minstrel with a voice like a songbird.

'True.' Lovell sounded satisfied. 'Very well. Gilmore vouches for you, so I'll hire you. I have some…supplies I must pick up from a merchant here. Then my business is done and I shall return to London.'

I waited. What supplies? What was he hirin' the minstrel for?

'I'll pay you sixpence a day,' Lovell continued.

I stuffed a fist into my mouth. What I could do with that much money.

'You'll go to London and find us accommodation. Then you'll shoot where and when I say. No questions. No arguments. Understood?'

'Understood,' the minstrel said calmly. 'But don't you think you're being a little hasty? I'll take ten and you'll put it in writing. Signed and sealed with that ring on your finger.'

'I'll do no such thing,' Lovell said, his voice harsh. 'I put nothing in writing that could be used against me. I'm not a fool.'

'And do you think me one?' Morrigan replied, still calm. 'Tell me now who I'm to kill or I walk. I don't need your job and I won't go in blind.'

'Who are you to speak thus to me? Do you know who I am?'

'Should I? To be honest, I'd rather not know.' Morrigan sounded amused. 'Your nobility is obvious, though.' Was there sarcasm in his tone, or were my ears playin' tricks?

There was a long silence. I held my breath in case they heard me.

'Very well,' Lovell said. 'My aim is to bring peace to the realm once and for all. And that cannot be under a Lancaster king. In the short time he's been in power, Henry has stripped families—including mine—of their wealth and is now planning such new taxes as will bring the nobles into revolt against him.'

I sneered. Typical lord, worryin' about his family's wealth and power. Not givin' a shit about how any taxes might hurt people like me and Helen and Aunty Lizzie. We'd be the ones payin', not him.

Hasty footsteps paced back and forth, only a few feet from where I sat.

Lovell continued, 'My chief concern is for the people of England. We have been at war too long. We need to put a man on the throne who will guarantee peace. Not one who will incite rebellion.'

Well, that was hard to argue with.

'And?' Morrigan prompted.

'And,' Lovell said heavily, 'in a week we kill Harry Tudor. His wife, Elizabeth, and their heir, if it's born alive. Then we'll restore the Plantagenet line in Edward, Earl of Warwick. Henry, the usurper, holds him imprisoned in the Beauchamp Tower of the Tower of London.'

I covered my mouth. A babe? He'd kill a babe for the sake of some family baubles and the hope of peace? I might not be a lord, but surely the rest of them would be up in arms if the royal family all up and died sudden-like. It'd be war all over again. But what did Lovell care? Our menfolk'd be the ones dyin', not him.

'When my wealth is restored,' Lovell continued, 'anyone who helps me will be well-rewarded. Are you with me?'

Morrigan's reply came quickly. Too quick for my likin'. 'Aye, my lord. And I believe I know of a few others who'd be willing to help as well.' He chuckled. 'Without them knowing the full of it, of course. How are you planning to do the deed?'

'It will need to look natural. We don't need any more turmoil. An illness.'

'I know exactly how to dispose of the traitor, my lord.'

'If you can help me achieve this, you shall have your tenpence a day.'

'Pleasure doing business with you, my lord.'

'Cooper,' Lovell called.

Heavy footsteps hurried close.

Lovell spoke again. 'Get the things I requested from the grain merchant. Make sure he knows where to deliver the bags of flour I requested and distributes the rest across the city. I depart for London at midday.'

'Aye, my lord,' Cooper said, greasy-like.

I held still as three pairs of footsteps faded. Should I tell someone? I screwed up my nose. Who would believe me over a lord and the reeve? If I stood witness they'd come after me for sure. Best I just forget the whole thing. I tried to set aside a twinge of guilt. After all, the king would have people protectin' the babe, surely?

Lovell appeared on the road headed south, with Morrigan beside him. They didn't look around and I heaved a sigh of relief when they were out of sight. But which way did Cooper go? Would he see me if I stood up? My arse was startin' to ache from sittin' on the cold ground. The sun inched higher and I needed to get to the forest. Especially if Cooper was goin' to be busy elsewhere.

I took a risk and stood up. All clear.

The sun was fair-up by the time I got to the woods. I paused and checked around. But outside the trees were only rows of wheat ready for harvest, hedgerows and a few cows and chickens. Inside the forest, cool light shone green through the summer-dark leaves. I breathed in a deep gulp of air, heavy with the smell of damp leaves and dirt. This was more like.

What would a forest in Wales smell like? The same? I fingered the leaves of an ancient oak. Would somewhere far off, like Spain, have oaks? What did the ocean look like? Was the water really salty, as that Frenchman who came through Isledon last year said? Didn't seem possible.

A rustle in the undergrowth dragged my thoughts back to here-and-now. No point in thinkin' about far-away places I couldn't get to for years and years, yet. I'd promised Ma to look after the littleuns.

Just in case someone watched, I picked a few mushrooms and stowed them in a cloth bag I carried in my pouch. Then I pulled an arrow from the cloth quiver around my hips, nocked it, and crept forward. A fallow doe and her fawn stepped soft-like into a sunny clearin'. I let down the string and watched. I didn't shoot nursin' does.

A young stag appeared and stopped, sniffin' the air. The wind shifted and he stiffened, his head turnin' toward me. I swore, drew the string, sighted and released. Then another. But the first hit him fair through the lungs. He leapt, staggered a few steps and fell hard on the mossy ground. The doe and fawn skittered into the forest.

I approached the stag careful-like, but it stared glassy-eyed back. I knelt on the ground and laid a hand on it's warm hide, offerin' thanks to the old gods, as my Pa had taught. So far, the Lord hadn't provided much and had taken almost everythin' from me. The old gods seemed to have a better idea of what was important—food and family.

The arrows came free and I cleaned and tucked them away. Now I had a problem. The animal was small, but too heavy for me to carry the long miles back home. And it wasn't yet dark. I couldn't exactly go prancin' about the countryside carryin' the king's deer for all to see. But I couldn't leave it here to be eaten by wild dogs, either.

I'd have to gut it, skin it, butcher some and string the rest high in a tree. I could take some home tonight and some tomorrow night. It was risky. The kill might be found by other poachers or even the reeve's men. But it would have to do.

Skinnin' and butcherin' was a messy business, so I took off my leather satchel and most of my clothes and laid them aside. Nothin' gave away poachin' like a bloody tunic. The job took an age and I was bone-weary by the time I wrapped a haunch and the brain, liver and kidneys in the skin and tied the rest up a tree. I'd use the brain to tan the hide. I scraped a hole and buried the offal. A stream gurgled nearby. The water was icy-cold, but woke me up and cleaned off the blood and stench.

Leavin' the skin and meat by the stream, I went back for my clothes and dragged them on. Slung my pouch over a shoulder and pulled out a cloth to wrap the haunch in. I'd missed a smear of blood on my elbow and wiped it on my tunic. A little blood wouldn't matter.

The sun rode low through the trees. Night would catch me soon. But there was the last-quarter moon tonight, so I should be able to make at least one more trip to collect more meat. I headed back toward the stream. Dusty gold beams of light played through the leaves and blackbirds warbled and sang in the undergrowth. Sounded like dozens of them, all callin' and singin' like their little hearts would break with the joy of livin'.

When I was halfway back to the stream, the birds fell silent. Black wings fluttered and flittered in the bushes. Somethin' stirred the fallen leaves behind me. I'd left my bow by the wrapped meat. All I had was my dagger and slingshot. I held it ready with a stone loaded. In these woods it could be anythin' from charcoal-burners or poachers, to dogs, or escaped pigs. All of them dangerous to a girl on her own. Though I was less afeared of dogs and pigs.

'What are you doing out here?' Jeff Cooper stepped out of the undergrowth and gripped his sword and dagger hilts. He pushed out his chest like a cockerel and swaggered closer. His lips curled up in a smile but his eyes were wolf-hard. I tried not to shiver or shrink away.

Maybe he'd think me a lad and leave me be.

He tipped his head to one side. 'You're Edward Barrowman's girl, aren't you?

'Aye,' I mumbled. 'Huntin' for mushrooms.' I held out the half-filled sack.

'Uh-huh.' He studied the sack like it was somethin' unlawful—which it wasn't. He came a couple of steps closer. I stood my ground, but tried not to look him in the eye. He was the sort to hate that in a woman.

I risked a quick look. Sure enough, he was leerin' at me as he had Mistress Helen. He licked his lips. The slingshot still lay hidden in my hand. But if I used it, I might kill him and I wasn't game to do that. No way of knowin' if he was here alone or with his men.

He moved closer. Now I could smell his ale-heavy breath and the rank sweat that stained his tunic.

'You're not such a bad-looking girl, now, are you, Tilda? But didn't your Ma teach you how to wear a dress? It's not seemly to wear hose.' His smirk shifted into a leer and I forced myself to stay still. No point in runnin'. No point in fightin'. He'd enjoy the chase and I was nobody's prey. The only way out was to be like a rabbit and trick him into thinkin' I was dead—or at least not worth eatin'.

His fat hand landed hard on my breast and squeezed. I kept still. He grabbed the bottom of my tunic and lifted it. Then he stopped.

'What's this blood on your tunic? You been poaching, girl? Tell the truth.'

'No, Master Cooper,' I whispered. I hung my head, thinkin' fast. 'It's the woman's curse. That's why I'm out here, really—collectin' moss.'

Cooper's lip curled into disgust and he dropped the cloth like I was spoiled meat. He backed away and wiped his hand on his doublet.

'Get out of here, then. Go home and stay out of my sight.'

'Yessir,' I mumbled, and ran, grinnin' from ear to ear. Men were stupid.

But I only ran until I was sure he couldn't see me. Then I doubled back. No way was I leavin' my bow and that meat behind. I circled around to the stream and followed it back to where the carcass hung. Blood dripped steadily into the stream. That should help hide it from scavengers, at least.

I wrapped up the skin and meat in the cloth. Then I threw my bow over my shoulder. Time to get home. Not a bad day.

When I turned, Cooper stood in front of me, smirkin', his arms crossed.

'God's teeth,' I muttered.

'So you're a blasphemer, a liar, *and* a poacher.' He looked me over again, slow-like.

I said nothin' but itched to grab out my dagger and jam it into his neck. Sweat prickled under my arms and my knees shook.

He jerked his chin at me. 'Tell you what, girl. We'll make a deal. I'll let you keep that haunch and the skin.'

Our gazes clashed and my jaw dropped open. He stepped closer. Still out of dagger reach though.

'And you'll meet me every Wednesday and Saturday behind the church. Ed Nash says you like paying him the rent between the sheets. Maybe you're in the wrong business.' His voice dropped to a low growl and he leered. 'You don't need money when you've got tits.'

'You can keep the deer,' I said, achin' to spit at him.

'No deal. I'll take you to the courts for poaching. Your choice, girl. You look after me regular-like, and I won't notice a deer missing every month. Maybe even a couple of pheasants. Not too much of a sacrifice for a girl like you.' His lip curled.

I hesitated. A deer and pheasants every month without havin' to watch over my shoulder. Meant I could sell the hides and feathers and even the meat. Meant I could feed the boys and maybe even set aside a little so I could get out of this place when they were older.

But the price. I stared at Cooper's coarse red face and his big, heavy body and knew I couldn't. I shook my head dumbly, afeared of what he'd do if I spoke my thoughts aloud.

'Fine,' he said. 'I'll take my dues whether you like it or not, then.'

He fisted my tunic and hauled me close. I drove a knee between his legs. He choked out a scream and bent over. I rammed my forehead into his nose and smiled at the crunch. He collapsed in a heap, curled around his cock, groanin' and burblin' as blood poured from his broken nose.

I ran.

I ran fast and hard, all the way back to Aunty Lizzie's house, the skinful of meat bumpin' against my shoulder.

When I got there, I slammed the door and leaned against it, gaspin'. Aunty Lizzie's brisk footsteps sounded on the flagstone floor. She and Mistress Helen appeared.

'Are you alright, Tilda-love?' Aunty Lizzie said. 'You look sick. You've got blood on your head!'

'Cooper's,' I managed.

Helen helped me over to a stool. I sat because my knees gave way and I couldn't stand any more. My whole body shook and I could hardly get the words out but I told them what he'd done. What I'd done.

'What'll I do? He'll come after me for sure. He'll charge me with poachin' and the boys will have no-one to raise them. I should have just done it.'

'Stop it,' Mistress Helen said sharply. 'He had no right to try and force you. But you're right, he won't let this go.' She shuddered. 'I know his type.'

'Aye,' Aunty Lizzie said darkly. 'We all do.' Her face brightened. 'I know. I've been worritin' about Mistress Helen goin' off to Lunnon on her own to chase this grain merchant. You'll go with her Tilda. That solves the problem.'

I gaped at her. 'But I can't. The boys need me.'

'Pshaw,' Aunty Lizzie said, pattin' my knee. 'They're almost grown. Young Joe was tellin' me he wants to 'prentice to the blacksmith. And I know you. You're itchin' to get out of here. I'll take the boys until you get back.' She smiled smugly. 'And you'll be back soon. As soon as you see what a dirty, sinful place Lunnon really is. You'll be wishin' yourself back here in no time.'

I looked between her and Helen, uncertain. 'But…'

Helen nodded. 'She's right. Come stay with me tonight. We'll leave first thing tomorrow and you'd best keep away a little while, at least. Cooper won't let that sort of humiliation go unpunished. We'll visit with my sister-in-law, Catherine. You'll like her.'

'Is she like you?' I asked.

Helen laughed. 'No. She's plump and dark-haired and calm. She and her husband run a bakery, although he's away. She'll help you find work. Then you can decide whether to stay or come home.'

'I can't,' I said again, but even I could hear the wishin' in my voice. Could I really? The boys needed me. No, they needed a mother, and Aunty Lizzie was better than I was at bein' motherly. I'd promised Ma to look after them. But she was the one who'd always said I should go when I was ready. After all, I'd only be there a little while. Like Aunty Lizzie said, I'd surely be back soon.

And maybe, in the city, I could find someone to tell about Lord Lovell's treachery. For the killin' of a babe and its ma didn't sit well with me.

Excitement fluttered low in my stomach and my heart sang like a bird set free of a cage.

'Here, Aunty Lizzie.' I handed over the haunch of venison and stood. 'I've got to pack and say goodbye to the boys. I'm goin' to Lunnon.'

4. Baked in a Pie

Catherine Miller, 25
Baker
Chepe Syed, London,

Wednesday (morning), 20th September, 1486

'Goodwife Miller. It's almost time.' The bishop's tithe-collector squeezed out a smile and flattened slick, thinning hair over a balding pate. He clasped thick hands together on a stomach fat-rounded by too much ale and rich eating.

I stopped kneading, staring at the pale dough pushing through my claw-curled fingers. Sweat stuck hair to my skin and ran down my neck and between my tits. With the ovens running since the churchbells rang at Lauds—before the sun was even up—the house was stuffy-hot even at this early hour of the morning.

I shivered.

'Good morrow,' I said, calm as I could. 'What can I do for you, Master Godwin?' Surely it wasn't yet time to pay tithes? I'd only counted the money last night. There wasn't enough to pay the church their tenth.

The roof shingles had needed repairs last week. Then there was Mother Miller's doctor's fees. Not that they could do anything for her but ease the pain. And with Paul gone, the bakery's income had dropped. But the Church wouldn't believe that. Or wouldn't care.

Master Godwin's lips stretched again. He picked up a manchet made of fine-ground wheat flour and waved it around at the shop. I chewed uneasily on resentful words. That bun would normally sell to a rich merchant for at least a ha'penny.

'Just a call of courtesy. Reminding you the tithes are due tomorrow.' He took a slow bite of the bread and watched me with those little black-ratty eyes.

I tried to look innocent. 'And, sir?' Heat flushed up from my chest to my hairline.

'And we wouldn't want you being late again,' he said, spraying crumbs. 'After all, I'd hate to see you lose such a fine establishment. Your husband's grandfather built it, didn't he?' He surveyed the thick stone walls, the big, open kitchen and the huge baking oven. 'Where is your husband? Paul, isn't it?'

I brushed my hands off, brisk, and straightened loaves that didn't need to be. 'My husband is away…on business. If that's all, Master Godwin, I have baking to finish.'

Godwin's uneven brown teeth flashed. 'Of course, Goodwife. I'll see you tomorrow, then.' He screwed up his nose, hesitated, then placed the half-gnawed bread back on the display bench.

Trembling, I waited until he was out the door and vanished up the street.

'You're a churl and a base skamelar, Master Godwin,' I yelled. 'A pox on your family.' Snatching up his leavings, I hurled the bun out the open window, into the street.

Agnes Webb, an underfed street waif who hung about Chepe Syed, snatched it up with a crow of delight and scurried away. Her skinny little brother raced after.

I stared at my plump hands, curled into doughy, useless fists. Light glinted off the silver and garnet poesy ring Paul had given me at our wedding. The only thing of value I owned. I sat heavily on a stool and twisted the ring on my finger.

A honey-bread off the display found its way into my hands. I rip-tore it into pieces, shoving each bite into my mouth as fast as I could chew and swallow. When it was gone, I licked my fingers.

Then I burst into tears.

'Catherine? Where are you?' The crotchety question floated down the stairs. 'Catherine?' Mother Miller thumped on the ceiling until dust drifted down into the shop.

'Coming, Mother,' I called, wiping my face on my apron. I kneaded the dough into the rough shape of a head, then hard-thumped it flat. I set it aside to rise and trudged upstairs.

Mother Miller sat by the bedroom window with the shutters wide open and morning light streaming into the room. Harry looked up when I entered. His little cherub face lit up, those blue eyes sparkling and fat cheeks rosy. He left the wooden horses and men his papa had made and ran to me. My heart nigh on burst when he wrapped his pudgy arms around my neck and bussed me on the cheek, quick and warm-wet.

'Mama,' he said, pointing to the toys. 'King Henry beat King Richard and everyone's dead.'

'Aye, lad,' I said, 'that they are. They always are, no matter who wins.' I forced a smile. 'But King Henry's pretty wife is about to have her own little boy to love, so maybe there'll be no more wars awhile. Now, do you need the privy?'

He shook his dark curls—so like mine—and pointed to the chamber pot under our bed.

'Well,' I said, setting him on the floor, 'maybe you can empty it for me. There's a lad.'

He pouted, but went to the chore agreeably enough. He carried it carefully down the stairs and headed for the back door to empty it in the privy outside.

'He's such a good boy,' I murmured, half to myself. He was why I kept getting up before Lauds to stoke the ovens and bake the bread. He was why I would find the money for the tithe tomorrow. He was why I had the strength to keep going until Paul came back.

'He'd be a sight better if you made him do more chores, instead of letting him waste time playing,' Mother Miller snapped. She twitched a grey wool shawl into place around her shoulders and shifted in the chair. I pressed my lips tight and said nothing.

'He'll have to start learning the trade soon, Catherine,' she added, watching me narrowly.

'He's not even four, Mother,' I said, calm as I could.

'When his father was four, he was helping his pa stock the baking oven and mix the dough. My Paul could run the shop by himself by the time he were twelve. You're spoiling Harry. If Paul were here he'd have summat to say.'

I turned away to hide the sudden anger-burn in my gullet. Appalled, I made a fuss of straightening the bed we shared and tidying Harry's toys away.

Paul had been gone three months. Sometimes it cut like it was only a week. Sometimes it ached like an old love-memory. Was he safe? I still looked for him in every man that entered the shop. Did he miss me, or Harry?

Mastering myself, I turned back. Mother Miller waved me over. Her salt-white hair glinted in the light. Paul said she used to be beautiful and happy. But in the five years I'd known her she'd only shown a face carved deep with lines of pain and bitterness. Her mouth pinched around an endless stream of hate-ugliness.

But it was not her fault the accident had left her crippled and in pain. I must be patient.

The street below her window was crowded with people and horses now the sun was fully risen. Hawkers of everything from apples to shoes cried their wares loud, trying to outdo each other. Children scurried about, doubtless thieving and getting up to make-mischief.

Young Agnes Webb dashed past, a purse in hand and an elderly man in pursuit. That girl would get herself killed one of these days. My Harry would never feel the hunger-ache enough to need to thieve.

Blackbirds Sing p65

Not if I had any say in it.

The stench of shit and piss was strong today. Sure enough, the night soil collector's cart stood not far away, taking buckets from those who didn't have a privy. Made me glad the tannery that used them was on the other side of the river, in Southwark.

My Harry would never stoop to that job, either. He would have the bakery when he was old enough. It was hard work, but he and his family would never want.

As long as I could keep it going until he was grown. With Paul gone, it was hard to do everything myself—and look after Mother Miller and Harry. But I couldn't afford to hire a man to do the heavy-work. I worried at my lower lip and fiddled with the poesy ring.

'Your eyes are red, girl,' Mother Miller snapped, glaring at me. 'What have you got to cry over.' She slapped one of her stick-thin legs. 'At least you're not stuck in a chair day in, day out, minding someone else's brat...' Her hand curled into a fist and she looked away, grimacing.

'Harry's your grandson,' I said quietly. 'Your only son's boy. You should be glad to help. After all, I'm the one up all hours running your son's business. If Paul were here—'

'You're the one should be grateful, girl.' She sniffed. 'When my Paul found you, scrounging in the gutters and stealing food, you were just another quean over in the Southwark whorehouses.'

I chewed down a spiteful-mad reply and dug my nails into my palms. Even after my first husband died and left me with nothing, I'd never stolen. Or whore-sinned so bad as that. Yet Mother Miller would only believe the worst of me.

She raked me with a scornful look. 'What was Godwin doing here? Tithes aren't due til tomorrow.'

'Just reminding us,' I said, stiffly.

'You've got enough set aside, haven't you?' she said, sharpish.

My cheeks burned and I studied my fingers where they turn-twisted my apron.

There was a long silence and Mother Miller's thin fists clenched in her lap. 'If there's not enough for the tithe, we'll lose the shop. My home. Your son's future.'

'I know.'

'Well, you need to stop stuffing your gob, eating all the profits, girl. Gluttony is a sin, remember. If you weren't so greedy, Paul would still be here, not off trying to earn gold sailing to foreign lands. And I wouldn't be afeared of being thrown out of my own house.'

I gasped and we stared at each other: her pale and bitter, me dizzy and guilt-sick.

'Mama?' Harry's piping little voice floated up. 'There's a lady and a man in the shop.'

I whirled and hurried to the stairs, glad of a reason to leave before anger took hold of my tongue and spat something hasty-hot at the old woman. All I'd ever wanted was a meal every day and to be a mother. I never wanted to run a business. Her family's business. But it kept my son's stomach full, so I would keep doing it.

For Harry and Paul. Not her.

I paused halfway down the stairs and took a deep breath to settle myself. I couldn't afford to snap at paying customers so I pasted on a make-smile.

'Good morrow, my good—' I stopped and gaped. '*Helen?* God's blood! What are you doing here?'

My sister-in-law's dark blue eyes widened at the oath. At her side, a wiry lad with a broad, cheerful face full of freckles smothered a snort-laugh. I mumbled an apology and opened my arms.

The troubled frown vanished from Helen's plain face and she

embraced me. We'd always got on well, for all she and my brother, John, lived all the way out at Isledon. I looked past her at the street outside.

'Where's John? And little Robert? Surely you didn't leave poor John looking after the babe? Not in the middle of harvest.'

Helen's sun-pinked cheeks paled. She stilled and one hand stole to her throat. 'I sent a message three weeks ago. John…and Robert…' A single tear slipped down her face and she brushed it aside with the habit of one long used to crying.

I covered my mouth and leaned heavy-like on the bench. My brother and my nephew. My last family. John had been much older, but he'd been kind. Now I was truly alone.

Heart-hollowed, I asked, 'How?'

'An…illness,' Helen said, her voice rough. 'But one I know how to cure, now. That's why we're here. I have to find a grain merchant who came through Isledon. Has he been here?'

'I buy from the market, not from the travelling merchants.'

'I'll have to go try the guild houses.' She cleared her throat and pointed at the young man by her side. 'This is Tilda. She was kind enough to escort me here. I said you might let her stay and perhaps have a little work.' Helen looked anxiously at me. 'Just until she finds her feet in London. I thought…maybe with Paul away…'

One more mouth to feed. I looked the girl over. Dressed like a boy. That would never do in my shop. Not here in London. The monks would haul her to the stocks for people to laugh and mock like a common whore.

Tilda gave me a big, hopeful grin. 'I can bake a bit, Goodwife Miller. And look after the little one. I'm strong, too.'

I sighed. There was every chance the Church would take the shop tomorrow, anyway, and we'd both be out on the street.

'Well, I can't pay you right now. Church tithes are due and I haven't got enough to pay them. Food and lodging. The bedroom's upstairs and there are spare floursacks in the storage room in the back for bedding. Take it or leave it.'

Tilda's smile shifted from sparkle to determination—which made me like her all the more. Not a pathetic little country flower who'd wilt in the polluted air of London, then.

Helen tucked her haversack under the stairs. 'I have to find that merchant. And…' she blushed and looked away '…I need to leave a message for a…friend…at the Minstrel's Guildhall. I'll be back later.'

'I'm comin' with you, Mistress Helen,' Tilda stated, laying aside her bow and satchel. 'Aunty Lizzie said I weren't to leave you alone in Lunnon.'

'Quite right,' I said. 'But keep your hat low, Tilda, and your dagger close. There's many a man who'd take offence at your get-up. Stay out of trouble. Be back before sunset. The curfew bell goes at nine, but you don't want to be out after dark.'

She grinned and tugged her floppy felt hat lower.

'Helen?' I wiggled the poesy ring off and held it out, ignoring the grief-lump in my throat. 'Take this to the Cahorsin down the road. The shop with three gold balls hanging out front. Tell Cecily Hayward it's for me. For the tithes. She'll do the right thing.'

'Oh, Catherine,' Helen said softly, holding the ring up to the light. 'Pawning it? Are you sure?'

My heart contracted as the sun glinted blood-pretty through the garnet. I'd buy it back before Paul returned. I nodded. 'It's the only way. It won't be enough, but I'll find the rest. Somehow.'

She slipped it onto her thumb and kissed my cheek, teary again.

'Go on,' I said gruffly. 'Before I change my mind. And try the grain market on Gracechurch Street, or the storehouse at Leadenhall on Corn Hull for your grain merchant.'

I watched them weave through the cartsellers and bystanders and shook my head. They were both so green. Hopefully they'd make it back with my money.

Harry tugged on my skirt and I swept him into a hug, burying my tears for John and little Robert in Harry's sweet neck, holding him so hard-tight he squealed and squirmed.

An hour before sundown, the women weren't back and I was starting to worry. Master Godwin strolled past the door and tipped his hat to me, smiling that knowing sly-smirk that made me want to slap his round, sweaty face.

As the sun softened to gold-dusk I checked the street again, hoping to see Helen and Tilda hurrying back. And there they were, only a few steps away, both looking hot-flushed and harried.

Helen dropped coins into my palm. 'The money from your ring. But we've had no luck at all, Catherine. The merchant must have sold his wares already and they could be anywhere.' She gazed at me earnestly. 'Whatever you do, *don't* buy any rye flour. Whatever you have here already should be alright, but nothing new.'

'You can't mean it, Helen!' I glanced at my loaves. 'Three quarters of my customers can only afford the rye.'

'If you don't do as I say, your customers could die.' She nodded sharply. 'Now I must go write a note to the Master of the Barber's Company. He must warn all the surgeons and doctors. Then I'll need to…' Her voice faded as she hurried upstairs followed by Tilda, who shrugged and took the steps two at a time.

Die? I gaped after them. What in the Lord's name was she on about? Maybe losing my brother had turned her wits end-wise. I couldn't stop selling rye bread. Might as well pack up and leave if I did that for then I'd have no hope of paying tithes. I checked the coins she'd given me. Not enough for tomorrow.

The sunset bells rang out and I grasped the door, ready to lock up.

Across the road, a pair of fine gents standing opposite caught my eye. Both with skin the colour of crusty bread, and dark-cinnamon hair. One was so tall and broad as to almost be a giant. And handsome. The other was like enough to be his brother, but thin and carrying a gittern and bow across his back. They were talking and pointing at my shop.

I twitched my apron straight and patted my coif, tucking a few loose hairs back beneath the cloth. One more customer was worth staying open for.

The larger strode off up the street. The thin man waited for a fish-cart to pass then crossed the road. He ducked to enter my doorway. I put on a beaming smile and curtseyed.

'Good e'en, good sir. What will you have?' I pointed at the display of honey breads and round loaves. 'We have the best breads in the city. Not just rye, but white bread, molasses bread. All sorts.'

He bowed and selected a small molasses bread. He placed a whole penny on the counter.

'Tis too much, sir,' I said. 'Take another few loaves as well.'

He smiled and suddenly I wanted only to please him so I could see that gentle-kind smile again.

'I have a commission, my good woman. And your honesty persuades me you are indeed the best person for the job.'

'I never cheat a customer, or steal, sir. What can I do for you?'

'I need you to bake a subtlety for me. Enough to feed sixty people.'

'A subtlety? For sixty? Good my Lord!' I'd heard of them, of course. The gentrys' cooks made creations of such beauty or strangeness that word of them filtered down to even the lowest folk. Peacocks and swans whole-roasted, with their feathers put back on so they looked alive. Breads and cakes baked into the shapes of animals and myth-beasts. Fruits and spices from far off lands. Things with saffron and clove and sugar in them. My mouth watered at the thought.

But those cooks had dozens of people to help. And huge ovens in big kitchens. I glanced doubtfully around my little shop with its one oven and two workbenches.

'Are you sure you have the right place, sir?'

'I am.' He spread his hands. 'Something called me to you. God, himself, perhaps.'

I crossed myself as his meaning sank in. Perhaps this was the sign I'd been hoping for; the sign that things would get better. Gloom descended again like a cloud of flour settling heavy on my shoulders.

'I wish I could, sir, but I don't have enough help or money to make something so important.'

'You shall. And the money. And, when the time comes, you'll also have a kitchen larger than this to work in.' He leaned close. 'But there are two things you must agree to.'

'What, sir?' In my experience, there was always a catch if something sounded too good.

'One: you must tell no-one the details of what you're making, where, when, or for whom it's being made.' He waited for my nod then continued, 'Two: you will use the ingredients I send over for you. Nothing else. If you do these things, you will have forty angel-nobles.'

Impossible hope swelled in my chest like rising dough. That much money…I totted up in my head. Forty gold nobles was thirty-two hundred pence. Twelve pounds worth. My breath hitched. I could hire help for two years, at least. More if I was careful and hired them casual-like. Maybe long enough to keep the shop going until Harry grew old enough to help.

Suspicion overtook hope. It was definitely too good to be true.

'This isn't nothing...wrong, is it, sir?' I glanced uneasily out the door, half-expecting a constable or the bailiff to come bursting in. 'I won't get into trouble?'

The beautiful man leaned in again, his smile melting my fears. 'No, child. Not at all. Not if you do exactly as I say.' He extended a hand and opened his fist. There, on his palm, lay my poesy ring.

I gasped, reached...and hesitated. 'Where did you get this?'

He placed the ring on the bench with a little tick of sound. 'I merely redeemed it for you from the Cahorsin. As a symbol of good faith.'

He withdrew a small leather purse from beneath his plain doublet. The purse clinked heavy-rich when he dropped it next to the ring.

'A downpayment of fifty pence. I'll send the ingredients over tomorrow. Rye flour, wheat flour, spices and a few other things. The messenger will tell you a recipe to follow. Exactly. No questions. No changes. When it's done, the rest of the money is yours. Do we have an agreement?'

I stared long at the ring, gleaming red in the sunlight. At the purse of dark-shining worn leather, weighted by the wealth inside. The coin that could pay the tithe, save my shop, my future, my son. But every bit of me cried out against the sin of it. No questions? No changes? And what of Helen's warning about rye flour? This couldn't be right. Couldn't be Godly or honest. And, in spite all the bad that had happened to me, I'd never done evil to another.

But the tithes.

Due tomorrow. And the loss of income if I couldn't sell rye breads, as Helen said.

I slipped the poesy ring onto my finger and nodded. 'Send the

Blackbirds Sing p73

ingredients.'

He bowed and left the shop. I still didn't know his name. Didn't want to.

Quick footsteps pattered on the stairs behind me. Helen, with her skirt lifted, raced down and hurried mad-like out the door. She caught up with my customer and caught at his arm. He bowed over her hand and kissed it. They exchanged a few words, then he nodded and strode away. She watched after him, cheeks flushed and eyes sparkling.

If she knew him, perhaps my choice to take his money wasn't so bad. I hefted the purse. No. It was too good a deal. But what options did I have? Damned if I did, or if I didn't.

I stood there for a long time. Then I took three soft, white-bread manchet's off display and carefully spread creamy butter on them. I carried them and the purse upstairs. In silent reverence, with the sunlight streaming through the west window like God's blessing, I lay the bread and the purse on a little table next to Mother Miller.

'What's this?' She stared at the objects, shrinking back from the bread as though it were diseased. 'You can't waste good wheat-bread on us. Harry!' But her warning was too late. Harry'd snatched a roll and stuffed half of it into his gob. The bliss-rapture in his blue eyes warmed me through.

I pointed at the purse. 'I'm commissioned to bake a subtlety. This is a downpayment. We can pay the tithes. We won't lose the shop.'

Mother Miller touched an unsteady finger to the purse. I tensed, awaiting a sharp-tongued slight. But her dark eyes overflowed and tears traced the creases of her worn cheeks. My heart melted with each unheeded drip to her coarse woollen kirtle.

'I won't have Harry go hungry,' I said. 'And I won't let you be beggared on the streets. Not ever, Mother. You're family. *My* family. All I got left. Even if you don't want me.'

'Oh…' She covered her mouth with one gnarled hand and gripped my arm tight with the other. 'You won't…leave me like Paul, and my husband?'

Gently, I hugged her and she embraced me back. I turned my thoughts away from the future. From what I'd done. From what I would do for that money. Only Harry and Mother mattered.

For them I'd do anything.

5. When the Pie was Opened

Agnes Webb, 10
Thief
Chepe Syed, London,

Wednesday (morning), 20*th* September, 1486

My stash was gone and vanished no matter how much I scratched around in the dusty little hole under the floorboard and swore by God's teeth, hair, and balls. Nothing. I sat back against the dirty-plastered wall and stared at the dark ceiling beams close overhead. Three days' work, a silver ring, six ha'pennies and four farthings; 'nough to keep Mama Rolfe off my back and still put two farthings away so I could take Jack outa the city one day.

Gone.

The thin wooden box that had held the pretties and coins lay open and smashed on the floor, like someone wanted to show they hated me. I grabbed the dagger at my hip.

My heart jittered and hopped like a skittish sparrow. What about my stash for Jack and I? Was that still there, did I dare check in the daylight hours when someone might see me? The stuffy attic room was empty but for piles of ratty cloth and bags that served as bedding for five of us, and Jack was downstairs in the alley playing cobnut with some of the other little ones, like the five-year-old kid he still was.

But there were holes in the plastered walls and any one of Mama Rolfe's thirty other runners could be watching; no telling who'd seen me put the box back in my hidey-hole yesterday, best wait til dark and check the other hoard when everyone but the lookout was asleep.

I stilled. Or, maybe someone else'd given the hiding place up.

I scrambled to my feet, shoved my torn felt hat back on my fresh-shorn hair and brushed at my tunic and hose, for I had to ask him, but then I'd best get moving as Mama Rolfe would check the takings at midday and that didn't bear thinking about.

My shoulders twitched. Nah. Wouldn't happen. I'd think of something and I was one of Mama Rolfe's best thieves, so she wouldn't throw me out if I came home with a little less than normal this once, and sure as the sun came up I'd get something and it'd be fine.

Down in the street, I collared Jack and dragged him from the rowdy game.

'Who'dja tell?' I whispered in his grubby ear. He said nothing but his big green eyes—just like mine—widened. 'C'mon. It hadda be you. No-one else knew.'

'S-sorry, Agnes,' he said. His lip quivered. 'I hadda. Big Jim said he'd kill ya if'n I didn't give over. But I didn't show him everything, I promise.'

'Jack, I'm your big sister an I'm twice your age.' I cuffed his head. 'We gotta trust each other 'cause God knows there's no-one else we can trust. Y'hear me? I can take Jim, so you keep your trap shut, y'hear?' I pulled the dagger I'd stolen last month outa my belt and thrust it at him, and he flinched and nodded respectful-like. 'Now we gotta go get more or Mama Rolfe'll give us hell come midday. Jim can't hurt me, but Mama'd beat us or throw us both on the street in a whistle if'n we don't pay our keep.'

Jack's head bobbled again and he followed me like a tantony pig toward Chepe Syed.

We squeezed behind some barrels in an alley off Bred Street. The place stank of piss and vomit, but we hunkered down opposite Goodwife Miller's bakery and waited for a mark to come by as they always did on this street full of folks with money to spend and half of them without the smarts to keep their purses tucked away and deserving to part with them.

Inside the bakery Goodwife Miller yelled out loud enough for the whole street to stop and turn and a chunk of bread came a-flying outa the door so I nipped out and snatched it up afore anyone else, and shared it with Jack. Good white bread. Rich folk stuff. Might be the only food we got today if my luck didn't improve, but it would, for sure cause I hadda good feeling.

A couple hours later and all I had for my troubles was an old man's flat pigskin purse with three farthings. So much for the good feeling and now the sun was too warm and the stench of piss and rotten food was worse than ever. The clocktower bells rang eleven and I fidgeted, watching the street close 'cause there was only an hour to go.

Jack nudged me with a sharp elbow and pointed a mark out, standing a few steps away, staring at the bakery like he couldn't decide whether to go in or not. He was tall and thin, wearing cheap clothes but with a musical instrument slung on his back and a longbow as well, so he was from outa town because no-one carried a bow in the city, and he had money, because travellers always did, but maybe not much. Enough to make it worth a try. I grinned. This'd be easy.

'You distract him,' I whispered to Jack. 'Tell him you've lost your mama or something. Look sad.'

There would be no trouble him doing that as he always looked sad, ever since our Pa died in the wars and then Ma died in the sweating sickness last year, anyway. 'When you see me run, you run too. Don't you get caught, y'hear?'

Jack's pointed chin set hard and he darted out and tugged on the man's shirt. I couldn't hear what they said but Jack was doing a fine job 'cause the mark's whole look was all for the poor little lost boy.

I snuck around behind them. One slice and the purse was mine, all heavy, supple leather and soft clink of coins as I dropped it inside my tunic and scarpered. But only a few steps down the road and there was no slap of Jack's bare feet behind me so I swore and turned around, heart dropping to my knees 'cause, sure enough, the big guy had my idiot brother by the arm and held him close, but his attention was on me, not Jack.

He smiled and I couldn't help smiling back even though I was in so much trouble it shoulda scared shit outa me. He waved me closer and I went, who knew why, not me, that's for sure.

When I got closer I realised he was a woman in men's clothing, well-hidden for sure, but not a man 'cause they smell different and move different. Her dark-rimmed grey eyes sparkled with laughter I didn't understand.

'Well, aren't you an observant little sprat? So…' she said, still holding Jack, but not so tight he squalled; he just looked miserable with tears streaking tracks in the dirt on his face and snot dribbling from his nose. 'I believe, young lady,' she continued, calm-like, 'you have something of mine. Perhaps you'd like to exchange my purse for this young gentleman?'

I hesitated, the purse's weight heavy and solid against my belly. If I said no and ran, she'd turn him over to the constable and there might be enough money in the purse to pay his fine and set him free and still keep some for Mama Rolfe.

The woman bent closer, and she smelled like cut wood, sweet and warm, but she had a hardness that would blunt axes. Her breath brushed my ear and I shivered but forced myself to stand still and lift my chin like it didn't scare me in the least.

'No,' she murmured, 'there *isn't* enough in the purse to pay his fine and keep some for yourself. Because he'd lose a hand, or an ear for this theft.'

My jaw dropped open and I held up a clenched fist, thumb stuck between two fingers, to ward off demons and curse her. 'Witch!' How else could she have known my thoughts so true?

She laughed, a merry sound that somehow settled my fear and dried up Jack's sniffling tears as well and he gazed up at her open-mouthed like a puppy that's found its master.

'Child, I'm no witch. But neither am I an easy mark, as you see.' She pointed at the bulge in my shirt-front. 'Let's make a deal. Give back my purse and I'll give you your brother. And I'll hire you to put those nimble fingers to work for me.'

'Hire me? To do what?'

'Exactly what you're good at.' She glanced up at the sun. 'But you'd best be off now or you'll miss your appointment, won't you? Come back at the two o'clock chimes and I'll have instructions and a new target for you. Agreed?'

I thought about it and gave a satisfied nod and grabbed Jack's other arm and tugged until he squeaked. 'Let him go and you gotta deal, lady. But I'm wishing I'd never set eyes on you.'

She chuckled again. 'I'm no lady, child. And I'm glad you felt called to accost me.'

I gaped at her 'cause no-one had ever been glad I'd stolen from them, so maybe she was mad and what was she going to make me steal?

She added, 'I promise I'll make it worthwhile. Give the purse back.' I threw the purse and she let Jack go then checked the insides like a smart person would, then made shoo-ing movements. 'Off you go. Best not be late.'

Jack and I sprinted toward Thames Street, but I looked back once and the lady was watching us with a twisted smile that gave me chills and I had a feeling that not showing up at two would be as bad as what we were headed into now.

We slunk into Mama Rolfe's chamber in the old boarding house off Garlyk Hill just as the churchbells all over the city rang out midday prayers and quieted all the kids' chatter, until the clanging stopped and we could hear each other again.

When the last rings died away Mama Rolfe shoved through the tatty curtain at the back of the room and plonked her skinny arse on the wood chair she'd had made to look like a throne—all big and chunky and decorated with anything shiny and cheap, bits of glass and copper, mostly.

She tucked her skirt around her ankles and smoothed the patched brocade then pasted on a smile all broken teeth and pretending. The wrinkles and bags around her eyes twitched and her fingers curled into sharp-ended rat claws that scratched at the chair arms and left pale marks in the worn timber.

I whispered in Jack's ear. 'Whatever you hear me say, don't you dare speak up, got it? Looks like Mama's been at the funny mushrooms again and she's not right in the head. You gotta shut up. Right?' I waited for his nod. 'It'll be ok. You know me. I'm always ok.' He nodded again, this time with a little smile.

'So, my filthy snipes,' Mama crooned in her voice like sand grinding underfoot. 'Whatcha got for me this week? Bring it on up.' She pointed to the wooden crate at her feet and Big Jim—who was about three years older than me and a head taller—threw a much-mended sheet of grey wool over the crate to make it presentable.

One by one the runners who stole for Mama in return for a place to sleep and a share of food dropped their weekly takings onto the table and Mama brooded over each little pile, sniffing and licking the metals, biting on any gold, stroking the silk purses and cackling like a broody hen.

Then it was my turn and I squared my shoulders and strode up with my head high. No point in pretending so I shrugged.

'I had a stash, Mama, but Big Jim nicked it so I got nothing but a promise from a mark that he'll hire me this afternoon to do a job and I'll get to keep some of what I lift. You know I'm good for it, yeah?'

Mama Rolfe glared at me with watery, red-rimmed eyes and drummed her black nails on the chair arm. Big Jim leaned his greasy black head in close to her ear and whispered something, then sent me a grin made of bile and hate.

'Jim tells it different,' Mama said. 'He says it was his takings and your brother filched it. Jim just took it back. I trust him. He's been with me since he was four. And I hear-tell your little Jackie-boy got caught and you had to give a purse back today. Get your brother out here so I can punish him.'

'No,' I jumped in hasty before she could drag Jack up. 'No. It wasn't him, it was me as took from Jim and it was me that got caught so punish me, not Jack.'

She smiled like she knew I was lying and didn't care a whit. 'You're a good taker, but you're too cocky by half, girl. Jim?' She lifted a hand and he placed a thin willow switch into it. 'Turn around. Lift your tunic. You're lucky I'm feeling generous. Five today. You don't bring me enough tomorrow and you and your little brat brother are out for good. Got it?'

I ground my teeth and stared black at Jim. Then I turned round, raised my tunic, and fixed my eyes on the bright patch of sunlight streaming in through a hole in the ceiling. All around, the kids' faces were mixes of horror and pity and fear and I ignored them all, even Jack 'cause he'd be crying and if he saw me break he'd break too and then we'd both be flogged. But there was no point in running 'cause

Jim'd catch me before I made the door.

The first lash fell and I set my jaw against a cry and clenched my tunic into tight bunches. Dust danced in the beam of sunlight and I watched a single mote with all my power as the next lash fell and the pain made tears that smeared the room into patches of light and dark.

Another and I had to bite my lip to stop the yell but I growled when the next one fell, pulling my lips back in a snarl I hoped Jim knew was for him. Darkness took my heart and buried it in an anger so red I could barely breathe.

Jim'd been my friend when we first came, before he got scared I'd be Mama's favourite. Just showed I couldn't trust anyone.

The last cut fell on my back but still I didn't cry out and it must have angered Mama for she threw one more at me in a fit then hurled the switch aside and yelled for ale. I dropped my tunic and walked out, straight like a sword, strong and ready to cut, too.

I grabbed Jack and we left the half-rotted room full of thief-kids and their Godforsaken whore of a leader. We could do better. We didn't need 'em.

Jack trotted at my side, looking fearfully up at me. 'You alright, Ag? Does it hurt? Where are we going?'

I wanted to bite out that of course it hurt you stupid fool, but I shook my head. 'Not so much. We're going to get our stuff and the stash and we'll go somewhere else, to another part of the city. At least until we have enough to get out to the country somewhere and we can get work on a farm or something 'cause Papa always said he wanted a farm. I dunno. Anywhere has to be better than London.'

'But who'll look after us? Where'll we sleep tonight?' Jack skipped a couple of steps to keep up with my longer legs and we ran up the stairs to the attic.

'We'll look after each other and for sure we'll find something,' I said. 'Remember we've got that job this afternoon.'

'You trust that lady?'

'Nope,' I said, grinning. 'But we're gonna make sure we keep whatever she wants us to steal.'

We bundled up our things, snuck back downstairs and opened the front door to freedom without anyone being the wiser and I laughed and lifted my face to the warm sun as we fled.

Two hours later and we'd hidden our things in a tucked-away alley-hole none of Mama's kids knew about and waited in the alley across from the bakery. My back was sweaty and stinging, the cloth sticking and tearing the whip-stripes every time I moved but there was nothing I could do but grit my teeth and pretend it was a scratch I couldn't itch. It'd heal in a few days and by then we'd be somewhere safe with food and work and a place to sleep and no-one would lay a hand on either of us again. Not if I could help it.

The clocktower chimed two and Jack's bony hand crept into mine and gripped it tight until my fingers tingled and I had to shake him loose.

'She's not coming,' he whispered. 'What'll we do?'

'She'll be here,' I said. 'I know it. Just wait.'

A shadow fell over us and I jumped up snatching, at my dagger. Someone grabbed my wrist and the lady's calm smile settled my thumping heart a bit. She let me go and I rubbed the white marks left behind.

'You're all bones, child,' she said. 'You need fattening up. But first, let me give you directions.' She crouched, lined her face up beside mine and pointed. 'See that man, with the grey hat and the matching grey doublet with the slashed sleeves? The one who looks like everyone smells bad?'

I snorted a giggle because her words were so right.

'On his left little finger is a ring. I need you to steal it for me. If you can take his purse at the same time, that's perfect. He keeps it tied close, though, so it won't be easy. But the ring is most important. Do you think you can do it?'

I studied the man, his swagger, the sword on his left hip and dagger on his right, the expensive cloth sewn to look like ordinary clothing, his long-toed shoes of grey leather stitched with red.

'I can do it,' I said. 'But I'll need Jack.'

Jack nodded. 'Lost again?'

'Yep. Hang off his hand and get the ring. Grease your fingers in your hair first and it'll slip right off. Don't get caught this time.'

He flashed me a worried little smile, ran his hands through his hair, and scurried up the street, dodging between a cordwainer's cart full of boots and shoeleather, and a horse-drawn cart stacked high with bales of hay. I followed, keeping a cart carrying cages of live chickens between me and the mark until I got past and could come at him from behind.

His purse dangled on his right hip in front of the dagger-sheath of tooled leather. Jack hung off his left arm, whining and begging like the actor he was and I eased alongside with my dagger half-hid in my hand. The mark raised a kerchief to his nose and a woody-sweet smell overpowered even the horseshit stink of the street.

'Get *off* you hedge-born churl,' the mark growled, shaking Jack loose. 'How dare you touch me? I'll call the constables. Get your filthy face out of my sight.' He backhanded Jack across the cheek and laughed when Jack staggered back with blood pouring from a cut near his eye.

Jack burst into tears and ran back toward the alley, and it was hard to tell how much was acting and how much was real pain, but no-one hit my little brother. No-one. I kicked at the back of the mark's knee with my bare foot. Hard. He yelled and stumbled and I kicked the other knee and he dropped to the filthy cobbles and rolled onto his back, blades sliding from their sheaths.

But I wasn't a fool and I'd already slipped into a crowd of goodwives hurrying toward the Shambles market, their chatter and long kirtles hiding me until I was close enough to the alley to slide out and round the corner.

Jack and the lady waited for me and I peered close at Jack's blood-streaked face. 'You alright?'

He nodded and sniffed and wiped his nose on a sleeve then held out his bloodied fist and opened it to show a heavy gold ring with a red stone glinting in the palm. The lady made a grab but I snatched it away quick and held it hard in a tight fist, pulling Jack a few steps outa easy reach.

'We get outa here first, 'cause he'll notice and come a-running and send the constables.' I glared up at her. 'I'm not taking the fall for this if we get caught so if'n you want the ring, find us somewhere to lay low until he gives up and the constables go home.'

'That's reasonable enough,' she said. 'Follow me. I know a place you'll be safe.'

I held Jack's blood-slippery hand and followed a few steps behind as she headed away from Chepe Syed street and turned east, which was fine by me as long as it was far away from the rich man with the swords and the too-quick fists.

'What about our things?' Jack whispered.

'We'll come back later.' I bent closer. 'When I say run, you run, right, 'cause I couldn't get the purse, so this ring is all we got and we can sell it to the Cahorsin on Watlinge Street for a small fortune. Enough to get outa this stinkhole town but first we hafta get far enough away from Mama's territory 'cause for sure she'll have Big Jim and his boys out looking when they find our stuff gone.' I jerked a thumb at the lady. 'Then we ditch her and find somewhere to hide.'

I glanced up at the lady to make sure she couldn't hear, and stopped dead in the alley 'cause she'd vanished and we were alone.

But not alone. The hair on my neck fizzed and I spun, pushing Jack behind me.

Big Jim swaggered down the narrow alley, a nasty grin on his pock-marked face and a sharp blade glinting in his fist. Behind him were three of his bully-boys, all bigger than me and meaner and all carrying clubs or knives.

I pretended to wipe my nose and shoved the ring into my mouth; no way was I losing it even if I hadda swallow.

'Whatcha want?' I jerked my chin at him and rested a palm on my dagger, casual-like.

'The money you owe Mama,' he said, his smirk wider now. 'And anything else you cleared out of the house when you left. I'm sure you took more of my stuff. Hand it over and we might let you get away with just another beating.'

'Hell with you,' I said, snarling. 'Run, Jack. Get outa here, now.'

'No,' he said, with that stubborn streak he sometime got at the stupidest times. He picked up a broken bit of crate-wood from a pile of rubbish heaped against the wall. 'We got each other's backs, remember? You said.'

'Looby,' I muttered.

Big Jim and his pals spread out but I put our backs against a wall so they couldn't get behind. In my ears it sounded like a thousand kids were roaring, and my back prickled with fresh sweat. I yanked out the dagger, pushed it in front of me and tried to watch all four of 'em as they crept closer.

Jim made a dive for me and I ducked his blade and slashed at his arm. Drew blood and a thrill rushed through me when he swore and jumped back.

'You little…' His thick lips twisted into a snarl and he waved the others forward.

Now we were in for it and I might not make it outa this one, but I'd do my best to take Jim with me and maybe they'd let Jack live.

'The first one to lay a hand on my young friends will die a quick death with an arrow through his eye,' a calm voice said from above me. 'Who shall it be?'

I shot a quick look up and, sure enough, standing on the roof of a lean-to building nearby was our lady-friend. With her longbow ready, and an arrow nocked, she had the tip pointed at Jim's head and a cool smile on her mouth that made me want to cheer.

Big Jim and his pals exchanged looks but they didn't want to lose face, even though they were all cowards. The lady drew the bow and lined Jim up nice and he paled and, with one glare at me and a quick nod to the others, he ran up the alley, back toward Mama's place like the big baby he was.

I held back the urge to yell a taunt after him. I wasn't that dumb.

The lady jumped off the high roof like it was a horse-mounting block and strolled over as she put away the arrow. She held out a hand like she wanted to shake, not like she was asking for anything, but I checked it suspiciously.

'I thought, perhaps, I should introduce myself. I'm Amsel,' she said. She kept the hand out and I kept mine safe at my sides, with Jack pushed behind me. 'You do realise,' she said, 'that I could have let them beat you, then taken the ring whenever I wanted? What will it take to convince you that I'm trying to help? I'll find you somewhere safe to stay. We can help each other. Deal?'

I shifted the ring around in my mouth. It meant freedom and escape from London and a chance for Jack to grow up away from the life we'd led since our parents died; always thieving and running and hiding.

Ma would have been horrified. I didn't mind it so much 'cause I was good at it. But Jack was always scared and I'd promised Ma I'd look after him.

If I gave the ring up I had nothing but a few rags for clothes and a couple of coins and nowhere and no-one.

'You may trust me. Truly,' Amsel said with that soft smile that made me want to make her proud.

I hesitated and looked into Jack's big, hopeful eyes. He needed somewhere; someone.

I spat the ring into my palm and thrust it into hers. 'Don't make me regret this, lady.'

She tucked it away and nodded toward the end of the alley. 'Come. We have a ways to go and I must be back here at sunset for an appointment.'

Jack stepped around from behind me and tucked his hand into hers, gazing trustfully at the tall woman.

'Where are we going?'

'Where would you like to go?' she said.

'To a house with a fire and food and a family,' he stated firmly.

Amsel chuckled and held out a hand toward me. 'Then you'll like my friend, Olivia. She lives in a lovely house with her parents and her husband, but she's quite sad because her little girl died and she misses her. I believe she will like you both very much.'

I looked back over my shoulder at the filthy rabbit-warren of alleys and broken lives around this part of town, then back at Amsel's gentle smile and a tiny seed of forgotten warmth grew in my stomach and I remembered what it felt like to have a grown-up I could rely on. Maybe.

I hesitated, then slipped my hand into hers.

6. The Birds Began to Sing

Isabella MacDonald, 29
Musician/Composer
Chepe Syed, London,

Wednesday (mid-afternoon), 20th September, 1486

'Isabella? Are you listening?' Nicola's light question interrupted me. 'Prithee, Bella, read it again to me?'

I sat back from my frantic search through our trunk. In truth I'd only been half-aware of her words; more attuned ta their cadence than meaning. Her voice always seduced me.

She held out the heavy, gilded tome her godfather, William Caxton had given her, and smiled that winsome, a-hoping smile. I'd read stories from it every day for months since it arrived. The book was her most-treasured object. And the most valuable thing in this tiny, musty room.

I wouldna miss this place, once I was in the Fellowship and earning decent money.

In the winter winds whistled through the gaps with notes that set my teeth on edge. In the summer we sweltered under the close roof and lay a-talking, and a-listening for the waite-musician-watchmen ta make their rounds and play their night-music ta lull us ta sleep.

But even in this poor garret bedroom overlooking Westchepe Syed, Nicola managed ta be lovely. She reclined in her chemise on the straw-stuffed mattress, amongst the rumpled bedsheets. A beam of sunlight painted red in her long dark hair and turned her sightless eyes snowy-white.

But I had ta resist her. Today, at least. I dragged a green surcoat from the trunk and held it up. Yes, it would do. No time ta steam the wrinkles out, though. At least it matched my eyes and showed off my red hair. I threw it on over my grey kirtle and white chemise and tied a coif over my hair.

'Aye, Nic, I'll read it,' I said, a-fumbling with the surcoat lacing. 'But not now. Remember? I have ta take Father's sword and my shawm ta the Cahorsin shop and get money for the membership fee. I canna be late. Harold's a-waiting. He's promised ta come with me ta see the Master.'

'Oh, but no, Bella.' Nicola's fine dark brows pulled tight in a rare frown. 'Not your shawm as well. You'll not be able to play this evening?'

I shrugged and fastened the lacing. 'I've still got my lute and the recorder. Quieter alongside your lute, anyway. And once I'm in the Fellowship of Minstrels I'll be able ta ask higher rates. Write music for the playhouses. Maybe get a noble patron. And the Fellowship can afford ta get my music printed on Master Caxton's new printing press. Then, God willing, the court'll hear my compositions and we can move ta better lodgings.'

I sat on the edge of the bed, set the thick copy of *le Morte d'Arthur* aside, and held Nicola's hands. 'I promise, Nic. Once I have membership, everything'll change. You'll see.' But I was a-sweating already. What if the Master of Minstrels said No?

Nicola stretched out a hand. I leaned inta it. Her calloused fingertips scratched my cheek.

'I know, love,' she said, soft and sweet. 'But it matters not to me where we live, so long as we're together. If I'd wanted a rich life could I not have married Sir Edward?'

I swallowed a lump in my throat. 'Aye, but I canna stand the way the men in this churlhouse gawp at you. An I canna always be here ta protect you.'

Her smile became wry. 'But I need no protecting and you need not join the Fellowship. You're better than any of them. But you'll not listen when I tell you that so, prithee, go. And good luck. But remember, we sing for our supper after the sunset bells ring.'

I kissed her soft, warm mouth and savoured the taste of mead on her lips. I sighed in regret for having ta leave and gathered my shawm and the sword in its sheath. 'Practice that new piece I wrote and I'll be back a-fore Vespers ta take you ta church.'

She kissed me again and shoo-ed me out, locking the door behind me. The first notes of my new tune drifted from her lute. She had a perfect ear. I'd only played it once for her.

Downstairs, Harold waited, his homely, broad face a-lighting up when I ran down the risers. 'You look a treat, all dressed up.'

I dipped a mocking little curtsey.

He grimaced. 'You sure 'bout this, Bel?' he said, scratching at his curly brown hair. 'I mean, you've gotta place to live and food for free for singin' each night. There's many-a member who can't even boast that. Do you—'

'Aye, I'm sure,' I said. I had my recorder and a roll of my music tucked inta the satchel over my shoulder. I'd *make* them see I was worthy. They'd print my music by the book-full. My hands shook and Harold snatched the shawm and sword a-fore I dropped them.

'Rollo?' I called ta the Broken Seld's innkeeper. He stuck his balding head out from the corridor at the rear of the taproom and lifted caterpillar brows. 'I'm a-going out. Make sure no-one bothers Nic?'

'O-course,' he said, sniffing. One meaty hand lifted a club he kept leaning up against the wall. 'Always.' The faint sound of Nicola's sweet voice carried from our room and his round face softened.

Harold and I a-hurried south ta Cecily Hayward's pawn shop on Bred Street. It was the work of moments ta sell her the shawm and my father's good steel sword. It cost me a pang ta part with both. But my father had always prayed for a boy, not a disobedient daughter who wanted nothing more than ta play music. Died still wanting a boy to protect him in battle.

Cecily sighed over the shawm, for she had a generous heart in her generous bosom. She hid the instrument away, a-promising ta keep it safe.

With coin-purse tucked deep inta my kirtle, we strode toward Bassing Lane. And everywhere music followed me. The chatter of passing goodwives a-carrying baskets of groceries rose and fell like partsongs. The pattering steps of apprentices running errands for their masters set up a rhythm counter ta the clip-clop of horses' hooves. A blacksmith's hammer struck a clear C on the anvil, steady and slow. I found myself a-humming a new melody round the hammerblows. A song about a smith and his lover. About a battle and a death.

'Bella?' Harold's deep bass voice interrupted the song. He'd stopped and stood a-pointing at the little stone hall on Bassing Lane. I came back and joined him, staring up at the front with its thick stone ground floor, and plaster and timber upper storeys. A sign with a lyre and a swan hung out front, a-creaking in the warm late-summer wind.

I pulled back my shoulders, lifted my chin and followed Harold up the two steps, through the thick oaken door. Harold snatched off his hat and twisted it in his big hands.

A servant showed us inta Master Smith's office. At the door, I gulped and almost backed out. What if he hated my music? What if I only *thought* it was good? Was I just a-fooling myself? Only a frowning look from Harold got me over the threshold.

'Master Smith,' Harold said.

The master looked up from his desk and nodded a greeting. 'Harold. Good to see you, boy. One moment.' His voice was smooth and resonant. I wanted ta write a part-song for him and Nicola. A love duet. His quill pen travelled over a sheet of parchment, a-scratching in the thick silence. I took the chance ta look around his cramped, dark office.

Two real wax candles lit his work and tallow ones stood in brackets around the walls. In between, hung more lutes, gitterns, viols, hurdy-gurdys, and other instruments than I'd ever seen. Some I couldna even name and shame a-flushed inta my cheeks. I oughta know. A real member would know. I chewed on my lip and fiddled with the satchel. I shouldna be here.

The scratching stopped and Master Smith carefully sanded his work then set it aside onta one of the enormous piles of parchment on his desk. So much parchment and vellum. Even some paper. What I could do with that. How much I could write, print—maybe even sell ta other minstrels.

Master Smith cleared his throat and looked over the top of his little round eyeglasses. He leaned back in his chair and swept a narrow hand over his smooth dark hair.

'So? What can I do for you, Harold? Time to sit for your Master's level?'

Harold shifted from foot ta foot and gave a nervous laugh. 'Nay, sir. I doubt I'll ever be good enough to make Master. I'm happy playing in the Broken Seld and makin' lutes and viols for folk.' He paused and shot me a quick look. 'This here is my friend, Isabella MacDonald, sir. I've come on her behalf. To beg a favour.'

'Oh?' Smith looked me up and down.

I dipped a quick curtsey.

'She—' Harold began.

'I'd like ta join the Fellowship, Master,' I blurted, unable to wait on Harold's slow words anymore. He groaned.

Smith leaned forward, his chair creaking. He gave a tired,

disdainful laugh and flicked ink-stained fingers at me.

'I'm disappointed in you, Harold. No women. You know the rule. Women don't have the intellect to understand music, to write it, to *feel* it. And the bishop certainly won't allow music written or played by a woman into the chapels and cathedrals.' His smug expression was the sort my father used ta give when I said I'd be a minstrel one day. 'Go back to your husband and your hearth, good woman. Leave music to men and look after your children.' He slid another piece of parchment before him and dipped the quill inta an inkpot.

Harold shuffled toward the door and grabbed my wrist. I yanked free and pulled my sheet music out.

'But sir,' I said, palms a-sweating. 'I can play five instruments. And look at—'

Smith shot ta his feet, scowling. 'How dare you, woman? I am Master here, and while I am, the rule stands.' He pointed at the door. 'Out of my office now before I call a constable. Out.'

I opened my mouth, shut it, whirled and stalked out the door with tears a-blurring the way so much I could barely see. Outside on the street I strode back and forth with fists clenched at my sides and anger a-burning a hellfire path through my whole body.

'It's not *fair,* Harold,' I railed. 'He didna even look. Didna even let me play.'

'I know, Bella,' he said regretfully. 'You shoulda waited for me to lay the groundwork instead of stomping in like you did. He don't like change. Not shoved at him sudden like that.'

'So this is *my* fault?' I said. 'It's *my* fault the Godforsaken Fellowship is like everywhere else and thinks women are fools?' Abruptly the fight went from me and I sagged against the warm stone wall. 'Maybe we are. Maybe I am for thinking I could do it as well as a man. Maybe I've been a fool all along and my father was right.'

Harold came close and put an arm around my waist, he tucked me against his body and I sighed and leaned on his shoulder.

'You don't need them, Bella,' he whispered. 'Marry me and we can play music together. I don't mind. And once you have a baby you'll be happy, anyway. You won't need to earn money playing in inns.'

I pushed away and stared at him in horror. 'Marry you? God's blood, I canna. I ran away from home so I wouldna have ta marry.' He didn't know about Nicola and I, for we hid from everyone. God frowned on our kind of love. But I'd never suspected Harold cared for me. I was too angry now ta hide my teeth or protect his feelings. 'And I don't play ta earn money. I play and write because I *have ta*. I canna sleep for music a-pushing its way inta my dreams. Everything sounds like a tune or a lyric. I don't want ta be a goodwife and have babies. I want ta play music. I want other people ta play *my* music. Canna you understand?'

He stood, stiff and pale, staring at his feet. 'I understand, alright. I understand you're a stubborn wench who would rather die poor and alone than be with someone who cares.' He slapped his hat on and tugged at the brim. 'I won't bother you again. Good luck.' And with that he spun on his heel and marched away.

I didna follow or call out. I was still too angry with him, with the Master, with God, with all of them. Instead I stalked back ta Cecily's shop and redeemed my shawm.

'Keep the sword,' I said bitterly. 'Idiot men and their idiot wars. Let someone else buy it and I hope they all kill each other.'

Cecily laughed, her deep bosom jiggling. 'Righty-o, love. I know how you feel. But I'm glad you've got your shawm back. I'll come tonight and hear you and Nicola play, shall I?'

Her good cheer settled me a little and I managed a smile.

'Gramercy, Cecily.'

I returned ta the Broken Seld and ran up the stairs without greeting Rollo or even a-glancing at the early drinkers in the public room. When Nicola let me in, I still couldn't speak. I held back the tide of pain pushing at my throat and curled up on the bed, saying nothing ta her questions. At last she stopped asking and lay beside me, stroking my hair.

The abbey bells rang for Vespers and Nicola stirred. 'We must go or we'll be late.'

'I'm not a-going,' I said. 'God hates us. Why should I care for him?'

'Bella! Prithee, tell. What's happened?'

'It doesna matter,' I said. 'Go, if you want. Get Rollo or Anna ta take you.'

'Please, Bella?'

'No!' I rolled over ta glare at her. 'I wanted one thing in this life. One thing! Ta make music that people all over knew and loved. But I canna because I'm a woman. I have nothing left. Leave me alone.'

She covered her mouth. 'Oh, Bella.'

I stayed silent, ignoring the break in her voice. She left and the place grew quiet as many folk went ta church ta pray.

Relieved ta be alone, I lay still for an age, a-holding back tears by force of anger alone. Finally, I took up my lute and Nicola's, my recorder, tabor, and shawm and headed downstairs. I didna want ta, but we still had ta pay for our lodging and food. I set up in our usual corner and tuned the lute, a-thinking about what ta play.

The room was dim-lit by oil lamps and the glow from the fire in the brick fireplace. Too warm, and smelling strong of sour ale, and the fish oil Rollo burned in the lamps when he was low on money. But empty and desolate, save for a few hardy souls waiting for their supper.

I plucked out a melancholy tune I'd composed a decade before when Nicola's father had betrothed her ta Sir Edward Sutton and we'd been forced ta part a-while. It suited my mood.

Alas, my love, ye do me wrong
To cast me off discourteously
For I have loved you so long
Delighting in your company.

Greensleeves—

The outer door slammed open and six men entered the public room.

'By Christ's hair, Calain, I hope you're right.' A man's thin tenor jolted me out of a daze. I scowled, resentful of the intrusion, but kept a-playing, quietly.

'House!' shouted the smallest; the one who'd spoken already. 'House? Damn.' He glared at me. 'Where's the innkeeper?'

Sarah Clark appeared, Rollo's strumpet of a housekeeper. She wiped filthy hands on a filthy apron. 'Whaddya want, then?'

'Keep a civil tongue in your mouth, woman.' The small man raised a hand as though ta strike her. Her piggy brown eyes widened and she shrank. The largest man in the group caught the strike before it landed.

'Nay, my lord,' his deep voice rumbled. 'She came as quick as she could. Folk are at Vespers. Don't take out your ire on those trying to help.'

Sarah's red cheeks reddened further and her look at the big man changed ta something like worship. 'I'll get you drinks, good sirs.' She hurried away with a backward glance.

'Very well, Calain.' The lordling sniffed and his gaze slid across me like I was of no account. 'Come. We have time to talk, then, before the place fills with dross.' He brought a kerchief ta his nose and the woody scent of moss and roses reached me. 'Could you not have found us a better hostelry, Alistair?' This last was addressed in a peevish tone ta the tall, thin man ta his left. The other three companions were a pair of thick-throated brothers and a mop-haired boy with a pout like a child's.

The one named Alistair bowed and drew out a bench not far away. 'Where, my lord? Lovell Hall, down the road, perhaps?' His voice was a gentle mocking tenor, round and smooth. He carried a gittern and a longbow on his back and lay the gittern on the table with particular care.

I liked him. Two good men in the company of an arrogant lord. Odd. You could usually tell the quality of a man by his lord, and visa versa.

The lordling cast Alistair a darkling look and sighed. 'No, you've the right of it. This hovel is all I can afford now that my own lands have been confiscated by that upstart on the throne. By God I'll be glad when he's gone and a rightful heir is back in charge.'

'The young Earl of Warwick is only eleven, my lord,' Alastair said.

'And? So he'll have a regent for a few years. That's not your problem. Getting him out of the Tower, is. Hurry the preparations.'

The one named Calain, huge with broad shoulders, rumbled a reply. 'Time will, my lord. We are laying the plans. Fret not.'

'Well, you'd better be.' The lordling held up a hand. 'And damned-well find my ring, while you're at it. That little brat who stole it must be around here somewhere. Check the pawn shops.'

Part of me wanted ta cheer whatever street urchin had stolen his ring. Instead, I played on in the shadowed corner. If it suited him ta pretend I didna exist, it suited me ta eavesdrop on their conversation.

Alistair bowed again. 'That we shall, my lord. Now, what did you wish to discuss?'

If these men were against the king, it might pay me ta hear as much as possible. Perhaps my way inta noble patronage could be bought by the sale of traitors ta the crown. I didna care whose arse filled the throne, but the means ta keep Nicola safe, publish my music, and keep war from a-killing more of my brothers, lay in the richest hands around. And, right now, those were Henry Tudor's.

A distant set of church bells a-rang out; a joyous cascade of tones. Somewhere in the eastern end of the city, by the sounds.

The men started and exchanged puzzled looks. I paused in my playing. What was it? Invasion? Another set joined in. And another, until the afternoon was a-wash with bells and I had ta clap my palms ta my ears.

A babble of voices arose outside. A thinner, higher bell jangled, jarring, and the trained shout of a town crier cut through the noise.

'The queen is delivered of a boy. The prince is born. God save the king. God save the prince.'

'God's body!' My lord struck the timber table with a fist and scowled at his companions. 'Sooner than I'd hoped. We must move.' He lapsed inta frowning darkness and I inta silence, a-straining ta hear.

'Alistair, the king will undoubtedly have a banquet to celebrate in a few days,' the lordling continued. 'I have contacts who can tell me when and where. And tradition says the king should grant pardons and invite me to the feast. Which means it's still the best time to strike.'

'So soon, my lord?' Alistair spread his lean hands. 'The preparations aren't complete.'

'Then *make* them complete,' he snarled. 'Calain, help him. This is too important. I'll pay you both double. Do we have a deal?'

Alistair inclined his head and the big man, Calain, did the same, but they exchanged a long, silent look. The other three men nodded like brainless lackeys.

'Good,' said the lord. 'I have an appointment in Southwark tomorrow morning. I shan't need an escort so you may both hasten your preparations in my absence. But Alistair, at noon I'll need your assistance at Derby House. I'm meeting Lady Roslyn Stanley and you'll be my lookout. Her uncle, Thomas Stanley, Earl of Derby, holds no love for me.'

'Very good, my lord,' Alistair said, a-bowing again.

Rollo and a crowd of church-goers burst through the door, a-cheering. Rollo started a-pouring ales as fast as he could. The lordling snarled at the bar wench, Beth, when she came with drinks. He shoved up from the table and stalked upstairs. A door down the hall from ours slammed shut.

I played a new song, one more joyous ta suit the crowd's mood—even if not mine. Nicola made her way slowly through the mob and took her place at my side. She said nothing ta me. It wasn't the time ta speak our thoughts, but I was grateful she was safe.

Harold didna join us, though. He probably never would. I hadna meant ta hurt him, but he deserved ta find someone who could love him. We did miss his rich voice for some of the madrigals and duets, though.

The crowd didna seem ta mind and we sang until we were hoarse and the candles guttered. Rollo shoo-ed those that could walk out the door around midnight. Those that couldna, snored under the tables with the dogs and the rats. We gathered our instruments and I guided Nicola through the mess of unconscious bodies, vomit and spilled ale.

In our room, Nicola was quiet, but so was I. Tired, dispirited, seeing my dream torn away, unable ta stop it. We barely spoke as we undressed and climbed inta bed.

In the morning the bells of Prime woke us after the first flush of dawn and I lay a-staring at the ceiling. Lead sat in my chest and my limbs were heavy. I was neither thirsty nor a-hungered and could think of no reason ta rise. The world was tuneless and flat, my hopes soured like a slipping string.

Nicola rose and made ready without her usual, cheerful chatter about what the day would bring. I was grateful for I couldna bear ta pretend happiness. She moved quietly around the room, a-washing her face, dressing, using the chamber pot.

Then she opened our trunk and withdrew her precious copy of *le Morte d'Arthur.* She carried it ta the bed and lay it gently on the mattress.

'Here,' she said, quietly.

'I canna read, Nic.' My voice cracked and I cleared my throat. 'Maybe later.'

'No,' she said. 'An it means so much to get your music sold to other minstrels, prithee then take this. Sell it. Go to my godfather and ask him to print your music. You can sell the sheets at festivals and in the inns and playhouses where other players work.' She touched my arm. 'For you to be so unhappy is something I cannot bear. Make your dream happen, an it is so important.' She rose from the bed and opened the trunk again.

I sat up, staring at the book in hope and guilt. She was right. Selling it would give me more than enough ta print hundreds of copies of my songs. Everyone who heard my music loved it. So surely this was the way ta fortune?

A soft noise from Nicola made me look up. She was carefully pulling her clothing out of the trunk, checking the little shoulder-knot that showed an item was hers. Then she folded each piece and laid them on a square of cloth. When she was done, she tied the cloth inta a bundle and stood. She collected her lute and felt her way ta the door.

'Where are you going?' I asked. 'I don't understand.'

She turned those pale eyes on me and her mouth drooped. 'I know. I always knew music and being successful was important to you. But that it meant more to you than I…I never realised. And I'll not stay and help you kill yourself working for recognition from the Fellowship. People who care not and matter not.'

'What are you talking about?' I ran ta her and tried ta pull the bundle from her arms. 'I love you, Nic. Why would you leave?'

'You said,' she started, then stopped and sucked a sobbing breath. 'You said all you'd ever wanted was for your music to be heard. That you had nothing, now. I'm nothing to you. Prithee, take the book. Sell it and be happy, Bella. That's all I ever wanted. For you to b-be h-happy.' Her lovely face crumpled.

'Oh, Nicola.' I threw my arms around her and held her tight as she cried against my shoulder. What had I done? She'd given up everything for me—the chance of a comfortable life, her family's protection and status, and now her most-loved possession. And I'd made her feel like she meant nothing.

I stared over her shoulder at the book and thought about our life. The times we laughed and cried and poured our hearts out. The times we huddled together under the covers in winter and a-giggled like children. The times we loved one another with such joy and pleasure it outsang the music in my head.

Releasing her, I carefully pulled the bundle and lute from her grip. Then I retrieved the book and placed it in her arms.

'Don't go, Nic. I'm sorry,' I whispered. 'I love you more than anything and I'm a fool for hurting you so. You are more important, I promise. Stay.'

She hesitated and swept her fingers over the tooled leather. 'What of your songs? Your music?'

'*Our* music is better.'

She gave a sobbing half-laugh and put the book down. Then she threw herself inta my arms and kissed me and cried all at once.

A light knock fell on the door and we broke apart, giggling.

I wiped my cheeks and hers and opened the door a crack.

'If I may, ladies?' a quiet voice intruded. It was the tall man, Alistair, who'd dealt with the lordling last night.

'What can I do for you, sir?'

He bowed. 'I'm sorry to startle you. I felt called to compliment you on your singing. And your playing. Both of you are most accomplished.'

'My thanks,' I said, and opened the door a fraction more, curious. 'If that's all?'

'Not quite,' he said. 'The song you were playing when we arrived last night…your own composition?'

I nodded. Where was this going?

'Excellent.' A sweet smile lit his angular face. 'I'd like to commission you to write a song for me.'

'For you?' I couldn't help the quick glance along the hall ta where his unpleasant companion had vanished. And I bit back an urge ta ask if it would be played in court if his lordly friend succeeded. Was there any harm in playing both sides? My father had died fighting for King Richard. Been put ta death by the victor for loyalty ta the wrong man. So perhaps hedging my bets and helping both sides was an option.

'For me.' His smile deepened. 'And you might get the chance to play it for the king. I predict the right song will go down in history, and you're the one to write it.'

I put out my hand. 'Deal, sir. Tell me what you want me ta write about.'

He chuckled. 'Blackbirds.'

7. Wasn't that a Dainty Dish

Beatrice Parry, 16
*Daughter of Eliza Parry, Brothel-owner
Bankside, London,*

Thursday (morning), 21ˢᵗ September, 1486

'Bea? Beatrice, dear?' Mama's liltin question floated up the stairs.

Me hand jumped and I smudged the number under me quill tip. I sighed and scraped at the parchment with a knife. Mama called again. When she had that sweet note in her voice, it meant she had someone important waitin downstairs.

And that were what I feared most. But refusin to go would earn me a tongue-lashin, so I cleaned me quill and set it aside. I'd have to ask Mama what *'pay IB for MS job'* meant and finish the creditors list later. Pity it were so much longer than the debtors list, but Mama never listened and spent money like water tryin to keep the fleshmongers happy.

I pinched out the tallow candle lightin me desk and tied an apron over me grey kirtle. Mama hated this dress but there weren't time to change. And she'd hate the apron more. That were the idea. Bawd's weren't allowed to wear them. Maybe she'd get the message and leave me be. I tied a coif over me wild brown hair—what Mama called me best asset, apart from me tits. She always laughed when she said that.

The narrow stairs from me garret room creaked. Mama never fixed them, so's she could hear if I tried to sneak out to meet William Hayward. As if I would. I might be the daughter of a stew-house-keeper, but I'd not be one of her plucked geese if I could help it.

If I could help it. Me hands shook as I smoothed the apron and came down the last risers.

Mama stood in the gaudy front room, with its clove oil smell and sinful paintins of nude women touchin themselves in the nothins. Mama were dolled up with face paint and a yellow silk dress, even though it were only just past the Prime bells. She dressed up whenever she could, but only in the house because a bawd weren't meant to wear silks like the fine ladies.

But dressed pretty she looked like the new queen, Elizabeth of York, and people were callin her Queenie. Which made her laugh because a quean were just another word for a whore. Today, with her gold-bronze hair long and loose like a maid's she looked closer to twenty than thirty. But I'd never say so. She were vain enough already.

Beside her stood a man only a little taller than me, with short dark hair and pale skin. His oversweet perfume smelled of damp wood and moss. His brown eyes were fixed on Mama and he barely noticed me. Which suited me fine. A ruby-hilted sword hung at his hip and a matchin dagger on the other. His clothes were plain, but good cloth. They needed a clean, though. A care-less man who had money. I shrank inside and dipped a curtsey.

'There now,' Mama said, throwin her plump arms wide. 'Didn't I tell you she's a sweet little thing, Lord Lovell? And ripe for the pluckin at sixteen.'

'Hmmm.' Lord Lovell walked slow around me until me cheeks burned. 'She's a little…plain. Her hair and eyes are so dark. I prefer blondes, like you. Who's her father?'

Mama turned away in mock shyness. 'Now, me lord, you can't expect a girl to kiss and tell.' Then she whispered loud enough for the cook to hear in the kitchen. 'Anyways, she's got a fine pedigree, does me little Bea. The Duke of Clarence, if you must know.'

'On the wrong side of George Plantagenet's bed,' Lovell said dryly.

'Oh no, we were married right and proper, the oldfashioned way—not in the church. And he up and died before we could tell the Bishop, so I weren't believed when I said, anyways,' Mama said, pettishly, liftin one shoulder. 'And with the crown jumpin from head to head the last few years and all the warrin going on... Well, it weren't *safe* to let on who she were.'

'If you say so. But she *is* a virgin?'

Mama simpered. 'Oh yes. I've made certain. *And* well-trained in all the arts of pleasurin a man. You don't get that pairin too often.' She elbowed him and winked. Lovell sent her a cold look.

I kept me head down and tried to hold back tears, for Mama would be sore angered if I showed fear. But with all me heart I prayed to the Lord to save me. To take me away. For William to rescue me and marry me proper. But his ma hated me. Wouldn't believe I weren't a bawd like Mama. Wouldn't believe I went to church and tried me hardest not to sin like the women Mama hired to work in the stew-house.

Straightenin her shinin yellow skirts, Mama cleared her throat. 'She'll fetch a fine price at auction tonight, me lord. Shall I put you in as a bidder?'

I dug me nails into me palms til it hurt. If word got out amongst the nobles and the people over the northside of the Thames about the auction, then Goodwife Hayward would never let William marry me.

But I couldn't think of any way to stop it.

Lovell checked me over again. 'I believe I shall bid. Tonight, you said?' His smile turned sly. 'And I have friends who might be interested, as well. I'll send them over, shall I?'

'Oh, aye, me lord,' Mama said, all but rubbin her palms together. 'And if you'd like to go through to the back room, you'll find some of The Cygnet's best girls waitin to entertain you. I'll be there in a moment.'

Lovell bowed. 'You're kind, madam, but I have no coin on me today.'

'Pshaw. You can pay next time, me lord. I'm sure you're good for a bit of tick, anyways.' She waved to Porter, our servant, and the two men headed toward the big hall in the back of the house. I stayed where I were, for me knees shook too much to let me climb the stairs.

'Ooooh.' Mama hugged me, squeezin so tight I could hardly breathe. 'It'll be summat special, girl. We'll get Isabella and Nicola from the Broken Seld to play and make it a dance. And Olivia Grey's sendin over a silk dress. Her customer never collected it so she's giftin it to you. Lovell'll bid and all his rich friends, too. And if they drive up the price, the Bishop of Exeter will have to pay more. Because he's bound and determined to have you. Mark me words, this'll save us and the business. And set you up for a secure future.'

'How, Mama?' I said. 'How'll sellin me make the Cygnet secure? The bishop'll get the money right back in twenty-shillin fines because a woman can't own a stew-house.'

'Now don't you be worryin your head about that.' She tapped me on the nose and grinned, showin teeth still white and even. 'His Grace said he'll overlook me ownin a house when he's made Bishop of Winchester and runs Southwark. As long as he gets you, anyways. If you're good he might even keep you as his mistress. And that's what I want most for you. I never want you to go hungry, Bea,' she said, serious. 'Or have a man's hand raised against you.' She stared through me. 'I'm determined, Bea. You'll have nothin but the best. That's why I waited so long. Not like me, havin to work since I was barely ten.' Her jaw clenched. 'With the bishop you'll be safe. You'll have everythin you want.'

Except a husband.

But I didn't say that aloud. She caught me in another suffocatin hug.

'You know I only want what's best for you, don't you, poppet?

Believe me, it's better to be a rich man's mistress than every man's whore. And there's nowt else for the likes of us, raised to this life.'

'So why not give me to the bishop now, then?' I said. 'Why the pretendin with the auction?'

'I told you.' She opened her blue eyes wide. 'Lovell will drive up the price.'

'And what if he wins?' I said, my voice small.

'Well, we'll have to make the best of all that lovely money, won't we?' She pinched me cheek. 'Now you run back upstairs and don't put your nose out of your room less I call you. I've set Porter to guard your door.'

'And what happens if Lovell wins and don't pay up, Mama? You've told everyone the winner'll have me the same night. I'd be spoiled goods and you'd have no money to show for it.'

'Don't be a looby, girl,' she snapped, then yanked a scrap of linen from between her tits and coughed until her eyes were red. I waited. Mayhap a cold in the chest could explain why she'd been so testy of late.

She wiped her mouth and tucked the kerchief away. 'Of course he'd pay. Or his friends would, anyways.'

'The same friends who fought for the Yorks and lost, Mama?' I asked sweetly. 'The ones who had all their lands and titles stripped by our new king?' I ran upstairs before she could think of a reply.

It were a small victory, but one I held close to me heart.

Upstairs, I opened me window and stared out over the stews and inns of Bankside and Southwark, then across the Thames, toward London city. Wind blew the rotten-meat stench of the tannery in and I coughed. The streets below were mostly quiet this early in the mornin. Southwark and Bankside bein full of stewhouses and inns meant a lot of business happened at night. And last night had been one long party celebratin the birth of the new prince. I'd barely slept for the shoutin and laughin. What I'd give to move over the river and live a proper life.

I sighed, sat at the desk and stared at the numbers lined up neat on the parchment. I'd been doin Mama's books for long enough to know the business were in trouble. It didn't help that she kept usin the old Latin numbers instead of the proper ones, and messin up me sums. But I'd checked four times today. Even runnin The Cygnet all day and night weren't workin.

She'd sold all the gewgaws given to her by the Duke, me father. Not that I really believed that story. The only thing left to offer of value were me maidenhead. I knew Mama were tryin her best to look after me. And without sellin me at auction, the house would be broke in six months and we'd both be out on the streets.

I shuddered and glanced out the window. I'd seen what happened to some of the girls who worked on the streets. Thrown in The Clink. Raped, even murdered. Mayhap bein a whore and havin a roof over me head weren't so bad. Most the girls as worked here rented rooms by the night and had to live elsewhere by law. I was lucky. If Mama could be happy with this life then mayhap I could, too.

A shout from outside distracted me. Someone called me name. I hurried to the window.

'William?' Me dear sweet William stood in the top-floor window of the Fleur-de-Lys stew-house next door, grinnin like a great looby. Behind him, Mary giggled and blew me kisses. I hurried to me bedroom door and slid the bar across to stop Porter comin in. When I returned to the window, William had a sturdy plank laid across the gap between the houses. I watched with me heart in me mouth as he crawled across.

Blackbirds Sing p117

He slid into the room and I threw meself into his arms and buried me face in his broad shoulder. He wore a rough woollen tunic and smelled of charcoal and hot metal. His face and arms were streaked with black and his blue eyes stood out vivid and sparkly. He kissed me sound and set me back a pace. Then he rummaged in the purse at his belt and produced a grubby scrap of paper.

'I got it,' he said, too loud. I shushed him.

'I got it,' he whispered.

'What?'

He waved the paper. 'The common marriage licence. All signed proper by the priest. We're both of age. There's no impediment. We can be married.'

Hope jumped in me chest, then sank again. 'But I got no dowry and your mama hates me. She'd throw you out. Where would we live? How would we live?'

'It don't matter. We'll work summat out. We'll find our own little place. I'll set up my own smithy. It'll be fine, you'll see, love. Come with me.' He pointed out the window.

How I yearned to go. To crawl out of the muck of this life and into his arms forever. A little house. Me own babes to love and suckle. I could see it clear.

But he were a dreamer. It cost money to buy an anvil and a forge. It took time to set up a business and years to make a profit. I knew that too well. And without a dowry from me he had no hope. I couldn't put him through poverty like that. And I couldn't let Mama down, either.

I pulled free and backed up.

'I can't, Will.' I turned away so's not to see the puppy-sad face he made. 'You have to stay with your mastersmith so's you can inherit his forge when he goes. I'm no good for you. Not without a dowry, or a decent family. Your ma would cut you off without a penny, too.'

He took me jaw between his big hands. 'Don't, Bea. Don't say such things. We'll be fine, I promise. You love me and I love you. That's all we need.'

I peeled off his hands. 'It's not, Will. Mama loved me father and he left her with nothin. Now look where we are?'

'I won't do that, I promise. I'll take care of you.'

'You can't promise! People die all the time.' I pushed against his chest, shovin him back. 'Go find someone with a dowry and a family your ma approves of.'

He hesitated and his shoulders slumped. 'You don't mean that, Bea.'

'I do mean it,' I said. 'Go. Forget me.'

His feet scuffed the timber floor but he went to the window and paused there.

'I'll come back for you, Bea. I'll convince Ma and earn enough for both of us so you don't need a dowry.'

'It'll be too late, Will.' Me voice broke. 'Go before you make a mistake we'd both regret.'

With one last look at me, he climbed out the window and crawled back to the Fleur-de-Lys. I slammed the shutters, threw meself onto the bed and cried fit to drown.

Porter knockin on the door and callin me name woke me. I blinked in the darkness. Only a faint strip of grey light crept around the wooden window shutters. Had I slept away the whole day?

I sat bolt up. The auction. What were the hour? The knock sounded again on me door.

'Anon, Porter. I'm awake.'

'Yes, miss,' he said. 'Only the mistress says you're to hurry. She's bringing up your dress and bath now.'

Me head were thick and me eyes puffy. Mama wouldn't be happy with me looks tonight. But I didn't care. Why did doin the right thing for William make me heart feel like it had been ripped out of me chest?

I unbarred the door and Mama bustled in with her little bag of facepaints, and a surcoat of the most beautiful blue brocade over her arm. Porter and the cook lugged in a half-barrel of steamin water and laid out lye soap scented with rose petals, and a cloth for washin. I couldn't remember the last time I'd had a hot water bath in a tub. Men could go to the bath houses nearby, but whores were the only women who went there.

The servants left and I undressed and stood in the warm water while Mama washed me all over and chattered like a magpie. I weren't really payin attention. Nothin seemed important anymore. I were doin right by William and by Mama, but I were dead already. I just wanted the night to be over.

By the time she were done with the washin and dressin, I could barely move in the tight-laced surcoat. She brushed me hair til it shone and then put a little paint on me cheeks and lips. Without a mirror I couldn't see how I looked. Didn't want to, anyhow. The priest at our parish church would be ashamed of me.

She produced a fine gold chain with three pretty little pearls danglin from it and tied the riband around me neck.

'The first thing your Papa gave me when we fell in love. I've been savin it for you. Swore I'd never sell it. Oh.' She dabbed at her eyes. 'You'll break hearts tonight, poppet.'

I tried to thank her, but the words stuck in me throat.

Then it were time and we went down the dark, creaky stairs, through the gallery of nudes and to the back of the house. The big room blazed with light from dozens of tallow candles mounted in holders along the red-painted walls. Fresh rushes lay on the floor and the wood benches and tables were all pushed back. Isabella and Nicola from the Broken Seld played a dance tune on recorder and lute, but it might as well have been a dirge. The half-dressed housegirls draped themselves on fleshmongers who'd come to bid and all eyes turned to me.

I shrank back and dug me nails into the door frame to hold meself up. There were upwards of thirty men in the room, from boys hardly older'n me to ancients of forty or fifty. Some wealthy merchants or nobles in their fine silks, some gross tallowcatches—horrible, fat men I'd seen here before, sweaty and lickin their lips, pawin at the girls. One were the Bishop, Peter Courtenay, fat as lard, red-faced, inspectin me like a horse-trader. Not far away, Lord Lovell stood with one hand on his sword and a smug smile on his thin lips.

'Gentlemen and ladies,' Mama began, throwin her arms wide. There were some sniggerin from the housegirls at bein called 'ladies'. 'As promised: me daughter, Beatrice. Sixteen and still untouched by a man. Come, come. Dance and look at her up close.' She gestured for people to approach. 'She don't bite—unless you ask her nice, that is.'

A burst of laughter. Me cheeks burned hot under the makeup. The room were stuffy and I couldn't breathe. The faces swam, hazy and blurry as men crowded close.

Someone put a hand under me elbow, holdin me up. Isabella. I leaned on her. She glared at the men.

'Back off you louts. Canna ya see you're scaring the poor child. Come,' she said, quiet, to me. 'Sit by us a moment and take a sip of ale ta cool down. You must be a-dying of heat in that ridiculous surcoat. What's your mama thinking?' She sat me on a bench, pushed a cool tankard into me hand and peered close at me. I gulped at the bitter liquid.

Blackbirds Sing p121

'Gramercy, Bella,' I managed.

Nicola kept playin the lute, coverin our talk, and Bella stroked me sweat-sticky hair back.

'Are you sure you want ta do this, Beatrice?'

I shook me head hard and me hand wobbled so's the ale almost sloshed out. 'I don't got a choice, though. Mama's almost penniless. But she's got the new Bishop pantin after me for a mistress. And now this Lord Lovell, too. He's got eyes like a wolf.' I shuddered.

'I thought you had a beau who was sweet on you. What was his name?'

'William Hayward,' I said, me throat tight. 'The blacksmith. But we can't marry. I've no dowry, he's got no money, and his ma won't have me.'

'Ah. Celia's son. I remember, now.' Bella cocked her head. 'I wasna sure if we should come, but I'm glad now we were a-called here tonight. I reckon we can help.'

I gave a little gasp and stared up at her. 'But Mama…'

'You go pretend it's all fine,' Bella said, helpin me stand. 'When the time's right, you'll know what ta do.' She leaned over and whispered to Nicola, who nodded. Then Bella waved over one of the pageboys Mama had hired for the night.

I had no choice but to let Mama tow me off into the press of men. What should I do? What would I know to do when the time came?

Leerin faces pushed too close. Hands squeezed me arse and me tits over and over 'til I were bruised. Coarse laughter and jests made me long for the cool of the church. Would God ever forgive me?

I were close to tears when Mama finally dragged me clear and lifted me onto a bench at the back of the room. She coughed into her kerchief, her cheeks going red. Porter passed her a tankard of ale and she quaffed it in two long gulps.

'Get on with the auction!' someone cried. 'I've got seeds to plant tonight.' A laugh ran around the room.

I twisted the brocade cloth of me dress until Mama slapped at me hands and bade me stand still. She pushed me chin up.

'Who'll start the biddin at two pounds?'

Lord Lovell threw up a white hand. 'Three,' he drawled.

His Grace glared. 'Four.'

Lovell grinned. 'Five.'

'Ten,' His Grace snapped.

Mama snatched at me wrist. Ten pounds were more than most folk made in a year. Me head spun. I'd never expected so much. A little more and Mama's debts would be paid off. So why did I feel like cryin?

'Twenty pounds,' Lovell shouted over the murmurs and laughter.

'Twenty-five, you base-born cur!' the bishop shot back, his face purple.

With that much the house were set for two years at least, as long as I could keep Mama from spendin it all.

There were a stir at the door. People shuffled aside. A tall, broad-shouldered young man pushed his way through. I almost fainted. William. With his leather cap a knot in his big hands, he stared at me and swallowed so his adam's apple bobbed.

All the noise and heat faded and I about drowned in those pleadin blue eyes. Why had he come? Was he tryin to torture me or himself? Next to him, Isabella's bright red hair caught me eye. She smiled and spread her arms wide.

By me side, Mama were almost havin an apoplexy with delight. Lovell had bid fifty pounds.

The bishop clenched his fists. 'A hundred pounds and that's my final offer!'

Blackbirds Sing p123

The crowd gasped and whispered. Mama covered her mouth and sat with a thud.

Lovell bowed low. 'I concede, Your Grace.'

The bishop looked smug and elbowed his way through the crowd toward me.

'I'm not a virgin!' I shouted.

The bishop froze, gapin.

'I'm a married woman,' I added. 'Just today. Wedded and bedded.' The lie fell easy from me lips into the shocked hush.

Mama's painted mouth fell open. 'What? Oh.' Her laugh sounded half-strangled. 'She's jestin. She's such a wit, me girl. She's been locked in her room all day, anyways.'

'Locked from the *inside,* Mama. Me betrothed climbed into me window today and we exchanged vows. We're man and wife. You can't sell me to anyone because I belong to William Hayward.'

Now it were my turn to plead with him. The marriage would only be legal if he agreed. Would he still take me?

He pushed through the crowd, and stopped afore me. He held out a hand and I took it, relief bubblin a silly giggle out of me. I fell into his arms and held him tight, afeared Mama would take him away.

'Now see here, young man,' she said.

William pulled out the common licence and showed it to her. 'It's all legal-like, ma'am. And I'll take my bride home tonight, if you don't mind. She's tired.' He kissed me forehead. I couldn't stop smilin.

The bishop muttered somethin that should never come from the mouth of a holy man and stalked from the room. Others turned to the girls for hire who'd been waitin to sard the disappointed bidders. Lovell swaggered up, clapped William on the shoulder and checked him out like a cow at market.

'A blacksmith, huh?' He smiled, all knowin and amused. 'You'll do just as nicely as the other plan. Best of luck.' He nodded at me. 'I'd keep this one on a leash, if I were you, son. She's got a trifle too much self-will for my liking.'

William stared down at the smaller man. 'Gramercy for your good wishes, sir. But forgive me if I don't take your advice. I like Bea just as she is.'

Lovell shrugged, kissed Mama's hand and whispered in her ear, then strolled out of the house. Mama watched him go, her eyes narrowed to shrewd slits. Then she turned to us and heaved a sigh.

'What am I to do with you, girl?' She sank onto the bench.

'You've nothing to do, ma'am,' William said cheerfully. 'I'm taking her off your hands.'

'Well, if you must, I suppose. You sure, Bea? Say the word and I'm sure the Bishop could annul the marriage. You'll be poor your whole life, married to this one.'

I sat and leaned me head on her shoulder. 'I'm not like you, Mama. I can't live this sinful, wicked life and be happy. I've never understood how you can.'

Her eyes glittered hard for a moment. 'I were never given a choice. At least you had a mother who loved you enough to keep you—and one who tried her best to care for you.'

'Oh, Mama.' I hugged her tight. 'I know you done your best. Really, I do. I can't be like you. God would never forgive me.'

'I hope you're wrong, Bea.' She shrugged. 'But I never thought God were half as vengeful as the priests'd have us think, anyways. If Christ forgave Mary of Magdelen, then surely God will forgive me doin what were needed to survive and bring up a daughter.' She flicked a hand at me. 'Well, be off, then. It's gettin late and we don't want you put in The Clink for walkin the streets after sunset.'

Blackbirds Sing p125

I started to rise but she gripped me wrist. 'What about his ma?' She glared at William. 'Will she treat you right? Comin from here, I mean?'

William pulled me into the curve of his arm. 'I'll make sure of it, Mistress Parry.'

'You'd best love her with your whole heart, boy,' she said fiercely. 'Don't make her regret marryin you, or you'll answer to me, mark me words.'

I kissed her cheek. 'I'll go upstairs and change. Oh.' I untied the necklace riband and handed it to her. 'I'm sorry I couldn't go through with the auction. Use this to pay off the debts? Please, Mama?'

She sighed and curled her fist around the gewgaw. 'And you keep the dress. That can be your dowry. Olivia said it's worth ten pound new.'

'Oh, Mama!' I hugged her tight and she squeezed me close.

She leaned back and sniffed. 'I only ever wanted the best for you, poppet. I'll be fine. You know me. You go be happy, now.'

I took William's hand, full of hope for the first time in months. 'I will, Mama.'

8. To Set Before the King?

Lady Roslyn Stanley, 20
Lady-in-waiting to Queen Elizabeth of York
Derby House, Pawle's Wharf's Hill, London,

Thursday (midday), 21ˢᵗ September, 1486

'My lady?' The servant hurried after me through the arch-roofed hall. 'A gentleman is at the entrance. Asking for you. Won't give his name. What shall I say?'

I paused outside the heavy oak door to the lady's bower. Excitement fluttered low in my stomach. Francis. He had responded to my message. Now I could tell him my news and all would be well. Soon, we would be wed. I bit my lip to hold in a squeak of joy.

But first I must speak to Lady Derby.

I schooled myself to calm. 'Tell him I shall be there quite soon.'

The servant bowed, opened the bower door and announced me. Lady Margaret Stanley, Countess of Derby, looked up and smiled. The hot midday sun slanted through stained glass windows and left pretty rainbows of colour on her pale skin. But the room was stifling, thick with the scent of roses. My head swam and my stomach churned—with excitement or illness, I wasn't certain.

I curtseyed low. Lady Derby set aside her embroidery and approached.

'Now, now, dear child,' she said, kissing me on both cheeks. 'Haven't I said before? You mustn't stand on ceremony with me. I may only be your aunt by marriage, but I stand in place of your Mama since she's so far away in the north. Your Uncle Thomas is out at present, so we may be quite at our ease.'

'Thank you, my lady,' I murmured.

'Well, let me see you, then. It's been an age, I swear.' She studied me. 'You're looking lovely. New surcoat and headdress? That shade of russet silk suits your pretty blonde hair and brown eyes, dear. But don't spend too much on fripperies, will you? Your father isn't very deep in the pocket, I know.'

'No, my lady.' I blushed. It was hard to be at court and not spend money. All the noble ladies dressed so elegantly and wore such beautiful jewels. Luckily my dressmaker, Olivia Grey, made cheap material look expensive.

Lady Derby brushed at the front of her severe black surcoat. She wore no jewels—only her rosary and house keys at her waist—and covered her luxurious dark hair in a tight coif. 'Is being the queen's lady-in-waiting suiting you?'

'Yes, my lady,' I said eagerly. 'The queen is sweet and so kind. Though she has been quite cross lately. But that's to be expected, I suppose, when one's so heavy with child.'

'Indeed,' Lady Derby said drily. My cheeks warmed, again, for the world knew she'd had her only babe—King Henry—when she was hardly more than a child of thirteen, herself. After such a difficult birth, it couldn't be easy for her, knowing she'd never again have babes.

'Thank you for recommending me to the queen's household,' I rushed on. 'My mother quite despaired of finding a suitable husband for me in the north country. But I'm sure I'll find one in London.' How much I wanted to tell her of my full heart and my hopes, of my future prospects. But I couldn't. Not yet. Soon, though.

'And so you will. You've only been here four months.' Lady Derby inclined her head. 'And you must make a good alliance to a man of breeding and money. Especially with so many younger sisters behind you, and your brother dead in the war. It's a pity your Papa is not here, but I'm sure we can rely on your good sense.' She patted my wrist. 'Now. Tell me of the new prince. How is my grandson? The

Tower staff must be at sixes and sevens after the birth yesterday. Was the queen able to spare you?'

'Oh yes, my lady,' I replied. 'She's resting quite comfortably. Her midwife, Mistress Laura Kennet, seems quite sanguine about Her Grace's health. The queen gave me leave three days ago to visit you and was kind enough to keep her promise. She also asked me to extend an invitation. She's hoping you'll visit your grandson tomorrow, if that's quite convenient?'

Lady Derby's rather sharp countenance relaxed into a pleased smile. 'Most convenient. I'm so pleased she's produced an heir for Henry. The country needs stability and a healthy male heir is just the thing. And Laura Kennet is an excellent midwife. I made a wise match for my Henry in young Elizabeth of York. Of course, she was the most eligible York daughter.' A swift frown knitted her brow and she shook her head.

'Very wise, my lady. And they quite dote on each other.' I glanced at the door. With the invitation delivered, I was anxious to leave. Then I remembered the second half of the message. 'Oh. His Grace, the king, would like Lord Derby to be the prince's godfather.'

A faint flush tinged Lady Derby's pale cheeks. 'Indeed, I'm certain he would be pleased. As I said, Thomas is out at the moment—some rumour about a conspiracy to release young Edward Plantagenet from the Tower. Which would be fatal to the peace my son has established.' She waved dismissively. 'Such a thing will not, of course, happen while Thomas is Lord High Constable. He's so diligent in his duties. But the rumour is vexing him. This news will make him most happy.'

'I'm glad, my lady.' I edged toward the door. 'But I can't stay. Her Grace is waiting for your answer, so I must take my leave.' Would Francis still be waiting for me downstairs? He took such a huge risk coming here. To the house of the very man who now owned his lands and monies. He must love me very much. I hugged a thrill of certainty close.

With Uncle Thomas's patronage of us, surely King Henry would return Francis's lands and titles and approve our marriage. Uncle Thomas loved me dearly. He would wish to see me well-wedded. And, he had so many estates, he couldn't possibly mind giving Francis back his lands. Not once he saw how happy it would make me.

'Of course,' Lady Derby said. 'You came with a servant, I assume?'

'Yes, my lady. By your leave?'

She nodded. I hurried from the room and ran through the hall with its exquisite tapestries and narrow, leaded-glass windows. Through them could be seen the courtyard, where Uncle Thomas's men at arms practiced swordwork, their weapons flashing and clashing in the bright noonday sun. But I spared them only a glance and ran on, my footsteps on the flagstones echoing off the oak-beamed ceiling.

At the arched wooden entrance gate, a guardsman pointed to the little guard-room to one side.

'Thank you.' I dropped a farthing into his palm. 'Please tell no-one. I'll only be a moment. Have my palfrey brought around and ask Spencer to attend me.'

'Aye, m'lady.' The coin vanished and he gave me a sly smile before disappearing toward the kitchen, opposite the hall. Undoubtedly Spencer would be in the buttery, drinking ale with the other servants. He, at least, could be relied on not to betray me.

I eased into the tiny guard-room and stopped. Two men awaited me, not one: my darling Francis and a tall, thin man with golden skin and grey eyes of such haunting beauty I had to hold back a cry of surprise. The men bowed then Francis caught me into a quick embrace. I melted into his strong arms and the world was right again.

'Francis, you came.' I threw my arms around his neck and kissed him, heat rising in my body at his touch. I sighed and laid my head on his shoulder, content to breathe in the warm, woody smell of eau de chypre that was uniquely his scent.

'Of course I came, love,' he murmured. 'For I have something important to ask you.'

I pressed two fingers to my lips to stifle a squeal. He was going to ask for my hand in marriage. Oh, this day couldn't get any better. Mama would be thrilled.

The second man cleared his throat. 'My lord, perhaps I should withdraw?'

'But I am remiss. Roslyn,' Francis said, 'this is Alistair Morrigan, my man.'

I extended a hand and Morrigan kissed it. 'My lady, I'm pleased we called upon you today, for otherwise I would not have seen such loveliness and my world would be poorer.'

My heart jumped and I gave a little gasp, then giggled. 'Faith, good sir, you flatter me.' I indicated the door. 'But would you bear watch whilst we converse?'

He bowed again and left.

'Oh, dearest, I have wonderful news,' I whispered to Francis.

His mouth quirked in that tiny smile I adored. 'Indeed, love, what's that?'

'No. You ask your question first.' I could barely suppress my excitement and clenched my fingers together to stop them fluttering.

'Very well.' He paced to the grimy window that overlooked the front gate. When he turned back his expression was grim.

'I need you to get me in to Beauchamp's Tower. I need to speak with Edward Plantagenet, Earl of Warwick.'

I stared at him in bemusement. Where had that come from? What did he mean by it? Was he not going to offer marriage? Yes, of course he was. He was an honorable man.

'My lord,' I managed, 'I don't understand. Why?'

Francis came close and caressed my cheek. My fears dissolved as he stared at me with an intensity that matched the first night we lay together, a month before. I swayed into him and he kissed me.

'It doesn't matter, love,' he murmured, kissing his way down my neck. 'I need your help. I can rely upon you, can I not?'

'I…I…' I wanted so desperately to feel his hands upon me again. I'd missed his touch these last five days he'd been away.

He cupped my face. 'How can I gain entrance to the tower where the young earl is being held?'

'I know not, my lord. Even if I could get you through the gatehouse, Beauchamp Tower is quite heavily guarded. And the king has chosen men of unquestioning loyalty.'

'Bah!' Francis thrust me aside and stalked back to the window. 'I have no money to bribe lackeys, anyway. There must be a way.'

'My dearest, forget that.' I hurried over and clung to his arm. 'I must tell you my news before I return to the queen's side.'

'Very well. What is of such import?'

I lay my hands across my belly. 'I'm with child, my lord. Your child. Ours. Is it not wonderful? But we must be married. And you will have a son to inherit your title.'

'An empty title with no lands and money.' His finger jabbed at me. 'Those lie in your uncle's hands.'

'But we can go to him. Together. When he knows I'm with child he'll talk to the king. They'll restore your lands, I'm sure. He loves me.'

Francis stilled. He leaned close and whispered, 'Let's make a deal.

Blackbirds Sing p133

You get me in to see Edward Plantagenet, and I'll beg Lord Derby and the king for your hand and my inheritance.'

I backed away, palms to my hot cheeks. 'But I can't! If I'm caught… If you're caught… It could mean the scaffold for both of us. What do you want with the boy, anyway?' Lady Derby's mention of a rumour flashed into my thoughts. No, Francis would not be so rash. Yes, he had chosen the wrong side in fighting against Henry Tudor. But he was changed. Humbled. Eager to win the king's favour.

But instead of answering, Francis dismissed my question and fears with a wave. 'None of your concern. Choose. Now. Get me access or bear the illegitimate child of one the king considers a traitor. See how your precious family name survives that scandal.'

'Francis!' My legs gave way and I reeled back to lean on the plastered wall. 'You can't mean that. It would ruin me. My sisters. And my father. My uncle. Even Lady Derby would be tainted. You can't…'

His brown eyes, usually so warm and loving, were stone hard.

'I…thought you loved me,' I whispered. Could I have been wrong? Surely not. His protestations of love; his assiduous pursuit of only me and no other woman. I'd never known a man so attentive. He loved to hear every silly detail of my life in the Tower because it made him feel close to me even when we were parted. He wanted to know things most men didn't care about—my maid's name, what I did for the queen, how I spent my time. Only a man who truly loved me would be interested in such things; would listen so close to my answers.

He studied me. Then the coldness in him vanished and he caught me in his arms, his lips hot and demanding on mine.

'My fairest,' he murmured. 'Of course I love you. With all my heart.' His kisses deepened and his fingers slipped beneath my surcoat, seeking out my breast. I groaned against his mouth and he pushed me up against the wall.

'Have I not risked everything, time and time again, to see you?' he whispered. 'To love you. And surely you love me well enough to do this one thing for me? For us. All I need is to speak to the boy. Nothing more.' His lips drew a fever into my skin until I burned and my mind fogged with desire. 'Get me into the Beauchamp Tower. Then we can be married and save your fair name. Such a little thing, for such an important result. Think how happy we will be. You, me, married. Our son, legitimised. Living on my estates. Say yes, my love. Say it.'

'Oh.' I gasped as he tugged the lacings on my surcoat undone and pushed his thigh between mine. 'Oh, yes. Of course. Anything.'

A knock sounded on the door and we jumped guiltily apart.

'We must leave, my lord.' Alistair Morrigan's voice sounded through the timber. 'Lord Derby's retinue approaches.'

I retied my lacings and patted at my hair.

Francis swore and kissed me once more, hard. 'I like you like this—mussed with loving. I'm staying at the Broken Seld. Send a message saying when and where to meet you. Get me in. Promise?'

I nodded but my throat closed. He left without a backward glance and I stared at the shut door until my heart slowed. I pressed my belly and fought the urge to chase after him. No. I was overreacting. Francis was worried about supporting his family, our son. He probably wanted to be sure Edward Plantagenet was no threat to the Tudor king. Of course, that was it.

The door opened again and Spencer put his grizzled grey head around the panel.

'Ready, my lady?'

'Of course.' My voice cracked but he said nothing, only opened the door wider and ushered me out.

'The midwife is with Her Grace, my lady,' my maid said, putting away my peaked headdress with its gauzy veil. 'Her Grace asked for you.'

'Thank you, Flora,' I replied absently. I hurried from my hot, airless apartment to the queen's brighter rooms. Her maid let me in. By the bed, Mistress Kennet was packing her things away into a satchel in her usual, calm fashion. Her small dark eyes flicked over me and she nodded in greeting.

'I'll be back later, Your Grace,' she said. 'And mind you stay out of the city. There's rumour of an illness going around. Not sure what, yet.'

An illness? My breath hitched. I'd just been to the city. But I'd not seen any ill folk. No, my babe and I would be fine.

I approached the royal bed and curtseyed low.

'Roslyn, what news?' Her Grace said. She lay propped up against goosefeather pillows, dressed in her chemise, her bronze-gold hair loose. The room was stuffy with late summer warmth and she had flung aside the gold brocade bedclothes. Beside the purple-velvet canopied bed, an oak cradle carved with delicate flowers and leaves held the new babe.

I crept closer to peek at him. 'Oh, Your Grace. He's perfect.'

The babe slept, swaddled in white linen, his tiny mouth sucking and red face peaceful. Warmth swelled from deep in me. Soon I would have my own dear child to love. My own home and hearth and husband.

'Roslyn?'

I looked up to find the queen watching me, her wide-set grey eyes troubled. 'Are you well?' she asked. 'You're flushed.'

I nodded and managed a bright smile. 'Lady Derby sent her

congratulations and said she will attend you tomorrow. And she seemed quite pleased that Uncle Thomas was to be godfather.'

Her gentle smile emerged. 'My husband will be glad.'

The bedchamber door opened and His Grace entered. I sank into a low curtsey. He stopped by the cradle.

'Well, ladies,' he said calmly. 'How are you today, my dear?'

I rose and watched in soft envy as he kissed his wife and stroked the baby's arm with one lean finger. With his dark hair neatly brushed and cut to his collar, and wearing no jewels and a plain forest-green doublet and hose, he seemed quite ordinary and approachable.

'Perfectly well, dearest,' Elizabeth said.

'Lady Roslyn?' he addressed me.

I blushed and stammered a greeting. The queen frowned. I retreated to the other end of the room to give them privacy, though I could hear everything they said.

'Any word?' Elizabeth asked.

Henry rubbed tiredly at his thin face. 'Only more rumours. Lovell's been seen around London, but I have no reason to suspect him of anything, yet. I just don't trust him. He was in too deep with Richard. I've doubled the guard around Edward Plantagenet.'

I bit my lip. How could I get Francis in to see the young Earl now? And how could I prove to my king that Francis meant no harm? That he was changed? Perhaps if I told the royal couple of my condition? No. The king was close to my uncle. He would speak of it and then my mother and father would find out. I must be wed before then.

My mother's final words when I left for London had been a warning to protect my chastity and reputation at all costs or my dowry would be forfeit. But she didn't understand! How could she when she'd been given into a loveless, arranged marriage? How could she understand the depth of my feelings for Francis, and his for me?

The royal couple spoke of other inconsequentialities—when to announce the banquet they planned to hold to honour and name the new prince on Tuesday; the state of other prisoners being kept in the Tower. I couldn't force my lips to form the words that would reveal my sinful behaviour or beg for Francis's reinstatement.

With a nod for me, the king left and the queen beckoned me closer. She plucked at the bedclothes and pressed her lips tight.

'Tell me the truth, Roslyn,' she blurted.

She looked young and vulnerable, worried—just as I felt. We were the same age, but she always seemed so calm and wise that sometimes I forgot she wasn't older.

'Anything, Your Grace. What troubles you?'

She blushed and looked away. 'Are you the king's mistress?'

I gaped in disbelief. 'Your Grace! No!'

She said nothing, only staring at me with hope and distrust writ large in her expressive face.

'I swear on all that is holy, Your Grace,' I said earnestly, crossing myself. 'The king has no interest in me. Nor I in him.'

'Then who? For I know the signs. You've been pale and peaky. Hardly touching food. And I've seen you sneak off to the garderobe dozens of times a day. You're with child. Whose, if not the king's?'

What could I say? How I wanted to share with her my joy and my fears. But what would she respond?

I strode to the narrow window and stared out over the spaces around the White Tower. West of the Green with its pleasant copse of trees, was Beauchamp's tower, where the young Earl of Warwick was held. To the north, on the Hill, stood the scaffold, stained black with blood. I shivered.

No, I couldn't risk telling her. Protecting Francis was more important. And he would care for me, in return. Of that, I was certain.

So I went back to her side with a fixed smile and a light voice. 'No, Your Grace, I'm not with child. I've just been much-plagued with stomach problems these last two weeks. I'm feeling quite well today, though. And by my troth I am no mistress of the king's.'

Elizabeth hesitated, sighed, and nodded. 'Very well. I shan't need you until evening, then.'

I curtseyed, but paused, unable to resist. 'Your Grace, I couldn't help overhearing. Why does the king dislike Lord Lovell so? Is there no hope for reconciliation?'

She studied me. I tried to keep an open countenance. Seemingly satisfied, she smoothed her chemise several times before replying.

'Francis Lovell was unfortunate in his loyalties. He was my Uncle Richard's sworn man. King Richard's little dog, they called him. Francis supported Richard at that final battle in Bosworth. So there's no hope, I'm afraid.'

The baby fussed and woke, his thin wail loud in the stone-walled room. I passed him to his mother. She inserted the tip of her little finger into his mouth and he suckled himself back to sleep. Then Elizabeth looked up at me, her mouth drooping.

'But it's not Francis you should concern yourself with, Roslyn,' she said, sighing. 'In these times, when men war over land and thrones, it's their wives and families who suffer most. Francis may have lost his lands, but he'll find men who will hide and succour him. It's his poor wife, Anne, who must be suffering. Abandoned by all because she had the ill fortune to be married off to a man like Francis Lovell.'

The queen shook her head. 'Choose well in your marriage, if you can, Roslyn. For it's only through marriage that a woman can have any kind of security at all.' The baby fussed again and she called for the wet-nurse.

Blackbirds Sing p139

Shaken and speechless, I retreated. Blindly, the world blurred by tears I could not yet shed, I hurried through dark halls to my room. I slammed the oak door and leaned against it, one hand to my mouth to hold back a sob.

Married. Francis was already married. He had deceived me. Oh, I was a fot, a simpleton, a fool. And he was a bedswerver, a leasing-monger who would sell his wife and child for power.

His unborn child. I laid both hands on my womb. As my belly swelled, I would be disgraced, sent home. My five younger sisters tainted as well. Every chance at making a good marriage gone in a sinful moment of weakness.

The life within me was sacred. Precious. But to birth this babe would be to condemn both of us, and my sisters, to a life of hardship and poverty. Or would some kind man take me in, regardless? I'd heard of women of the lower classes who still found husbands even though they had children out of wedlock. Could that be my path as well? I racked my mind, trying to think of a noblewoman who had done the same.

'My lady?' Flora emerged from her closet, pale blue eyes large against her creamy skin. She hurried forward and helped me to a stool. 'What's amiss? Is the queen unwell? The babe?'

'No, no,' I managed. 'I'm…a trifle tired. Leave me awhile to rest. The queen has given me the afternoon off. You may go.'

She curtseyed and moved toward the door.

'Flora, wait. Send Mistress Kennet to me, if you will?' I turned away so she couldn't see the blush rising in my cheeks. The door closed and I stared at the gilded painting of the Madonna over my bed, my mind blank.

A knock fell on the door. 'Enter,' I called.

Mistress Kennet entered and curtseyed. I had come to know her well over the last few months of her attendance on the queen. Her calm good sense settled me now.

'Mistress Kennet, may I beg your silence and your help on a delicate matter?'

Her shrewd dark eyes narrowed. 'Of course, my lady. What do you need?'

I paced the room. My rosary lay on my desk and I gathered it up, slipping the beads through my fingers, praying to the Lord for forgiveness and understanding. Praying for the strength to make the right choice. But what was the right choice?

Finally, a kind of peace stole over me and I kissed the rosary and murmured a prayer.

I drew a deep breath and faced the midwife boldly, though my throat tightened.

'I'm with child.' My voice cracked. 'But I know…I know you can make a special tisane. I heard you speak of it with one of the maids.'

'A tisane, my lady?' she said carefully.

'A drink that will make it all go away.' I burst into tears. She held me tight against her shoulder and stroked my back.

'There there, child. It's alright. You'll be alright,' she murmured.

And I wanted to believe her.

9. The King was in His Counting-House

Cecily Hayward, 44
Pawn shop owner
Bred Street, Chepe Syed, London,

Thursday (late evening), 21st Sept, 1486

'Righty-o, thou great lummox,' I said, nudging Rollo in the ribs. 'Away with ya. There's the waite-watchmen on their rounds.' The reedy wailing sound of shawms and the thud of tabors swelled and faded down the street. Beside the bed, the tallow candle guttered and shadows danced across the low ceiling.

Rollo grumbled and rolled over, the straw-stuffed mattress rustling under his bulk. He wormed an arm under my neck and pulled me close. And promptly fell back asleep. I laughed and kissed his forehead.

'C'mon sleepy. Hie thee home. That inn of yours won't run itself.'

He yawned. 'This'd be a sight easier, woman, if I didn't have to sneak home in the middle of the night like a guilty boy. I'm forty-six years old and you're forty-four. We should be wedded proper-like and not hiding from kith and kin.'

I leaned on one elbow and grinned at him. 'Ya great looby, Rol. Aren't we having fun?' I prodded his ample stomach. 'Admit it. Sneaking around adds spice.'

He gave a reluctant laugh and finally opened his warm brown eyes. 'Aye, love. Takes me back to when I were a handsome lad with all the lasses after me.' He turned serious and stroked my cheek with his calloused thumb. 'I fancied nobbut you, even then. And you made me wait. Twenty-seven long years. Don't make me wait more. Marry me, Cecily?'

'Oh, getaway with thee, Rol. Don't be daft.' He didn't reply and I frowned. 'Serious? I thought 'twas a jest.' With a sigh, I kissed his palm. 'Ya know my mind. I put up with Matthew's mastery for twenty-five years because I had no choice in the matter. My parents married me off too young to argue. I got choices now.' I sat up. 'I love thee dearly, Rollo Chambers, but I won't marry again. In the eyes of the law, the shop and house are mine 'til I go, and then William gets it.'

He pushed up onto his elbows. 'And? I got no beef with that, love. You've worked hard to keep the Cahorsin shop going after Matt passed. Your children deserve what's yours to give. But I'm not sure your Reina wants it. And your William's dead keen on setting up as a blacksmith. And that'll be sooner now he's wedded young Beatrice.'

I shook my head. 'I can't believe he did that today—went and got married without saying! Anyway, not the point.' I waved his objections aside. 'An we marry, Reina would have to live in the inn, and everything I own goes to thee and I'd get no say in it.'

'Well, the Seld's no place for a lass like Reina, that's true.' Hurt flitted over his swarthy face. 'But I wouldn't take anything of yours. You know I wouldn't.'

'No, ya wouldn't.' I patted his cheek. 'But if I married thee, I'd have to give the shop to William now, and he's not ready. I can't sell it, either. The books are in such a state that no-one would buy the place. No-one's got the money! And if I could somehow keep it despite the law, what about those boys of yourn? Three sons and two businesses? If summat happened to thee, they'd fight amongst themselves over who got the Broken Seld and the shop. What would happen to my Reina and William, then?'

He sighed and hauled me back to his side. I pillowed my head on his bare chest and listened to his steady heartbeat.

'Aye, love. I know you're right. My boys can be greedy bastards and all. But I worry about you. It's not safe here.'

Blackbirds Sing p145

'What, a few blocks away from the inn? Ooh yes, it's a right nasty neighbourhood, Chepe Syde is.'

He raised a brow.

I chuckled. 'Well, alright, it's not the best neighbourhood, I'll grant ya. But no-one's been murdered hereabouts for ooooh at least a month.'

'Don't make fun, Cec. You know what I mean.' His big hand stroked back my greying brown hair and I snuggled closer. 'You keep all sorts of valuables here. William's away at the smithy all hours. And with your boy Peter killed in the wars—'

I stiffened and he paused, then continued, rubbing my back. 'Sorry, love. We all lost boys, I know. But without him to take over the shop and protect you, there's only Reina, old Carter and Sarah. Well, and young Beatrice now, but she's just a slip of a thing. What would you do if someone broke in?'

'Ya worry too much, Rol,' I said. 'All the valuables are hidden away under the hearthstone and Carter sleeps on that.' I caressed his broad chest, tugging at the coarse dark hairs there. 'Tell ya what, if you're not going to get up and go…then get up and *come*.' My hand slid lower and he rumbled a laugh.

'Insatiable woman,' he murmured. 'C'mere.'

When I woke again, I was alone and grey dawn light crept around the shuttered window. Horse-drawn carts rattled in the street below as early farmers brought their goods to Market Street. The sunrise bells carolled across the city. I stretched away the softness of a night of good loving and flung aside the blanket.

The household would be a mite edgy today if I was any judge. When William had come home late last night and declared himself married, he'd about caused old Carter's heart to fail. Then thrusting that mouse of a girl, Beatrice, into the house and swearing he'd leave if I didn't accept her. Well, that took some gumption. Lucky Reina had been abed asleep or she'd've screeched the roof down.

By the time I'd settled old Carter and shooed him off to his hearth-bed in the hall, William had calmed down too. I'd been expecting Rollo to knock any minute, and was too tired to argue, so I'd sent the blushing bridal pair off to William's bedchamber.

Now I'd have to deal with it and what choices did I really have? William had a common marriage licence, of all things. Who'd've thought the boy had the wit to make all the arrangements and sneak out to Bankside to carry a girl off? And he swore black and blue she was a virgin, in spite of growing up in a stewhouse with the worst doxy for a mother as I ever saw.

I laced a brown kirtle over my chemise. Well, nowt to be done about it now. It'd serve no-one to have the marriage annulled for William was as stubborn as his father when he put his mind to it. I'd have to make the best of the girl and hope Reina grew to like her. If the two took to being old-cattish this house would get mighty small, mighty fast.

At least the silk dress Beatrice brought as dowry would fetch a good price in the shop. I knew two merchant's wives who'd probably give their eye teeth for it. Lord knew we could use the money. Everyone seemed to be feeling the pinch at the moment and I'd been doing more buying than selling. Too much stock, too little coin.

Never mind. We'd make do. I always found a way.

I made my way down three flights to the ground floor, paused to press at a stitch in my side, then headed out to the back of the house. Old Carter already had the hearthfire going and Sarah had a pot of porridge bubbling over the low flames. I sank onto a stool and leaned my back against the cool brick wall, relishing a few moments of quiet before the day's madness started.

Carter shuffled over, shoulders hunched. 'Sorry Missus. Broke two eggs meant for Miss Reina's breakfast this mornin and she's reet cross at me.'

I groaned. 'Nevermind. She'll find summat else to fix on soon enough. Stay out of her way a tad til she settles.'

'Mama!'

I jumped. Reina's call repeated and I sighed. At least she sounded excited, not angry.

'In the hall, lovey.'

Carter cast me a hesitant, worried look and I silently shooed him from the hall. Knees creaking, he shuffled out to the vegetable plot in the back yard that was his special care. How the man loved plants. It was a wonder, what he could grow in that tiny patch of dirt.

'Mama,' Reina cried, appearing in the oak-framed doorway. She held out the blue brocade surcoat Beatrice had brought home. Reina's brilliant blue eyes—darker than mine—glittered and she held the surcoat up to her ample bosom. It matched her eyes exactly and showed off her spun-gold curls. I should have known. She checked the shop each morning to see what I'd bought the day before.

'Mama this is *perfect* for me,' she breathed. 'I must have it. Please? Where did it come from?'

'Your brother brought home his bride last night and that's her dowry. I reckon we could sell it for ten or fifteen pounds if we're smart.'

Reina gaped, her hands falling until the silk dragged on the rush-strewn floor. She lifted the cloth clear, folded it carefully and sat on a stool like her legs had given way.

'Bride?' Understanding hardened her eyes to sapphire chips. 'Not that stewhouse whore of his?'

I nodded and rose. 'Best get used to it, lovey. It's all legal-like and everything.' I wagged a finger at her. 'Don't ya be a hag-wife to the girl. She came in last night acting like she expected us to sell her into slavery. Her mother dressed her in that getup to sell off her maidenhead.' I chuckled. 'Still want it?'

Reina screwed up her perfect little nose and sighed. 'I suppose not. I'll take it back to the shop.' She rose, dragging her feet.

'And put your father's silversmithing tools away, too,' I said. 'It's good you're using them. Ya need summat to keep thee busy that's not just thinking about marrying a lord. But clean up after yourself, would ya?'

'I *will* marry a lord,' she snapped, stamping a foot like the child she still was. I grinned and she huffed and turned away.

'Marry young Luke from next door,' I called after her. 'He's a good lad. He'll never lay a rough hand on thee, I'll say that for him.' I didn't want to marry again, but Reina's heart was set on being well-wedded, bless her.

'Oh, Mama,' she said, rolling her eyes. She left, tossing her hair. I smiled. She was determined to marry into nobility and I hadn't the will to tell her it was a silly girl's dream. She was strong-minded, our Reina. If anyone could make it happen, she could.

Carter crept back in with an armload of beets, parsnips, and skirrets for Sarah in the kitchen. I called him a cowardly old coot and he bobbed a bow, smiling his mischievous, gummy smile. He'd been with my family since before I was born. Came with me to this house when I married. Tried to shelter me from Matthew's heavy-handed rage. Cared for my babes. Wept for the three who'd died. The least I could do was protect him from Reina's sharp tongue.

The bridal pair still hadn't made an appearance when I opened the shop, mid-morning. I certainly wasn't going to interrupt them. The shop needed a good dust and re-arranging, but I hadn't the energy. Under the counter, the accounts ledgers lay unbalanced for the last six months. I'd listed sales and purchases, but put off the balancing, knowing how it would look. I was doing everything I could but the shop was still losing money and if that didn't change soon…

Matthew hadn't been perfect, but there was no denying that running the shop in a businesslike way had suited him better than me. I was too soft. Well, no use worrying. I'd make it work, somehow.

I lit as many candles as I could to make the place cheerier. With the shutters open and the late-summer breeze blowing in, the room was almost fresh. Well, apart from the smell of horse-dung and piss from the street. But everyone was used to that.

Outside, the sky clouded over with a promise of rain later to clear the streets and water the vegetables. Everything always felt better for a good wash, even if it did keep folks indoors and their purses tied shut.

Shadows darkened the door and I smiled broad at the customers. Three men stood outside and three more came in: two tall and one a squib only about my height. But he wore silks, carried a ruby-studded sword, and sniffed like the room stank. The other two were like enough to be brothers—sharp-cheeked and gold-skinned—but one with shoulders as broad as the door and the other thin as a rake. The thin one seemed familiar but it took me a moment to recall.

Ah. He'd come in on Wednesday and redeemed Catherine the baker's poesy ring for her. And…hadn't he done summat else? I thought a moment. Surely he'd also pawned summat? Why couldn't I remember?

I opened my mouth to greet him but a warning in his clear grey eyes stopped my tongue still. Strange. I couldn't speak his name, though I remembered it, now: Alistair Morrigan. But my mouth wouldn't form the words.

'You! Woman.' The small man swaggered to the counter.

'Aye, sir,' I said, reluctant to curtsey though he was probably of a station to expect one. Summat about this man made my teeth itch.

He ran a disparaging eye over the stock on display—some of Caxton's new leatherbound books piled on an iron-strapped oak trunk; a gittern and a tabor hanging on the plastered wall between two large paintings of noble ladies with their gauzy veils and surcoats studded with gems. Reina liked to sigh over those. All sorts of chairs and sideboards, pretty plates, rusted pig-stickers and daggers, trinkets, and a rack of clothing. The blue silk was still missing. Undoubtedly the dratted girl couldn't resist trying it on.

'Get your husband. I wish to do business here.'

I sucked up my pride and pasted on a wide smile. 'Pardon sir, there's only me. My husband passed away two years agone. What can I help with, then? We have a nice shiny suit of armour over in the corner there.' I couldn't help the dig for he struck me as the sort whose parents likely paid a scrutage fee to the king so's to keep their precious boy from doing his knightly duties to his liege.

He sniffed. 'Don't waste my time. I want my seal-ring.'

'Er…' I cast a helpless glance at the other two men. The large one's brows pulled tight like he was troubled; the thin one, Alistair, wouldn't meet my eye.

'Righty-o sir. I can't say as I know what ring ya mean, exactly, but I've several ya can look over.' I pulled out the lock-box that Carter brought in daily. I fumbled with the iron house-keys while the customer tapped one booted foot impatiently.

I opened the lid and sorted through the boxes and trays within. I upended one little box on the wood counter. 'There, sir. All the rings we have. Pick the one ya fancies and we can come to a deal.'

His cold dark gaze slid over me. 'We shall see.' He pushed through the jumble of gold, silver and copper rings. The metallic jingling got on my nerves.

'Bah!' He thrust the pile aside. 'It's not there. Tell me where it is, woman. It was stolen from me on this street two days ago by a pair of little cutpurses. They must have brought it here. It's a garnet cut into the shape of an L, set in gold. Where in God's name is it?'

Something about the description seemed familiar, but I couldn't pin it down and shook my head. 'Sorry, sir. Nothing like that's come in, nor been sold in the last two days. Mayhap your mistaken. Try old man Birch's shop over on Walbrooke Street.'

His dagger was out and at my throat before I even saw him move. I froze, my heart a-thudding. I couldn't even squeak. I just knew I couldn't be killed. Not when my children still needed me.

He leaned closer. His breath reeked of ginger hum—the strong ale and wine mix inns served to their richer patrons.

'I want my seal-ring. You have it here. I have it on good authority that those two cutpurses came here with a cloaked man the same day my ring was stolen. Give it to me. Now. What else are you hiding in that box?'

'I swear. On my troth, my lord,' I managed. 'I know nowt of it and I was the only one in the shop that day. Believe me.'

The door opened and a cheerful voice greeted me. One of my regular customers. She hurried to the clothing rack. The dagger vanished from my throat. I sagged against the counter.

The three men stood back, the small one muttering. 'I'll give you until the sunset bells tonight to produce my ring. If you don't hand it over, I'll send a message to the king's tax auditors and have them go through your books line by line.' His lip curled. 'I have no doubt they'll find a great deal to ponder in an establishment such as this. They may even suspect you of being a Jew.'

'My lord,' the one called Alistair said. 'I'm sure you'll not be called upon to go to such lengths. The goodwife will find it.'

I quaked, crossed myself, and clutched at the countertop to steady myself. How was I to find something I had no memory of?

'Aye, m'lord,' I finally muttered. 'I'll find out who has it. I'll send runners to the other Cahorsins and see if it's been pawned there.'

'I'll be back at sunset,' the lordling said. 'See you have it.'

This time I did curtsey. And it was long before my heart stopped hammering.

While I was still staring blank at the empty doorway, Reina tripped in carrying sunshine and the scent of oncoming rain with her. She wore the blue silk and carried a muddied blue silk bubble-bow.

'Mama,' she said gaily, 'I've met the most delightful gentleman.' She held up the spoiled silk pocketbook and her full lips turned down. 'I dropped my bubble…purse and he was ever so kind as to pick it up. Admired my surcoat and paid me the prettiest compliment.' She kissed my cheek. 'I think he was a lord and all, for his companion addressed him as 'my lord'.' She paused, studying me uncertainly. 'Mama? Are you alright? You're pale.'

'Aye, lovey,' I said, smoothing the front of my kirtle over a few times to still the shakes in my hands. 'Aye, I'm fine. Righty-o. Go take the surcoat off now you've had your fun. There's some clothes on the rack that need your fine touch with a needle.'

She pouted and sighed, but went off to change.

I covered my mouth. I had no doubt a lord could alert the king's tax collectors. Truth was, I'd no idea if we'd paid the right taxes. I'd no head for figures and paid whatever I could and told the collector and the titheman firm-like that it was right.

If the lordling kept his word when I didn't produce the seal-ring…

I peered under the counter for the ledger book. The shelf was empty, just a dust-free square where the leather-bound journal usually sat. My heart sank. What had I done with it? I checked the tiny, cluttered back room with its toppling piles of vellum and boxes of useless junk I'd never cleared out after Matt passed.

Nothing. It couldn't be in my bedchamber, that held only my personal things. Where had I put it?

'Mother Hayward?' A timid voice from the back of the shop interrupted and I whirled. Beatrice stood there, wearing a plain grey kirtle, with her wild brown hair loose to her waist.

'Lordy, girl,' I said, one hand on my bosom. I fanned myself. I couldn't take much more of this. 'Ya frightened life out of me.'

Beatrice bobbed a little curtsey, her dark eyes wide. 'Pardon the intrusion.' She held out a thick leatherbound book. 'William left early this mornin. He gave me this and asked me to—'

I snatched the book from her and glared. 'How dare ya poke your nose into my ledgers, girl? Not one day in the house and you're sticking into private matters that don't concern thee? I should ha' known a girl from Southwark wouldn't behave in a seemly manner.'

'But I—'

'Get out of my sight. Don't come before me until ya can behave at least a little more ladylike. I never!' I turned my back and held the heavy book to my hot cheek. This was my only chance to prove I wasn't cheating the tax collector and that little strumpet had the gall to steal it. I had vowed to try and accept her, but this was beyond anything. She had no right.

Her light footsteps hurried away; the faintest ghost of a sob followed. The stairs creaked and upstairs a door slammed.

I sighed and dropped the ledger onto the counter with a thud.

The day passed too quickly as I tried to make sense of the numbers crawling twisty-wise across the pages. I snapped at Reina twice so she left in a huff to go visiting just before the Nones bells carolled across the city. With an extra set of ringing—probably to celebrate one more time the little prince's arrival up in the Tower. Not that princes and kings had much to do with me and mine, except to kill our men when the nobles got to fussing over thrones and crowns and such.

By the time the sunset bells were due to ring, the promised storm broke over the city. There'd been hardly any customers. Carter and Sarah were carefully avoiding me and young Beatrice hadn't come out of William's bedchamber.

I bent over the book again, struggling to read Matt's crabbed writing. Damn him for not teaching me this while he lived. He'd always been secretive. How was I supposed to fix this? The seal-ring was impossible to produce. Runners had come back empty-handed from the other Cahorsins. I was close enough to penniless already so we couldn't afford to close the shop while the king and Church pried into our finances.

Now it was almost sunset and I still had no answer for either the lord or the taxman.

I considered burning the ledger, but then the king's men and the Church would take everything and I'd be left with nowt.

Finally, I set the book aside, took the strong box and passed it to Carter to hide under the hearthstone. Then I returned to the shop as the bells chimed in St Paul's on the hill. There was no point hiding. If I locked the door tonight, that arrogant lordling would come back in the morning with the taxmen, anyway.

The door opened and the smell of evening rain drifted in. Outside,

Blackbirds Sing p155

water gurgled along the muddy street and poured from the roofs. Thunder rolled and a flash of lighting silhouetted the lean figure in the doorway.

'My seal ring?' he said quietly, shaking rain from his cloak. He'd come alone this time, but that didn't help me. I had no skill with weapons, so I couldn't even act on my fleeting wish to stab him with his own ruby-crusted dagger.

'Sorry, m'lord,' I said stoutly. 'No-one knows of it. I don't have it, nor do any of the others. Mayhap the thieves had a private buyer.'

'Then how do you explain their presence in your shop two days ago?'

'I can't, m'lord. Mayhap twere a mistake.'

His glare turned icy. 'I think not. You'll regret this.' He said no more, but spun sharply about and left.

I stood awhile, shaking, one hand over my mouth.

I locked the door and went straight to bed. Couldn't even bear the thought of eating. Couldn't face William or Reina, knowing I might lose their inheritance—and my independence. I lay in bed, staring into darkness. Rain drummed on the roof and thunder rumbled.

What would I do without the shop? What could I do? Carding and weaving was all well and good, but I'd need a place to live. We all would. My only choice might be to marry Rollo after all. But he couldn't take on more servants so I'd be turning Old Carter and Sarah out into the streets. And Reina's dreams of a good marriage would come to nowt without a dowry. And William and Beatrice, just starting out. Oh, that poor girl. I'd bitten her head off for no reason but that I was scared.

With a sigh, I got back up. I couldn't let her go any longer believing I thought ill of her. 'Tweren't her fault.

Downstairs, timber splintered. Summat smashed. A broken chair?

Was anyone hurt? Summat else broke. Pottery of some sort. Or mayhap glass. A voice cried out. Old Carter. But he sounded angry, not in pain. What in God's name was going on down there?

More cries. A scream. More breaking. A crash of thunder and flash of lightning. The torrent of rain outside almost drowned out another scream.

I stumbled in the darkness, too hasty to light a candle. The stairs were in the black but I knew my way well enow. Was that Reina's voice calling me? I hurried down, my breath coming short and quick.

On the ground floor I hesitated. A cold, damp breeze blew in from the shop. I peered in. A flash of lightning. The front door hung askew on one hinge. Water puddled inside. A big urn lay smashed, pieces scattered across the brick-tiled floor.

Another scream and sobbing, this time from the hall. I clutched my chemise close and swallowed, though my mouth was dry. Behind me, a stair creaked.

'Mother Hayward?' Beatrice's timid voice in the darkness.

'Aye, lovey.' I reached out. Her small hand tucked into mine. I wasn't sure who was comforting who. 'C'mon,' I said. 'Let's see what's happening.'

We crept into the hall on tiptoes. I hesitated, then straightened.

'Rollo? What are ya doing here?' Gathered around the hearth were Sarah, William, Reina and Rollo, all staring down.

'Mama!' Reina flung herself into my arms, sobbing. She was soaking wet, her nose red and clothes sodden. She wore the blue silk.

'Reina Hayward,' I said. 'Ya ruined that surcoat. Now go upstairs and change before ya catch your death.'

'But, Mama,' Reina sobbed. 'He's—'

'Go. Now.' I glared.

'But I know who did—'

I pointed. 'Now. We'll speak later about your disobedience.'

Meekly, she left, still crying.

The others hadn't moved. Beatrice hurried to William's side and slid under his arm. She crossed herself. Rollo held out a hand to me and moved aside.

I gasped. On the floor before the hearth lay Old Carter. His rheumy eyes were pale and blank. His mouth open. His knotted hands stretched toward the door like he'd fallen trying to grab at something. Fresh blood matted the thin hair on the back of his head. A scarlet puddle spread beside the hearth and smeared a great streak across the floor.

The hearthstones lay upturned, the space beneath them empty.

Unable to stand, I sank to the floor beside the body. For there was no doubt he was dead. I rested my hand on his bony shoulder and closed my eyes. He'd been like a father to me and to my children. He was my real family. A little piece of me broke into slivers of pain that stabbed into my chest.

Rollo knelt and gathered me into his arms. I buried my face in his shoulder, but couldn't weep. Not yet. He couldn't be gone. I just needed to understand and it would all be fine.

'What happened?' I asked,

Rollo shrugged. 'I was escorting Reina home. Three men came running out of the shop, carrying a box. We came in to find this. Can't say more, I'm afraid. Sorry, love. Right sorry. Wish I could have been here to protect you, like I wanted.'

I let him help me up. Maybe he was right. Maybe I did need him. I couldn't run the shop. Couldn't protect my people. It was just luck none of my children were hurt.

'William?' I turned to my son. 'Alright, boy?'

'Aye, Mama,' he said, deep and sad. 'I got here a moment before you, so I didn't see what happened, either. I shoulda been home. But I'm trying to work more so's I can get my Master's ticket and set up a house for Bea.' His young wife cast him a glowing look and me an anxious one.

'No,' I sighed. 'It's not your fault, either. Rollo's right. Maybe a woman's not fit to run a business and manage a house on her own. Not if it gives thieves cause to believe they can steal and kill without come-back.' I looked at Carter's broken body and grimaced. There was a vice around my chest, tightening til I could barely breathe.

Sarah pressed a tankard of strong hum into my hands and I gulped it down. My shivering eased and I stared glumly at the gaping hole beneath the hearthstone.

'We've got nothing left. They took all the valuables. Went straight through the shop and left all of those things. Came right for the strongbox.' I threw back the last mouthful. 'Makes me so mad, it does. Chitty-faced, craven varlots the lot of them. Killing an old man for some baubles.' My voice broke and I closed my eyes. Maybe, when I opened them, it would have all been a dream. Carter would be just sleeping.

Rollo hugged me close. 'Well, you can't stay here anymore. It's not safe. We'll board up the door here. You can all come back to the Broken Seld. I'll look after you.' He puffed out his chest. 'Your ma's going to marry me. She won't have to worry then. Right, love?'

I sagged. 'Aye. Righty-o, I suppose.' With one last look at Carter's shrunken form, I turned away. Tomorrow we would lay him out proper. I couldn't do it now. He couldn't be dead. Not yet.

'Mother Hayward?' Beatrice crouched by the hearth, staring at the stones. They lay scattered, thrown hastily aside. She touched one. 'How did they know? I mean. Where to find the box and what order to move the stones? William told me it was like a puzzle.'

She was right. Carter had long ago devised a clever method of locking the stones together in a certain order so they didn't move easily.

I stilled. Beside me, Rollo shifted.

'C'mon, love,' he urged. 'Best get away from here and get some sleep. We can go to the church and be wed tomorrow. Then you'll be safe.'

I broke free of his embrace and stared at him. 'Ya knew. Thou'rt the only one outside this family as ever saw me put the box away.' I stepped back when he moved forward.

'Now, love,' he said. 'Be rational. Who would I tell?'

I pushed him back, acid bubbling up. 'That lordling. The one who came in today threatening me. He's staying at your inn. I saw him the other night when I came to listen to the music. Smelled your ginger hum on his breath today. He didn't believe I didn't have his seal-ring.' I jabbed a finger into his chest. 'So ya told him where to find the strong box, didn't ya?'

How could he? How could he do it?

Rollo's shoulders hunched and he shuffled backwards. 'I'm sorry, love. Lord Lovell threatened you, and Reina, and my inn, and my boys, too. Said he'd see us all before the courts for evading taxes and tithes. He's a lord, love. What was I to do? He said his men wouldn't hurt anyone. Just take the seal-ring.' He pointed at Carter. 'I thought it might help you decide to have me. I didn't think they'd…'

'No,' I said. 'Ya didn't. And ya don't do this to someone ya love. Ya loved the *idea* of owning me after all this time waiting, that's all. Get out. I never want to see thee again. We'll find some way to get through. We don't need the likes of thee. Go.' I showed him my back.

William stood tall and glowered at Rollo until the older man sighed and left.

Then all my rage and certainty slipped away and I was left with a hollow core and nothing to fill it. Carter dead. All the valuables gone. It didn't matter if the lordling called the tax collectors or they came as they did, regular. We'd no money.

I grimaced. At least the lord would leave us alone, though. His seal ring had been in the box the whole time. Hidden beneath a gold chain. He would find it.

I remembered it, now. Remembered Agnes Webb bringing it in with that Morrigan man. How had I forgotten? I sank onto a stool and buried my head in my hands. Carter's death was my fault. If I'd remembered earlier, I woulda given the thing to the lord with my blessing. What was wrong with me? Why had I forgotten where it was? Was I going mad?

There was a long, bitter silence, broken only by Sarah's snuffling sobs and the crackle of the dying fire in the hearth.

'Mother Hayward?' Beatrice's cold hand touched my arm. 'I know I made you angry readin the ledger before, but—'

'Nay, lovey.' I pressed her fingers. 'Twasn't thee I was angry with, but myself for not knowing how to keep the business afloat. Ever since Matt died, I've not been able to balance the books or keep enough money aside. I'm not cut out for it, I guess. I don't know what we're going to do, now.' Colour had leeched out of the room. Even the banked coals of the hearthfire seemed grey and cold and I stared hopelessly into them.

Cloth rustled and Beatrice crouched before me. 'That's what I were tryin to tell you, Mother. Your husband. He set money aside. Hid it in the ledger by makin it hard to read. But I've been doin me Mama's books for years, an I know all the tricks. I like numbers. I can help run things. But first we need to find it.'

I stared at her, brain fogged and blank. 'I don't know what you're saying, lovey.'

She said, tentatively, 'Goodman Hayward, Mother. He hid a fortune for you. Somewhere in this house. And I think I know where.'

'But the taxmen, the church,' I said, helpless. 'They'll take it.'

Her nose wrinkled and she glared toward the door. 'That Lord Lovell the innkeeper talked of? Same one as bid for me maidenhead.' She sniffed. 'He's a traitor to the king. He won't go near the king's men to report anythin. So we just need to find it before the tax collector's regular rounds.' She rose and held out a hand. 'Shall we?'

I laughed a sob and let her help me rise. It wouldn't bring Carter back, but maybe I could protect the rest of my little family from the likes of Lovell.

And maybe, in time, forgive myself.

10. Counting Out His Money

Reina Hayward, 17
Daughter of Cecily Hayward
Chepe Syed, Bred Street, London,

Friday (afternoon), 22nd September, 1486

'What say you, Luke?' I twirled then sank into a deep curtsey, holding out the shining blue skirts. I sent him a mischievous look beneath my lashes. 'Is it not lovely? Does it not suit me?'

The Nones bells chimed and clanked—with extra ringing for some reason. Maybe 'cause of the baby prince. They almost drowned out my words and I sighed, resigned to waiting before I could hear his reply.

My best childhood friend stopped his work and gazed steadily at me for a long moment. Then he shrugged and returned to his rhythmic scraping of timber with a plane. Long curls of pale wood spiralled to the ground like shorn locks of hair. I stroked my own gold ringlets and adjusted the gauzy blue wimple draped over them. I studied the brown bubble-bow...*purse*. Pity the blue got muddied, earlier, for the brown was so dull. And now Mama was cross with me over that, as well.

Luke still hadn't answered so I poked him in the ribs. 'Well?'

'Aye,' he said, brushing wood dust off the timber plank. 'Tis a fine surcoat alright, Reina. But...nay.' He grimaced and shaved off another curl.

'But what?' I inspected myself and could find no fault.

Luke straightened and pushed a strand of curly black hair from his dark eyes. He put the plane neatly in line with his other tools and folded his arms. 'But tis not for the likes of us. You, me, our families—we're not nobles. You get caught dressing like that and talking all breakteeth, playing off airs and graces—it'll be no good for you or your mama.'

I hunched a shoulder and sniffed disdainfully. The warm smell of oak and elm wrapped me in comfortable memories of a childhood spent playing under the workbenches and sketching animals on scraps of wood on rainy days like today. Bah. A peasant-child's memories.

'I won't get caught.' I smirked. 'Or I will, but by a *lord*. I'm determined, Luke. I'll not end up like Mama—married off to some hoddypeak…I mean some base churl who hits me when I say what I think.' I flung my arms wide. 'Or like your mama—working all hours making wax candles for the lords while you and your Papa work all hours to make their fine furniture. I want to *be* rich, Luke. I've seen how the grand ladies get treated—like they're delicate and precious. I'm going to snaffle…marry a lord. I know it.'

I hugged myself and hid a smile. A certain handsome, pale face danced in my head; white smile and charming voice as he complimented my surcoat and returned my muddy purse this morning. He was the one. And he had *five people* in his retinue, all handsome and dressed in fine linens. And after he'd strolled on, his thin, gold-skinned companion had bowed over my hand and said my lord would be pleased if I called on him. All formal and proper, like I were…was already a lady.

'Noble blood don't mean noble actions, Rei.' Luke picked up another plane and set to work again. 'Just watch yourself. We've been friends a long time and I don't want to see you get hurt.'

I kissed his dusty cheek. 'You're a dear. But I'm a sight…quite a bit tougher than you think, Luke Jacobson.' I brushed at the blue brocade. No dust.

On the bench nearby lay a drawing of a huge sideboard. I studied it critically and picked up a piece of charcoal and a flat piece of scrap timber. 'The top would look better like this, don't you think?' I drew a curled decorative back piece to the sideboard and held it up.

Luke considered it long. 'Aye. That it would. You've always had a good eye, Rei. Gramercy.' He lined my sketch up beside the vellum and went back to scraping.

'I should like to do more drawing again. But Mama says women can't be artists. Or at least, not poor women.' I wiped charcoal dust off my fingers.

'You could be a silversmith, like your father was before he started the Cahorsin shop.' Luke looked at me beneath his lashes. 'He taught you how. Have you still got his tools? It's an honest trade. Good money.'

I wrinkled my nose. 'His tools are there. I used them on Wednesday night to make…' I paused. What had I used them for? I couldn't recall. No matter. 'Anyway. The point is: I don't want to work.'

Luke opened his mouth again and I cut him off. I didn't need any more lectures—or questions.

'I must go.' I shook out my skirts and nodded. 'Mama's been a bear all day. She's snapped at me twice for nothing. Old Carter dropped two eggs that were for my breakfast this morning and he's sulking because I cuss…reprimanded him. And that whey-faced bride of William's has locked herself in her bedchamber. So I'm going to visit Nicola and Bella at the Broken Seld.'

And a certain lord who was staying there. But I wasn't telling Luke that for I didn't want a lecture. With a giggle, I blew him a kiss and ran out.

Outside, the sky was a tumble of grey and black. God's teeth. I hadn't brought a cloak if it rained. Should I go home and get one? No. If Mama caught me out again in this silk she'd have a fit. As long as it rained *after* I met Lord Lovell, it would be fine.

The Seld had only a few people sitting at the tables when I arrived and luckily Rollo wasn't around. He could be *so* vulgar. Forever lecturing me about not visiting because the inn was no place for women. Silly, because Nicola and Bella lived there and they were women. And Rollo's housekeeper, Sarah Clark, was a woman. So were his two maids.

I paused inside the doorway, waiting. The quiet conversations stopped and I nodded graciously. How could they help but look at me in this beautiful surcoat? Sarah hurried from the back room, brushing at the food stains on her apron and patting at her frizzy blonde hair. She bobbed a curtsey.

'Beggin your pardon, m'lady,' she mumbled. 'Was you looking for someone? Afraid the master's not ere.'

I giggled. 'It's me, Sarah, Reina Hayward.'

She gaped like a simpleton. 'Lordy. I fair didn't recognise you. Don't you look a treat? Oooh.' She reached out but I twitched the blue silk away from her filthy hands. She hung her head. 'No, you're right, m'lady. Don't wanna spoil it. But why're you here?'

I could get used to being called m'lady. I leaned closer, ignoring the stink of wine and old meat that hung about her. 'The lord you have staying invited me to visit.' I put a finger over my lips. 'But don't say a word to Rollo.'

Sarah's watery brown eyes widened. 'But m'…Reina, you don't wanna be a-visitin with that one.' Her voice dropped to a harsh whisper. 'He likes to…' She made squeezing motions. Whatever did she mean?

I pursed my lips. 'Don't be a blob-tell…gossiping about your betters, Sarah. Which room is he in?'

She bobbed and pointed up the stairs. 'Third door on the left. But I don't wanna know what Master Rollo will say when he finds out.'

Blackbirds Sing p167

'I forbid you to tell him,' I said, and marched up the stairs.

I hesitated outside the door and smoothed the blue silk with sweaty palms. My hand shook as I knocked on the oak panel.

'Enter,' a male voice snapped.

The door opened under my touch and I stepped boldly in. It was Rollo's best room. Big and with a window that looked out over the back garden, rather than the noisy stench of the street. Next to the window stood a small oak desk and Lord Lovell sat there, with his back to the door, writing. The goose-feather quill scratched across cream vellum, leaving strong black marks. Against the opposite wall, a huge bed stood, unmade, the fine linen bedclothes rumpled.

I gulped and closed the door then stood on tiptoes, trying to see what he wrote in such a swirly, elegant hand. He finished the note, signed it with a flourish and sanded the wet ink dry. After sealing the noted, he muttered an oath and pressed his thumb into the soft blue wax. Then he cursed, used his belt-knife to slit the letter open again and re-read it, adding a few words.

I cleared my throat. He cleaned the pen and laid it and the letter aside before turning around.

A small smile curved his lips. My cheeks burned. The room seemed hot and airless. Lovell rose, smooth like a cat, and circled me.

'So, I see you accepted my invitation.' He leaned closer and his lips brushed my ear. 'I'm so glad.'

Hot and cold shivered across my skin, leaving goosepimples and a strange ache behind. He laughed softly and trailed one finger along my cheek, down my neck, across my bosoms. I gasped and his smile broadened. He tugged my wimple free and dropped it on the floor. His fingers slid into my hair and I swayed into him, hungry for summat, but I didn't know what.

His beautiful dark eyes roved over me. 'That blue dress. You must be another daughter. And much more my type.' He twirled a gold ringlet. His lips kissed my throat and my knees turned to mush. 'Remind me to thank your mother when we're done.'

That made no sense, but my mind was all mixed-up anyway. All I wanted was for him to kiss me. If he kissed me, he'd want to sard me. Then we'd marry, right and proper, and I'd be a lady—treated nice and never having to work. Never having my sons go off to war and die if I didn't want them to.

Someone rapped on the door and Sarah's thin voice called out.

'You've a visitor below, m'lord.'

I swore an oath and Lord Lovell laughed.

'Indeed, my fairest. But hold that thought while I get rid of our uncouth messenger.' His warm lips found my throat again and I groaned.

He strode to the door and yanked it open. I fanned myself and fluffed my skirts, trying to get a cool breeze onto my heated nethers. I wandered to the window while Lovell sternly told Sarah his visitor could wait until later.

A quick look at the letter on the desk showed it was written to *'The fairest in all England.'* My heart skipped. He'd just called me 'fairest'. There was no time to read the rest. I snatched the thin vellum up and stuffed it into my purse. Then I carefully tipped the inkpot over the blank page left behind. Let him think he'd knocked it over and ruined his own letter. I hurried back to where he'd left me with blood thudding in my ears.

Lord Lovell closed the door and returned to my side.

'Now, where were we?'

I tilted my head and looked beneath my lashes. 'I think, my lord, you were going to show me how soft the bed is?'

He chuckled, low in his throat. 'That I was. But first we need to get you out of this creation, lovely as it is.' His fingers worked at the laces of the surcoat and they were undone in a trice. The material slid off my shoulders and pooled in a puddle of shining blue at my feet. I kicked off my leather slippers.

Then he scooped me into his arms and I giggled, breathless, half-frightened. He laid me gently down, kneeling at my feet. He pushed my chemise slowly up my legs, scraping my skin until I quivered from head to toe.

'My lord,' I groaned. His touch tickled my inner thigh.

'Relax, my love,' he murmured.

I caught his dark gaze and stilled. The eyes of a hunter. Glittering. A cat crouched for the kill.

Cold sense washed desire from my blood. 'My lord,' I managed. 'will you make me my lady Lovell? Or are you just after a quick swyve?'

His lip curled and a hand slid further up my leg. 'My lady Lovell? High ambitions, indeed, for a common Southwark goose. I think that dress went to your head, girl.'

I pushed upright and shoved his hand off my leg. 'I'm no strumpet, my lord. I'm an honest girl. When you invited me I thought…'

Lovell laughed. 'Not a whore? In that dress? Of course you are. I knew it the moment I saw you. You're obviously the sister to the other slut and I'll take great pleasure in making sure you've no claim, either. But if you're after money, then you can wait until we're done. Now lie back and stop putting on airs.' He grabbed the hem of my chemise and pushed it roughly up to my hips.

I struggled to hold it down. 'No! I'm not, my lord. Please?' Fear fogged my brain as desire had before. 'I'm not a whore. I'm not any slut's sister. I have no sister. I thought you'd marry me. Stop.'

He did. I gaped, sniffling.

He sat back and scowled. 'Stop blubbering, you stupid girl. Tears never fix anything, so I don't know why your sex resorts to them in every circumstance. I've never had to force myself on a woman and I won't start now.' His expression turned knowing. 'But I'm quite certain I can convince you to change your mind, if you give me a chance. And you'll enjoy it, I promise.'

I shrank back and hugged my knees to my chest, pulling my chemise over my bare legs.

A brisk knock sounded on the door.

'Oh, for the love of—What now? Can I get no peace?' Lovell strode to the door and yanked it open.

I scurried off the bed and grabbed up the surcoat, my face aflame. My hand shook too much to tie the lacings properly so I held it together and slipped on my shoes.

'Well, then, m'lord,' a hearty voice said, overloud in the chamber. 'Entertainin I see? Don't let me interrupt.'

'You already have, Queenie,' Lovell said dryly, 'but it appears I wasn't going to get any satisfaction. At least, not with her.'

I glanced up in time to see him give that same, animal smile to the woman standing in the doorway. She was tall, and curvy, with shining bronze-gold hair, grey eyes and creamy skin. When she opened her rain-dewed cloak I blinked at the splendid emerald velvet surcoat beneath. She held herself like a queen and checked me over critically.

'Where'd you get that surcoat, girl? Tell me, now.'

There was no pretending with this woman. She terrified me as much as Lovell had. I curtseyed automatically. 'My sister-in-law brought it home last night after she wedded my brother. I wanted to be a lady. I *felt* like a lady and I thought…I thought.'

Queenie burst out laughing and prodded Lovell in the chest. 'There's a turn-up, m'lord. Looks like you were tryin to bed me daughter's new sister-in-law.' She strode forward, all businesslike, tied my laces and collected my purse and wimple from the floor. 'Go home, girl. Don't tell your mama you've made a fool of yourself with this one. You're nowt but a silly child. Believe me,' she added, 'lord or not, you wouldn't want the likes of him.'

'Kind of you,' Lovell said, bowing.

I fled from the room, holding onto the remains of my shredded dreams and dignity as I ran downstairs. I headed blindly toward the inn's front door and bumped heavily into someone. They laid a hand on my shoulder and I squeaked.

'My lady.' It was Lovell's tall, gold-skinned servant. He held out my purse. 'I think you dropped this.' I accepted with a disjointed murmur of thanks and hurried out the door.

Outside, I wandered aimlessly around the Chepe Syde streets for an age, lost and broken, ignoring the light autumn drizzle of rain. All around, shops were closing their shutters for the evening. Men streamed into inns and the sound of coarse laughter and bawdy music drifted into the darkening street. Candles glowed in house windows as families sat around their hearths. The smell of woodsmoke and rain grew strong.

I turned a corner at random, barely thinking past my own stupidity. The scene in Lovell's room played over and over in my mind. How close I had come to throwing away my maidenhead in the veriest hope of marriage to lord. Was I mad? No, just foolish. Next time I would be smarter.

At least it proved lords were honourable, as I thought. He could have forced me, but he didn't. So I was right to find a husband higher up, where men were more refined and gentler with their women. And maybe, now he knew I was an honest girl, Lovell would look at me differently. Yes. I shouldn't give up hope, yet. I just had to try a new way of winning his heart. Or, if not his, another would do.

The storm broke just as the sunset bells pealed. Rain poured from the black sky and drenched me as I headed home. Mud splattered onto the blue silk surcoat and rain soaked it through. But I didn't care. It would clean and I would wear it again to entrance Lovell or another like him.

'Reina, love? Is that you?' Rollo appeared, hurrying through the storm, his cloak hood up. 'What are you doing here? Nevermind. Let me take you home. It's not safe for a girl to be out alone at this time. C'mon.' He lifted his cloak over me so I could take shelter.

I smiled and tripped along by his side, giggling as water splashed under my feet.

When we reached the house we stopped and peered through the rain. Why was the front door open after sunset? And all the lights in the shop doused? A faint scream cut through the torrent of rain. I took a step but Rollo gripped my wrist so hard I cried out.

'Wait,' he said. 'There's summat wrong.'

'I know. We have to go in. Let go!' I wrenched free.

A dark figure plunged out of the door and barrelled into Rollo, knocking him over.

'Rollo!'

He struggled to his feet, muddied and soaked. 'I'm alright.'

Two more men emerged, one carrying a wooden box. Lightning flashed and I caught a glimpse of a plump, girlish face and rain-flattened dark curly hair. The three men ran up the street and vanished into the blinding rain before I could call for help.

I hurried into the house, calling for my mother and William. A woman screamed. I ran.

In the hall, William and our servant, Sarah, stood by the hearth, staring down. Sarah's hand covered her mouth but great, gulping sobs escaped her and her thin shoulders shook. My brother stood there, silent and grim.

I froze. Old Carter lay, bloodied and broken beside the fire. The hearthstones were scattered about, Mama's strongbox gone. My throat tightened. I'd thrown harsh words at him for some silly mistake, only this morning. How could I have done such a thing? Carter had been part of our lives since I was born. Since William was born. Before, even. How could he be…was he? No, he couldn't be. I didn't want to touch him. Didn't want to know it was true.

A gnawing, horrible sickness twisted my stomach and tears made the room shimmer. What had I done?

'Rollo? What are ya doing here?' Mama's surprised question made us all turn.

'Mama!' I flung myself into her arms, sobbing.

'Reina Hayward,' she said, pushing me away. 'Ya ruined that surcoat. Now go upstairs and change before ya catch your death.'

'But Mama.' How could she even worry about a stupid surcoat right now? 'He's—'

'Go. Now.' She glared.

I'd seen the face of one of the men. I knew who had done this. And who must have ordered it, though my heart rebelled against the thought. But it must be true. We had to send a messenger to the magistrate of the King's Court.

I tried again. 'But I know who did—'

She pointed. 'Now. We'll speak later about your disobedience.' There was nothing but anger in her. No point in trying to explain.

Would no-one listen to me? Would no-one treat me as a grown woman? My limbs were heavy with new awareness of the extent of my naïve silliness.

I ran out into the storm again.

'Luke?' I pounded on his front door. 'Luke? Let me in, it's Reina.'

A light flickered under the door and it creaked open. I stumbled into the front room and threw myself, sobbing uncontrollably, onto Luke's broad chest. He carefully put his candle aside and wrapped me tight, stroking my back.

'What's the matter? You're soaked. Why are you crying?' He gripped my arms and held me away, staring. 'Wait. Did summat happen at the inn? Or on your way back? You're not hurt? My ma's over at my aunt's house, helping deliver her babe, but we can send for her.'

The words tumbled out: Lord Lovell, my hopes, my stupid belief that he would marry me, how close I'd come to making the biggest mistake of my life, the broken door at home, the stolen box, Carter's blood on the floor. Everything.

Luke's grip tightened on my arms until I lost feeling in my fingers. 'Carter's dead?' He blew a thick breath and sat me on a bench along the wall. 'That's hard to think on. And you say Lovell must have ordered it? How do you know?'

'It was his men that ran out of the house,' I said, my voice wobbling. 'They carried our strong-box and knocked Rollo over. I recognised them from when I met Lord Lovell on the street today. But what should I do? Mama won't listen. He's a lord and I'm...' I leaned my head on Luke's shoulder. 'I'm just a stupid peasant girl.' I scrubbed at my eyes. 'I thought I was special. That I could be more by marrying a lord. But you were right: noble blood doesn't mean noble actions. I can't believe I was such a simpleton.'

There was a long silence and Luke let out a heavy sigh. 'You're not a simpleton, Rei. A little spoiled, maybe, but smart and far braver than most. Remember the time you stole apples from old Widow Henderson's yard?'

I chuckled weakly. 'Her dog chased us for two blocks. You climbed a building and pulled me up. Seems you're always rescuing me from my follies.'

'It's my honour.' He looked at his hands in his lap. 'I wasn't going to say anything, Rei, but after tonight…' He shrugged. 'Maybe I've a chance after all.'

'What are you talking about, Luke?'

He threw his broad shoulders back and cleared his throat. 'I want you to marry *me*, Rei, not some lord. I've loved you since I was ten. Since the first time I saw you draw a bird and thought it looked so real it ought to fly off.' He faced me, anxious. 'I can't give you the rich life you want. But I think, together, we can make a better one than our parents. Y'know where me pa is?'

I blinked at the change, hardly able to keep up, still reeling from his proposal and Carter's death. It was too much to keep in my head.

'Remember that drawing you did of the sideboard?' Luke glanced across, so I nodded. 'The customer was so happy with that design that he's ordered five other pieces of furniture to match. Pa's off measuring his house, now.'

'Umm…good, but I don't see—'

Luke gripped my hands so hard I winced. 'Nobles and merchants pay top money for good furniture. You design and I'll make. You have an artist's eye, Rei. Don't waste it being some frippery wife who can't do more than embroidery. Marry me. We can build things. A life. Furniture. A family. Together.'

I stared at our hands intertwined; his large, strong and calloused, mine small and soft. Perhaps he was right: I was spoiled and aiming at a life out of my reach. And if I married some lord, he could turn out like Lovell and want me for nothing but my face and my body. But money made life easy and lack of it meant sickness and starvation and fear. Children lost to wars. If I married Luke, I might be happy. I could draw again and our business might be successful—or it might fail. He could go off and die, leaving me poor and alone.

I glanced up and found him watching me, his cheeks flushed.

'I'm not sure, Luke,' I said on a sigh. He flinched and tried to pull free but I clung tight. 'I'm not saying 'no'. I just need time to think on it.' I leaned on him again. 'It's been a horrible day and you surprised me, that's all. Will you give me some time?'

He said nothing for a while, then rested his cheek on my head. 'I've waited seven years, I can wait a mite longer. I want you to be happy.'

'I always thought I could only be happy if I married someone rich.'

He sighed. 'I know, Rei.'

'Now, I'm not so sure.' I snuggled closer and tucked my arm through his, content for the moment.

p178 *Aiki Flinthart*

11. The Queen was in the Parlour

Eliza (Queenie) Parry, 30
Brothel owner
Chepe Syed, London,

Friday late (afternoon), 22nd September, 1486

I studied Lovell from beneath me lashes. How should I play this?

He was the sort to think women fools but he weren't stupid. And with that silly girl, Reina, gone he'd like as not be frustrated as well. Mayhap I could let him think I'd help ease his achin—'til I got what I'd come for, anyways.

I tilted me head, smiled coyly and swayed forward. The last rays of sunlight slipped under the stormclouds, through the unshuttered window, and lit Lovell's room at the Broken Seld a soft gold. I weren't a young girl anymore, but in this light and wearin this emerald velvet I should pass for twenty. Lovell clearly liked his women young and naïve.

'Now, m'lord…'

'Now what, Queenie?' He snatched his leather purse from a bedside table and yanked open the top. 'I suppose you've come for money? Seems everyone does.'

I chuckled low in me throat. 'Well, you do still owe for that tumble in the sheets with me stewhouse girls yesterday mornin when you came to see Bea. Three girls, in fact.'

He plucked a couple of silver coins out and thrust them toward me. 'Take it and go. I have important matters to attend to and I'm expecting visitors.'

'No.' I pushed his hand back. 'You have summat I want more, anyways.'

'Ah.' He stared at me a long while, searchin me face for summat. 'Yes. So very like.' Then an arm slid around me waist and he pulled me close. His lips trailed hot down me throat. 'You're beautiful, Elizabeth.'

I rolled me eyes but didn't protest. Men. Always thinkin with their yards. He tugged at the lacins on me surcoat. A hand slid inside. I buried an irritated sigh.

He groaned and nibbled me ear. 'You should be mine. You were always meant to be mine. Richard promised.'

Now that was gettin a bit strange, even for me. I didn't know any Richards as could promise me to anyone.

A crack of thunder slapped hard overhead and we both jumped. Rain tumbled down and a chill breeze wafted into the room. I slid free of his embrace and kissed him lingerin-like to soften the partin.

'Didn't you say you had visitors comin? Maybe we can do this later, when we've got time to really enjoy ourselves.'

Lovell frowned, his eyes still love-glazed and hungered. He focussed on me and disappointment flickered across his sharp face. Then he shook himself and smoothed his tunic. 'Yes. You're right. What do you want, then?'

'Information,' I said, retyin me lacin. 'Tell me what I want to know and we'll call our other debt clear. I'll even let you have a free swyve with any girl in me house you want.'

'You,' he shot back. 'You. On your knees, then tied to your bed, begging me to sard you.' His pupils darkened and his breath quickened. 'Give me that and I'll tell you whatever I can.'

'Done, m'lord.' We shook hands like the business deal it was, with Lovell flushed red and practically pantin, me keepin scorn safe-hidden. Men were all the same. After eight years workin and ten runnin the house, you'd think I'd've found one decent man. Well, apart from Georgie, anyways. But he'd gone and died before we could tell the world we were wed and I'd been lucky to get away from the rest of the Plantagenets with me head still on me neck.

A cough tickled in me chest and I buried it hasty in a kerchief. Me breath rattled and I wiped me mouth.

Lovell cleared his throat. 'So, what do you want to know? Though I can probably guess.'

'What did you mean last night at Bea's auction?' I said baldly. 'When you said her marryin William would do as well as your other plan?'

His smile broadened, cunning. I wanted to slap him but instead I fiddled with me lacins again, slowly tuggin one free. His gaze dropped to me tits.

'Do you know who your parents are. Your mother?' he said, his attention still on me breasts.

There it was. What I needed. I stilled then relaxed, not wantin to let him see how much I had to know what he knew. I shrugged one shoulder like it weren't the question that'd bothered me since I were old enough to ask it.

'Does it matter, m'lord? I'm a whore. We don't have parents, anyways. At least, not ones who care.' Bitterness crept into me words and I ground me teeth.

Lovell chuckled. 'You do. Although they may not care, as you say. But I had to be sure about Bea. Things are muddy enough as it is.'

'Don't give me riddles, m'lord,' I snapped. 'Mark me words: if you've nothin of sense to say, the deal's off.' I retied me lacins, gathered me cloak and headed for the door. I should have known he was a liar as well as a bedswerver.

'Go ask the midwife,' he called as I yanked the door open. 'Laura Kennet,' he added, sly.

'Laura?' I frowned. 'I see her regular. She looks after me and me girls. Good woman. Good midwife.'

'Your father's dead, but your mother could well be alive. Mistress Kennet knows who your mother is,' he said, secret amusement lightin him. 'I almost wish I could be there to see your reaction. But I have things to do. I'll come and see you to complete our agreement.'

'If your information's true, m'lord,' I said, 'But don't come tomorrow, I've a large party booked. And the next day is the Sabbath and the house is shut by law.'

'And I'm rather busy. I'll send word.' With a languid wave, he sauntered to the desk by the window. He swore an oath and picked up a pile of ink-stained vellum and hurled it out the window into the rain.

I went slowly downstairs and took a seat in a darkened corner, cloak hidin me fine surcoat from the few men slurpin at ale. The slattern of a housekeeper thumped a mug of ginger hum onto the table and snatched up my coin. I sipped and thought.

I'd grown up a foundlin in the very stewhouse I now owned. Wetnursed by the owner's wife. Laura Kennet had been called in to midwife one of the whores when I was eleven. She'd taken me to her heart. Treated me like her own daughter. When I was fifteen, she'd brought Bea into the world. Later, she'd helped me girls get rid of unwanted babes early. For the laws said pregnant girls weren't allowed to work.

But in all those years Laura'd never mentioned me mother bein alive. Why would she hide such a thing?

Footfall on the stairs made me look up. Lovell left the inn, cloaked against the drizzlin rain. He didn't see me and I didn't want to see him so I stayed mum. He returned a short while later, just after the sunset bells, lookin darker than the thunder as growled outside.

Outside, rain splashed harder. I finally bestirred meself and rose from the rickety table.

I had a choice to make.

The Broken Seld's front door crashed open and three men stumbled in, soaked and pantin. They headed for the stairs. One carried an iron-strapped oak strongbox. I stepped aside and waited for them to pass.

They knocked on Lovell's door and he let them in with a sharp comment about their tardiness. After the door closed I couldn't hear nothin, but a few seconds later a whoop of delight rattled the walls. Lovell's voice drove me toward the outside. Storm or no, I did not want to be around if he came out of his room.

At the door, I about bumped into a tall, becloaked man and pulled up short with a breathless apology. He bowed. I almost curtseyed out of habit then recalled I were dressed as a lady and that wouldn't do.

I sniffed and curled a lip, instead. The stranger's smile widened. His grey eyes were startlin against gold skin. I studied him closer. Not a man. A woman. Interestin.

She pointed toward the top floor. 'Have you just called on Lovell?'

I started, recovered and cleared me throat. 'I don't believe that's any of your business. Excuse me.' A bout of coughin stole breath for a time and I clung to the wall with a kerchief to me lips. When it was done I stepped around her and yanked open the door.

I glanced back and she was watchin me with a soft smile and a hint of sadness that made me throat ache.

The storm had washed away the worst stink of horseshit but left the street a muddy swamp. The rain eased to a drizzle. Me thick wool cloak protected me precious green velvet and hid it from those that might take exception to a Southwark goose wearin finery on the northside of the river. A few bronze and horn street lanterns were lit, but the side alleys were darker than sin. I hoiked up me skirt and drew out a dagger from the sheath strapped to me thigh. George had long ago taught me to defend meself and I'd never scrupled to use it when needed. Me life might not be much, but it was mine to say when it ended, if I could.

At the crossroads of Grasche Street and Fanchurche I hesitated. Did I go home, or did I go speak to Laura? Did I want to know the answer? I'd lived a life so far without knowin who me Ma was. Did I really want to know why she gave me up to a whorehouse?

I stared down the dark road toward the London Bridge; more than just tolls and shops, it was the barrier that separated Southwark from the London that despised me and my girls.

A half-dozen tosspots stumbled out of an alehouse, along with a gust of warm, yeast-scented air. They staggered along Grasche Street and stopped, yellin crude words at anyone nearby as they pissed against the wall.

'Heya. You'll need another dagger if you're think'n to go home past that lot, Your Grace.' A shadow detached itself from the alley nearby and drifted close.

'God's balls, Ingaret Leon,' I said. 'You about stopped me heart, girl. You followin me? I don't owe you money, do I?'

Wearin a dark tunic and hose, with her black hair short and skin smudged with charcoal, Ingaret was barely visible in the gloom. She shrugged.

'Probly. You always do.' Her stiletto dagger gleamed in a flash of lamplight. 'But tonight Bea asked me to shadow you.'

'Dratted girl,' I said. 'None of her business what I do now she's good an married.'

Her teeth flashed white. 'That's what I said. But she paid me. She's worried about you. Says you've been poorly.'

I suppressed a cough. 'She should know I'm too tough to die. Tell her to leave off.'

Ingaret smirked. 'Too shrewish, more like. If you're goin home at this hour you'll need help.'

'Well, I'm not. Get home, girl.' I glanced over me shoulder in the direction of the Broken Seld. 'But I might have a job for you soon. Someone who's gettin a mite under me skin. That Lovell bastard.'

'He'll cost you some.' She sniffed. 'Quick with a blade, that one.' Her grin flashed. 'But I'd be glad for his sword and dagger.'

'If I know you, you've got a bunch already, hidden away. No wonder you ain't married. No man'll wet his wick in a girl who'll stab him in the mornin.'

'Good.' She chuckled. 'Anyway, I like my job too much to marry. Sides, there's still a sight more to learn. Found new teacher. Italian style. Neat. Quiet.' She flourished the stiletto.

'Killin folk for money's not a job. Not a Godly one, anyway.'

'Says the quean?' She shrugged again. 'Pays pretty well. But time's money and you're cost'n Bea a penny stand'n here. You stay'n or goin?'

'Fine. I'm goin thataway, anyways.' I pointed up Fanchurche Street.

When I looked back, Ingaret was gone on the whisper of a laugh.

'Pesky child,' I muttered. I kept the dagger ready and turned up Fanchurche Street instead of headin for home.

I paused outside a modest brick and half-timbered house, tucked between the St Dionis Church and the Pewterers Hall halfway up Lyme Street. Laura Kennett had lived here as long as I could recall. Her mother before her. She'd outlived two husbands and three of her own children. Five more were grown and had left a home I remembered fondly for its welcomin warmth.

Yet now I stood outside in the wet-dark, reluctant to go in.

The front door opened and golden lamplight poured onto the shiny steps. A dark-silhouetted female figure stepped out and hesitated.

'Eliza? Is that you?' Laura's deep, calm voice broke the silence between us. 'Bless me you gave me a fright an all. What in the Lord's name are you doing here at this hour? Are you alright? Bea? Come in, come in.'

Words of greetin stuck in me throat so I took off me muddy boots and said nothin. She ushered me inside and into the cosy kitchen-hall. Seated by the hearthfire, her husband, Oswin, looked over his little round glasses and nodded. He rose.

'I was just off to bed, so I'll leave you to talk, shall I? Eliza.' He bowed cordially, kissed Laura on the cheek and shuffled upstairs with a candle.

Laura put down her midwife's bag and tossed aside her cloak. She gestured me to a seat by the fire and took one opposite.

'I can't stay long, Eliza,' she said. 'Just got a call to another miscarriage. Third one today an all. I'm afeared they may be connected to the illness I hear is in the town. But I met a young healer by the name of Helen O'Reilly, from Isledon. With her beau, a young man by the name of Alistair Morrigan. Tis a wonder but she says they might be able to cure it.' She shook her head. 'But you didn't come to hear me talk of work. You're pale. Are you well?'

I shrugged impatiently and swiped rain off me face. Me careful makeup must be smeared, me curled hair limp and draggled. But it didn't matter. I studied Laura, lookin for clues. Her narrow, dark eyes were creased by fifty-six years of life and worry for women and their babes. She'd seen more of both die than anyone had a need to yet her calm good cheer remained undimmed.

Blackbirds Sing p187

'Who's me mam?' I forced the words out quiet when I wanted to scream them at her and shake her plump shoulders.

She stilled, her strong hands clasped so tight in her lap that the nails turned white. She stared into the fire.

I bore the silence as long as I could, fiddlin with the dagger still in me hand. When I could stand it no longer I spoke, hard and low. 'Who, Laura? And why'd you never tell me? You knew how unhappy I was in the stewhouse as a girl. If you know me family, why didn't you tell me?' I swallowed a hard lump of fear. 'Are they dead?'

Laura shook her head and snatched the white coif from it, leavin her wiry grey hair stickin out askew.

'I'm sorry, Eliza. More sorry than you'll know.' She heaved a sigh. 'I tried. Tried to find you an all. When I did, I tried to get your foster mother to let you come to me. But she'd already started you working and you were her big money-earner for the house. What with how pretty you were an all.'

'I never knew. Why didn't you say?'

Laura's wrinkled lips stretched into a weary smile. 'You were only a girl. I didn't want to get your hopes up an all.'

'But why?' I glared. 'There were three other girls the same age there. Why were you lookin for me?'

'I can't…' She rose and paced the room a few times. She were normally so calm I couldn't help but gape at her. 'Your father's long dead. Your mother's name was Philippa.' She wrung her hands then sat heavily on the stool again. 'I should have done more, an all. I tried, but his family…oh, I was young and afeared and stupid!'

'You're makin no sense, Laura. Tell me, straight up. Was I born on the wrong side of the bed? What does that matter, anyways? I kept Bea, didn't I?'

'Yes. No, but you're a—'

'A what, Laura? A whore, a quean, a strumpet? And whose fault is that? Why did she give me up?'

Her dark eyes pierced me soul. 'Why? In the Lord's name, Eliza, why do you need to know, now? You're a businesswoman in your own right. Bea is married, I hear. What good will it do, an all?'

I stared at me hands. Still smooth and soft like a lady's, lyin on the soft green velvet over me knees. But it was all an illusion. Me whole life had been a pretence. With George I'd thought—for one heady year—that I could have summat better. Be summat better. Or be loved, anyways.

Then he'd died and I was thrown back to the fleshmongers. I'd hidden me pregnancy until it was too late for me foster mother to do anythin. And Bea had been me light. But I'd never understood her—pious, quiet, fussy thing she was. I were glad she were out of the life. But jealous, too. Jealous with a chest-deep ache that stung me eyes with hard tears when I thought on it. She and her children would have what I never did.

'I need to know, Laura,' I managed at last. 'I need to know who she is and why she gave me up to that life.'

'Oh, Eliza. She didn't want to, I promise. But I'm sworn to silence. Her family watches me. I don't dare—'

I shot to me feet and touched the knife blade to her jowly throat. 'They aren't here, Laura Kennet. I am. Mark me words, I will end your life now if you don't tell me.'

She didn't flinch or cry out for her husband. She just waited. Only pity and worry showed.

'Then you'd never know, Eliza.'

Fire drained from me and I fell to me knees before her, me head pillowed on her lap as I'd done in years gone by when I was angry or afeared. She stroked me hair.

Blackbirds Sing p189

I sniffed, feelin like a girl of twelve again.

We stayed that way a long while, starin into the cracklin fire. Outside the storm thickened up and thunder rolled.

'I'm dyin, Laura,' I said at last. I'd known it for weeks. Since a winter chest ague had turned to coughin blood into me kerchief.

Laura's hand on me head stilled a moment then took up the rhythmic strokin again.

'Thomasine Smith,' I added, 'the barber-surgeon on Crokyd Lane said it's the consumption alrigh. Gettin harder to breathe every day.' I raised me head. 'I want to speak to me mam before I die. I need to understand.'

'Even if it would make you both unhappy?'

I gave a watery laugh that ended up as a chesty cough. 'Her unhappy, you mean? What else can happen to me?' I gripped her wrists hard so she flinched. 'Give me this, Laura. You say you couldn't help me when I were younger. Help me now.'

'And what about her?' Laura searched me face. 'Are you so cruel? She's old. She thinks you were given to a loving wetnurse who raised you in a family, an all. I did too. I checked on you, but then your nurse died and no-one told me you'd been sold to your foster mother in Southwark. Would you wreck your mother's peace of mind to satisfy your hurt?'

I shoved up from the floor and strode away, picked up a thick clay mug from the slab oak table and set it down again. I'd never thought of me mam's feelins. Me own pain had burned away any thought of her except anger and longin. Laura was right. Findin out I'd been sold into the stewhouses would break any lovin mother's heart.

But that was what I needed to know. Was she truly a lovin mother? Why had she given me up at all? What mother would choose her own freedom over her babe's, anyways? And why not just kill the child rather than leave it alive, if it were unwanted? Lord knew hundreds of babes a year died, abandoned by girls who couldn't rear them for one reason or another.

I rounded on Laura and held the knife out toward her again. 'No. Her feelins be damned. I've a right to know—before I die—why I was thrown out like dirty water while she lived on free and clear.'

Laura rose and brushed at her skirts. 'Very well. It's not my tale to tell and I don't know the full of it.' She cocked her head. 'I'll send her a message, an all. But I warn you she may not reply. She's close-watched, too. As soon as I hear back, I'll try to find a way to bring you together.'

Her words were a blow to the stomach. I sank onto the stool. A kind of fluttery excitement built in me chest until I could barely sit still.

Laura gathered her midwife's bag and laid a light hand on me shoulder. 'Stay here tonight. It's too cold and wet out for someone with your condition. The gable room is made up for guests. Go get some sleep an all. We'll speak more tomorrow.'

She left and I stayed by the fire, unable to think beyond hope and fear, unable to let go the wish for life lived different, unable to imagine what I would say to a mother who'd chosen to give me up when she could have kept me.

But at least now I had a hope of findin out the truth.

And that were enough for tonight.

12. Eating Bread and Honey

Emma Turner, 50
Apiarist
Outside Aldgate, London,

Saturday (early morning), 23rd September, 1486

'Ma? We need ta talk.' My son, Adam, stood outside my workshop, bright-lit from behind by the morning sun, turning his straw hat in his hands like he was a boy of ten not a man of thirty.

'Hey, m'lad.' I peered at him then went back ta scraping caps off the honeycomb. Honey dripped inta the pot beneath, golden and rich, the smell warmly familiar.

Adam cleared his throat and toed at a clump of grass.

Something rattled against the outside of the old wattle and daub hut I used as a workshop. And slept in most nights these days. This was more my home than in the main house, now. I glimpsed a shock of scruffy brown hair—same dark shade as mine, but with less grey—and a mud-stained tunic. Paul, my eight-year-old grandson. Lurking, listening in ta his betters. A pair of blue eyes—again like mine—peeked around the corner; full of youthful mischief and no-good. Brat of a boy. A care-for-nought who backtalked his elders with every mouthful of words.

'Ma,' Adam continued, oblivious ta his son's presence, 'it's about the field.'

'Oh?' I went on scraping at the honeycomb. I wasn't about ta encourage him. It was my last field. Only ten wooden box-hives left, scattered among the wildflowers I'd spent years planting. Columbine, borage, lavender, thrift, milkmaids, foxglove, clover. Every colour, every delicious scent, throughout spring and summer. And then there were my huge herb gardens where I grew what went inta the theriac cure-all for bee stings.

'We need the land. For more sheep,' Adam finished in a hurry. 'Money's in wool, they say. If'n we want Paul ta have a good life, we need ta get more sheep in.'

I shot him a long, steady look. Our family had supplied honey ta London and the royal family for five generations. Yet he wanted ta be rid of the hives and graze sheep. Sheep! As if'n there weren't enough of the pesky animals around already. Seemed every field was thick with woolly white coats and loud with their sorrowful bleating.

Adam shrugged and cleared his throat again. 'Think on it, Ma. You could go live with Aunt Margaret in the city. Stop working so hard. You know you can't manage on your own anymore. What with your eyesight and the bone-aches. Help Marg with her grandkids, like she asked. She's poorly and needs you.'

At least he had the wit ta hold back the 'and we don't'. Still stung, though. I said nothing, just kept staring. He sighed and strode toward the cottage. Paul appeared from nowhere and skipped alongside his father, chattering and asking a dozen questions one after another as he always did. He asked about the hives and the bees and sheep. And whether Grandmama would be staying or going.

I couldn't hear Adam's answer.

I slammed a palm flat on the workbench and dust rose inta the warm, thick air. Forty years I'd tended the hives and flowers. First with my pa, then alone when he'd gone. Now all my work would go ta waste. Dug inta the soil, along with my body.

Adam and his little family cared not a whit for me or what I wanted. Just concerned about how much money the farm could make if'n the bees were gone.

If'n I were gone.

A drone bee buzzed in through the open door and landed on the honeycomb.

Blackbirds Sing p195

'Hey, m'little one.' I put out a fingertip and he crawled on. 'Almost time for you and the other drones ta be pushed out, hmmm? Left ta die in the cold winter.' His wings fluttered and settled. 'I know how you feel.'

I carried the drone ta the window and flicked him inta freedom. He buzzed off over the field and returned ta the drone-gathering site on an alder tree.

Hasty footsteps pattered outside.

'Mistress Turner, come quick! It's me ma.' The youngest Wallis boy burst inta my workshop, panting, face red.

'Hey, m'boy. What's amiss with your ma, hmmm?' I said.

'Beestung, Mistress.' He pointed back the way he'd come, down Aldgate Street, toward Hogg Lane. 'Out checkin the sheep in the cloverfields. She's swelled up something awful.'

I grimaced. Sheep in the clover in flowering season. Happened every year. Most the time folk were lucky—like me—and the stings just hurt and itched a few days. Sometimes it was worse. And sometimes people hardly noticed the first few stings, then next time they swelled up in horrible pain. Sometimes they died afore I could help.

I licked honey off my fingers and squinted up at the top shelf. There it was. The ceramic jug almost slipped from my sticky grasp but I caught it afore it hit the oak workbench. I measured a large dose of the bitter-smelling black liquid inta a smaller jug.

'Beestings make a body too wet. Give her this theriac. It'll dry her out. Rub some on the stings. Mind she drinks all the rest, hmmm? Off you go, boy. Quick now.'

He held the jug close ta his chest and bolted, his bare feet splattering along the path muddied by last night's storm.

I huffed. There was a time when I was that important ta Adam.

Years ago. When he would have done anything for me and I for him. Now, all I had left was the bees. At least they needed me.

I resumed scraping.

'Mistress Turner?' A light male voice sounded behind me.

I jumped. 'Lordy, boy, you scared the life out of me.' I squinted and gave a little gasp. No peasant lad, this young man had the air of nobility about him. Ruby-hilted sword, arrogant lift ta his chin. A leather satchel hung over his shoulder and pulled at the set of his grey silk doublet.

A worker buzzed and landed on his arm. He flicked the bee off with a middle finger and thumb, so hard the animal fell ta the dirt, wounded. The stranger crushed it beneath his boot.

I pursed my lips but dipped a curtsey. 'Pray your pardon, m'lord. What can I do for you, hmmm?'

He picked up a small pot of my honey, dipped in a finger and stuck it inta his mouth. He pursed his lips and set the pot back in its place. His gaze flicked around the workshop and I suddenly wished I'd dusted, made up my bed, and tidied all the pots and tools away.

'I understand yours is the best honey to be found,' he said. He glanced toward the hives. 'And that you work seven days to keep your hives in good order.'

'So I'm told, m'lord. But the bees do most the work I just help.'

'Tomorrow's the Sabbath,' he said. 'Surely you'll be resting, not working?'

'I go ta dawn service, m'lord,' I said. 'And we'll go twice more, as we always do. But the bees don't know it's the Lord's day, so I have ta tend them. I'm sure the Lord'll understand. After all they're His creatures, too, hmmm?'

The stranger looked down his sharp nose at me. 'Don't presume to know what our Lord thinks, woman. That's for the clergy to decide, not you.'

I bowed my head, cursing my prideful tongue. I should have lied and said I rested.

He wiped his fingers and, from his satchel, produced a large clay pot. 'Later this morning you'll get a visit from a young lady. A maid named Flora Leon, from the Tower. She comes every month and buys honey for the king, I hear. And at this time of year,' he added drily, 'I'm told she also buys a small pot for herself.'

This time I waited. It was common knowledge the new king favoured my honey. But Flora was one of several people who slipped inta my workshop at this time of year, wanting honey for special reasons. I pretended not ta know why they came. They were good folk, Jews or not. Why did he mention it? Did he expect me ta admit I knew what she was? I wouldn't be part of helping the Church kill innocent young girls because they worshipped the same God in a different way.

'This month,' he said, 'you'll give her this as a gift for the king's table. To be used at the banquet celebrating the new prince's christening.' He thrust the pot at me. I stared long at it but my hand wouldn't move.

'If you don't,' he added, 'I'll inform the Bishop that you work on a Sabbath *and* that you can identify the Jews who buy honey for their unlawful rituals. The Church will confiscate your land, expel your family from England and burn your fields to ash.' He placed the pot precisely on the workbench.

Still, I said nothing. My heart fluttered, mind buzzing, but what could I say?

'I'll take that as consent,' he said. 'Wise woman.' He turned away, then back again. 'And yes, I will know if the honey is not on the royal table that night. I'll be there to watch him eat it. And I shall know if the seal's been broken. So don't fail.'

After he left, I could do nothing but stand and stare at the pot. The top was sealed tight and stamped with red sealing wax. I sniffed at the edges, catching a whiff of the contents smeared on the outside. Honey, alright. But with a hint of something bitter I couldn't quite name. Nothing good. I replaced the pot carefully and thought long and hard.

He must be meaning ta poison King Henry. But what if'n the king didn't eat enough ta die? Or if'n the pretty Queen Elizabeth of York ate it instead? Or someone else? It seemed like a very uncertain way ta kill a man. So what was he meaning ta do, then?

Could he be aiming ta get the girl, Flora, accused of trying ta kill the king? What good would that do? She was just a maid. But who did she serve? I'd never asked. And if'n she was accused, then I would be, too. And my family.

It seemed ta me there was no good answer and no good reason for any of this. If'n I gave it ta Flora, we'd be accused of treachery ta the crown. If'n I held it back then the Church would take the farm and destroy my family. And I didn't know the lord's name, so I couldn't even report him ta the reeve. Besides, who would believe an old woman over a lord, anyway?

There was no right choice. I asked the Lord for guidance. Nothing. He'd never spoken ta me. Not once. Most likely I wasn't worthy.

What did I do?

I gazed long at the little stone cottage where Adam, Sarah and young Paul lived. They cared nought for me, but I couldn't let the king kill them or let the Church take the farm. Nothing I could do would keep them safe.

Unless…

I sat hard on a stool and rested my weary head on the bench.

It was the only answer. The only thing that might save my family.

I carefully put away my tools and set the cleaned honeycomb

Blackbirds Sing p199

aside. I'd have ta be rid of everything later, tell the Church or the king that I'd got rid of the hives last month, and hope my neighbours would stand behind me. It was a risk, but also the only path that gave us a chance.

Misery clouded my world as I pulled on leather gloves and donned a wide straw hat with its veil of coarse-woven linen. I collected Adam's big wooden wheelbarrow from the barn and trudged toward the hives.

As I neared, worker bees buzzed placidly, landing at the hive entrance and doing their little dances ta tell where ta find the best flowers. I lowered the barrow. I'd spent so many years watching them they were like family. I knew each hive. The queens from this one always laid six new queens each season and swarmed at least twice if'n I let them. The workers were the nastiest, too. I'd been stung most gathering honey from this box. Lucky I didn't get sick.

'Hey, m'little ones. Time ta go. Forgive me, hmmm?'

I set my jaw against the ache in my throat and pulled free the wooden dowels that held the hives firm ta their stands. The buzzing grew louder. I hefted the whole box inta the wheelbarrow, grunting at the effort for it was heavy. The sick-sweet smell of fermenting honey surrounded me.

The workers swarmed out by the hundreds, buzzing and circling, landing on my thick woollen clothing and taking off again. They climbed all over my veil, darkening the world with their heavy bodies.

One managed ta crawl beneath the veil and sting my neck. I hissed, flicked the poor thing off and pinched out the stinger. There would be more. I'd survive. They never bothered me much.

I trundled the hive across the field, toward the little patch of woodland that separated our farm from the neighbours. I couldn't bear ta burn the hives, but maybe if'n I put them in the woods, they'd survive and someone else could care for them. Then Adam could plough in the wildflowers and plant grasses for the sheep in spring.

Another bee stung me. I welcomed the pain. I deserved it for what I was doing. They had kept my people for a hundred years. And I was betraying them for a son who would be happy ta see them go. But family was family. He and Paul deserved the best chance I could give them.

Another sting.

I reached the edge of the field and lowered the barrow for a spell. Must be getting old. My chest tightened, each breath a struggle. The skin on my cheeks and eyes felt hot and stretched, my lips thick. I wheezed. Dizzy, I backed away from the barrow, stumbling on the uneven ground. A few bees followed, but most returned ta the hive, protecting the queen.

I stripped off the hat and gloves. My fingers were clubs, my cheeks hard lumps, my eyes almost swollen shut. I tried ta call out, but the breath wouldn't come.

This was God's revenge for abandoning his creatures. I would die here, in my own field, killed by the bees I loved.

It seemed only fair.

I sank ta my knees, gasped in the sweetness of honey and flowers, and prayed.

The blue sky darkened and the joyful sound of churchbells carolled from our little parish church. A wedding, a christening, a funeral? Calling them, and me, ta God.

'Grandmama! Grandmama!' Young Paul's tousled head blotted out the sun and I squinted at him. He shook me, crying my name over and over. I dragged a wheezing breath, but couldn't speak ta let him know it was alright. Then he vanished.

I'd be alone ta die, then. Not surprising.

Blackbirds Sing p201

Light footsteps pattered close. Paul's thin arm slipped under my back and he raised me up. His forehead was knitted, his dirty cheeks smeared with teartracks. Tears? Why?

He held something against my thick lips. 'Drink, Grandmama. You must. It's your own thria...theriac. You said it fixes people. I heard. Please?'

But it was too much effort. Each breath was harder than the last. Why bother? At least God wanted me.

'Please, Grandmama?' Paul's blue eyes drowned and spilled tears. 'I know I make you cross and you don't like me. But I want ta learn about the bees. I want ta help. I don't want Papa ta grow sheep instead of flowers. And I don't want you ta go live in the city. Please drink?'

He thought I didn't like him? He wanted me ta stay?

He tipped the cup and the bitter liquid dribbled inta my mouth. I managed ta swallow a few dregs. My tongue softened. I sipped more. My throat eased. I raised a shaky hand, dipped two fingers inta the cup, and smeared the theriac on my eyes and face. The effort was too much. But Paul got the idea and copied. Then poured more inta my mouth.

Bit by bit, the swelling went down. My breath came easier. The wheezing stopped and my eyes cleared. I took the cup and gulped the rest, gagging at the bitter, woody taste. Lordy, that was foul stuff.

Paul burst inta wild sobbing and threw his arms around my waist.

Sitting amongst the flowers, I gazed at him in wonder and stroked his bony back.

'Hey, m'little one. No need for tears, hmmm?' My voice was the barest whisper, but at least I could speak.

He raised his face. 'I thought you was gonna die, Grandmama. Promise you won't?'

I managed a wheezy laugh. 'Not today. And that's because of you. Hey, m'boy, God's truth now. You really want me ta stay?'

He nodded vigorously. 'I want ta learn about the bees, too.' He pulled back, plucked a crushed flower from the grass and twisted the stem. 'But I didn't think you'd want me around.'

I gathered him close and held him hard. 'Ah, Pauly. I'm so sorry, m'boy. I thought you all wanted me gone, so I was angry.' I put a finger under his chin and raised his tear-streaked face. 'But if'n you want me ta stay, then I will. Mind, somehow we need ta turn your Pa's mind ta bees instead of them blasted sheep.'

His lightning grin showed. 'He'll do it for me. I know he will.'

But that recalled ta mind the problem that had brought me here: the poisoned honey for the king. I sighed, leaning my aching head on one hand.

'What's the matter, Grandmama? Can't you get up? Are you still sick?'

'A little,' I said. 'I just need some time ta rest.'

He glanced up and whispered. 'There's folk here, Grandmama. A tall man with skin the colour of honey, and a woman with gold-red hair.'

I squinted at the two figures hurrying through the flowers, but my eyesight wasn't good enough ta see their faces. My legs were too wobbly ta rise and greet them, so I stayed put on the ground. They crouched beside me, concerned.

'Goodwife Turner, are you in need of succour?' The man's smile made me want ta dance. He exchanged quick looks with the woman. She was plain compared ta his sharp beauty, but kind and sad. She nodded.

The man reached out to me. 'Come. I'm glad we called in today. Let us help.'

I gaped, hesitated, then took his hand. A strange feeling oozed along my arm. Like honey, warm and golden, slipping through my blood and flesh. He hauled me upright with seeming no effort. When he let go, the aches that plagued my bones these last few years were gone. I blinked. Was I dreaming or could I see better, too?

'I'm Alistair Morrigan. This is my…good friend, Helen O' Reilly,' he said, bowing.

The red-headed woman threw him a funny look, half amusement, half longing.

'I'm grateful for your help, sir,' I said, brushing down my skirts. 'If your goodwife needs honey we'll have ta go back ta my hut, hmm?'

Helen blushed prettily. 'We're not…I mean…'

Alistair glanced at her, his expression softening. 'Helen would like to buy honey. And a great deal of your herbs. She needs them to cure an illness in the city.' He tilted his head. 'And I think you may need our help with another matter, too. A little question of honey for the king?'

Somehow, it seemed right that he should know all about it.

Master Morrigan strolled ta the hive and gathered it inta his arms like it weighed nothing. Helen stretched out a hand, her eyes fearful. But he spoke ta the bees like they were old friends and they settled, calm.

'Shall we return this?' he said. 'I think you'll be needing it.'

I grasped Paul's warm little hand. Together we led the way back toward my workshop.

13. The Maid was in the Garden

Flora Leon, 23
Maid to Lady Roslyn
Tower of London,

Saturday (early morning), 23rd September, 1486

I crossed myself and asked Jehovah's forgiveness for doing so. The gold cross on the white altar gleamed in the blood-red light stream'n through the stained glass, mock'n me. Would Jehovah hear me pray'n to him from inside a Christian church? My chest ached, empty, like He'd abandoned me for betray'n Him.

Saturday's dawn service finished and Lady Roslyn rose from her prayers. I followed, a few discreet steps behind, as she left St John's chapel in the White Tower.

She chattered non-stop to Lady Anna; all lightness and laughter, her elegant hands gestur'n to explain a silly story about Rose Griffiths, the quiet Mistress o the queen's hawks and greyhounds. But when we turned a corner and the ladies separated, the joy fell from Lady Roslyn and her shoulders slumped. I hurried to slide an arm around her waist.

'Oh, m'lady,' I whispered, 'you should still be abed, I'm sure. Mistress Laura, the midwife, said you shouldn't be up. You only miscarried the child yester e'en.'

She pressed slim fingers to pale lips. 'No-one can know I was with child. I must keep pretending all is well.' She gave me a wan smile. 'Thank you for your loyalty, Flora.' Her gaze sharpened over my shoulder. 'I'm quite sure I can make it to my chamber. There's someone waiting for you.'

I glanced back and heat rose in my cheeks. 'Oh, he can wait.'

Her rosebud mouth downturned. 'No. Don't throw away real love. It's too rare.'

I hesitated, astonished. She was much-changed these last two days. Los'n the babe and her hope o marriage had squashed the sparkle in her. And made her more thoughtful, perhaps, for she'd never have considered my lover important before.

Edmund waited, patient as ever, handsome in Lord Morley's dark blue livery with its gold embroidery and black leopard coat o arms. He grinned and leaned his broad shoulders against the stone wall o the Coldharbour gate. Lady Roslyn pushed me toward him.

Another group o noblewomen emerged from the chapel, the sun gleam'n off coloured silks and brocades. Lady Roslyn raised her chin. Back straight, she headed for the queen's chambers with two other ladies-in-wait'n. The sound o chatter and laughter died as the other churchgoers scattered to all parts o the Tower.

I turned to Edmund with a leap o joy in my heart, only equalled by the quiver o worry. He caught my hand and coaxed me out o the cool morn'n light and into the gate's shadowed doorway. I brushed at my grey kirtle and tucked stray long dark hairs back under my hairnet and veil. He laughed, teeth white against skin the colour o acorns.

'You're beautiful, my sweet. As always.' He kissed me, soft. 'But those pretty blue eyes of yours, they seem too worried.' He kissed my eyelids. 'I've got you now. I'll never let anything hurt you.' It wasn't true, o course, but I put aside fear a moment and let myself rest against his warmth.

'Have you decided, love?' he whispered. His wiry black hair tickled my cheek.

'Edmund Moorson.' I glowered at him. 'You said you wouldn't press me. Chang'n my belief…it's chang'n my whole life, not only which build'n I worship in. I must talk to my rabbi, and my family. But my lady has been unwell. I haven't left the Tower for two days.'

'You're not having second thoughts?'

'Oh, yes.' I sighed. 'And no. Oh, I don't know.' I twisted his

Blackbirds Sing p207

livery doublet between my fingers. 'I want to marry you. So much. You're the only man I've trusted and the only man I've loved.' I gazed up at him, warm inside at the sight o his ador'n half-smile. 'And the only man I'll ever love. But if I give up what I believe my family will cast me out. And it's part o who I am. Can we not continue as we are a little longer? At least until after the Sukkot festival is finished.'

Edmund gripped my arms. 'It's too dangerous to be a Jew in England, my love. Just last week His Grace, Bishop Kempe, had a whole family executed. You must convert. Only then will you be truly saved…safe.'

I broke free, wring'n my hands. A faint breeze fluttered the veil over my hair and brought the smell o stagnant water from the moat surround'n the Tower.

'Oh, I know,' I said. 'I know, Edmund. Very well. My lady has asked me to take a message into the town this morn'n. I'll try to see the rabbi as well, I promise.'

He snatched a kiss and beamed. 'You've made me so happy, my love. I must go. Lord Morley requires his clothes steamed before he consults with the king in the Privy Chamber.'

'And my lady must be measured for a new gown for the prince's christen'n feast. I'm to go order it from Olivia Grey.'

He kissed me again and strolled away, whistl'n, toward his Lord's chambers in Lanthorn Tower near the king's rooms. My footsteps dragged as I returned to the chambers for the Ladies-in-Wait'n in the Queen's House. Everyth'n was so simple when I was with Edmund. His love and acceptance made it all seem possible.

But it wasn't.

'You must give Francis Lovell this note.' Lady Roslyn pressed coins and a folded piece o vellum into my hand. 'No-one else. Then go to

Emma Turner's farm outside the city walls and get the king's honey, as usual. Then to Olivia's.'

I nodded and tucked the message into my bodice.

She walked with me to the door. 'Do you have quite enough coin for your own honey? I know your mother loves it at this time of year. And it's your sabbath today. I'm sorry to send you on errands, but we must, I suppose. You may take a little extra time to visit your family, but be back before the Sext bells at noon.'

'Oh yes, gramercy m'lady.' I hesitated, not want'n to overstep the bounds o our relationship. 'M'lady, you won't…'

Lady Roslyn shook her head. 'You're keeping my secret, of course I'll keep yours.' Pink spots burned in her pale cheeks and she played with her rosary beads, tugging them restlessly through her fingers. She embraced me. 'Now hurry. I was to meet Francis at St Anna's chapel on Syvedon Lane at the mid-morning Terce bells.'

'Oh, don't worry, m'lady.' I curtseyed. 'I'll deliver it safe. Do I wait on his reply?'

'No!' She bit her lip. 'No. That is…I quite think…no, I shouldn't.'

I left her still unsure and hurried through the Tower grounds. I covered my nose as I crossed the stone causeway over the stink'n moat. To my left the Tower wharf teemed with men unload'n boats and carry'n goods for the Tower—spices from the East, steel for the smithy, silks from Italy. Even a cage with a spotted cat for the royal menagerie. When I reached the St Martin Tower and the barbican at Lion's Tower, the big cats roared and the guards whistled and made lewd comments. I ignored them all and strode on.

Once across the drawbridge, I picked up my skirts and ran, for there was little time before the Terce bells rang. Even at this hour, Tower street was crowded. I dodged past carts laden with hay and barrels o wine, jumped over deep muddy ruts, and pushed aside the hawkers who tried to sell me brooms or unkosher foods like mussels. A farmer drove a squeal'n herd o pigs along the street and I stepped aside with a shudder o distaste.

When I reached Syvedon Lane, I slowed to catch my breath and pat my hair into order.

Someone latched onto my wrist and dragged me into an alley reek'n o cat piss. I opened my mouth to scream and a palm slapped over my lips. A pair o fierce blue eyes gleamed at me and I sagged. She let me go.

'Oh, Ingaret,' I scolded, 'you scared the life out o me.'

She shrugged and stowed a wicked-sharp knife back in its scabbard at her belt. 'Heya, nice to see you, too, sister. Look'n clean and pretty, I see.'

'More'n I can say for you,' I snapped. She wore a man's tunic and hose, dark and dusty with little wash'n. Her dark hair was hacked off short—shorter even than most men's. If it weren't for the swell o her breasts and the delicacy o her jaw, she could pass for a boy o fifteen rather than a girl o eighteen. 'Does Mother know you're dressed like that?'

She shrugged. 'Haven't seen her for a few months. You know she don't like me. Don't mind the money I make, but not how I do it.'

'I'm not surprised,' I hissed, glanc'n about. 'You *kill* people for money!'

She smirked. 'But good money. I earn more'n you do.'

'But you spend it all on…' I shuddered '…weapons and that horrible man who teaches you. Go home, Inga.'

Ingaret curled a lip. 'He's a sight less horrible than the handsy old lickspittle bedswerver Mother lined up to marry me. That's why I left. You're more to her taste. All prim and proper and work'n in the Tower. She brags on you all the time. Marry a Jew and produce little

Jewish babies and you'll be set for life in her eyes.'

I hunched a shoulder. 'I have to go. I have to deliver a message for my lady.'

She grabbed my arm, lean fingers bit'n into my flesh. 'Heya, watch yourself, sister. I've been want'n to warn you. There's someth'n going on in the city. Not sure what, but it ain't good.'

'Oh, there's always someth'n going on.'

'Not like this. There's a sickness for starters. Some are say'n it's St Anthony's Fire. And there's a healer woman from Isledon says she can cure it. But the priests are start'n to talk o witchcraft.' She glanced around as someone passed by the mouth o the alley. 'And rumours o someone want'n to kill the king.'

'Nought to do with us, sister. The king's well-guarded in the Tower.'

'If it's true, it'll be more wars and you know what that does to the city,' she warned.

I swallowed. Men and boys gone, clank'n and stink'n o rust; com'n back dead, wounded. The smell o death over everyth'n like a hot, heavy blanket. Food scarce and mouldy. Fights in the streets over scraps fallen off fishcarts. Women try'n to run their husbands' businesses; try'n to do their husbands' jobs and still feed bairns and care for old folk.

Surely it wouldn't happen again.

I pushed Ingaret away. 'I have other things to worry about.'

'That betrothed o yours, by chance?'

I gasped. 'How did—Don't you dare tell Mother. I'll do it in my own time.' I wrenched free o her grip and stalked from the alley.

'When?' she called after me. 'In the cathedral, when the priest paints a cross on your head with holy water and puts the wafer in your mouth?'

I reached the little chapel o St Anna's, pant'n, just as the first bells chimed for Terce. I slipped into the nave and peered through the gloom. This was a little-used chapel, it seemed. Only a few people knelt in the pews, await'n the priest. The windows were small in high walls o dark oak, and the place smelled o dogs and tallow candles.

'My love,' a man's voice whispered from a shadowy corner. He stepped into the half-light and frowned. 'What's this? You're her maid, Flora. Where's Roslyn?'

I dipped a curtsey and pulled the vellum out o my bodice. 'Oh, I'm sorry, m'lord. She bade me give you this.' When I turned to go, he yanked me back. I cried out as he pulled me further into the darkness. He shoved me hard against the chapel's cold stone wall. His dark eyes glittered and the sick-sweet smell o moss and ambergris filled my nose.

'You'll leave when I give you permission, wench,' he muttered. 'Do you know what this says?'

'Oh, no. m'lord.'

'Then stay here until I read it and take her my reply.'

'C-could you not send her a note, later, m'lord?' I regretted the words as soon as they left my lips for his glare was colder than winter.

'I put nothing in writing, unlike your lackwit mistress.' He moved into the light and unfolded the note. A gem-studded sword and dagger glinted on his hip.

I stayed where I was, my heart thudd'n. I could guess what the note said and I didn't want to be here if he unleashed anger on me. My lady had loved him, but every sight I had o Lord Lovell gave me the shivers. She'd not told me why she spurned him now; nor why she'd deliberately miscarried his child. Look'n at his scowl I was glad not to know. I wished myself far away and waited.

'Damn her to Hell,' he growled, screw'n up the vellum. I gasped at the oath and inched toward the entrance. His arm shot out, fingers circl'n my throat.

'It seems my plans must change,' Lovell murmured, study'n me thoughtfully. 'And I require your assistance. Understand?'

I nodded and his grip relaxed but didn't release me.

'I know all about you,' he said. 'I know your secret for your Mistress's tongue is easy to loosen. It's shutting her up that's difficult.'

My mouth dried to ash. She had betrayed me? How could she when I kept her secrets faithfully? But maybe he didn't mean what I thought. I held my peace.

He cocked his head. 'You doubt me?' He leaned closer and whispered into my ear. 'You bathe on Fridays, don't eat pork or cook on Saturdays, and your next errand is to a certain farm to buy honey for the king. And for your own family—for a special occasion. Am I right?'

Fear clawed at my throat, caging words so I couldn't reply.

'Excellent.' His smile widened. 'Now, since Roslyn won't help, you will. If you do not, I'll walk up to the priest in this chapel and denounce you as a Jew right now. Understand?'

I nodded. My breath rasped loud.

'Here's what I want,' he said, lean'n his hands on the wall on either side o me. 'On the night of the feast to celebrate the heir's birth, you will let me into the queen's chambers. Clear?'

I nodded again, paralysed by the darkness in him.

He traced one finger down my cheek. 'What a scared little rabbit you are. Never fear. I simply wish to pay my respects to the queen and her son. Nothing else. I was quite her favourite two years ago. She'll be pleased to see me. And pleased with you for letting me in. Now.'

He straightened and tugged at his grey silk doublet. 'Go about your errands and return here at the Sext bells at midday. Bring me a servant's livery I can use to get into the queen's chambers without arousing suspicion.'

His heels tapped on the brick floor as he left the chapel. Shak'n, I slid down the wall, sat on the ground and buried my head in my arms. At the altar, the priest droned on about Christ and God, but in Latin so I couldn't understand or take strength from his words. I yearned for our rabbi's soft voice, murmur'n passages in Hebrew from the Tanakh, whispered in the quiet o our kitchen on days like today, our Sabbat.

There was no comfort here and no help, either. I struggled upright on weak legs and left the chapel. The other errands yet had to be run for the king must have his honey for the feast—whenever that was to be—and I had to deliver the measurements to Olivia, the dressmaker. The honey to my family would have to wait for I couldn't face them. Not yet. Not know'n my existence put them in such danger.

I returned to the Tower with no memory o the long walk out through the Aldgate to Emma Turner's beehives, and little thought for the redheaded woman and the beautiful man with golden skin I'd met there. He'd called me by name before we'd been introduced, and had spoken at length about the king's honey. The honey that rested heavy in my satchel.

I barely heard the Tower guards call out and whistle as I passed through the barbican gates.

When I curtseyed before my lady, I couldn't look her in the eye. I passed her the honey and rushed through the message from Master Morrigan.

Lady Roslyn turned the pot around and around. 'I shall deliver this to the queen, myself. She'll know what to do. Gramercy, Flora. You've done quite well.'

Her pretty thanks left me cold. She had given away my secret to a man who used it against me. How could I forgive her? I gave short answers to her questions about Lovell so she asked instead about the dress she'd ordered from Olivia Grey's busy dressmak'n workshop.

'Oh, I'm sorry, m'lady,' I said, keep'n my eyes fixed on the patterned-timber floor o her bedchamber. 'M'lord Lovell kept me so long I ran out o time to go across to Mistress Grey's shop. I'll go now.' It was the best excuse I could think o to return and meet Lord Lovell at the Sext bells. After a swift, worried look, Lady Roslyn dismissed me to the errand.

I hurried downstairs and across the greensward toward the laundry rooms. It was my only hope. My luck was true. Wash'n flapped from cords strung in a courtyard hidden from the noble lords and ladies o the Tower. I snatched the livery tunic o a yeoman o the wardrobe and stuffed it under my chemise. Breathless, expecting a cry o 'stop thief' any moment, I ran back toward the Lion Tower and barbican.

'Flora!' Quick steps chased me along the causeway over the moat.

I stopped at the familiar voice. 'Edmund. I can't stay.'

'What did your rabbi say?' he whispered, glanc'n about.

We were alone on the causeway with only the seagulls' cries and the creak o ships at the wharf in the background. I hardly noticed the stench o fish and nightsoil from the river when the wind changed direction.

I gazed into his lov'n charcoal-dark eyes and managed a smile. Perhaps here lay my safety. If I gave up my way o life, maybe I could protect my family. But could I forsake them and my God, as my lady had betrayed me?

Blackbirds Sing p215

No. I couldn't. I wasn't fickle and feckless like my lady.

'Oh…I'll marry you, Edmund. We can pledge our troth the old way—by declar'n our love before God and shar'n a hearth and a bed. But not in a church. We'll make it work, I promise.' I glanced at the ragged grey roofs o the city, where Lord Lovell waited, and back to the Tower's neat stone walls where my lady stayed, safe from him. 'But please don't ask me to give up my way o life? I need it more than ever right now.'

He worried at his lip. 'But you—'

I touched his fine mouth. 'We'll talk later. I've another errand to run in the city for my lady.'

'But I missed you.' He cornered me against the crenulated sun-warmed wall and kissed my neck, his hands slid'n up my arms to cup my jaw. I groaned as his warm lips explored mine and he stroked my neck.

'Can't it wait until tomorrow?' he breathed. 'Then we could find somewhere quiet now and…celebrate.' He smiled wickedly.

'Oh, no,' I murmured, kiss'n him back and wish'n I could say yes. My body ached for him. 'Tomorrow's your Sabbath, remember? Rest and prayer.'

He laughed. 'With the prince's christening tomorrow? My Lord Morley'll be all Ed, press my clothes. Ed, find my kerchief. Ed, where's my shoe? So stay with me.' He nibbled at my earlobe, send'n pleasant shivers across my skin. 'Not for long. I'm away into town for my sister's wedding, soon.'

I giggled, my heart lift'n for a moment out o darkness. 'Oh, I wish I could. I truly do. I must go see the dressmaker.'

Edmund stilled and pulled back. 'I thought you did that this morning.'

Heat rose in my cheeks and I edged away, duck'n under his arm.

'Oh, yes, I was supposed to, but I ran out o time. I'll be back soon.' I blew him a kiss and turned to leave.

He caught my wrist and hauled me back. 'Flora, if your faith means that much, then I'll convert. I'll become a Jew. I love you and that's all that matters.'

'You'd do that? For me? Oh, Edmund!' I kissed him hard. 'You don't know what that means to me. But we'll talk later. We'll meet before Vespers, I promise.'

I fled, full o happiness and fear at once. I feared if I stayed, as I wanted, he'd find the uniform if he held me too tight; feared he'd ask questions and I'd blurt out the truth. Feared he'd try to stop me meet'n Lord Lovell, and so condemn my family to death.

The sun inched higher, hot on my head. Sweat prickled under my arms and down my back as I ran through the city. No time for manners. I shoved and pushed my way through women chatter'n as they headed to market or to church. A cart driver cursed me when I ducked across the road. His pony skittered, whinny'n in distress. Mud splashed on my boots and kirtle.

The Sext bells clamoured and I ran faster, my breath hot and sharp in my throat. Outside the chapel I paused to settle my stomach's churn'n, then stepped again into the cool darkness.

Lord Lovell waited in the same shadowed corner. I yanked the uniform out from under my chemise and thrust it at him. He shook the cloth out and held the tunic to his shoulders.

'Very good.' His words were a whisper, almost drowned out by the priest's prayers in from the altar. 'Now,' Lord Lovell added, 'where will the christening feast be held?'

'Oh, I don't know, m'lord. They haven't even said what night, yet.'

'God's blood!' His lips peeled back in a snarl. 'As soon as you know, you must send a message to the Broken Seld. On the night of the feast, when the queen has withdrawn, I'll slip away from the banquet and you'll meet me outside her chambers and let me in. Understood? If you don't…' He pointed toward the altar, hidden from our view by a pierced wooden screen. His other hand rested on my neck, fingers loosely circl'n my throat.

I gathered my courage and whispered. 'You…you won't hurt the queen or the babe, though?'

His smile turned sour. 'That's—'

'Flora? Who's this man?' Edmund's sharp question echoed loud in the nave and the priest shushed him. Edmund stalked closer, peer'n at us. 'Is he hurting—'

Lord Lovell moved, quick like a cat. Steel glinted in the half-light. The lord seemed to embrace Edmunc, who gave a strange, burbl'n gasp and sank to his knees. Lovell wrenched his dagger free o Edmund's chest and wiped scarlet onto Edmund's blue livery tunic. I gaped, the breath frozen in my lungs, my heart still in my breast.

My betrothed, my love, my future…toppled sideways, his black eyes stark and star'n blankly at me. Blood flowered across the cloth o his tunic and seeped through to drip on the floor under him.

I drew breath. Lord Lovell's palm silenced my scream.

'Not a sound. Not a whimper,' he murmured. The point o his dagger flashed before me. He would kill me and I wanted him to. Then the pain would go. None o this would be real. It wasn't. It couldn't be.

But he didn't drive the dagger into my heart a second time, and Edmund still lay on the floor.

Lovell's ironic smile appeared. 'Gramercy for the second uniform, though it will need some cleaning and mending.' He plucked at his own grey doublet, now stained with Edmund's blood. 'As will mine. Luckily, I know a laundress. Now, you will leave and return to the Tower. If you don't do as I ask, I will hunt down your family and send them all to the gallows. Along with everyone they know.' The dagger tip pointed at Edmund's still form. 'Right now it's one dead. Betray me and everyone you love will die. Go.'

He released me and I closed my lips against the cry that struggled to escape. Tears drowned darkness and the room shimmered. I clenched my teeth on a scream as I edged past Edmund's still body. Every part o me ached to hold him, to beg his forgiveness, to tell him I would convert to Christ if I could just hear him laugh and say he loved me one more time. But his body lay unmov'n, his warm skin already waxen, his eyes soulless.

He couldn't be dead. But he was and it was my fault. How could I have been so doltish? How could I have trusted my mistress and not trusted Edmund? He could have helped. Now it was too late. He had missed his sister's wedd'n. His blank stare accused me.

His life was over. And so was mine.

I covered my mouth to hold in the screams and tears and vomit, and fled.

Aiki Flinthart

14. Hanging out the Clothes

Griselda Moor, 40
Washerwoman
Hosyer Lane, London,

Saturday (midday), 23rd September, 1486

'Mama, has Edmund come home yet?' Ava's shrill voice drifted down from the top floor and I rolled my eyes.

'Not yet, poppet,' I yelled. 'Y'know he said he'd be home at Nones for Trea's wedding at Vespers. It's only just past the Nones bells now. He'll be here.' I waited but my youngest daughter just grumbled and stomped about in the garret room she shared with her sister. I grinned. She adored her brother—everyone did—and hated that he rarely came home from the Tower to visit her these days.

'I'm heading back to the washrooms, poppet,' I added. 'Make sure you finish that spinning. Y'know there's cheese and fresh rye bread on the table?'

'Mama?' Ella, my eldest daughter, stuck her head out of her chamber at the back of the house and hurried into the hall. She bounced her first-born on her hip, her belly big with the second. Her brown kirtle was bespawled with milk and food, her curly black hair wild and matted with something sticky from Conrad's pudgy little hands. She looked like I did at seventeen: pregnant, big black eyes, pretty. Before four children thickened my waist and greyed my wiry hair. But her skin was a shade lighter brown than mine and she was far too serious.

I tickled young Conrad under the chin. He giggled and held out his arms. I kissed his forehead. 'I must get downstairs, poppet. Maybe later.'

He scowled and buried his face in his mother's neck.

Ella huffed. 'You said you'd mind Con while I spun the new batch of wool. Y'know I have to finish the broadcloth for Olivia this week.'

'Well,' I said, hands on hips, 'happen I doan have a lotta choice. I got four washer girls away with this sickness that's going round. Thomasine Smith, the barber-surgeon, says it's looking bad. St Anthony's Fire. They might not live. But the customers doan care, do they? Laundry's still gotta get done, y'know.'

'Seems you've never gotta choice, Mama. The laundry always comes first. Will you make it to Trea's wedding?' She glared.

With a laugh, I headed toward the narrow stairs. 'Watch that shrew's tongue, girl, or that husband of yours woan stay around to see my next grandbaby born. Someone's gotta earn a living for this family and y'know it's always been me. My ma came out—'

'I know, Mama.' She sniffed. 'Grandmama came out from Spain and Grandpapa from Marrakesh and started this place. It's just…' She sighed. 'You never have time for us. For Con.'

'Well.' I wagged a finger. 'Y'know your father was a lazy fopdoodle who would've gambled the house away if he hadn't died in the king's war. We've got debts to pay and more mouths to feed. The laundry's all I got. You make sure Trea's ready and I'll be back up in a trice. As if I'd miss my daughter's wedding.'

'You missed Conrad's birth!' Ella shouted after me. Her heavy footsteps sounded along the timbers overhead. 'And I bet you doan even know Ed's got himself betrothed!'

I paused on the dark-timbered stairs. My boy? Betrothed? His first love had been a feather-headed scullerymaid in the Tower, who'd left him for a knight's better-paid bed two years after the wedding. Ed had been broken, but he was after my own heart and came around quick. But still, it'd been two years and this was the first new woman in his life. Happen he'd chosen better this time. Well, he'd bring her home to meet me soon. Maybe today.

Blackbirds Sing p223

With a light heart, I hurried to the washrooms. Five women in sweat-soaked chemises stirred huge timber vats of soapy grey water. Three more vats stood empty, those girls away sick. Warm steam coiled up to the timber ceiling and cool water rained back down. Piles of unwashed linen threatened to tumble off the long wooden table, onto the stone floor. Over a huge fire in the brick hearth, a great copper kettle boiled water for washing out the most stubborn stains. The room stank of soap, cloves and sweat, but I hardly noticed after all these years.

'Beth,' I called to the eldest of my washerwomen, 'send over to the soaphouse in Bishshopsgate. We're almost out of the rose-scented, y'know.' On a shelf above the hearth, neat bundles of soapwort leaves lay ready to soak for washing regular folk's clothes. Nearby were stacked cakes of rose or clove-scented castile soap for the clothes of my wealthier customers.

'Aye, Mistress Griselda,' Beth said, wiping sweat from her reddened face and patting at her hair in its long grey plait. 'And we've had some clothes come in from a lord, no less. Very full of himself. Wants them washed and ready for tomorrow.' She pointed at a neat-folded stack separate from the rest. A doublet of grey silk, stained with something reddish, lay atop.

'Did he pay in advance?'

She shook her head, stray long hairs escaping her coif. 'Said he had more to come and would pay tomorrow.'

'Pah!' I laughed. 'Then he can wait. Lord or no lord, I doan give credit. Learned that one the hard way years ago, y'know.' I rolled up my sleeves, grabbed the copper kettle and tipped hot water into a washing tub. A huge splodge of beetroot stained the first shirt in the paying customers' pile. 'Right. Let's get this done.'

Two hours later and we'd barely made a dent in the stack, for more work kept pouring in. Seemed everyone wanted clean clothes to celebrate the new prince's christening on the Sabbath tomorrow. And often their best clothes, needing soaking, with ingrained stains they'd left for weeks out of laziness.

I'd long since taken off my heavy green kirtle and laid it aside so it wouldn't get mucky. I was sticky with sweat and my hands were wrinkled and red. I licked salt off my lip and glanced despairingly at the dirty clothing. We'd be here until midnight at this rate. But, it was good money at least.

The street door burst open and Cecily Hayward from the Cahorsin shop on Bred Street bustled in bearing a blue silk surcoat bespattered with mud and who knew what else.

'Gris, lovey,' she said, 'I got summat needs done right-quick.'

I wiped wet hands on my apron and inspected the silk. 'If we soak it in verjuice most of this'll come out.' I grimaced. 'I doan know as we can have it ready fast, though Cec. We're a bit behind and four girls off sick, y'know.'

'I'll pay double, Gris.' A stricken look around Cecily's blue eyes brought to mind recent gossip.

I laid a hand on her plump arm. 'I heard about your house being robbed and old Carter. I'm sorry, Cec.'

She heaved a sigh and nodded. 'I won't lie, we're all pretty cut up about it and the house is at sixes and sevens.' She shook the surcoat. 'But this is more important right now. A customer wants it for the christening. We need the money. The thieving bastards took everything valuable and we haven't yet found—' She stopped, cleared her throat and thrust the silk into my hands. 'Can you do it?'

'Well…' I studied the stack of waiting clothing. 'Course, Cec. It'll have to soak awhile, y'know, then we'll wash in castile and rose.

Come back in an hour. Woan be dry, but you can hang it up at home.'

'Righty-o.' She leaned in and bussed my cheek, hers flushing. 'Thanks, Gris, lovey. I owe you. I'll pay you as soon as the dress sells. The buyer's coming back at sunset.'

For an old friend I didn't mind a little credit. She hurried out and I set the surcoat to soak in the sharp green juice of unripe grapes that was so good at taking stains out of silks. Then I scrubbed at linens from Sarah Clark, the housekeeper at the Broken Seld. She was another regular of ours. Drank too much of Rollo's ale and wine, sharp-tongued as the Devil, but always paid well, so I liked to keep her happy—even though the sheets from her guest beds were sometimes disgusting. Someone called my name and I waved them away, concentrating.

The linens done I pulled the blue silk out and washed it through with a bar of rose castile. When I was finished it looked like new and I hung it on a pole in the back yard to drip until Cecily came.

Across the city, bells rang out. I straightened my aching back and used my apron to mop at my neck.

'Lordy,' I said, checking the table covered in clothes. 'Does it ever get smaller?' I hadn't done this much washing myself for years.

'Mistress,' Beth said, frowning at me. 'Weren't it Trea's wedding today?'

'Is it Vespers already? Oh, Lord, Ella'll kill me.' I stripped off the apron and hauled my kirtle on over my sweaty chemise. No time to rush upstairs and change. 'Why didn't they come get me?'

Beth threw me a strange look. 'They did, Mistress. Just after Goodwife Hayward came in. You told them to go off and let you be.'

I scowled. 'I never!'

She shrugged and turned back to her work.

Had I?

Outside the day's worst heat had faded into a cool autumn sunset of golds and reds. The last bells died away as I ran toward the St Pancras church on St Pancresse Lane. Huffing and swearing I pushed through a crowd of pilgrims, still dressed in their sweat-stained travel clothes, heading for St Pauls on the hill. Then I ducked through a back alley to make up time.

I paused a few steps from the chapel to pat vainly at my hair. The damp washroom air had turned it wild and I'd forgotten to put the coif on, so it stuck out all over like black sheep's wool. I yanked a kerchief from my pocket and tied it quickly over my hair then rounded the corner.

'You're too late, Mama,' Ella's sharp voice brought me up short. She stood outside the chapel's heavy oak doors, dressed in her finest surcoat of dark yellow broadcloth, arms folded across her bulging belly.

'Oh, Lord, poppet,' I said, sighing. 'I tried, y'know. We've got urgent washing up to our ears to do for tomorrow. And Cecily Hayward needed—'

'What about what Trea needed?' Ella glared. 'And her husband. And me, and Conrad, and Ava? When are we more important than dirty washing?'

'Doan be daft, girl,' I snapped. 'I'm doing this for you all. Y'know that. So you can eat and feed that little boy of yours.'

'Oh, no, Mama. You doan get to lay the blame on me and mine. I earn enough spinning and weaving for Olivia Grey's dressmaking. You work so hard because you doan know how to stop.'

I pursed my lips and bit back a sharp answer. 'Where's Trea?'

Ella sniffed. 'They all went back to our house for supper. I waited for you.' She checked over my shoulder. 'Is Edmund with you?'

'No. I thought he'd gone straight to the chapel with you.'

She gathered her skirts and stepped onto the muddy street. 'Happen he'll be at home.' She walked off with the waddle of the heavily pregnant.

We reached our place in Hosyer Lane only to find Thomasine Smith on the stoop, surgeon's bag under one arm.

'What's amiss, Thom?' Had another of my washers fallen ill? We were so behind already, how would we get it all done?

The barber-surgeon hefted her leather satchel of medical gear, her amber eyes narrow. 'Your Trea sent a messenger. Seems your Ava's sick.'

'Pah,' I said, chuckling. 'None of my children have been sick a day in their lives. Healthy as horses, y'know. She's trying to get out of doing her spinning. She hates it.'

'Mama!' Ella pushed past and shoved the door open.

Beth appeared at the entrance to the washrooms. 'Mistress Gris, so glad you're back. We got another rush-job and the work's piling up something terrible.'

Ella frowned at me. 'Mama, Ava needs you and Trea's just married. The laundry can wait. They can't.'

Beth leaned in close and whispered. 'The rush-job's for Lady Derby. Not sure you want to make her wait?'

My stomach flip-flopped. Last thing I needed was my best customer getting snarky with me. I flapped my hands at Ella and Thomasine. 'You go up. Beth says it's important. I'll be up soon.'

Ella glared and her jaw worked as though she chewed on words she wanted to spit at me. She turned away and led Thomasine up the stairs.

In the big washroom, two of the girls were resting, feet up on stools, chewing on great chunks of rye bread and cheese. Beth had returned to the vats with the others. At least the pile of clothing was smaller. Sunset kept many folk indoors so we shouldn't get more tonight.

Cecily's dress was gone. She must have collected it, already. My eye fell on the lord's neat-folded grey silk doublet and underclothes. Beth had moved them close and reached for them now.

'There's still more paying customers, y'know Beth-love,' I said. 'Leave that for later and work on Lady Derby's lot.'

She shrugged easily and dumped Lady Derby's lavender silk into a bucket of verjuice and sloshed it around, saying over her shoulder, 'The lord with the grey silk sent one of his men with coin and paid, Mistress. Brought a whole lot more clothes, too. One to be mended. Paid double if we could get them ready by Monday.' She pointed at a second pile of clothes. The tunic was a dark blue with gold embroidery and a large, dark stain on one side.

I picked the tunic up. The stain was sticky-damp and a neat hole sliced into the cloth. My hand came away red. I sniffed the stain.

'That's blood, that is, Beth.' I stuck my finger into the hole. 'And a blade's done this, y'know.' Shaking the tunic, I held it up by the shoulders to see the whole. 'Oh, Lord Almighty. That's right through the chest, y'know. Wasn't that grey doublet stained, too?'

Beth nodded, her eyes sliding away from mine. 'Best we doan ask, Mistress. He's a lord and it pays not to meddle in their affairs.'

I wasn't listening, for my ears were full of a strange roaring and my clothes were too tight, strangling me. My legs collapsed and I sank onto a stool. The tunic slipped from my grasp to the wet stones underfoot. It couldn't be. It wasn't possible.

'Mistress?' Beth gathered it up and peered at me. 'What's amiss?'

The blood on my fingers mocked me.

Blackbirds Sing p229

'Edmund,' I said, though the word broke. 'That's Edmund's tunic.'

Beth gasped and held it out. 'No, Mistress. Can't be. Could be anyone's.'

'Dark blue. Lord Morley's livery. The embroidery. The black leopard. Stitched that myself. My stitching. I know it. I know it, Beth. My Edmund. Oh Lord, my Edmund. What's become of him?'

'I'm sorry, Mistress. I'm so sorry. Happen he's alright. I'll ask Mistress Thomasine if she's heard of a man a-lyin injured, shall I?' She rose.

A tall figure darkened the door.

I gripped Beth's wrist. 'No need,' I whispered.

The stranger entered the washroom, bearing in his arms my son's limp body. Edmund's laughter was washed away, his skin grey, dark eyes filmed the colour of soapy water. Blood coloured his undershirt red from shoulder to hip. One lax arm dangled and blood dripped to the floor.

My washerwomen shrieked and fell back, huddling against the walls in frightened silence. Beth shoved clothing off the long table. I could do nothing but stare, my voice stolen. The room's steamy air pressed on my lungs til my head spun. I couldn't stand but had to stay sitting, dumb and broken while my son came home for the last time.

The man laid my Edmund's empty husk on the table and straightened the limbs. A look of regret passed over his golden face. He sighed and stroked Edmund's wild dark hair back. Then he turned wide grey eyes on me and I flinched beneath the depth of old grief there.

'I'm sorry,' he said. 'I wasn't there, but I know who did this.'

I didn't trust my legs to work, so stayed where I was and stared at my dead son. My first born. My light. My joy. More reliable than my husband had ever been. Quick with a joke. Ready to forgive. Never complained about my work, just pitched in and helped raise his sisters. Came back alive from the battle at Bosworth when I thought I'd lost him.

Gone. And I'd never had a chance to say gramercy. To make sure he knew I loved him. To meet his betrothed. See him be a husband and a father.

I was a fool.

The man who'd brought my baby home crouched before me and gripped my hands so hard I cried out. The pain broke the thrall of grief over my mind and I looked at the stranger.

'You're not a fool, Griselda,' he said gently. 'But we must act. And I'm called upon by a higher power to help you. Will you help me in return?'

I gulped, the weight of his expectation adding to the heaviness that nailed me to the stool. 'Yes,' I said. 'If it will bring the man who did this to the king's justice, then, yes. What do you need?'

He smiled and the blanket of darkness around my heart lifted a little. 'Just a piece of clothing. Your son's undershirt. And don't wash the stains completely out of his doublet. Or out of the grey silk one I see over there.'

I nodded, not even caring enough to ask how he knew of them. 'That we can do. Just you make sure…' My voice broke again and I stopped lest the unshed pain drown me.

He nodded. 'I'll do my best, I promise. Trust me.'

And somehow, I did, though I'd no idea why.

I looked at my son's body. 'I can't…'

The stranger patted my arm. 'No. I understand. Is there someone who can help me undress him?'

'Beth?' I glanced at her.

'Aye,' she whispered. She swiped tears away and sniffed, for she'd known Edmund since he was born and loved him like a son.

I gazed past the stranger, toward the stairs leading up to my family. To my sick little girl who needed me. To my baby grandson who wanted only my time. To my pregnant daughter who'd tried to tell me.

My legs were weak, but I forced them to raise me. I paused by Edmund and stroked his cheek, singing the lullaby I'd put all my babies to sleep with so long ago.

Hush pretty baby, don't say a word
Mama's gone and called you a sweet black bird
And when that little black bird doth come
Mama's gonna buy you a big war drum

Then I closed his eyes, shutting him away from the world he loved. His forehead was cool against my lips as I kissed him one last time.

'I'm sorry, poppet. I'm so sorry. Be at peace.'

I barely glanced at the stranger as I strode to the stairs.

'Beth will help you. I have to go. My family needs me, now.'

15. Along Came a Little Dog

Rose Griffiths, 32
Mistress of Hawk and Hound to Queen Elizabeth of York
Outside Aldgate, London,

Sunday (early morning), 24th September, 1486

I stopped exactly twelve hundred steps from my chambers in the Tower and lifted my face to the morning sun. Three deep breaths, taking in the scent of wildflowers and honey from Goodwife Turner's farm just north. The blush of dawn light sparkled on the dew dusting the homefield of St Mary Malfelon. I looked back the way I'd come, at the line of grass untidily bent by my passage. My long grey skirts, soaked with dew, clung to my ankles.

Prime bells rang out from St Clare's behind me, and from St Mary Grace's and St Katherine-by-the-Tower's ahead. Too many clashing chimes to count. Time to get back to the Tower before the streets and fields grew too crowded. Though belike I'd not meet many here. Most folk weren't allowed to hunt these fields. And those that did see me would scurry away.

I was used to it. My white hair, gold skin, and dark-rimmed, icy eyes marked me as strange everywhere I went. Yet another reason I preferred solitude.

But Sister Philippa of St-Clare-without-Aldgate knew me and knew whose dogs I exercised. I had her permission to walk here. It benefitted the nunnery to let the queen's falconress hunt where she would, for the king set guards to protect the nuns and gave deeply of the privy purse to the Poor Clares.

I stared south at the distant grey Tower buildings, where my mistress, Elizabeth, now lived, and I with her.

Little though I cared for people, it puzzled me to see how they hurried to do the gentle Elizabeth of York's bidding. For a woman who rarely raised her voice, my mistress had people scrambling to do her will. Twas one of the reasons I followed her to the Tower when the Lancasters and Yorks finished their squabblings and she wed the new king.

The decision had been a poor one, though. For me, anyway. Her Grace loved her greyhounds and falcons as much as I, and begged me to come with her, assuring me of gentle treatment in our new home. But the king's men, with their swaggering boorishness, were wont to despise a woman falconer and dog handler. And, with a new babe and a palace to manage, Her Grace was not close by to ward me from their dislike.

I shook my head, rehashing an old argument with myself. Was there some way of convincing Drake Wright, the king's new Master of Hounds, that I was no threat to him? I'd yet to think of one and his snide remarks became daily more vicious.

A confrontation would come and I had no idea how to handle it. People's minds were an impenetrable wall of confusing, conflicting emotions; untrustworthy, unreliable, unpredictable. Animals were simple to understand and dependable.

'Jakke, Bo, heel,' I murmured. My words drifted, carried south by the lightest autumn breeze at my back. Jakke and Bo, running helter-skelter two hundred yards away, skidded to a halt in the long grass. Jakke cocked his smooth grey head and bounded back across the field, his ears flying and tongue flapping. Bo leapt after, her lean brindle body almost matching his for speed. A small herd of sheep bleated and trotted out of their path.

After all these years, I no longer questioned how animals heard me from such a distance. Nor how Merri, flying in her waiting-on pattern overhead, kenned my wishes without word or signal. The animals knew my mind, knew I preferred silence to speech, and knew I couldn't bear a raised voice or an out of place item. Twas just one of the many reasons I enjoyed their company and loathed that of ordinary folk. An I never spoke to another person again, I'd be content.

I lifted a gloved hand and the peregrine plummeted from the sky, stooping with breathtaking grace. At the last moment she opened her wings and extended her legs. The bite of her talons through the glove was the grasp of an old friend.

I waited til she settled then transferred her to the padded perch on my shoulder. She creeled and hunkered down, balancing easily as I strode across the field toward the Tower.

Jakke and Bo, panting from their exertions, followed at my heels. The three rabbits they'd hunted—their supper and mine—dangled from my belt, and a headless pigeon rested in my belt-pouch for Merri's meal later.

Jakke yipped and nudged at me. I petted him, uncertainty easing. No, I couldn't let Drake drive me away. How could I bear to leave the dogs? Or their energetic, curious, half-grown pups?

The dogs darted off, sniffed at an old rabbit warren, then returned to my side when I turned west on Hogg Lane. Swallows flittered and darted through the air. Merri creeled a question and I hushed her. Swallows were her favourite challenge.

We trotted along the narrow lane between Tower Hill and St Mary Graces Abbey, then crossed the field at the base of Tower Hill. To my right the ground sloped down toward the Tower moat's stinking waters. Beyond that the imposing grey stone wall of the Tower.

On the left we passed the one hundred and seven tiny cottages and weatherbeaten tenements huddled together outside the grounds of the St-Katherine-by-the-Tower hospice and church for the poor. Skinny mongrel dogs slunk out of sight. Filthy, canker-ridden children made the sign of the cross as I strode by. I ignored them, counting steps.

We left behind the last, straggling huts and were within a few dozen paces of the causeway leading across the moat to the Iron Gate Tower, when the sound of chanting wafted from St Katherine's. I paused to listen, entranced by the precise, layered voices of the church choristers.

My soul lifted with the notes and was carried close to God at that moment. Jakke whined and cocked his head. On my shoulder, Merri shifted her wings.

'Pray tell, do they sound good to you?' I stroked her breast and she gave a soft cry, her focus fixed on something ahead.

I turned to look and gripped my dagger, only to release it as recognition shocked through me, almost painful. I dropped instinctively to one knee. Merri cried shrilly and extended her wings for balance.

'Your pardon, my lord,' I said humbly.

'Pray, don't.' The tall, gold-skinned man—no, woman—in everyday woollen tunic and hose, grimaced and made a dismissive gesture. 'I'll not be called what I've no right to. Do stand, Rose.'

'But you've more right to it than any in the Tower, my lady.' I rose carefully, petting Merri to soothe her.

The woman chuckled, low and liquid. 'Nay. Twas my mother, The Morrigan, who used the title of Lady. I'm no-one. Call me Alistair, if you will, for I'd rather the humans didn't know I was female.'

She tilted her head, grey eyes narrowed. 'So, you know your *sidhe* heritage?'

I shrugged one shoulder. 'Only quarter-caste, on my mother's side.' I stroked Bo's pate. ''Tis from her I inherit the ability to control animals.'

'Useful,' she said. 'I left my hound at home and miss her dearly.' She settled a longbow across her shoulders and adjusted a leather satchel. 'Our mothers were war companions at one time, I believe. What did your mother tell you of mine?'

I gaped, unable to imagine my quiet, gentle mother at war by the side of The Morrigan. I shook myself and replied, 'Your pardon, my lady. She sang the songs, of course, but said only that when The Morrigan called I should offer all assistance. What can I do, my lady?'

She nodded slow and tapped at her lips. 'Tis not so much your help, as your dogs' I need.' From her satchel she withdrew a bloodstained linen undershirt. 'So they'll be ready, when the time comes.'

The encounter was over in less time than it took for Merri to catch prey on the wing. The Morrigan's daughter left my side and strolled toward the Postern gate where the old Roman wall ended against the Tower moat. I watched her out of sight, more awed than I liked to admit. I'd counted my mother's tales as bedtime stories and lullabies and no more. Seemed I was wrong.

I spoke to Jakke. 'Now you've been in the presence of true royalty, Jakke. Pray, what think you?' He whined at me.

'I know what you mean,' I said. 'She has a way of making you want to please her, doesn't she?' But I was dubious about her expectations for me and my charges. She needed me to be at the feast on Tuesday night to celebrate the prince's birth. But amongst so many people? And so much noise.

I couldn't do it.

But The Morrigan's daughter had asked it of me.

Doubt, fear, and duty roiled sickness in my stomach. I counted windows in the distant buildings of St Katherine's to calm myself.

Footsteps crunched on the dirt path behind me.

Merri launched herself into the air without leave, shrieking a defiant cry. I spun back to face the Tower. At my side, Bo and Jakke growled, low in their throats, and moved half a pace ahead of me.

'So.' Drake Wright folded his arms across his broad chest and curled a lip. 'More unseemly, unwomanly behaviour. Tis not enough you do a man's job, I see.'

He pointed toward the village. 'Now you walk unescorted and endanger the queen's hounds? His Grace shall hear of this, you can be assured.' Beside him, the king's two wolfhounds strained at their leashes, growling.

I kept a still countenance, for any reply would enflame him.

'What say you, woman?' he said, sneering.

'Pray, let me pass,' I said quietly. 'Her Grace is expecting me. Tis the prince's christening at the Sext bells and the dogs are to be part of the procession to the chapel.'

He swaggered three steps closer. 'And what if you never came back? Do you really think she'd miss you? My brother was owed your duties.' He poked himself in the chest, his cheeks reddening. 'My family have been hound- and hawkmasters to the kings for five generations.' He spat at my feet. 'No woman'll push us aside.'

Jakke's growl took on a fierce note and he barked. Bo took up the challenge. The wolfhounds echoed them, deep and chesty. Drake yanked at their leashes and swore, half-strangling them into pained yelps. He lashed out with a kick and the bigger hound yipped.

'Jakke,' I said softly. 'Enough.' He whined but sat obediently and Bo copied. Overhead, Merri shrieked, a wild, fierce cry that made Drake flinch.

'Pray, stand aside,' I said. 'I've no quarrel with you.'

Drake's hot brown eyes narrowed. 'But I've one with you. You

Blackbirds Sing p239

need to learn your place.' He released the leashes. 'Whoops. Sturdy. Troy...hunt.'

The wolfhounds leapt, barking ferociously, showing huge white fangs. Unperturbed, I gestured Jakke and Bo behind me and crouched to a height with the massive, shaggy beasts.

'Stop.'

They sat back on their haunches in mid-gallop, dust swirling, an expression of surprise in their doggy faces. I pointed at Drake and whispered, 'Hunt.'

The two spun and fixed intent looks on their master. His jaw dropped and he whimpered. They advanced, creeping like big cats. Drake retreated.

'Troy! Sturdy. Heel. Heel, I say!' His tone rose to desperation as they kept advancing, growling now so low it rumbled through my chest.

Drake screamed and ran, heading for the Iron Gate Tower. The dogs bounded after him, barking full-throatedly. Merri dove from the sky and harried him. She snatched off his felt cap and dropped it in the moat. He screamed again and covered his head. Her talons tangled in his dark hair, tearing loose great hunks.

I covered my mouth to stifle a laugh. 'Enough, Troy. Stop, Sturdy. Go home.' The wolfhounds slowed and glanced back at me, then followed their master, tongues hanging out like it was the best game they'd had all day.

'Merri. Return.' She flew back to my wrist and I used my dagger to slice off a wing of the pigeon as a reward.

I waited until Drake was well within the Tower before heading through the Iron Gate myself. As satisfying as that had been, twas a poor decision to antagonise him. He'd been digging at me since the day he'd inherited his father's duties six months gone, trying to get me to argue. I'd resisted, sought the queen's protection, hidden, done everything I could to avoid and calm him. Now all that was undone. He would not take such humiliation well.

The guards at the gate barely looked at me, crossing themselves as I paced through. What was that about? I hurried across the bare ground between the outer defensive wall and the inner. Again, at the gate to the inner courtyards, the guards crossed themselves and edged away.

Uneasiness scrabbled like claws in my stomach. Belike Drake had come this way and used his serpent's tongue to good effect against me. As I passed across the inner courtyard, the echoing conversations and laughter of servants and yeoman died away.

Eyes followed me and my cheeks grew warm. I lowered my head and counted each step.

On the third riser of the stairs leading into the Queen's House, a young woman sat, sobbing. I hesitated. Flora Leon, her name was. A pretty little thing with dark hair and solemn blue eyes. She attended Lady Roslyn Stanley. She sometimes visited the stables and played with Bo's pups.

Her shoulders shook and her awful sobs wrenched at me. I didn't know her well enough to offer consolation and words were awkward on my tongue at the best of time. But something called me to her aid and I approached. Jakke shoved his nose into her hair and licked at the salt on her cheeks. She flinched away, then gave a watery chuckle and threw her arms around Jakke's slim form.

I waited, silent, until her tears dried and she mopped her face on her apron. Her smile wobbled into view.

'Gramercy, Rose,' she said, stroking Bo and scratching Jakke behind the ear, where he liked best.

I waited. She bit her lip, flicked a quick look at me, then stared fixedly at Bo's head.

'Oh, I don't know what to do, Rose. I have a terrible secret and no-one I can tell.' Her petting slowed. Jakke nudged her.

I hooded Merri, set her on the stair handrail, and waited. The silence lengthened and still I waited. Flora would fill the emptiness if she felt the need, and trusted me. I didn't want her secret, but somehow I knew it was part of this *sidhe* web The Morrigan wove. Which meant I had to help—even if I didn't understand.

Finally, she cast me a frightened look and blurted her tale in a hoarse, hurried whisper. She burst into tears again when she reached the murder of her betrothed. I listened, aching for the poor child.

Hesitantly, I touched her arm and she grasped my fingers, pressing them to her cheek.

'Oh, gramercy, Rose,' she whispered. 'I was going mad not being able to tell anyone. But oh, what do I do? I can't let Lord Lovell into the queen's chambers.' She gazed at me, trusting, and I sighed.

'Your pardon but I'm better with animals than people, Flora.' I glanced in the direction of the stables where I could safely hide from all this confusing messiness. 'But I think I know someone you should tell of this. Sh…*he*'ll be able to help.'

We spoke for a few more moments and she agreed to send a message as I directed. As I suspected, she'd already met The Morrigan's daughter, though she clearly didn't understand the significance. Then again, I didn't, either, in some ways.

When we parted Flora hugged me and I stiffened, unsure how to respond.

'Gramercy.' She whirled in a flurry of skirts and vanished up the stairs.

I took Merri up and clicked a tongue at the dogs. I didn't understand why Flora hadn't yelled bloody murder in the church and had this Lord Lovell imprisoned by the bailiffs. But undoubtedly her mind was too disordered at the time to think clearly. The extremes of human emotion baffled me but I didn't know if it was a *sidhe* thing, or just something different with me.

The Terce bells rang and the sun peeked over the top of Constable Tower just as I returned to the stables with its warm animal smells and human silence. I greeted the queen's horses like the old friends they were. They whickered and snuffled my hand, searching for apples. The dogs ran ahead and stood before the unused stall they called home. I opened it and their four half-grown pups came tumbling out, yipping and gambolling. They followed me into the mews, where I fed Merri and her mate, Sky, with the pigeon.

A measure of peace returned with the quiet routine of caring for the animals.

I closed the mews door and began to muck out the dogs' stall in preparation for cleaning them for the christening procession.

Unease prickled the back of my neck and Jakke growled, low in his throat.

A shadow darkened the stable doorway.

'You need to leave, woman.'

At Drake's rough words, I faced him. But this time he was not alone. Three of his brutish friends flanked him, all wearing the king's insignia on their livery tunics. No hounds with them and I had no influence over a human mind.

'Your pardon, but I'm here by Her Grace's request,' I said, keeping my voice low and calm. 'I'll go if she asks me to.'

'We're here by *His* Grace's order,' Drake shot back. 'And the king's word is law above the queen consort's. So leave or we'll call in Bishop Kempe. I'll tell him what you *really* are.'

'What am I, pray?' My heart fluttered. Could he possibly know I was *sidhe*? How?

'A witch.' His companions crossed themselves and Drake pointed at Jakke and Bo. 'And those hellhounds are your familiars.'

I almost laughed, but the bitter seriousness in him stilled my tongue. We stood in a silent tableau, with only Jakke's low growl and the stomp of horses' hooves on straw to break it.

'What will you do if I stay?' Part of me rebelled against the idea of abandoning my animals, and Her Grace. I loved both. I touched Jakke. He stopped growling.

'See!' Drake pointed at the dog and looked to his companions. 'They obey her without commands. Hold her.'

Three pairs of hands grasped me, holding my arms and waist so firm I struggled in vain. They wrenched my arms painfully. Cold metal of a knifeblade pricked my throat. My heart raced and knees weakened.

Though my *sidhe* blood made me stronger than most women, I could not break free of three big men. I watched, helpless, as Drake grabbed Jakke by the collar and kicked one of the curious pups aside. The pup yelped. Jakke twisted and pulled backward, trying to slip his collar.

Drake pulled out his belt-knife, curled a lip and hissed at me. 'You stay, witch, and I'll make sure you're tested. Trial by water, by prayer, by torture if we have to. You'll confess to your sins with the Devil and your familiars will be slaughtered.'

He laid the gleaming knifeblade across Jakke's slim throat. Bo tilted her head and looked to me, but I couldn't risk Jakke by commanding her to attack. The greyhounds were no match for Drake and his cronies.

'I'll go!' I cried. 'Pray, let the animals be. I'll go. After the procession to the prince's christening. I'll pack, go and you'll never see me again.'

He let out a coarse laugh. 'You'll go right now. With nothing but what you have on your back. And this will make sure you have nothing to stay for.' He pressed the blade into Jakke's skin and blood dribbled along the steel. Jakke yelped and writhed.

'No, please! I'll go now. Don't hurt him.' I struggled again, to no avail.

Bo and the pups set up a ruckus, barking and yipping. The horses in the stalls whinneyed and kicked at the timber walls. In the Royal menagerie, lions roared and wolves howled. I hovered on the brink of calling every animal in the Tower to my aid.

'What is the meaning of this, sirrah?'

Drake gasped and released Jakke, who slunk into a corner of his stall, followed by Bo and the pups. The horses quieted, snorting and stomping.

'Your Grace.' Drake bowed low, the bloodied knife still in his hand. My arms were released and his three men backed away, casting fearful glances at each other.

Elizabeth of York stood in the stable door, flanked by three of her ladies-in-waiting and eight yeomen of the guard in their scarlet tunics. Her wide-set grey eyes were narrowed and her soft lips thinned. A glittering net held back her bronze-gold hair and she stood tall and regal, the sun gleaming off her cloth-of-gold surcoat embroidered with pearls and sapphires.

'I asked,' she said, 'what is the meaning of this? Why do you hold my mistress of hawks and hounds prisoner? Why is the blood of *my dog* on your knife, sirrah?'

I massaged feeling back into my hands and summoned Jakke to my side. He came, circling to avoid Drake.

Drake straightened, his expression condescending, pitying almost. 'Your Grace, this woman is a witch. She made your dogs her familiars. Consorts with the Devil, she does. I believe she's conspiring with others against the king. You must get the Bishop and test her. You must—'

'I must?' Elizabeth said, her tone soft and dangerous. 'I must do nothing of the sort, you base churl. How dare you lay a hand on my attendant and my animals without leave?'

'I'm His Grace's man, Your Grace.' He bowed low. 'I oversee all the animals in the Tower. Yours included. I shall inform His Grace soon.'

Elizabeth's eyes flashed. 'You'll do no such thing. I've known this woman my whole life. She's the daughter of an Earl.'

Drake blanched, his gaze shifting to mine and away again.

You, however…' She raked him with a sneering look '…are not even a yeoman. I believe you only came to us six months agone. If anyone is to be suspected of ulterior motives, it is you. My husband will certainly hear of your actions today. Guards.' She gestured and the yeomen stepped briskly forward. 'Put him into the Julius Caesar Tower until after the christening. Then His Grace will pronounce sentence.'

'Your Grace,' Drake cried, 'I protest. She bewitched the animals—you heard them caterwauling. And she made my dogs attack me. I can prove it.'

'Oh?' Elizabeth said, lifting her fine, arched brows. 'I doubt that, somehow. I've seen how you treat the king's dogs and horses. If they attacked you, it was only your due. Take him—and his men. And see he speaks to no-one.'

The yeomen drew swords, surrounding Drake and his men.

I leaned against the stable wall, quaking and panting like I had run a race. Jakke pushed himself against my leg and I checked his throat. The cut was superficial, already sealing and drying. I held him close, trying to soothe his shivering.

'Is he well?' Elizabeth came close and ran her hands over his dear head.

I nodded and rose. 'Gramercy, Your Grace. A few more moments, though…'

'I'm sorry. I should have kept a closer watch on how things were. I convinced you to come against your will and now this…' She embraced me, her rose perfume sweet and comforting. 'Somehow, I think you and Jakke would both be happier resting here with the pups than being part of the procession.'

I curtseyed. 'Gramercy, Your Grace. So much happier.'

'Then stay,' she said, 'and I'll make sure none disturb you ever again.' She turned in a swirl of gold skirts and regal confidence. Her ladies-in-waiting surrounded her like colourful butterflies, shining in the morning sun.

'Your Grace,' I called after her.

She looked back.

I hesitated.

Could I do this, even for The Morrigan? Even for Elizabeth? After Drake's lies, could I face a feasting hall full of people who feared me?

Elizabeth waited, gentle and kind, as she had always been. Never afraid of my strange appearance and solitary ways. She had always championed me and asked little in return. I owed her this much, and more. Especially if what The Morrigan's daughter said was true about the forces conspiring against Elizabeth and Henry.

I buried my fear. 'I'll bring Jakke and Bo to the christening feast for the prince on Tuesday e'en, if I may? I would like to be there—for you, and for your son.'

She clasped my large hands with her tiny ones, her face alight.

'Oh, Rose. You're my oldest, most-trusted friend. I should like that very much.' She gave a little giggle. 'But I shan't call on you to make any speeches, I promise.'

I chuckled, my heart lighter. 'Gramercy, Your Grace.'

16. And Nibbled Off Her Toes

Thomasine Smith, 45
Barber-Surgeon
Crokyd Lane, London,

Saturday (early evening), 23rd September, 1486

I spoke the words I hated most in the world, 'There's nowt else I can do, Maria.'

I stroked her daughter's sweat-plastered hair. In the tiny bedchamber, the grey light of evening faded toward Saturday night. Had I been here so long? And for nowt, it seemed. I'd tried everything. I pushed back wayward grey hair and rubbed at my face, feeling dry skin, slack with age and sleeplessness. The weight of loss to come pressed on my chest. Familiar, but still painful.

Clara moaned and thrashed on the straw pallet. Green vomit stained her lips. The room reeked of it, and piss and sweat.

'Hold her. It's the fits again.'

Maria clamped down on her daughter's convulsing limbs. When Clara lay still again I picked up her limp, arm and tested her pulse. Barely there. Her fingers had been bloated, but were now thin and an unhealthy shade of grey. Toes the same.

'Christ's teeth,' I muttered, reluctantly meeting Maria's anxious, dark-circled eyes. 'It's the St Anthony's Fire alright. And you said she lost the child about an hour before I came?'

'Aye, Mistress.' Maria petted her daughter's hair. 'She don't even know. Is there nothing you can do?'

'No-one's found a cure for it. Especially not once the toes start to blacken.'

Outside, a crier's shrill voice echoed in the street. Tomorrow was the new prince's christening day. Poor Clara might never have a child to baptise. She was scarce more than a child, herself. Only a little younger than my Anne.

I grimaced and tugged my night-grey kirtle straight. All I could do was keep Maria busy. We both rose. Maria stood half a head over me and she wasn't a large woman.

'Don't fret,' I said, 'for it won't help. Keep her warm and try to get ale or milk into her. She's lost blood. What she's got's not getting to her fingers and toes. Get her into a warm bath if you can. God willing she'll come through it, somehow,' I lied, in the hope of comforting her.

I pulled a sheet of parchment, quill and ink from my satchel. Most of my patients didn't keep such things in their homes. I cut the parchment in half with my belt knife and scrawled two notes.

'Take this one to the apothecary. These herbs might help ease her fits and the nausea.' I passed over the other. 'Take this one to the midwife, Laura Kennet. She should check Clara now the baby's been lost. Just in case she pulls through.' More lies. But words I'd want to hear in her place.

Maria clutched the parchments to her spare breast.

I gripped her shoulder. 'And pray. Send for me if she worsens.'

She gulped. 'What about…what about if she don't start getting better? Me grandma died of St Anthony's. At the end her feet and hands were black and she were in such terrible pain.' She glanced again at Clara. 'If it gets that bad…Mistress Thomasine I can't watch my daughter go through that. Ain't there summat we can do to help her…pass?'

I hardened my myself. 'You know it's a sin, Maria. If I were found out by the Company of Barbers my husband and I would both be brought before the magistrate. Bad enough a woman practicing medicine. If I did something wrong…' I sighed. 'But even then, there's nowt I know of as will help her pass painless.'

Maria stifled a sob. 'God can't mean for innocent children to suffer so.'

'I long ago gave up wondering why He makes us suffer. No-one's sinned this bad.' I gathered my things. We trudged downstairs and she

Blackbirds Sing p251

thanked me brokenly, pressing two farthings into my hand. I returned the coins. They were a poor family and I'd done very little.

'Use it for the apothecary.'

Outside on the street, I stared back at the tiny, two-storey house. People passed me, heedless, uncaring. Hurrying to get home or to the alehouses. Faces intent. A swollen jaw that might be a tooth or a tumour. A red rash flaring up a thick neck. Hands knotted and painful with age.

All of them worm-food soon and me not able to stop it. Nor even ease their passing.

I hefted my satchel of medicines and surgical tools and sighed.

'Bad, love?' Robard's deep voice pulled me out of my dark thoughts. My husband slid his arm about my waist and bussed my cheek. My head barely reached his shoulder and I rested on him as we strolled toward home.

'Aye,' I said. 'Clara Devon's the tenth one this week with St Anthony's Fire.'

He groaned. 'Make that eleven. Young Harald Metcher as well, right next door. And rumours of more, scattered about the city. Not as bad as the sweating sickness last year, but bad enough.'

'How did the meeting at the Company of Barbers Hall go?' I asked. 'What news?'

His jaw hardened. 'No word of a cure. Not even a reliable means of easing the symptoms.'

'Well, you'd best get home. Nobbut there'll be more, soon. I have one more visit to make.'

Rob hesitated. 'There was word of a female healer who offered a cure.' His nostrils flared. 'But apparently no woman could possibly do medicine, so they ignored it. Lord knows, I tried to get them to find out more. Fools.'

I stopped in the middle of the walk and pulled him down to kiss, soft and loving. He tasted of ale, and the dark bristles on his chin scratched my skin.

'Lord, how I love you, Robard Smith. Bless you for trying.' He'd stood by me for thirty years. Taught me everything he learned from the Company of Barber-Surgeons. Worked by my side to build our practice. And he was still prepared to fight battles for me where I couldn't go.

He laughed and lifted me up in a bear hug. 'And I love thee, Thom. I still remember the day we met. You were the prettiest slip of a thing with eyes the colour of amber and hair the colour of the sun.'

I patted my big hips and grey hair self-consciously. 'I recall you saying you wanted to be a barber-surgeon. And me telling my ma you were the man I was going to marry.'

Rob grinned. 'And I recall you saying *you* wanted to be a barber-surgeon. I went home and told *my* ma you were the only woman I would take to wife. And here we are, thirty years later.'

I stroked his cheek. 'And here we are.'

I couldn't imagine life without him.

We parted ways with a lingering kiss at my next call. I promised to let the man of the house escort me home if the time ran after sunset. Rob waved and strode into the darkness, taking my heart with him.

I ended up sending a message home, instead. A babe with a fever needed more care than the sick mother could give. I stayed the night on a pallet on the floor, and not for the first time. My bones ached in the morning but the child's fever had broken and the mother's too. So I left them in the care of the eldest daughter and headed home with the Prime bells in my ears and the early sun at my back.

It had been a long night after a series of long days. But there was no time to rest. With the dawn would come a flood of new illnesses and injuries into the consulting room. Sunday might be God's day of ease, but people still got sick and needed help.

Perhaps tonight I'd get some rest. Safe in Rob's arms.

I trod through alleys full of broken timber and rotting sacks. Finally, into my own yard with its neat vegetable garden and scratching chickens, and the little three storey house on Crokyd Lane that was my haven. Inside the house, I slumped against the plastered wall. Lord, but I was tired. Tired of blood. Tired of death. Tired of feeling helpless. I lowered my satchel onto a bench and sat beside it in the tallow candles' flickering light.

'Betsy?' I croaked. 'Is there nowt to drink in this house?'

'Mistress!' My young housegirl poked her curly blonde head into the room and scowled. 'Don't you half look awful. Here.' She handed me a mug brimming with ale and I tossed back its earthy contents in three long gulps.

Betsy plonked a bowl of porridge onto the table and I scooped a mouthful in haste.

'None of that loaf you baked yesterday left?' I mumbled.

She shook her head. 'The master were powerful hungry last night. He et up half. And this morning Miss Anne et up all but a scrap of the heel. I et that.' She pointed at the flour-dusted table. 'I'm bout to bake another.'

'Where are Anne, and Rob?' I asked.

'Miss Anne's been poorly and stayed in bed. Hardly et anything for supper, but had that bread and cheese this morning.'

I put the bowl aside and started to rise. Betsy clucked her tongue, pushed me down and gave it back.

'Don't be silly, Mistress. A bit o sickness is normal for a woman with child, you know that!' She patted my shoulder. 'She'll be hale in a few weeks.'

I sank back. She was right. But after seeing Clara's miscarriage and illness… I'd already lost two daughters. I couldn't lose Anne, too.

'And Rob?' I asked, eating again.

Betsy added a little wood to the hearth fire and thumped at the lump of rye dough on the board. 'Master Rob came in so wearied last night. He's still abed. I didn't want to disturb him. You've both been working far too hard.' She screwed up her freckled nose and glanced toward the front of the house. 'But there are a few people already a-waiting. D'you want me to wake him so's you can rest awhile?'

'Nay then, don't fret him.' I said and put the empty bowl aside. 'He's worked longer hours than me of late. Let him sleep. I'll go.' I held out a hand and she pulled me creakily to my feet. I stretched my aching back.

'Haircuts or teeth?' I collected my satchel.

'I sent the haircuts away,' she said briskly, brushing at her apron. 'Knowing the master was asleep and men are silly about a woman cutting their hair.'

'Funny how they don't fret about who pulls their teeth when they're in pain, though.'

She snorted a giggle and kneaded the dough again. 'Oh, there's one who looks like a fine gent. Seemed a mite resty, too. Might want to see him first. Snippy tongue he has, though.'

'Just what I need.' I squared my shoulders and headed through to the consulting room at the front of the house. It took only a moment to tidy the surgery tools away. Some people got a touch squeamish seeing the tongs and cutting knives. The room seemed dark, for grey clouds crowded the autumn sky, promising rain. If not a storm. I lit an oil lamp to fend off the gloom.

Then I opened the door to the waiting room.

Only one man waited. I peered around, looking for the others.

He rose, his movements abrupt and impatient. 'I sent them away. My need is more urgent. I demand to speak with Master Smith, immediately. I've been waiting half an hour already.'

I curtseyed. 'Beg pardon, sir, but my husband's indisposed this morning. But I'm a surgeon as well. Come in, if you will.'

He lifted his nose, sneering.

'Or don't,' I added. 'I'm tired and I don't much care. Stay or go. Choose.'

His pinched nostrils flared. 'I haven't time to seek another surgeon and they all seem mighty certain their time is more valuable than mine.'

'Perhaps it is, sir,' I snapped.

'My *lord*,' he shot back, then his dark eyes flashed like he was annoyed for saying as much. 'However 'sir' will do for I have a desire to keep my name to myself.'

I pressed my lips tight and opened the door wider. 'Come in.'

This was all too familiar. Men of his ilk came nameless when they'd cheated on their wives and caught a sickness from the Southwark geese. I had little time for them. They usually got more sympathy from Rob. I'd treated enough of Eliza Parry's girls to know their customers got off lightly and suffered little by comparison.

He hesitated, then strode past me and took a seat without being asked.

I sat behind the desk Rob and I shared and leaned forward on my elbows.

'Are you unwell?' He didn't seem sickly. His movements were easy, his face unbloated, skin and eyes clear.

He waved aside my query with a languid gesture. The other hand rested casually on the ruby-studded hilt of his dagger. Was that a threat?

'No,' he replied. 'I have a proposition for you.'

I kept my face blank and waited.

He withdrew a small cream clay phial from his belt-pouch. It clicked loud in the silence when he placed it on on the stained wooden desktop.

'I wish you to test this on one of your patients.'

I picked it up, worked the stopper free and sniffed. Bitter, hints of something earthy and mint—to disguise the bitterness, perhaps. I tipped a drop onto the desk. Black as night. Perhaps a taste?

'I wouldn't,' he said with a hint of amusement. I snatched back my hand.

'Poison?' I asked. Stuffing the stopper back in, I thrust it away. 'Nay, then. Unless it'll cure St Anthony's Fire, I've no time for you. We don't poison our patients.'

'Cure St Anth…' He smirked then shrugged. 'Definitely not a cure. But by all means, use it on someone who's dying, if you must. I need to be certain of the efficacy.' He tapped the phial. 'One drop won't kill you, but it may make you unwell. This is one adult's dose.'

'Nay.' My chair scraped unpleasantly on the bare timber floor as I rose and pointed. 'The door is that way.'

He pulled a handful of coins from his purse and silently counted them onto the desk. Gold and silver glittered and tinkled musically onto the timber.

I ground my teeth and stared steadfastly at him. 'Keep your coin, sir, I don't want it.'

He studied me for a long time. 'I'm surprised. But I believe you mean it.' The coins vanished back into his purse and he touched the phial. 'Then I appeal to you as a surgeon. I'm told this is quick and painless. How many patients could you save from days or weeks of agony?'

I froze. Could it be a release young Clara from her pain when the time came? If she didn't get better, she would die in horrible agony, swollen, blackened, delirious. As would many others suffering from the same disease already.

Nay! Murder was a sin and so was suicide. Would I send either her or me to Hell for a little ease here on Earth?

His voice dropped to a coaxing murmur. 'Think of the pain you could save innocent children with this.' He watched me from beneath half-closed lids. 'If you test it, I'll give you the recipe. No-one need ever know, except those you've released from their torture.'

'Stop.' I snatched up the phial and stowed it into my belt-purse. 'Get out.'

'Send me a message at the Broken Seld. To…Alistair Morrigan.' His lips twitched in an ironic smile I didn't understand. The name seemed familiar for some reason. 'Just your name and a Yes or No to tell me if it worked.'

I bowed my head, hating myself and him. His light footsteps tapped across the floor and the door slammed behind him.

The rest of my morning was taken up pulling teeth and lancing boils. But my thoughts stayed with the phial. What had I done? No. Nothing, yet. I could still give it back. Still change my mind if Clara got better. Yes. This was a backup. In case.

At Sext the black sky hid the midday sun and bells all over the city chimed in celebration. The prince's christening. I'd forgotten. Cheering and laughter mingled with horses' hooves and the rattling of cartwheels in the street outside. Toasts to the prince's health rang out. Even with the lawful alehouses closed on a Sunday, there would be sore heads tomorrow, for many goodwives brewed their own ale.

I trudged to the waiting room door to let in the next patient.

'Mistress!' Betsy's shrill cry halted me. She flung open the back door to the consulting room. Her cheeks were ashen. 'It's Master Rob. There's summat wrong, Mistress. Come quick.'

'Rob? I stared stupidly at her then snatched up my satchel. No. He was never ill. Hardly ever in all our years together. But my children… 'Anne?' The memory of Clara's illness and miscarriage sickened me.

'Nay, she's fine. Threw up all her breakfast, but she's sleeping. I checked her a minute ago.'

'You're sure?' Relief warred with fear.

'Yes, Mistress. I checked her pulse and everything, like you showed me. Her colour's good, too.'

'Right. I'll look in on Rob. Send a message to Laura Kennet, just in case. I want her to come and visit with our Anne. She has to keep some food down.'

'Yes, Mistress.' Betsy hurried away and I faintly heard her yell out the door for a messenger.

In my bedchamber room, the stink of vomit made me gag. I swore and prayed in one breath. Repeated the prayer in hopeless hope as I stepped toward our bed. To no avail. My husband lay writhing amongst the crushed bedlinen, his skin waxen, his mouth agape. His head turned and he stared sightlessly at me when I sat beside him.

My stomach seized up and my mouth dried to ash.

'The light is too noisy, Thom,' he muttered. 'And the sky hurts. Shut the window.' The window shutters were closed. 'Thom! Thom? Where are you? I can't...I can't...'

Betsy returned, puffing from her run up the stairs.

'Nay then, love,' I whispered, stroking his dark hair. 'Don't fret. Don't fret thyself.' My voice caught on the last word. 'I'm here. I'll be here.'

His eyes rolled back and his body stiffened.

'Hold him, Betsy. He'll hurt himself or swallow his tongue.'

When the fit passed and his body softened, we stripped the soiled bed and his nightshirt. Then we cleaned him and remade the bed, working in stoic silence. Betsy cast me frequent, frightened looks.

'What is it, Mistress?' she whispered. 'Not the plague?' She crossed herself.

I checked Rob's pulse. Barely there. His fingers and feet swollen. Hopeless fear welled in my chest and strangled my voice.

'The St Anthony's Fire,' I choked. 'Oh, Lord. Help me.' I bent my head. I couldn't lose him. Couldn't go on without him. He was the rock that anchored this family and held us up to greatness.

'What do we do, Mistress?' Betsy stood beside the bed, wringing her hands, watching me.

But my mind was thick and heavy. I couldn't think straight. 'I don't know, damn you! I don't know.'

She blanched and crossed herself again.

'Nay, Betsy, I'm sorry. I just…' I stared at my husband's pale, drawn face. He had to live. I was nothing without his gentleness, his compassion, his abiding love. 'Stay, Robard Smith,' I shouted, fists clenched. 'Stay, you hear me!'

Betsy tugged at my arm. 'Mistress, stop. He needs your help, not your anger.'

'But I don't know what to do,' I repeated, sinking to the floor. 'There's no cure.'

'Master Robard spoke of a woman healer when he came home last night, Mistress,' Betsy said. 'Someone the Company of Barbers and Surgeons wouldn't listen to. Could she…?'

'They wouldn't even speak to her. And you know they won't speak with me, so I can't find out.'

A loud knocking sounded on the outside door and a voice called my name from the street below.

'I locked the door.' Betsy ran to the window. 'It's a tall man and young woman, Mistress. Reddish hair. Shall I send her away?'

'Yes. Yes.' I rubbed at my face. 'And bring up hot water and the big cauldron. We'll try to warm him and get the blood moving.'

After she left, I simply sat by Rob's side and stared at him. There was nothing in my satchel that would help. I knew that. I'd tried every herb and tincture we knew on the other patients. Even dangerous ones like aconite and belladonna.

The stairs creaked and the door opened. Betsy entered, followed by a plain young woman wearing a sky-blue kirtle, her reddish gold hair under a linen coif. Behind her stood a tall, lean man with almost jaundice-yellow skin and the eyes of someone who'd lost many loved ones. The young woman curtseyed. He bowed, graceful.

'Sorry to intrude, Mistress Smith,' he said. 'I'm Alistair Morrigan and this is Helen O'Reilly.'

Alistair Morrigan? Had the lord sent him to check on me?

He shook his head. 'But we've called on Laura Kennet's behest.'

I held a hand to my forehead. Had I said that aloud?

'Are you a midwife?' I asked Helen. 'I wanted Laura to check over my Anne.'

Her eyes flicked to Robard's restless form. 'I'm a healer. Oh, I've delivered my share of babies, too. But Laura sent me so I could speak to you of the illness in the city.'

'A healer.' Confusion and worry fogged my brain. But Rob's words echoed back at me. 'A woman healer? Are you the one they say can cure St Anthony's Fire?' I leapt up and rushed to her, grasping her hands tight.

She flinched but didn't pull away. 'I can try, Mistress. I've had some success. Especially with early cases.' Her gaze travelled to Robard again. 'But…well, we can try.'

'Can you do it or not?' I said, harshly.

This time she did flinch. She cast a quick look at Morrigan, who grimaced. Then she said, 'Do you have any other choice?' When I didn't reply, she turned to Morrigan. 'Go.' She glanced at Rob. 'I'll be a while. I'll let you know what comes of it.'

'I'll try to visit, later, if I can slip away.' He kissed her cheek lightly, his thumb lingering on her jaw, his wistful smile just for her. 'Have care. He may return and he would certainly recognise you from Isledon.'

My heart ached, for Robard often looked that way at me.

Her cheeks coloured rosy. 'I will. You have care, too.' Morrigan left with a nod for me and Helen spoke with Betsy at length. She handed over several packets of herbs and gave her a long list of instructions.

'Soup,' I said. 'You're going to give him hot soup and you think that will help?'

Helen ignored the question. 'We'll give it to your daughter and Betsy as well.'

'Why? They're fine.'

'It's the bread. The rye bread,' she said. 'There's something wrong with the flour. It causes this illness. But it's only certain batches. You city folk don't see the rye before it's milled, mostly. The raw rye can have black grains in it. They taint the flour. If you eat too much you get sick. And it stops blood flowing. Causes miscarriage, fits, hallucinations. And the black fingers and toes.'

I sank onto the bed. 'We got a new bag of flour yesterday. Betsy baked and Robard ate most of the loaf. Anne threw up hers because she's with child and feeling poorly. I didn't eat any.'

Helen laid a slim hand on my arm. 'I'm sorry. The more you eat, the worse it is. All we can do is try the soup and hope. It will help Anne and Betsy. Robard…I'm not sure.'

Her face said otherwise and I thrust her hand away. 'You're lying.'

She bit her lip and watched me, wary. 'It always helps those who've eaten less. But those like Robard…' She shook her head. 'If there's no change by Vespers then it won't work at all. And he'll be in more pain than you can imagine by this time tomorrow.' She rubbed at her throat. 'After that…well, you've seen it, too. A few days, a week. Hard to be sure.'

I covered my face and held back a sob by force of will. Finally, I lowered my hands but couldn't look at her.

'Right. Make the soup. Do what you can.' I headed for the door.

'Mistress?' Betsy said. 'Ain't you staying?'

'I have patients downstairs. Get a priest. Maybe prayer will help if this soup won't. Call me if there's a change. Rob doesn't even know I'm here.'

Helen touched my wrist. 'Don't be so sure, Thomasine.'

I snatched my arm away and hunched a shoulder. 'I can't…I can't watch him die. I've seen too many deaths. I can't watch the man I love suffer like that.' I bolted from the room and hurried to the surgery.

Once there, I buried myself in work with fierce concentration. Pulled rotting teeth, infected splinters, shards of metal from eyes. Anything to keep out the image of Robard's agonised expression and blankness.

Nothing helped.

The priest came and went, and Betsy reported Rob showed no improvement afterward. Which didn't surprise me, but cut away one more thread of hope. By the time the bells rang for Vespers I could barely think straight. The room swayed and the floor shifted underfoot. I stumbled, clinging to the wall as I climbed the stairs.

In our bedchamber, Anne sat quietly by her father's side, her eyes red from weeping. Betsy was in the hall below, preparing an evening meal none of us would be able to eat. Helen stood looking down at Rob.

She glanced up when I entered. Rob lay still beneath light covers, his body hidden. He seemed calm, his breathing easy. Joy leapt in my chest and I hurried to him. I flung the covers aside and snatched his hand.

Helen reached toward me. 'Don't—'

I dropped Rob's icy hand and covered my mouth. His fingers were dusk-dark, shrunken and wrinkled. He moaned, tossing his head, muttering senseless words in which only my name was clear.

'It didn't work,' Helen murmured brokenly. 'I'm sorry. I'm so sorry. He'd eaten too much and I was too late. I've given him willowbark to help him sleep and ease the pain.'

'Amputation?' I asked, choking. He was a barber-surgeon. If we amputated his fingers and toes to save his life he'd be a helpless cripple. But maybe he'd still be alive; with me. Surely that would be enough?

Helen shook her head. 'I'm sorry. It doesn't help. I tried on other patients, in Isledon.' She hesitated. 'My…my husband and son died of this, too. I do understand.'

I whirled on her. 'Nay, you do *not*. We've loved each other for thirty years. You have no idea what that means.' Pain in my palms brought me to my senses and I opened my clenched hands. Blood trickled from where my nails had bitten through the skin. I stared stupidly at them.

'Oh,' Helen said, 'let me—'

'Just get out,' I said. 'Everyone. Get out.'

Anne tried to speak to me but I cut her off. The door closed, leaving me alone with my husband. I sank onto the bed and kissed his pale cheek then touched my forehead to his. Tears dripped onto his skin but he made no move. His breathing was shallow and quick. The pulse in his neck rapid. But his hands and feet were even darker.

He moaned, his face twisting in agony despite the willowbark.

I kissed his cheek. 'Don't go, Rob. Please? Don't leave me. I can't do this on my own.'

His eyes opened and he focussed on me. 'Thom,' he croaked. 'It hurts. It burns. Make it stop, please?'

I dashed tears away. 'Aye, love. I know. I'm sorry.'

He lapsed into silence, his eyes drifting closed. Then he cried out: my name, the Lord's name, a guttural scream of pain. I wrapped my arms around his broad shoulders and buried my face in his neck.

I couldn't bear to see him in such pain. There *had* to be something. Some cure. A miracle. Surely we'd worked hard enough to help the poor to deserve God's favour? Just this once.

I prayed. Prayed to the Lord to save Rob, to cure him, to heal him.

'Thom?' Rob's voice was a whisper. His face was grey, drawn in pain. He lifted his blackened fingers and stared at them. He groaned and let the hand drop to his side. 'Help me, Thom. I can't…Don't make me…'

I stroked his cheek. 'Nay, love. You might come through. You might live.'

'Not this time We both…know…how this ends. Please?'

'Oh, Rob, nay.' My voice cracked.

'Please,' he said. 'As you love me, make it stop.'

My heart broke, but I nodded. Forcing him to go through more agony because I was scared was the most selfish thing I could do. I loved him too much for that. Blinded and aching, I pulled the cream ceramic phial from my belt purse and unstoppered it. I shoved pillows under Rob's head to raise him. Then I carefully tipped the black liquid into his mouth. He swallowed, coughed and grimaced.

'That's awful, Thom.' His eyes drifted closed. 'Add more mint next time.'

I couldn't laugh. I kissed his cheek and lay beside him in the bed, holding his warmth close.

A few minutes later I rose, took out my quill and ink and wrote the word YES, on a piece of parchment.

p266 *Aiki Flinthart*

17. And the Blackbird Still is Waiting

Scientia Wilson, 21
Daughter of Hugh Wilson, tutor to nobility
St Marie Street, London,

Sunday (midday), 24th September, 1486

'Would you...stand still, woman...so I can...hit you!' James puffed and hacked at my offside, trying to break through my defence.

I spun easily aside, conserving energy. His wooden bastard sword glanced off the leather pauldron protecting my shoulder.

'No, indeed. Defeats the purpose...of learning to fight if I stand still.' I jabbed but he drew back, crowing in triumph, his face red, dark hair sticking out from beneath the leather helm. His boots were dusty, his linen shirt sweat-stained and grimed.

I was probably just as dishevelled, even though I'd plaited my long dark-blonde hair back. With every panting breath I smelled damp leather and sweat from my tunic and leather armour. We'd been training for an hour in the courtyard of my father's house on St Marie Street, and I'd never felt so alive.

James struck at my legs. I deflected and feinted with my dagger. He dodged, crying out in surprise and skipped back, panting. I grinned at him and dropped into a fighting stance again.

Oh, to be able to live always thus—like a man, free to read, to travel, to train with sword and bow. Being female and unwed was the most restrictive, unpleasant... I stopped the useless thought. I should be grateful. At least Sir Belmont had stopped offering his corpulent self for my hand. I shuddered and refocussed.

Clouds boiled overhead. A gust of wind picked up leaves and swirled them into James's face. He flinched and lifted his sword. I struck at his exposed ribs. The thwack of wood on leather echoed in the courtyard.

'Unfair, Tia. I was distracted.' James pressed his ribs and groaned. 'I think you broke something.'

'Oh, dear. Did I, indeed? I'm so sorry!' I dropped my sword and threw aside my helm, hurrying to help. He was my best friend. I couldn't bear it if I'd hurt him. 'Take off the plackart so I can see.'

James grabbed my arm and laid his sword across my throat. His blue eyes gleamed with mischief.

'Ah-ha! Got you that time. That will teach you to be so soft-hearted. Remember what I said? Your biggest strength can also be your biggest weakness.'

'Yes, indeed. Look down,' I whispered. My dagger-point rested in his groin, at the vulnerable gap in his leg armour.

He released me with a rueful laugh. 'I'm beginning to regret teaching you to fight, Tia. I swear you could best some of the knights in my father's precious Order of the Garter.'

'Don't be silly.' I tucked my dagger away with a twinge of unease and turned the subject. 'Is your father at the Tower chapel for the christening today?

James glanced south, as though he could see his father, chief bodyguard to the king, through the stone walls and timber of our manor. He jammed his swordpoint into the dirt. 'Yes. Didn't want me there, though. Apparently, I'm not trusted enough to attend.'

'Oh, James,' I rested my head on his shoulder. 'No, indeed—I'm sure he doesn't think that. You're only one-and-twenty. Give him time to get used to the idea that his only son is a man. *Your* biggest strength *is* your impulsiveness.' I kissed his cheek. 'And it's what makes you so lovable, too.'

He stilled, his smile slipping. The atmosphere between us changed and I backed away.

'Don't, James,' I said. 'Indeed, you know I cannot leave Father.

He needs me. And I love you as a brother, no more,' I lied, fiddling with the end of my braid.

'I need you, too.' James frowned. 'Many marriages start with far less than liking and work out well. It's the only solution that suits us all. You get a home and freedom to do as you please. I get my father to stop hounding me about marrying.'

He held my shoulders and turned me around. I didn't resist, for my heart was daily torn asunder and his words were only what I'd told myself—and talked myself out of.

'Please…' My voice broke. I pulled free, gathered up my weapon and discarded helm and hurried toward the store room through the stables.

James followed, stripped off his armour and tossed it aside in the musty tackroom. 'You can't waste your life caring for your father. Your brother and a sister-in-law are moving in soon, aren't they? They'll care for him. Then you'd be free to marry me. Why *are* they moving in?'

'You're most kind—reminding me that David and Judith arrive on Tuesday.' I drew a deep breath, regaining my poise. 'Apparently David's selling his house to raise funds for expanding his business. But Judith won't care for Papa as I do.'

I avoided James's searching gaze. He knew me too well and I couldn't bear to argue with him. Even the thought of confrontation made me ill. 'I cannot leave Papa. With no-one to talk philosophy and history, he would be miserable. David has no thoughts but for his stonemason's business and Judith has none but for her children.'

'Lord save us,' he said, rolling his eyes. 'I never met such a bore as your brother. And the way he constantly belittles you makes me want to strangle him. You won't have a moment's peace.' He scowled. 'Why doesn't your father lend David the money?'

I flushed and hunched a shoulder. 'There's little besides my dowry left. David's spent it all on building up the stonemasonry. We can't afford to run this house on Papa's pension from the Duke of Suffolk. Indeed, it seems David holds the purse strings now. We must put up with his complaints as best we can.'

My throat tightened. Papa had been strong and independent his whole life. He allowed my care because we shared so many interests. But to have David—a boorish clod we both detested—control our lives, our finances, our home… I wrapped my arms about myself and stared into the shadows of the tackroom.

James caught my face between his hands. 'See? All the more reason to marry me. We can help each other. You would have a house, money, servants. Especially now my father has been made Baron Cheyne and given lands. You'd have everything you want.'

A fist tightened around my lungs, stealing my will to defy him. I shuddered, hating the argument that must come if I denied him. Yet deny him, I must. I ached; my body ached; my heart ached. How I wanted to be everything to him. More than a wife—a partner, a swordsister, a lover. He, of all the men I'd met, saw me as more than just my father's dutiful daughter.

But he would never love me. Could never. Not the way he loved Philippe.

I pushed him away.

'I'm sorry, James. We can't. You must go manage your father's Enborne estate in Berkshire. I must stay and care for Papa.' I turned aside. 'It's the way things have to be.'

'God's teeth!' He thumped the wall beside me and ran a hand through his dark hair.

I shrank, my heart pounding.

'Your father could come with us.' He whirled back, hope lighting his expression. 'We're only in Berkshire for a few months each year. And then Philippe could come too, for one more would go unnoticed in my entourage.'

'Papa won't leave London. His particular friends visit him. They bring him books and talk of world affairs. What would he do in the country? He can't walk or ride a horse.' I fussed with the leather armour, stacking it neatly. 'Besides, your father's a Baron now. He won't let you marry the daughter of a tutor. Even if Papa did teach lords and ladies when he was younger. We're not nobility.'

'I suppose you're right.' James grimaced. 'Don't look so frightened, Tia. I'm sorry to pressure you. I know you hate it.' He wrapped his arms about me and I wanted more than anything to melt into him. But I hardened my resolve and broke free.

'Come into the house and bid Papa farewell,' I said. 'He'd be hurt if you didn't.'

James's shoulders slumped but he followed me out of the storeroom without further protest.

Philippe met us outside the stables, intelligent green eyes smiling beneath lazy lids as he twirled a yellow rose in his fingertips. His scarlet doublet and cream hose were pristine, his black hair waving neatly to his shoulders.

I kissed his cheek, tasting the subtle, warm scent of his skin. 'I'm sorry, Philippe. Indeed, I wish I could help. I can't. It would make all of us vilely unhappy.'

He took my fingers and kissed them, bowing gracefully. 'Non, ce ne serait pas, Tia. Nous t'aimons.' A pleasurable frisson passed through me, as it always did when he touched my skin. How could I feel this way about two men?

'Merci, Philippe.' My voice broke and I pulled free. He and James might love me, as Philippe said, but not the way I wished to be loved.

They were my oldest, dearest friends. I would long treasure the last five years—the hours the three of us had spent under my father's tutelage, arguing Plato, translating the Bible from Latin, reading Chaucer.

And I was happy James and Philippe had found each other, even though they risked much. Their love was forbidden by the Church. If my heart were not given to James, already, I might even marry him to help them hide. But I could not watch him love another, day in, day out, and be left out of that love. I would go mad.

I hurried away. Their footsteps followed me. I ignored their whispered conversation.

We were halfway across the courtyard when the great timber street gate swung inward. A vaguely familiar male voice echoed.

'Visitors,' I said. 'I can't be seen like this!' Brushing at the dirt and sweat patches on my tunic did no good.

Two men swaggered through the gate, accompanied by our servant, Louis. The tallest had an arrestingly beautiful face—all sharp angles and golden skin, with dark-rimmed grey eyes. I could barely drag my gaze from him.

'God's—!' The shorter, dark-haired man cleared his throat. He swept off his burgundy silk hat in a low bow. 'Scientia, is that you? It's been an age. You've grown.'

I blushed and curtseyed awkwardly. 'Francis? I-I mean Lord Lovell. Indeed, it's been five years. It's good to see you.' I plucked at my tunic. 'I'm sorry, indeed, that you find me in such unseemly disarray.'

Francis kissed my hand. 'You look quite delightful, I assure you. Perhaps you'll set a new fashion.' He directed a cool, inquiring look at James and Philippe.

'Oh.' I stuttered the introduction. 'L-Lord Lovell, these are my friends, James Cheyne and Philippe Bisset.'

James managed a creditable bow. 'My lord.'

Francis's mouth thinned. 'You would be John Cheyne's whelp, then?'

James flushed and his hand dropped to his hip, but he hadn't yet put his real sword back on. Francis's gaze followed the movement. His lips twitched into a sardonic smile.

'I shouldn't, boy.' He rested one hand on his sword's ruby-studded hilt and plucked a hair off his dark burgundy doublet with the other. I hesitated, unsure what to do. He was a guest and my father's old student, but he should not insult James, so. Why did he?

I jumped into the silence. 'Will you go inside, Francis. And…?' I looked askance at his companion.

'Your pardon.' Francis waved his friend forward. 'Scientia Wilson, Alistair Morrigan.'

The tall, gold-skinned man bowed over my hand. 'I can see we've called at an inopportune time, Mistress Wilson. Shall we come back later?'

I gaped at him, mesmerised by his melodious voice and beautiful way of enunciating every word. My father would love to hear him read Chaucer's Canterbury Tales. Would it be too bold to ask it of a stranger? I shook myself.

'No, indeed, good sir.' I indicated the house. 'Pray follow Louis into the house. He'll take you to Papa.' I smiled ruefully. 'I'll change and join you shortly.'

Master Morrigan gave a singularly sweet smile and the two men headed into the house, leaving me staring blankly after them.

'That Lovell has some nerve,' James snarled. Philippe mumured an expostulation and laid a calming hand on his shoulder.

'Why was he rude?' I asked. 'I was a child when my father tutored him and the Duke of Suffolk's children in the Duke's household. He visited Papa often, after we left. But not for a few years, now.'

James snorted. 'Hardly surprising. He was thick as thieves with King Richard. There were three of them, fawning over Richard: Sir William Catesby, Sir Richard Ratcliffe and Lovell. They used to call them the cat, the rat, and Lovell, the dog.'

'But why was he annoyed about your father?' The answer clicked. 'Oh! King Richard made Francis a Knight of the Garter, but then King Henry degraded him from the Order, didn't he? Oh, dear.' I touched James's arm. 'Perhaps you should go. Indeed, it might not be politic to be seen in his company.'

He scowled. 'Have care, Tia. That man's a slippery levereter. I'd give a deal to know what he's here for. Seems more than a bit fishy to me. I wonder if the king knows he's in town?'

I smacked his wrist. 'Don't you dare tell tales that might imperil my father. We live by the generosity of the Duke of Suffolk's pension, and the Duke's position in King Henry's favour is precarious at the best of times.'

The Sext bells rang out and James grimaced.

'Very well. I'll stay mum.' He squinted at the blackening sky. 'We'd best go. Father asked me to hold house and make sure the servants don't empty the buttery of ale in celebrating the prince's christening.' He brightened. 'I am invited to the feast on Tuesday night, though. Pity I can't bring you along.'

'No, indeed!' I shuddered. 'I should hate to go to something so loud and boisterous. Now, go.'

He collected his sword and hat from a bench nearby and saluted jauntily. Philippe linked arms with him and they strolled out the gate, laughing. I watched them out of sight.

In my bedchamber on the second floor I bathed quickly with a basin and cloth, then dressed in a modest cream silk surcoat. There was no time to wash my sweat-soaked hair, so I tucked it into a cream velvet caul behind a gable headdress that framed my face in red and gold embroidered silk.

I crept downstairs. My father had converted the back of the hall into his bedchamber and cabinet, because he could no longer manage the stairs. The servants' entrance to his cabinet was tucked beneath the stairs. I turned the handle gently and eased inside, emerging behind a painted oak screen.

There I paused, listening. Eavesdropping was wrong, but Papa never minded. He wanted me to be able to discuss the meetings he had with the men of all ranks who valued his opinion. But, of course, a mere daughter of the house could not attend such meetings. So I hid here often, learning.

Afterward, Papa would call me out to talk over the ideas. Philosophy, science, history, theology, politics. They fascinated me in a way sewing, dancing, children, and housekeeping did not.

'Master Wilson, you must see the wisdom of my plan.' That was Francis's voice, persuasive and gentle.

'No, my lord,' my father's rounded, familiar tones soothed a fillip of fear in my belly. 'I cannot support such a mad venture. Twould destabilise the monarchy again. It matters not which family runs the country, so long as we have a chance to recover awhile.'

A chair scraped and footsteps tracked hastily back and forth across the chamber. 'You need not fret over the outcome, Hugh,' Lovell said, his words now condescending. 'Just get me into the tower. When I was a child you told me about the hidden entrance to the Beauchamp Tower. I *must* get in to see the boy. Edward is the last heir. The rightful heir.'

'Enough, my lord.' My father's voice held a stern note that usually subdued even the most headstrong student. A long silence followed and I held my breath lest they heard me. The room was close and stuffy. The smell of leatherbound books and dust caught in my nose and I pinched it to hold back a sneeze.

My father sighed. 'Francis, you always were a stubborn boy. Let the past be done and gone. Plotting with Edward Plantagenet is not the way. You say you've been invited to the feast on Tuesday night?'

'Yes,' Lovell replied shortly.

'And you know Henry will likely offer pardons to those that swear allegiance. Take what's offered and go home to your wife.'

'Bah!' Lovell growled low in his throat. 'And do what? I want my lands back, Hugh. Why should I be punished for doing what I thought was right?'

'Did you?' Papa said, weary. 'Or did you back Richard because he promised you even more lands. You let greed overcome sense. Don't make the same mistake twice. Take the pardon. Regain Henry's trust and in time you will regain your estates, I'm sure.'

'Your advice is useless, old man. Tell me where the secret passage is into the Beauchamp Tower and we can stop wasting each other's time.'

Another long silence followed. Nails drummed on something wooden. My father's nails or Francis's? I held my breath, afraid they might hear me.

'I cannot tell you, my lord,' my father said stiffly.

'Cannot or will not?'

'Does it matter?'

The slick sound of metal against wood brought a rush to my blood. A weapon had been drawn. But whose? I had nothing on me. My father was helpless; crippled and unable to walk. He had no way of defending himself. Should I scream and call for help? But Lovell could kill my father with one thrust of his sword and any help would be too late.

'It matters,' Lovell said quietly, 'if you wish Scientia to live another day. She trusts me. She won't even see the dagger that cuts her heart out, old man.'

I leaned against the wall, my head spinning. There were two men in there with my father and no fighting men in the household. If I went in now Lovell would hold me to hostage. I could do nothing but listen and hope.

'Very well, my lord,' my father whispered. 'You enter the passages through the cellars of the Robin-the-Devil's Tower, north of the Beauchamp Tower. The southernmost cellar. There's a pile of wine casks stacked before a small wooden door. The passage leads directly into the cellar of the Beauchamp Tower. Now get out. And never come near me or my daughter again.'

Lovell chuckled softly. 'I shan't, old man. Unless you lied, or ever breathe a word of this. If you do, Scientia's life is forfeit. And you will watch her die. Morrigan, let's take our leave. We have a rescue to plan. Farewell, Hugh.'

'Get out of my house, Lovell.'

Footsteps sounded and a door closed. I released a shaky sigh.

'Tia?' Papa's quavering voice lifted in question.

I slipped from behind the screen and hurried to his side. He sat in his favourite, big timber chair with its green velvet cushions. His drawn face was almost as grey as the wool blanket across his withered legs. A small fire crackled in the brick fireplace set in the eastern wall and cast skittering lights across his pensive expression.

He looked up at me, haunted, and stretched out a thin hand. I clasped it and sank onto a footstool at his side.

'You heard?' he asked, staring at the flames.

'Yes, indeed, Papa,' I returned, uncertain what to say. 'Enough to know he gave you no choice. I cannot believe Francis could behave thus to you. What has come over him?'

'Greed. Desperation. Desire for revenge.' My father's lips thinned. 'The usual follies of men.'

'Should we...should we do something? Warn the king, perhaps?'

He shook his grey head. 'You heard him. I wouldn't put it past him to set watch on me and follow any messengers to make sure I don't send word straight to the king. I'll not put you in danger, child. And you will hold your tongue as well. Don't speak of this to anyone. Not even young James Cheyne. Understand?'

'But Papa—'

'No. Do not defy me in this. I allow you a slack rein, child, because I take pleasure in your company. But in this you will obey me.'

I bowed my head. 'Yes, Papa.'

'We must get you out of London. I don't trust him to keep his word, even if he succeeds. He will wish to eliminate anyone who helped him plan this treachery.' His gaze sharpened on me. 'Louis said James proposed to you today in the courtyard. What was your answer?'

'I refused,' I murmured, my cheeks hot. What had this to do with getting out of London?

Burning wood crackled in the silence and I cast an anxious glance at my father. His jaw clenched tight.

'Are you in pain, Papa? Can I get your medicine?'

He waved me away. 'It's not that. Why did you refuse him? It's a good match. You have enough dowry to be eligible, even if you're not of noble blood. And it would see you out of London and far from

Lovell's reach. So why?'

I plucked at a loose thread on the hem of my dress. 'I...I don't love him. And you said you'd never make me wed where I couldn't love.'

His hand curled into a fist and thumped at his legs. 'Don't *lie,* girl. I've seen the way you look at him.' He squeezed his wasted thigh and his lips pulled back in a snarl. 'You refused because you feel tied to an old cripple. Hell and damnation! I should have died in that fall. I'm helpless to protect you.'

'Papa! No, indeed.' I knelt before him. 'Don't say such things. If you'd died we would never have had these last five years together. David would have married me off to Sir Belmont to further his ambition.' I gestured around the walls, lined with rank upon rank of leatherbound books. 'And I would have missed learning all this. How could you wish that on me?'

My father chuckled wryly, the pain around his mouth easing into humour. 'How can I argue with such logic?' He sighed. 'What do we do? I won't be here forever. I would like to see you safe. Surely you want a home and family. With James, or another. Sometime.'

'Perhaps,' I said, rising and twitching my skirts into place. 'But for now I'm quite happy for it to be just you and me.'

He caught my wrist. 'But it won't be just you and me. Not after Tuesday. And...' His jaw worked as he ground his teeth. 'David intends to reopen negotiations for your hand with Sir Belmont.'

I pulled my arm free. 'And you would let him sell me like some sort of...cow?'

'I seem to have little say any longer, Tia. I'm sorry.' He covered his eyes.

My knees gave way and I sat back down with a thud, my skirts billowing up. With a shudder I curled in on myself. David disliked me as much as I disliked him. I would be wed to Sir Belmont—a man twenty years my senior and three times my weight—before the year was done.

'And what of you, Papa?' I asked, choking. 'If I were to wed…Sir Belmont, or even James, what would become of you?'

He sighed. 'I delayed telling you of David's plan because I'd hoped young James would propose. And that you would…perhaps…be willing to house an old man with your new family.'

'But you know James's estates are in Berkshire. You'd be willing to live there? So far from your friends?'

'It wouldn't be such a sacrifice if I still had you to talk with. And I hear the Baron has a decent library, as well.'

Hope lifted me for a moment, only to be dashed again by the memory of Philippe.

'Indeed, I cannot marry him, Papa,' I said. 'James's love belongs to another. He proposed only to stop his father's complaints.'

With a dry chuckle, my father leaned back in his chair and threaded his fingers across his stomach. 'My dear girl, sometimes I forget how young you are. How untried in the ways of the heart. James might love Philippe, but I guarantee he loves you, too. As does Philippe, if I am any judge.'

I gasped and stared. 'You know about Philippe?'

'You think James is the first to love a man? The heart loves where it will. Before I met your mother…' He shook his head. 'Suffice to say, it's entirely possible to love two people at once.'

I stilled, words escaping me, thoughts twining around a tiny glimmer of joy I was afraid to look at too closely for fear it would vanish. 'But the Church…'

Papa gestured dismissively. 'You've read Plato and the other ancient scholars. Enough to know that opinions on love change. You know I believe God will not condemn the loving and compassionate to eternal hellfire.' His fingers hooked under my jaw and tilted my face up. 'And you are both, my girl.'

'What...what should I do?' I whispered. 'I do love James so much. And...admire and respect Philippe a great deal.' My cheeks burned.

Papa patted my wrist. 'Then you have the makings of an excellent marriage. I suggest you send a message to young James and Philippe. Invite them to dinner this evening.'

Still, I hesitated. 'But James is the heir to a Baronetcy. He needs royal permission to marry and I'm nobody.'

With a snort, Papa waved away that objection, too. 'Leave that to me. I'm about to invite our old employer, the Duke of Suffolk, to your wedding. He's in town for the prince's christening. And perhaps I'll let slip some information about Lovell that will put him in Henry's good books for a long time. He will owe me.'

Excitement leapt in my chest; the flutter of a new book's pages.

'Go.' He nodded at the door. 'We have a wedding to plan. David arrives in two days and I'd like you to be married before he moves in.' He chuckled wickedly. 'If for nothing else than to see the look on his face when I break the news.'

I laughed in delight and flung my arms around him.

18. And Her Eyes Have All the Seeming

Nicola Willoughby, 26
Musician/singer
Chepe Syed, London,

Sunday (after midday), 24th September, 1486

I bound a strip of thin silk across my eyes. People gave more and hurried past less if my milk-white eyes were hidden. Apparently, a pretty young woman with a bandage hiding her deformity was easier to cope with.

Rollo, the Broken Seld's innkeeper, fussed about me as he always did. Timber scraped on stone as he settled a stool against the inn's warm wall. His thick, strong fingers grasped my elbow and he guided me to the seat. I let him because it was easier than protesting I could find the seat myself. And it was nice to be looked after.

I trod in a puddle and water seeped in through the hole in my shoe. Perhaps we could afford new ones, soon, if Bella's music sold.

'Now,' Rollo said, his deep voice so much kinder than my father's had ever been. 'Don't you stay out here too long. It's almost the Nones bells and the sky's come over all dark. Could rain.'

I sniffed the cool autumn air. He did like to mother me, but he was right. Beyond the usual smells of manure, rotting food, and mud, was the warm smell of distant rain.

'I'll not die for a little rain, Rollo. But come inside, I will. I promise.' I set my wooden bucket between my ankles and stretched my legs out so passersby could see it. 'A little extra coin will help pay for Bella's music printing. Folk will be feeling generous with the prince's christening, think you not?'

'They'll be drunken louts, is what they'll be,' he muttered. 'I don't like you being out here alone, but the inn's so full, Sarah and the girls can't keep up. I have to go back inside.'

'I'll come back in when Bella returns to play her shawm alongside me.' On nights like these, when things got rowdy, I needed someone to keep the men I couldn't see away. Bella was quick with her dagger. I shuddered at the memory of hot, groping hands and the stink of ale and sweat. Never again.

Right now, it was safer outside, where I could hear people coming.

'You've got your belt-knife?' he said, sounding anxious.

I patted the dagger at my hip. Rollo had been a squire when he was younger and had taught Bella and I the basics of using our knives. I tried, but being blind meant there was little I could do and we all knew it. The training made them feel better, though.

He sighed. 'Well, make sure you use it if anyone tries anything. When's Bella getting back?'

'Not long,' I lied to reassure him. Truth was, I had no idea. Bella had gone off this morning with Alistair Morrigan on some task or other and hadn't come back, yet. It always worried me when she left for long, for I had no one else to rely on; no family. Without her I was lost. But she could look after herself, and Alistair Morrigan I would trust with my life—and Bella's.

Rollo muttered and stomped away, the inn's wooden door slamming behind him. I checked the tuning on my lute.

Then I paused and listened to the street. Hurried footsteps on the packed earth. Chickens squawking, getting further away. People laughing and talking, making jokes about the new prince. A crier ran past, giving the prince's name after the christening: Arthur Tudor, heir to the throne of England. The Broken Seld's door opened again and bawdy offkey singing swelled then faded. I grimaced at the flat notes.

I plucked out a jaunty little tune to warm up. Bella's new composition. But she'd asked me not to sing the words. Not yet. Not until Tuesday night. So I played and improvised around the melody, the gut strings digging into my fingertips. The notes fell true and sweet and I lost myself in the joy of it. Bella truly had a gift for writing memorable music.

One of the strings slipped a fraction. Most people wouldn't notice, but even the slightest untrue note grated on my ear like a fingernail on slate. I tightened the peg.

The breeze shifted, fitful and storm-driven, ruffling my hair beneath the coif and fluttering the skirts around my ankles. A familiar scent teased my nostrils. Ambergris and moss. I froze for a moment, then plucked a soft tune to cover my reaction. Stealthy footfalls scuffed in the narrow alley beside the Broken Seld, to my right.

I waited, my fingers working of their own accord, ears straining. A coin plonked into my bucket and startled me.

'Gramercy,' I murmured, smiling mechanically, still listening for noise in the alley. My fingers stumbled on a difficult run of notes. A murmur of voices in the alley was almost lost in the clatter of hooves and wooden wheels as a fishmonger's cart rattled by, trailing the smell of eel.

A group of people passed with their chatter about Prince Arthur's christening feast on Tuesday night at the Tower. I frowned, unable to shake the feeling that someone waited, close. Watching me.

Overhead, distant thunder rumbled and the smell of rain and mud grew stronger. Not yet, though. I had a little more time before I must go back into the stuffy, thick atmosphere of ale, rancid wine and old vomit. And perhaps Bella would be back to escort me in.

I raised my voice in song. A merry tune about a foolish, clumsy lover who couldn't win his love. Footsteps paused. More. Coins plinked into the bucket. A few more and I could buy vellum for Bella. I smiled, anticipating the honey-mead taste of her lips as she kissed me.

People greeted me by name. Voices I recognised I returned a greeting to. Those I didn't I merely smiled and nodded toward. Then the voices stopped. Thunder rolled and footsteps pattered away.

A light mist of rain dusted my skin and I sighed. Time to go in.

'Humphrey, you're late.'

I froze. The light male voice in the alley was one I recognised and disliked: Lord Lovell. And he must be speaking to Humphrey Stafford, one of the two brothers who followed him.

'I were detained, my lord.'

'You lie. You were seen with a known Lancaster supporter. You will not betray me again, that I can assure you.'

I forced my fingers to play a simple song, though they trembled.

'But, my lord! Weren't my fault. It were that Morri—' A grunt. A scuffle of feet on dirt. The crash of falling timber. Crates stacked in the alley, perhaps. A gasping, gurgling cry and the thud of something falling to the dirt. The metallic tang of blood in the air. The musical jingle of a sword sheath. The tick of a loose shoe nail. A bubbling death-groan.

And the smell of ambergris and moss.

I swallowed bile and fear and stilled the humming lute strings.

Silence. A roll of thunder.

The first bells of Nones carolled out and I jumped. By the time the bells had rolled across the city in a wave from tower to tower—and died into afternoise—I'd had a chance to decide what to do.

If I panicked and ran, the killer would know I'd witnessed his act. And Lovell knew who I was. So I pretended. Picked out a new tune and sang loud to cover the tremor in my voice. Where was Bella? I needed someone to protect me.

Footsteps stopped nearby and his distinctive perfume grew

stronger. My hands shook and nausea twisted my stomach. A coin clinked in the bucket and I forced a smile.

'Gramercy, friend.' I carefully refrained from saying 'sir' or 'my lord'.

His heavy breathing steadied and he gave a satisfied little grunt. The tick of his loose shoe nail dwindled and the Broken Seld's door creaked open, then slammed closed.

I stopped playing, wrapped my arms around my lute and hunched over it, shivering uncontrollably. What should I do? Should I report a murder to the constables? But who would believe a blind girl over a lord? Who would believe I could identify him? And what would stop him from killing me if I tried?

I'd given up the security of my family and name years ago and nothing could reverse that.

'Nicola? Sweet Lord above! Husband! It's Nicola! Right where the message said—'

'Margaret.'

Small hands grasped my arms and pulled me upright. Someone gently took the lute from me and I—still shocked and trembling—didn't resist. An old, familiar scent caught at my heart. Lavender and the warm smell of her skin took me back to childhood, safe, comfortable, sheltered.

'Mother!' I sobbed and buried my face in her neck. Lace scratched my cheek and her plump arms engulfed me.

I was home.

But no. I wasn't. I wasn't sixteen anymore; a frightened girl being sold into marriage. I was a grown woman. I'd left home ten years ago when my mother wouldn't protect me from my father's autocratic orders.

Or from my betrothed.

I pushed free. 'Mother. Why are you here? How did you find me?'

'Why...why, Nicola, dear.' She cleared her throat.

I could still picture her and father—fuzzily—from a time before God took my sight and made me their puppet, helpless. Was her hair still glossy, dark and straight like mine? Was her pale skin still flawless? And my father, was his back still as rigid as his distaste for me and Isabella?

'We've come from the prince's christening,' my father said, stiff.

'Really?' I couldn't hide the sarcasm and didn't try. He was lying. Mother had said someone sent them a message about where to find me.

'It was wonderfully grand,' my mother put in hastily. 'The queen's sisters were there. So pretty. *And* we've been invited to the feast on Tuesday night. I must get a new surcoat, Christopher. Oh! Sir Edward Sutton was there, too, Nicola. He asked after you.'

I made a gesture, trying to push away her words. Then I put out a hand. 'My lute, Father. Before the rain returns, I need to get it inside.'

There was a long silence and I tensed, my arm still outstretched. It would be like him to hold it to ransom. To demand my obedience as he had last time. To threaten again to destroy the instrument I treasured if I didn't comply and marry Sir Edward.

I dropped my arm. Surely he must know I'd leave it behind—like I had last time—rather than fight him.

Snatching up the coin-bucket, I hesitated. The last thing I wanted was to show them where I lived with Bella. My cheeks warmed for I knew how my father would disparage the Broken Seld.

'Christopher,' Mother said. My father pressed the lute neck roughly into my hand and I grabbed it.

'She must come home, Margaret. We agreed,' he muttered.

'She will,' Mother said, confident. 'Sir Edward has renewed his suit, Nicola. His wife died in childbirth last year. The babe with her. He still wants you.'

'Needs another wife to kill, does he?' I said. 'And again you thought of me. Why? Because I'm a cripple and of no other use to you? What do I get out of this bargain? Let me be, why can't you?'

Someone grasped my elbow, digging in painfully. 'Because you are our daughter, and obey us you *will*,' my father snarled. 'The law says you obey your parents or your husband. Sir Edward is a good man. He'll provide you with a secure, stable home.' He sniffed loudly. 'Not this disgusting shithole of a place. It's not fit for the daughter of the tenth Baron Willoughby de Eresby.'

'A good man?' I hunched my shoulders. They hadn't listened last time. Why would it change, now? 'I have a home with someone I love, who loves me. I'm not interested in Sir Edward. A brood mare is what he wants, nothing more. Two wives already, he's killed.'

'Someone you love!' My father sputtered and made a noise of disgust.

'Father,' I said, pleading, though I hadn't meant to.

'Father, nothing,' he snapped. 'I've had enough.'

'Christopher,' mother begged. 'Don't make a scene.'

'Silence! Both of you!'

I froze, shrinking in on myself, waiting for the thrashings and endless scolds—for laziness, for being too lighthearted; not mindful of my elders; too much singing of music that wasn't the Church's.

For being myself.

My father's fingers tightened on my elbow. 'You will obey. Marry Sir Edward and do your duty to your family. If you don't...' His nails broke the thin skin on my inner elbow. I cried out.

'If you don't,' he repeated, 'I will denounce you—and Isabella— to the Church for your sinful lifestyle. I'll put you in a nunnery and you'll never see her again. Isabella, I will have pilloried, flogged, and exiled from England. Your choice, girl.'

'Father!' I wasn't shocked, not really. Only surprised he hadn't done so years ago.

'I will see you wed proper, before God,' he growled. 'No daughter of mine will defy me—or God—thus. You're not fit to live without someone to look after you. A *man*.'

The Broken Seld's door creaked open again.

'You! Woman,' my father said. 'Know you this girl?' He shook my arm.

'Course, sir.' Sarah. Rollo's housekeeper. 'She's Nicola Willoughby. Lives—'

'Sarah, no!'

'—right ere in the gable room of the inn. What, Nic? Beggin your pardon, did I…did I say summat wrong?' The too-innocent tone of her voice told me who had sent them a message. Sarah had never approved of me and Isabella. And Isabella described Sarah contemptuously as a daggle-tail, disparaging her unkempt appearance and shrewish tongue.

'Nothing at all, my good woman,' my father said, smug. 'Here. Show us her room. We're her parents.' Coins clinked and I slumped. Sarah had never refused a bribe in her life. And my little hoard of coins was nothing to my father's fortune.

They dragged me inside and I went, unable to fight back. At least five sets of footsteps followed us. My father's yeomen; his entourage. Always ready with their swords. What could I do, but go along? And maybe Father was right. If I married Sir Edward, I would be safe from Lovell. I remembered the horrible sounds of death in the alley and shivered. And safe from the men here in the tavern who tried each night to find their way under my skirts. Safe from the death and disease that scourged London's filthy streets regularly.

But who would protect me from Sir Edward? No-one could. But, perhaps now it was my turn to protect Bella.

I gripped my lute like a shield. If I went, Isabella would be safe. Remembering that was the most important thing. As long as I was with her, Isabella's future would be uncertain. Without me she could keep pursuing her dream of writing and selling her music. She was just getting a foothold. How could I destroy her dreams and her life when the solution was so simple?

So I didn't argue when we entered the bedroom and my mother rummaged through our clothes trunk. She sniffed disparagingly over the two surcoats, four kirtles and four chemises Bella and I shared.

'You won't need any of these, dear,' she said. 'Is there anything you truly value?' Her tone made it clear she thought there was nothing in the room I should want.

I thought about the copy of *Morte d'Arthur* my godfather, William Caxton, had given me. But Bella would be able to sell it, so I simply shook my head.

'Only my lute.'

'You won't—'

'Oh, Christopher,' my mother said, wearily, 'let her keep it. I'm tired. I want my daughter home. Let's go.' She threw a cloak over my shoulders and clasped it at my throat.

As we left the Broken Seld, Rollo made a half-hearted protest, but my father overspoke him, threatening, blustering, until Rollo backed away with an apology. Half of me hoped Bella would come. The other hoped she wouldn't.

I paused at the door. 'Rollo?'

'Aye, Nic?' he said.

'Tell Bella what's happened.' My voice cracked. 'And tell her not to come after me. My father has vowed to denounce her to the Church if she does. Make her understand?'

He kissed my cheek. 'Aye, love, I will.'

I took a risk. I had to, for a warning needed to be passed on.

'It was Sarah who sent for them,' I whispered. 'Watch her. And tell Morrigan for me? Tell him, too, that Lovell killed Humphrey Stafford. Tell no-one else.'

'Killed!' Rollo lowered his voice. 'Why Master Morrigan?' His confusion was almost palpable.

'Just do it,' I hissed.

'Come along, Nicola,' my father said. 'It's getting late. We need to get back to the town house.'

And so, I left my small life behind. Much as I had ten years ago, but before I'd been filled with joy, lifted like a major chord. Now resignation and fear dragged me into the depths of darkness; dissonant. But what choice had I?

We walked as briskly as my sightlessness would allow through the crowded, boisterous streets of London. I rarely ventured far from the Broken Seld so could only guess at where we went. Somewhere to the east. Towards the cleaner parts of town where the houses were undoubtedly larger, the alleys wider, the money piled higher. Father must have bought or rented a house in London.

The street grew steeper and I stumbled on ruts and potholes. My father's strong grip held me relentlessly upright. Rain splashed and thunder rolled. Mud soaked into my patched and holed shoes. I tucked the lute under the cloak and prayed it would survive the cold and wet.

By the time we reached our destination, I was shivering and drenched.

Mother hustled us into a house, warm and redolent of roasting meats. The door closed behind me, shutting out the bleak, beggarly world I'd spent the last ten years surviving. Now I was back amongst the privileged people of my own class and I should be grateful. But all I wanted to do was cry.

Mother led me up a steep flight of stairs and into a chamber. Underfoot were soft floor coverings and a fire crackled to my left.

'There's someone here you'll be glad to see…meet,' my mother said, smug.

Surely she wasn't presenting me to Sir Edward looking like a beggar off the streets. My kirtle was patched and thin at the elbows. My hair soaked, my skirts splashed with muck. Then again, it might discourage him.

'Help her bathe, Katherine,' she said, 'and then bring your sister down to supper.' She took my cloak. The door closed behind us and the lock snicked.

'Katherine?' I set the lute on the floor by my feet. 'Little Katherine?'

Cool, slim hands grasped mine. 'Not so little now, Nicki.' She threw her arms around me. 'Oh, I missed you so much! You're so thin. And your clothes are so…so…Oh dear, I've made you cry. I'm sorry.'

I snuffled and held her close, marvelling at her height and the soft fullness of her woman's figure. I held her away.

'You've grown, sister.'

She laughed, light and sweet. 'I was ten when you left. I'm a woman, now.'

'And not married? I'm surprised Father hasn't sold you off.'

There was a long silence. 'I was,' she said, her voice low, sad and distant. 'My husband died in the sweating sickness last year.'

I embraced her again. 'I'm sorry, Kathy. Did you love him?'

I felt her shrug.

'Not really. He was twenty years my senior. A kind man, but distant.' She led me forward. 'But come, let me help you bathe. For I hear Sir Edward Sutton is renewing his suit and will be at supper at the sunset bells.'

I pulled free. 'So soon? I didn't think…' Old horrors strangled the words in my throat. I wrapped my arms around myself. 'Why, Kathy? Why have they dragged me back? Of what possible use am I?'

She was silent a moment, then said, 'Let's sit. There's a chair by your left hand.' Cloth rustled and timber and leather creaked.

I felt for the seat and sank into it.

'Father needs your dowry,' Katherine said, bluntly. 'I don't understand all of it, but the estate rents are down. The only capital is Grandmama's money that was settled on us and is tied up in our dowries. Yours, mine, and Lizzy's. Mine was returned when my husband died. Meg married last year and moved away. Her husband wanted nothing to do with Papa's investments. And Lizzy's not yet fourteen, so she can't marry.'

I laughed bitterly. 'So they are happy to sell me to Edward Sutton. And he, I presume, has agreed to invest my money in Father's plan. Oh! I *hate* them. I hate them both.' My fingers curled into my palms and dug deep. The pain distracted me from the hurt I'd buried deep in my stomach and tried so hard to forget in Isabella's love.

Isabella. Her future still lay in my hands. If I refused to marry Edward, Father would make good on his threat. He was a man of his word. I covered my face. The scrap of silk still shrouded my eyes and I tore it off. The darkness didn't lighten—neither for my eyes, nor my heart.

How could I sell myself to a man like Edward Sutton? But I was helpless to prevent it. Helpless to stop my father. Helpless and drowning in blackness.

Or not. I raised my head.

Perhaps there was another way. But did I dare? I had to. Father had left me no choice.

'Kathy, help me bathe and dress?' I rose.

She joined me, her hand soft on my arm. 'Of course. We're much of a size. I have a green surcoat that would be lovely on you.'

'Then there's a letter I need you to write.'

The Vespers bells rang. We had an hour before I must confront Sir Edward again.

Bells farewelled the sun just as Kathy and I descended into the great hall. I hesitated on the last step. Kathy squeezed my hand.

'It's alright, Nicki. I'm with you.'

'Is Sir Edward here?' I whispered. Sickness burned in my belly and my stomach roiled. I couldn't do it. How could I possibly stand against him and my father, both?

'He's here,' she murmured. 'With Mother and Father. They approach. Ware.'

I gripped her fingers so hard she protested. Footsteps, quick and assured, marched across the stone floor.
Kathy withdrew and I stood, alone, helpless, in darkness and a jumble of unwanted memories.

'Nicola,' Edward's smooth voice broke through my stasis and I raised my chin. 'Still so lovely.' He took my left hand and pulled me closer.

I stepped in, snatched out my belt-knife and pressed it against his throat.

'Nicola!' My father's shock was echoed by my mother's horrified cry.

I ignored them. 'You will take your hands off me, Sir Edward.

And touch me again you will not. For if you do, I'll draw this blade across your throat, I promise.'

I could feel his heart racing and it gave me pleasure to know he feared me, even if it was only a little. He released me, moved back and laughed.

'What a spit-fire you've become,' he said. 'I shall enjoy our wedding night. Come, Sir Willoughby. Let's go to supper and finish the negotiations.'

'There will be no negotiations, Father,' I snapped.

'Nicola,' he said. 'Think of Isabella.'

'I am. And I'm thinking of myself, this time.' I kept my dagger ready. 'Ten years ago, you tried to sell me to this…devilspawn. Did you never wonder why I ran away?'

'You ran away with…with *her*.' My mother spat the word like a curse.

'No,' I said. 'I ran away *from* him. Neither of you protected me. Bella did.'

'Protected you?' My mother's question fell into the silence. 'I…I don't understand.'

Edward made a scornful noise. 'A girl's silliness, my lady. We were betrothed. She shrank from my touch. I merely schooled her.'

I lifted my dagger again. 'You *raped* me, you whoreson. In my own house. And my father wouldn't hear when I told him. *That's* why I ran.'

A loud knocking fell on the door. A voice, raised in anger, called my name. I smiled.

'Christopher?' My mother's sharp question. 'Is that true? You never told me. Nicola, dear I—'

'Kathy?' I cut Mother off, for I couldn't give in to the hurt in her voice or I would lose all power. One chance is all I had. One bargaining chip. 'Kathy, give Father the letter.' Stiff vellum crinkled.

'What's this?' my father blustered.

'That letter gives you total control of my dowry, Father,' I said. 'Do as you wish with it. The second copy is for you to sign. By agreeing, you keep my money and give up all ties to me and you agree to leave me and Bella alone. Sign it and the money's yours. Don't sign and I'll kill Edward the minute he lays a hand on me. Yours is the choice, now.'

The front door rattled and Bella's voice broke the silence, strident and rage-filled.

'I'd be quick, Father,' I said. 'Bella's not known for her calm temperament.'

'To Hell with you, then, girl,' he snarled. 'Get out of my house.'

'With pleasure,' I replied.

Kathy took my hand and led me to the door, to my love, and to freedom.

19. Of a Demon that is Dreaming

Sarah Clark, 43
Housekeeper at the Broken Seld
Chepe Syed, London,

Monday (early morning), 25th September, 1486

I chopped and the head fell to ground. Blood spurted and the Hellborn animal kicked in my hand. I hated it when they did that. I grabbed the chicken's scaly feet and shoved the flopping bird at my doltish son, George.

'Ere. Go'n pluck'n draw this thing quicksmart. Giblets to the dogs.' I squinted at the brightening sky and wiped bloodied hands on my apron. 'Be dawn soon. Gotta get the pottage on. House'll be up and hungry. Too many guests, if'n you ask me.' I straightened and pressed at my aching ribs. 'Rollo never asks me, though, does he? Just crams em in, up to the rafters, without a by-your-leave or any warning. After all, I'm only the Broken Seld's housekeeper. No-one important.'

George said nothing, as usual. He turned dull brown eyes on me, yanked great handfuls of feathers from the dead bird and scattered them about the back yard like snow.

I whacked him about the ear. 'Oi! Makin a mess. Feathers in the bag over there and we'll use em for pillows and such.'

He did, carefully collecting every feather and putting it away. I left him to it. He was safe enough if told what to do and kept away from sharp things or fires. I took the huge kitchen knife with me and limped back inside. Every breath hurt.

Might have to get Thomasine to check for broken ribs. Wouldn't be the first time. But there'd be no chance today. Not with all the guests. No one would care how much pain I was in. Only that they got fed and had candles and clean linen.

Which reminded me. Had to send a girl to collect the linens from

Griselda Moor's laundry, and to Dorothy Jacobson's shop for more candles. Lord Lovell insisted on beeswax candles in his room and went through six or seven a day. Expensive, he was. And no telling when he'd pay the bill. Rollo hadn't the sense to see the man was trouble with a stick up his arse. Never listened to me.

I pushed through the low door and into the kitchen. Mary and Beth were up, finally. Lazy things they were. Rollo'd hired them for their looks more'n their smarts. All tits and hair, both of them.

But they cleaned floors and rooms alright and gave me a goodly portion of the money they took for being friendly with the male guests, so we all rubbed along well enough.

'Oi, Mary, you stoke up that fire and get the water heating. Beth go out back. Get some leeks and broadbeans from the garden and start chopping. Keep an eye on our George, too.'

Beth hurried out the back door.

The big kitchen was stifling with its low, dark ceiling and two brick fireplaces. One big enough to roast a deer—as if Rollo'd ever get the chance to feed royalty with venison.

On one of the long oak tables, Mary had dough lined up, ready for baking in the hearth-oven next to the smaller fire. Three loaves of good white were already baked.

She added wood to the fire and went back to kneading. I scowled. No rye bread. Not with the St Anthony's Fire bringing God's wrath to London. The healer woman Alistair Morrigan knew said rye was the cause.

I pursed my lips. Morrigan, I didn't trust. Or the healer either. But Calain Gilmore had backed her, so I had to listen. I patted my wild hair back into order and rolled down my sleeves to cover the bruises on my arm. A woman could depend on someone like Master Gilmore. So calm. So polite. So gentle. He'd never raise a hand to his wife, that was certain.

I touched the bruise under my eye and hissed. No point in dwelling. God had punished me for marrying an oaf. But maybe He'd shown me a way out.

'Oi, Mary? Any of that roast pig left from last night?' Rollo'd had me go all-out to celebrate the christening. But if I knew Mary, she'd hidden some away. We all did. I wanted her portion for Master Gilmore's breakfast. Mine, I'd eat later.

Mary's pale blue eyes slid from mine then she sighed and nodded. From inside a pot on a shelf, she pulled out a linen-wrapped lump and passed it over. When she returned to kneading, she thumped the dough like it was a wilful child.

I cut the meat into slices, tore off half the white loaf and laid both on one of our new wooden trenchers. I added a hunk of goat's cheese to the plate and poured a mug of fresh-brewed ale. Then I untied my apron, washed my bloodied hands in a basin of water and retied my hair neatly. There wasn't much I could do about the faded grey of my patched kirtle, but at least I was tidy.

When Mary's back was turned, I took a deep draft of the ale, wiped my mouth and refilled the mug.

'I'll take this up to Master Calain. He's always up early.' I left afore Mary could reply.

At the top of the stair I paused and listened at Bella and Nicola's door. No sound. I smiled. Good riddance to Nicola Willoughby. Always playing the helpless little girl because she was sightless and pretty with her long dark hair. Ungodly, the pair of them. Living together like that. And Rollo turning a blind eye. I didn't regret sending the messenger to the Baron to come and get his daughter. Someone had to help her find God again. Women were meant to marry men, serve men. That was our lot.

I knocked on Master Gilmore's door and entered at his call. I carefully pulled back my shoulders to show off my tits—still firm and full, even after two brats—and smiled through the stab in my ribs.

'Master Gilmore I brought you—oh! Beggin your pardon, sir.' I bobbed a curtsey. 'Didn't know you had Master Morrigan with you. I'll come back.'

Calain smiled in that easy, gentlemanly way he had and waved toward his desk. 'Nay, good Sarah. Prithee, put the tray there. But be so kind as to bring an extra pot of ale? We'll share the bread and meat. Most kind of you, indeed.'

Disappointment fisted in my stomach but I hid it, feeling Morrigan's cool gaze on me each step. He didn't like me, nor I, him. Not since the first day when he'd found me taking two bottles of Rollo's new wine, three loaves of bread and a handful of farthings home. He'd said nothing, just raised his thin brows. And he hadn't told Rollo or I'd know it. No, he held it over my head, waiting. But for what?

I slid the food onto the desk and fussed with straightening the bed until I couldn't delay any longer. Morrigan wasn't going to leave. The men stayed silent while I was in the room but Calain nodded, gracious-like when I curtseyed and left.

Shutting the door, I glanced about the dark landing, and put my ear to the keyhole. There had to be something I could find out about Morrigan that would stop him telling on me. I worked hard running this place and Rollo didn't pay what I deserved. The wine and bread was…perks. The money was important. And if I lost the job, I'd feel the back of my husband's hand again.

I quaked. No. I'd find a way. When Calain left London, I aimed to be with him. He needed a woman to care for him. And the way he looked at me…My nethers throbbed and I shivered.

'We must bide our time, Calain,' Morrigan said in that soft drawl he put on. Footsteps creaked across the wood floor. 'Tomorrow night. That's the moment.'

'You do have a flair for the dramatic, I'll allow that. But we don't yet know all his plans,' Calain's deep voice rumbled. 'He still hides much and even I cannot read him, so strong are his shields. And that message from the Willoughby girl. It troubles me.'

'You worry to excess.' Morrigan chuckled. 'Lovell suspected Humphrey with good reason. Stafford's death is no loss and it evens our odds.'

'Not as much as you'd think,' Calain returned. 'Lovell has more followers than we realised. We have no way of knowing how many will attend. An unknown number of seasoned fighters? Too much could go wrong.'

Morrigan laughed again. 'Trust me, Calain. You underestimate my people. Rest easy.'

A door opened further along the hall and I scurried away, my heart a-fluttering. When I got back to the kitchen I sent Beth up with the extra ale, then told her to go off to Dorothy's for the candles. Then I sat with my aching feet up on a stool and drank a long mug of ginger hum.

What was Morrigan on about? And Lovell? It was clear the pair of them were up to no good and Calain had been dragged into something against his will. How could I get him away from their bad influence? If I could only get him to *see* how much he needed me. Perhaps I could sway him to get out of London before whatever Morrigan was planning happened?

Or… If I could prove to Lovell that Morrigan had turned on him, then their little plan—whatever it was—would fall apart and Calain would have to leave town.

Yes. So now I needed to find something to use against Morrigan. Something that would stop him telling Rollo of my theft, as well. Kill two birds, so to speak. But what?

I poured myself another mug of hum. The warm smell of baking bread and of chicken soup made my stomach rumble. I helped myself to a slab of bread and spread it thickly with butter and honey. Munching, I stared into the fire.

The kitchen door swung open so hard it cracked against the timber panelling and I jumped.

'Lordy, Rollo!' I sprayed crumbs and brushed them off my skirt. 'Don't you know how to enter a room quietly?'

The smile fell away from his round face and his beady dark eyes glared at me. 'It's my inn, woman. I'll enter a room how I please. I've a bone to pick with you, anyway.'

I looked sharpish at Mary. She'd paused in her kneading. I didn't hold with having a set-to in front of the servants.

'Oi, Mary, take the dirty linen over to Griselda's laundry and pick up the clean. Finish the bread when you get back.'

She left the room with a quick backward glance.

I folded my arms. 'What's got you in a lather, then?'

Rollo towered over me. I tried not to shrink but he was solid, like my husband. With hands like dinner plates. I heaved to my feet, trying to make myself taller.

He wagged a thick finger at me. 'Young Nicola told me you'd sent a message to her father. He came and took her away yesterday.'

I shrugged and put the bread-making table between us. 'So? Her living with Bella was unGodly, and you know it.' I pounded the dough with a fist. 'She needs a husband to control her.'

'Not for us to judge,' he snapped. 'It's between them and God. She's a good girl. You're lucky she came back alright last night or I'd be sending you about your business right now.'

I gaped. 'She came back?'

He poured himself an ale. 'Some deal she struck with her father. I don't know all of it.' He pointed. 'With the house so full I need you, but you leave those girls alone, you hear me? Anything happens and I'll send you packing, make no mistake.'

I ground my teeth and slapped the dough onto the table. 'Aye.'

He nodded and headed for the door, then paused with one hand on the bolt. 'One more thing. The constables found Humphrey Stafford's body in the alley outside last night. Knifed in the heart.'

Dough squeezed cool between my fingers and I stilled, waiting for more. Rollo cleared his throat. 'They'll be coming to ask questions of us and the guests today. Trying to find out who did it.'

'And? Nothing to do with me.'

His eyes slid off mine. 'Keep them away from Nicola. Tell them whatever you have to. That she was away. That she's sick. Make sure they don't talk to her. Got it?'

'Aye,' I repeated, pulling my mouth down.

'And keep a watch on Mary and Beth.' He glowered. 'I'm sure someone's stealing coins.'

The door slammed behind him and I stared off into nothing. Well, this could be useful. Nicola Willoughby must know something about Stafford's death and Rollo was protecting her. And Morrigan clearly knew something, too.

I turned his words to Calain over in my mind. Did he mean that Lovell had killed Stafford? Or had Morrigan killed on Lovell's orders?

Well, one of them did it, and that was a useful tidbit to know. Now, what to do with it?

The answer struck me like an angel's voice in my head and I

smiled. Yes. That would do. In one move I could be rid of Morrigan, Nicola and maybe Lovell as well. That would leave Calain to me.

I dusted flour off my hands.

The Prime bells rang and guests bestirred themselves.

No time now with both Mary and Beth away. I'd have to tend to the guests myself and try to catch Lovell alone, later. I stirred the pottage. The chicken's headless carcass, stripped of its meat, rose to the top then sank again out of sight.

In the end, it was near to Compline in the evening before I finally caught Lovell without Morrigan or his other hangers-on around. The front room was packed, as usual. Louts and drunkards the lot of them. Laughing and carrying on. Layabouts too willing to spend money on ale rather than give it to their wives at home. Wives who needed coin to feed their brats, and needed a husband who'd do more than stagger home drunk and yelling.

Nicola and Bella played some tune or other in the corner, both right smug. Bella sent me a glare but I curled a lip and ignored her.

I caught Lovell as he came back into the inn from the back-yard privy. He ducked to enter the low back door. I stepped out from the shadows and curtseyed. My mouth went dry.

'M'lord,' I whispered. 'I've something to tell you.'

He looked me over and lifted a pomander to his nose. I dug my nails into my palms.

'Indeed?' he drawled. 'Speak quickly, woman. I've business to attend to.'

'Aye, m'lord,' I said. 'It's about your business I need to talk.'

He stilled. 'What, pray, could someone like you know of my business, wench?'

I pressed my lips together. I must speak nice, now. For Calain and for me. So we could be together and get out of this cesspit city.

'I overheard Master Morrigan talking to that blind musician girl, Nicola,' I said. 'They were saying something about Master Stafford. The one the constables found in the alley, I mean.'

Lovell stiffened. One hand dropped to his dagger and I shrank back.

'I didn't hear much, m'lord,' I blurted. 'Nicola sounded worried. Master Morrigan thanked her and told her not to be afeared. That he'd protect her against you. That he had something planned. I thought you should know.' I finished in a rush as the vicious glint in his eye deepened.

Five breaths we stood there in the dark passageway, the bawdy music and shouts from the front room the only noise. A great roar of laughter shook the inn and Rollo stuck his head around the corner. Lovell stepped back into the shadows of the storage room door.

'Sarah!' Rollo squinted and I scurried to his side, relieved to be away from Lovell's blade.

'Aye?'

'Mix up more ginger hum,' he said, rubbing his hands together. 'Looks like it could be another good night. Hopefully this queen'll pop out a babe every year.'

I shrugged. Queens and kings. Who cared? If I had my way I'd be long gone by the time the next royal brat was born.

In the kitchen, I tapped a barrel of wine and poured a third into the bung-hole of a half-empty barrel of ale. Stirred in some ginger and sent Mary out to the well to draw water. We topped up the hum with water. Together we carried it out to the main room and heaved it onto the stand behind the serving bench.

Rollo beamed and set a mug under the spigot.

I slid a look around the room. There, in the far corner. Lovell had

Morrigan backed up against the wall. Thomas Stafford and the boy, Richard Clinton, stood protecting their lord, glowering at the room as if daring anyone to interfere. Calain hovered nearby, his gaze flicking between Morrigan and Lovell.

I handed Rollo another five mugs. When they were full, I weaved through the crowd and carried them over to Lovell's table. Hum helped loosen a man's tongue and fire up his temper. That, I knew. I offered one to Calain, who waved it aside, his whole focus on the lord. Lovell's men accepted and quaffed theirs down. I set the other three on the table and backed up a few steps, but not too far.

'Twice, now,' Lovell growled. 'Twice your name has come up as that of a traitor.' He slid his dagger free of its sheath and touched the tip against Morrigan's throat. 'What say you, Morrigan? You say you've been working to my ends, but where's the evidence? I have my seal-ring back, but through no effort of yours. And I've still no certain way of getting to Elizabeth's rooms tomorrow night, or to the babe, *or* to the boy.'

'But you have, my lord,' Morrigan said, his throat working. He leaned back from the knife. 'You know the entrance to the tower where the boy is kept. You'll be at the feast with some of your men. We'll find a way to the…Elizabeth's chambers, I assure you. I have people inside working on that. Tell me who else will be there for you and I might be able to use them, too.'

I chewed on my lip. No good would come if Morrigan convinced Lovell of his honesty. I would still be at Morrigan's mercy. He could tell Rollo of my thefts any time. I needed more money to travel. A few more nights like this, skimming coin from Rollo's box, and I'd be right. *We'd* be right.

A quick glance at Calain showed him watching me with those eyes the colour of my grey kirtle and a frown on his smooth forehead.

I smiled then lowered my gaze and started gathering up empty mugs from a table nearby.

Lovell's eyes narrowed, still focussed on Morrigan. 'You've asked me more than once now to tell you who else supports me. Is that your game? Are you a traitor, Morrigan?'

Calain exchanged a quick look with Morrigan, who sighed. His head came up and he curled a lip.

'Believe what you will, my lord,' Morrigan said.

'I believe,' Lovell drawled, 'that many of my plans have gone awry since you joined us. I believe that you may not be as loyal as you say. I believe I was wise to put more plans in place than any one person knows of.' He switched to Calain. 'And you vouched for him. Can I trust you?'

'Of course, my lord.' Calain bowed.

'Easily said.' Lovell picked up a mug of hum and downed it. Then he angled the empty mug toward Calain. 'Prove it. Take Morrigan into the storeroom at the back. Dispose of him. We'll remove the body later. The blind girl I'll take care of myself.' His mouth curved into a cold smile.

'My lord!' Calain's eyes widened.

I slipped away to where Bella and Nicola sat.

'Oi! My lord wishes for a dance tune,' I snapped. 'Get everyone on their feet and he'll make it worth your while.'

Bella glared at me. 'Fine.' She put her lute aside and picked up the recorder. Nicola followed her lead and the drinkers in the room let out a whoop. Beth and Mary hauled men to their feet. More joined in, stomping and shouting.

Under cover of the sound and movement, Calain led Morrigan toward the back of the inn. I followed, easing from shadow to shadow.

Morrigan didn't resist and Calain pushed him into the storage room, closing the door. I crouched, listening at the keyhole. This would bind him to me. Morrigan would be dead. Lovell would send Nicola to Hell. Calain would show my lord he could be trusted and I would know both men's secrets.

Calain would take me away. But I would turn Lovell over to the constables. Send them a message when we were gone. He could take the blame for Morrigan's murder, too. Calain need never know, and he would be free. I could see our lives together, already. Happy. Safe.

'You must do it, Calain.' Morrigan's voice was so quiet I almost missed his words.

'I cannot,' Calain replied. 'You know I cannot. There's not enough forest here.'

'But it's crucial. I must die and he must see my death. Otherwise it's all been for naught.'

'God's blood, Morrigan, you ask too much.'

There was a soft laugh and a rustle of cloth. 'Then go, my friend. Send Stafford. You've no stomach for politics, yet.'

'Damn you to Hell, Morrigan,' Calain growled. Footsteps scuffed on dirt.

The bells for Compline rang. I leapt away from the door as it opened and Calain stalked toward the front room. His hands and blade were clean. No! He had to do the task Lovell had set or all was lost. Lovell must see the body and trust Calain. Otherwise the lord might kill Calain, too.

I ran to the kitchen, snatched up the kitchen knife and a taper and lit a candle. Then I hurried back, flung the storage room door open and thrust the candle into the darkness. The dim light clawed at the shadows. The place smelled musty and damp after the rain yesterday.

'Ah,' a soft voice spoke from the darkness and I jumped. 'There you are, Sarah.' Alistair Morrigan leaned against a stack of old barrels, arms folded. His angular face looked more resigned than afeared.

I gripped my big kitchen knife more tightly. He wasn't armed, but he was taller and stronger than me.

He tilted his head. 'I wasn't sure what to do with you,' he said calmly. 'But I'm glad, now, you've called in. For someone has to undertake this task and Calain was always going to be too squeamish.'

I gasped and took a back step.

Morrigan straightened and spread his long arms wide. 'Well, go ahead, then. Kill me.'

I hesitated, gripping the knife so tight my bones ached.

He stepped forward. 'Come on. It must be done. To protect Calain. That's why you're here, isn't it?' He moved closer, still. 'Best make it quick. Lovell's demanding to see my body and he's getting suspicious because Calain is stalling. Any moment he'll come down that passageway.' He pointed behind me.

I resisted turning to look. He was probably trying to trick me. The knife handle was slippery in my palm and my heart beat like a fist against my ribs.

Morrigan moved closer again. He was close enough for me to strike, but I didn't. His eyes held something I'd never thought to see: understanding, sympathy; love, even.

'I know what needs to be done, Sarah.' He raised his right hand, palm open. 'I know what will make you do it. But I'd rather not. Please? Use the knife.'

Still, I hesitated.

He grimaced. 'Very well.' His hand struck me hard across the cheek. A stinging slap that made my eyes water.

I tasted hot metal in my mouth and spat blood to the dirt floor. White rage blossomed from my belly and burst as a scream from my throat. I thrust the knife. Once. Twice, the blade sank deep into

Morrigan's stomach. He gave a horrible, gurgling gasp and folded in the middle.

I yanked the blade out, ready to drive it deep again if he came at me. But he collapsed to his knees, blood blackening his brown surcoat. He fell onto his side, fingers pressed to the wound.

The rage in me slipped away to cold realisation. I stood over him, wanting to vomit, shaking from head to toe.

'Go,' he whispered. 'Clean the knife. Let…Lovell and Calain find me.'

I sank to my knees beside him and crossed myself. 'Oh, Lord! What have I done?'

'Only what was… necessary,' he gasped. 'Go, now. You needed to do this. For yourself, for Calain. Lovell needs to… trust him. You need to trust yourself. Don't ruin it… by staying.' His eyes fixed on mine and I had no choice.

I stood, though I hadn't meant to. I turned away, though I tried to stay. I left and closed the door behind, though I fought against the urge.

When my mind cleared, I stood in the kitchen, knife cleaned and tucked away in its place, hands cleaned, cloak over my shoulders as though I was ready to go home.

Home. To the miserable shithole cottage with its leaky roof and rat-eaten furniture. To my bed-ridden mother-in-law whose sharp tongue cut open her son's heart each time they spoke. To my husband who took that anger out on me each time he drank. Every day. Every time.

I looked again at my hands. I shivered and pushed aside the memory of Morrigan's blood pumping out. Alistair Morrigan was bigger and stronger than my husband. My cheek still stung from the blow. Yet the knife had slid into his belly, easy.

Perhaps that's what he meant by saying I needed to do it. Perhaps it wasn't enough just to leave my husband.

I picked up the kitchen knife again and tucked it into my belt, hidden beneath my cloak.

Then I went home.

20. And the Lamplight O'er Her Streaming

Dorothy Jacobson, 36
Candlemaker
Bred Street, London,

Monday (midday) 25th September, 1486

'I suppose I must go back.' I rose from the nuncheon table and brushed breadcrumbs off my apron. The midday sun peeked from behind thin clouds and flooded the kitchen with warm golden light.

Nick slid an arm around my waist and drew me onto his knee. He nuzzled into my neck and groaned. Then he smiled at me, his dark-as-night eyes dancing like candlelight.

'Don't go, Dot, my sweet.' He twirled one of my untamable black curls around his lean finger. 'Leave the candle shop closed. I'll shut the workshop and finish the cabinet tomorrow. Let's take the afternoon off.' He grinned. 'We haven't done that since before Luke was born.'

'And that's because those afternoons are the *reason* Luke was born.' I kissed him to take away the sting. 'You know I'd stay if I could, love, but I have that big order for beeswax candles to fill for the Tower. The christening feast is tomorrow night and I've still got a hundred candles to make. Lucky Emma Turner called in to deliver a new batch of wax on Saturday afternoon.'

Nick grimaced and set me aside. 'Aye. And who was that strange fellow with her? Handsome. Tall and thin with gold skin.'

I shrugged one shoulder. 'A friend of hers. Alistair something. He wants me to make some special sealing wax.'

'Ah.' With a rueful laugh, Nick kissed my cheek. 'I'm a jealous fellow, aren't I? Well, I should finish the cabinet.' He shook his head, blond curls slipping over his shoulder. 'Luke's right. The nobles love young Reina's drawings—as long as I don't let on they're by a woman. I'll take the latest pattern over to Lady Derby. If she likes them…' he lifted me by the waist and swung me around '…we could be on our way to making furniture for her son. King Henry's cabinetmaker. What say you? Fancy a bigger shop and a bigger house?'

I patted his cheek. 'Nay, love. I'faith I like my little candle shop. Twould be too much work and discord to move, now.'

He kissed me. 'Aye, sweeting. You're a creature of habit, aren't you? And a good thing that is.'

I fiddled with the ties on my apron. 'I hear Lady Derby is quite lovely.'

Nick guffawed. 'Lady Derby is forty-five if she's a day.'

'Not so old,' I snapped. 'I'm thirty-six and you're forty-two. Or had you forgotten?'

He sobered and slid his fingers into my hair. He smiled, a little sadly. 'You've no cause to fear. I'm not leaving you for another woman. I'd never betray you.'

I lowered my gaze and pulled away. 'Don't mind me. I'm out of sorts today, what with Luke a-courting young Reina Hayward. Makes me feel old. And she's such a thoughtless, feckless child. Her head's stuffed with ambition and nonsense.'

'But Luke loves her. Since they were littleuns under my feet in the workshop. And when a man loves a woman that much, she can do no wrong.'

'Aye, certes. But I misdoubt me that she loves him. He'll get hurt. If they marry and someone better comes along she'll—' My throat constricted and heat burned in my cheeks. I headed for the stairs.

'Dorothy?' Nick called after me.

'Tis naught, husband,' I flung over my shoulder. 'I must get back to the shop. I'll see you at supper.' I hurried downstairs, into the shop at the front of the house.

With the door closed, windows shuttered and candles doused, the room was dark and stuffy, smelling of rancid animal fat, walnut, and honey.

I stood in the middle of the room, sickness churning in my stomach. Still, after all this time? Seventeen years, and every day remembering, awaiting discovery. Would time never dull the guilt? So many moments I'd thought to tell him and lost courage. The way he would look at me… I couldn't hurt him so. Or lose him. No, I'd made the right choice. Father Greene had absolved me.

I flung open the door and shutters, letting light chase away darkness. With a cloth, I dusted the bronze and steel chandeliers hanging from the ceiling, even though I'd done them only on Saturday.

Methodically, I checked the shelves: clay oil-lanterns in neat rows; the candles arranged; tallow the largest pile, for they were the cheapest. The costly beeswax ones behind the counter. Great barrels of oils lined one wall. Walnut, olive, castor, flax.

Finally settled again, I moved into the back room and added wood to the little hearth-fire I used for melting wax. I became immersed in the process. Melting the wax. Dipping the braided-cotton wicks over and over and over for the long candles. Pouring wax into little pots for the short candles.

The work soothed my stretched nerves and time flew past. When the Nones bells rang, I had ten more candles done for the feast.

The shop-bell tinkled, brassy and thin after the deep church bells. I stretched out my aching lower back.

'Anon! I'll be right out.' No reply, so I stripped off my work apron and hurried into the front room.

A man stood in the doorway, haloed by the afternoon sunlight.

Unevenly cut dark hair feathered around his head. His face was in shadow, but light glinted off the steel sword at his hip—and drew his outline in darkness on the stone floor.

'Dorothy.' His deep voice blazed into my soul.

'T-Thomas?'

He stepped into the shop-candles' warm glow and my heart lurched. Thomas Stafford. The years fell away. I was, again, a breathless young woman, dazzled by the young noble who came a-courting when my husband was away at war.

'Well, little Dot.' His gaze swept from my burgundy skirts to my loose hair and warmth burned up my neck. 'Lovely as ever.'

I curtseyed to cover my tangled tongue.

Thomas glanced around my orderly shop. 'You made the business work. Well done.'

'Gramercy, sir,' I muttered. I tried to still the flicker-jumping of my heart. What did he want of me after all this time?

'Sir, is it, then?' Thomas stepped closer. 'Once it was Thomas or dearheart, as I recall.'

I glanced uneasily over my shoulder. At the back of the house, Nick and Luke laboured together in their joinery workshop. If one of them should come out… I moved behind the counter.

'Sir,' I repeated. 'How can I help?'

Those sin-dark eyes measured me for a long time. And that mouth…oh, that mouth. His hair was touched with grey, now, for he must be close to fifty. But it only made him more handsome.

Finally, he opened the purse dangling at his belt. 'Very well. I do need your help.'

I folded my arms. 'After all this time, that's all you have to say to me?'

'What would you have me say? I'm sorry?' He scraped strong

fingers through his hair. 'For I have regretted leaving you every day of the last seventeen years.'

I clasped my hands together until the knuckles whitened. 'So why did you? I would have followed you anywhere.'

Thomas sighed and reached toward me. I jerked back.

'I know you would have, doveling.'

I flinched at the pet name. 'So why, then? I was with child. *Your* child. I thought Nick was dead in the battle at Edgecote Moor against King Edward. I was a widow. Why did you leave me?'

'Ah! Dot-love.' His brow furrowed. 'My father had arranged a marriage for me. A powerful Yorkist family. I had no money but his. I had no choice. You must understand.'

I unclamped my fingers and smoothed my skirt. 'Certes. We always have choices, Thomas. You chose a powerful wife with money over a commoner who loved you. I understand, alright.' And, in a way, I did. It was the lucky woman who got her choice of husband, or to have one she loved. More often she got neither. The hurt had long since faded to an ache that still tasted of bitter guilt.

'For what it's worth,' he said, his voice quiet and rough, 'I am sorry. I still care for you, Dot.' He cleared his throat. 'What of the child?'

'None of your business, Thomas Stafford,' I said. 'You gave up the right to knowing seventeen years ago. My husband came home. I love him and I'll not have you ruin my life again. Go.'

He sighed and nodded. 'And go I shall, doveling. But I need your help, first.' He placed a small, cream clay phial on the bench and tapped it.

'I don't understand. I sell lamps. What's this?'

Thomas moved forward. His breath, sweet with ginger and wine, brushed my cheek. My thighs melted and heat pooled in my nethers.

'I believe,' he murmured, his gaze dropping to my bosom, 'that you're making candles for Prince Arthur's christening feast.'

'Certes.' I leaned back. 'Tis true.'

He tapped the ceramic again. 'Then all you need do is soak ten wicks in this before you set them in the wax. Then mix what's left with the candlewax. Nothing else. Set those candles aside for the king and queen's own use.'

I picked up the phial. 'What's in it?'

Yanking open his belt-purse, he placed a gold angel-noble on the counter and slid it toward me. 'It doesn't matter.'

I studied the coin's sheen in the afternoon light. Worth six shillings and eight pence. More than I'd usually make in a fortnight. I could set it aside; save it for Luke when he married.

With a shudder, I shoved it away. 'Keep your blood money, Thomas. Secret potions for the king's candles?' I glared. 'Your family were always Yorkists. Belike you're trying to poison the king. His son is a York *and* a Lancaster. Why would you kill them that's ending a stupid war?'

His hand curled into a fist and his teeth showed in a grimace. 'You can't understand, woman. The Lancasters took everything. My lands, my wife and child. Everything. Now Humphrey, my brother is dead. Likely by some Lancaster's blade.' He spat to one side, his mouth set grim

My heart contracted at the pain in his face. I touched his hand, lightly. His fingers opened and gripped mine.

'I'm sorry, Thomas. Truly. I liked Humphrey.' I squeezed his fingers. 'But I can't help you poison a king who's our first chance at peace in my lifetime.'

'Dot-sweeting?' Nick pushed open the back door and halted on the threshold. Luke stood close behind, his dark hair a foil to Nick's blond, his shoulders broader than his father's for all he was not yet seventeen.

I snatched my hand from Thomas's and patted at my hair. 'Yes, love?'

Nick's mouth thinned. 'Tis naught. Reina's in the kitchen, hoping to speak with you. I'll tell her you're with a customer.'

'I'll be right there,' I said. 'I wasn't able to help this gentleman and he's about to go.'

Thomas bowed. 'Not quite, Mistress. I still need an oil lamp.' He sauntered over to the shelves and inspected the display.

An awkward silence fell, broken only by the occasional scrape of clay on timber as he picked up and set down one after the other. I managed a small smile at Nick. His eyes were darker than midwinter night as he retreated into the corridor and closed the door.

I sighed. He'd never met Thomas. Never knew of him. But he wasn't a dullard.

Thomas strolled back to the counter, his lips stretched thin. 'So that was Nick, huh? And the boy?'

'My son. Mine and Nick's.' I met his gaze steadily.

One of his brows rose but he said nothing. He placed the gold coin and the cream ceramic phial on the counter again and pushed them both toward me.

'You'll do as I ask, Dot,' he said. His jaw hardened. 'Or I'll tell your husband and son the truth about what happened here seventeen years ago when Nick was at war. You'll be shamed in the stocks for being an adultress; ridiculed in public for all to see. Your head shaved. Paraded in your shift.'

My lungs turned solid as wax in my chest. I leaned heavily on the counter. He didn't love me. Probably never had. I'd been too young and flattered, too full of fire to see. And now he was using that old mistake against me. If he told Nick I would lose the only good things in my life. Nick loved me, but to find I'd hidden an affair would be unforgivable.

In God's eyes, too. I'd always feared confession and penance were not truly enough to absolve me. Seemed I was right. God had more punishment in mind for me.

Help to kill a good king and be branded a traitor and executed if they caught me. Or lose my husband, my son and my business and be cast out as an adulteress.

Shaking, I gathered up the phial and the coin and stowed them away in my belt-purse.

'Get out,' I muttered. 'Now.'

He bowed. 'We'll send someone tomorrow to help carry the candles to the Tower. Just so they don't get lost.'

The door shut behind him. I sank onto the stool behind the counter and buried my head in my arms. Only by gritting my teeth could I prevent the tears from falling.

The back door creaked and I jerked upright, scrubbing at my cheeks.

'Dorothy?' Reina peeped around the corner, her sky-blue eyes wide and flame-gold hair falling in long curls onto her bosom. She wore a plain brown kirtle, but nothing hid her youthful loveliness. 'Am I interrupting?'

'Not at all, child,' I said. My voice came out calm and easy; a far cry from the churning sickness in my gut. 'What can I do for you?'

She held out a shilling and a folded piece of vellum. A letter with the blue wax seal broken open. A second scrap of vellum lay beneath it. Unsealed. 'These are from Master Morrigan.'

I took both and read the scrap, first, stumbling over some of the unfamiliar words.

Dorothy. You'll remember I called on you with Emma Turner on Saturday. Pray reproduce the sealing wax as quickly as you can. We'll require it on the morning of Tuesday 26th. Please deliver it, and the letter, to Eliza Parry by Terce bells.

Yours,

Alistair Morrigan.

Next, I examined the letter with the broken seal. A love letter, containing vague promises of great happiness, to someone named Anne. Signed, in a flourishing way, *Lovell*.

My heart had settled now, though the ceramic phial still hung heavy in my belt purse. I tapped the letters and looked to Reina.

'What do you know of these?'

She blushed. 'I went to see Lord Lovell the other day. At the Broken Seld.' She shook her head. 'I know it was wrong. Pray, don't you lecture me, too. I took the letter and Master Morrigan handed me his note and the coin as I left. I know nothing more but what the letter says.'

Reina had ambitions to be a lady one day. It didn't surprise me that she'd chased after this Lord Lovell. Only that she'd come away with her maidenhead intact—if she had, indeed.

I read the scrap again. 'The blue is an odd shade, but I think I can do it. But who's this Eliza Parry?'

Reina curled a lip. 'Beatrice, my new sister-in-law, is Eliza Parry's daughter.'

'Oh, yes. Luke said William had married. And you don't like her?' I said, neutrally.

She raised a pettish shoulder. 'Oh, Beatrice is no-one special. She's a devoted little mouse of a wife to William. Always pandering to him. Mama thinks she's perfect because yesterday she found money Papa hid and she's helping run the Cahorsin shop now.' She rolled her eyes. 'But Eliza Parry owns a stewhouse. She's a Southwark goose.'

I crossed myself hastily. 'I'm surprised your mama let William marry the daughter, then.'

'Pah,' She sniffed. 'No choice. He married her before we knew.' She touched the vellum. 'But at least she can get this to her mother and we don't have to go. *I'd* certainly never be caught dead over the river.'

She dropped her voice to a whisper. 'They say Eliza Parry used to be the mistress to the old Duke of Clarence, and who knows how many other lords and gentlemen. Even married ones!' She shook her head with the naïve arrogance of youth. 'I don't understand men. I can't imagine a woman ever betraying her husband the way men betray their wives. So easy, they do it!'

Blood drained from my head, leaving me queasy.

'You'd best go, child,' I said. 'I've work to do. Twill take time to match the blue of this sealing wax.' I dug a groat out of my belt-purse, trying not to touch the ceramic phial, and placed the coin into her hand. 'Fetch me some indigo blue colouring from the apothecary?'

She hesitated and I shooed her out. 'Hurry! I have yet to make the rest of the candles for the prince's christening feast.'

Reina cast me a curious look beneath her pale lashes, but dashed out the door, into the bright, noisy street beyond. She wouldn't be gone long, for the apothecary was only a block away on Watelyng Street.

I slid the bolt on the back door and put up the red sign on the front door that meant the shop was closed. For a long time, I stood in the middle of the shop, breathing in the familiar smells of beeswax, tallow, and oils. Then I returned to the back room and pulled the phial from my belt purse.

What choice had I? I couldn't lose Nick and Luke and ruin their lives, too, because I'd been a stupid girl overwhelmed by the attentions of an older nobleman.

Perhaps I could dilute the liquid enough that it wouldn't do any harm when the candles burned. Or perhaps I could *say* I'd mixed it in. But what would Thomas do if his plan didn't work? If the king survived?

I opened the bottle and tipped a drop onto a length of cotton wick. It stained the material the dark purple-grey of heavy twilight. The bitter, earthy fumes caught in my nose. A touch of mint as well. There would be no diluting. I couldn't risk Thomas coming back and threatening my family if it didn't work. My only option was to help him murder the King of England.

Clasping my hands, I offered up a prayer for forgiveness to the Lord. *Lucerna pedibus meis verbum tuum, et lumen semitis meis.* I would have committed two of the deadly sins. How could the Lord forgive that?

With a heavy soul, I tipped the inky liquid into a bowl and dipped in the first wick.

By the time Reina returned, I had the ten wicks done and the remaining liquid mixed in with wax for the candles. My head spun and my mouth was dry. The room seemed unsteady but I didn't stop. There were still eighty candles to complete. Reina offered to help and I accepted reluctantly. I was so dizzy and weary I could barely stay on my feet.

Reina proved to be a quick study and I soon let her pour the bowl-candles alone. While she worked on the ordinary candles, I finished the grey ones. Then I started on Master Morrigan's order. It was the work of moments to mix the apothecary's indigo in with beeswax, Venice turpentine, and larch-tree resin. Three tries produced a seal-wax the same colour as that on the letter. I poured it into two stick-moulds and set it aside to cool.

We worked through until after the Compline bells had fallen silent, Reina occasionally chattering away about silly, girlish things.

'Gramercy, Reina,' I said as we finished the last candles and wrapped them for delivery. 'Certes, I could not have finished without you. Best go home, for your Mama will be fretting.'

The girl studied my face. 'If I may be so bold, Dorothy, you don't seem well. I…' She glanced over her shoulder at the darkened shop. 'I could come back and help tomorrow, if you like? Luke says you throw your own pots to make the clay oil lamps? I'd like to learn, if I may?'

I stared at her long. She'd never shown any interest before. Perhaps her brush with nobility had been as disastrous as mine. But perhaps she had learned her lesson before losing anything truly precious, where I had not.

'Very well. I'faith I could use the help, I think.' I sighed. 'With winter coming tis always hard to keep up with demand. I'll pay you a wage, of course.'

A brilliant smile lit her face. She kissed my cheek, unbolted the back door and skipped away, leaving the room duller and shrouded in gloom. I doused the candles and lamps and sat awhile, thinking.

'Dot-sweeting?' Nick's deep voice broke the dark-silence. He came in, holding a candle so it fell soft and gold on his face and showed the worry there as shadows.

'Aye, lov…Nick.' My throat closed. I loved him. With all my heart I loved him. How stupid I had been to keep secrets from someone so wonderful. But my path was fixed into darkness, now, and I could see no way clear.

He set the candle down and gathered me into his strong arms. Warm smells of wood, smoke, glue and something just…him seeped into my body. But his protection didn't ease the hurt as it normally did. As it had all those years ago when he returned from the dead, to find me weeping for losses I wouldn't explain; yet he'd asked no questions.

'Oh, Nick,' I said, wrapping my arms around his waist. 'I don't deserve you.'

A low chuckle rumbled through his chest. 'I'm no angel, sweeting. Tell me what ails you. Is it that gentleman in the store, earlier?' He swiped a stray hair from my cheek.

I nodded, my throat thick. 'I have to tell you something about him. And me. But I'm afeared.'

'Then you've no cause to fear,' he said softly. 'For I've always known.'

I pushed free. 'Known what?'

He sighed and sank onto the stool behind the counter. 'That you loved someone while I was away fighting for King Edward.' His shoulders drooped. 'That you'd lost a child not long before I returned.'

Hope guttered and I sagged against the counter. 'How…?'

'You know the women around here.' His mouth twisted. 'Nothing stays secret for long.'

'But the child. No-one knew.' He'd known? All this time.

'Laura Kennet,' he said. 'When you were with child with Luke, she attended you and let slip she was worried because you'd lost the other child.'

'But you never said anything,' I whispered. 'Why did you let me carry this burden for so long?'

Nick stood and ran his hands down my arms, clasping my fingers.

'You thought me dead, Dot. I was glad you found solace. I only ever wanted you to be happy.' His thumbs stroked the backs of my hands. 'But the burden was yours and you never asked for my help to carry it. I would have. In a minute. I just didn't know how to tell you without shaming you.'

I threw my arms around his neck and he held me tight, both of us crying for the years of lost closeness.

Then I leaned back. 'Will you help me, now? Thomas has asked me to do something awful. I can't do it. I can't. But I don't know how to gainsay him without endangering you and Luke.'

Nick kissed me, long and loving. 'Of course, sweeting. We'll work it out. Together. You and me. Like always. No more secrets.'

'No more secrets.' A long-held place of lightless fear withered under the glow of his smile.

'Then,' he whispered, 'tell me this one and we'll find a way. I promise.'

Aiki Flinthart

21. Throws Her Shadow on the Floor

Ingaret Leon, 18
Assassin
Chepe Syed, London,

Monday (evening) 25th September, 1486

I crept up behind the small figure and drew my stiletto. She didn't hear and stayed, crouched in the alley, focussed on the Broken Seld

I whispered, 'Heya. Whatcha doing here, sprat?'

The girl jumped, squeaked and turned a glare on me. 'Hush, Ingaret, you scared the life outta me for sure, an I'm busy watching over The Morrigan for my stupid little brother cause Jack's worried about something happening.' She whispered, 'You know Morrigan's a woman, don't ya?'

'Agnes Webb, shut your hole.' I wedged a word in when she paused for breath. 'O course I know. But she's smart to dress like a man, stay'n in the Seld. Now keep your trap shut while I think. I'm here on a job.'

She glared, but quieted. I peered around a barrel and checked the front entrance to the inn. Lights seeped around the edges o the window-shutters, and glowed from oil lanterns o bronze and thin horn that hung on the walls, cast'n odd shadows across the road. I wrinkled my nose. Rollo used rancid fishoil in his lanterns. Cheapskate.

The Compline bells had not long died into silence. I had an hour before the curfew bells sent most folk scurry'n home and the constables and watchmen started hunt'n for those—like me—who spent their most profitable hours roam'n the city after dark.

'Bit late for you to be out, sprat,' I said to Agnes. For me, it was early. I'd just finished a job. A message delivered, for Laura Kennet, to one o the sisters in St Clare Without Aldgate. Midwives were not my normal employer, but times were lean. Assassins weren't needed so much dur'n peacetimes, so I turned my hand to whatever earned a few coins. I was good at gett'n into places unseen, and Laura needed that.

'I'll go before curfew,' Agnes muttered but kept her gaze fixed on the Seld's door.

'Good.' My second job lay inside the Seld. Then there was one more and I could relax for the even'n. But both jobs could be tricky if Agnes was fix'n to get in my way. Morrigan had sent for me to get Nicola and Bella away from the Broken Seld. For some reason she thought tonight was going to be worse than any other night in that rathole inn.

But the late hour meant I'd have to dodge the constables, for they patrolled Chepe Syed like terriers on nights like this. Nights o celebrat'n. Dark-o-the-moon nights. Last thing I wanted was to be thrown into a magistrate's cell. Once was enough. I shuddered at the memory. Still, money was money and I was older and smarter.

Morrigan's second request was to capture someone named Thomas Stafford. Which might be even harder, since I had no idea who that was.

I studied Agnes again. 'Maybe you should go now. I'll keep watch. You don't exactly fit in anymore. Not wear'n that getup.' The little thief wore a rust-coloured kirtle and white chemise, both smell'n o expensive, rose-scented soap and new-dyed wool. Her only weapon was a long dagger stuck into her belt.

'Come to think on it,' I added, 'ain't seen you and Jack about much. Whereya been? Someone made you take a bath, huh? Didn't recognise you.'

'Ha ha.' Cloth'n rustled and her warm arm brushed mine. 'Morrigan took us to live with Olivia Grey, the dressmaker, and we got all new clothes and don't have to thieve no more but I dunno…'

She folded her arms and scuffed a toe.

'Don't know what?' I pulled her back into the shadows, still hold'n my stiletto. We waited until a group o people passed by with their chatter about Prince Arthur's christen'n feast tomorrow night at the Tower. Mostly women. Wear'n beltknives. One skinny guy about eighteen or so, with a rusty shortsword stuffed through his belt. No scabbard. Amateur.

'I just…' Agnes scuffed at the dirt again and yawned hugely. 'I dunno for sure if Olivia even wants me there cause she talks to Jack all the time but of course she never laughs and she hides her face and won't hardly even look at me—'

'Why's she hide her face and not laugh?' I interrupted. She barely left space for a thin blade between words when she got talk'n, so it was the only way to get a thought in. I'd heard of Olivia Grey's skill with a needle, o course. Few folk in London didn't know o her deft touch with silks and laces.

Not my kind o thing, though. I wore a dark, short tunic and dark hose, soft boots, and my stiletto and little one-shot crossbow at my belt. Practical.

'Morrigan said,' Agnes rattled on, 'Olivia's house was burned last year and her face, too, and her daughter that she couldn't save, and now she's sad, but she seems to like Jack, for sure.'

'Ah,' I said. 'Maybe she—'

'Ware!' Agnes hissed.

We both stilled. The Seld's door crashed open and three men staggered out, sing'n someth'n bawdy and off-key. All armed with beltknives but noth'n worse. No threat. Especially not when they were that drunk. Music and the smell o stale beer wafted out the open door.

'I hear Bella and Nicola play'n,' I said. 'And I saw Morrigan.' That was a lie, but I worked best alone and I didn't need to babysit a ten-year-old kid tonight. 'You go home. I'll watch, I promise.'

Agnes hesitated. 'Really promise for sure not a fib to me because you want me out of your way, cause I know you, Ingaret Leon, you live all by yourself, you hide from everyone, you ran away from home years ago, and you kill people for a living, so why should I trust you?'

I snorted. 'Because I also kill people who give me the squits and I ain't killed you yet, have I? When I give my word I mean it. Go.'

'Fine,' she huffed. 'But I wanna a report in the morning or Jack'll get all pouty and try to come and check on Morrigan himself and he's about as useless at hiding as a hungry puppy in a slaughterhouse.'

The Seld's front door swung shut, dull'n the light and noise. I opened my mouth to answer, but stopped and cocked my head.

'Hear that?' I whispered.

Agnes stood stiff and pale like a corpse. 'A woman screamed somewhere out back, this way!' She darted off down the alley beside the Seld, vanish'n into the black.

I cursed and ran after her. I shouldn't have said anyth'n. Just let her get on home while I dealt with it.

My longer legs caught her up as she squirmed through a hole in the back fence. Too small for me. I flipped over the wooden palings and landed lightly in the middle o their lush vegetable patch. Mint broke underfoot. Well, at least that might hide my scent if the constables put the dogs on me tonight.

I grabbed Agnes by the collar and slapped a hand over her mouth when she opened it.

'This is why I work alone. Let me check before you rush in, sprat. Get behind me.' I drew my stiletto then cocked the little crossbow and loaded a bolt. She gulped and retreated, her dagger ready and glint'n in the light o the lantern hung on the privy.

I eased in through the back door. I'd been in the Seld many times, usually through the upper windows, though. I slipped into a shadowed corner full o hang'n clothes. By the rank smell, one o them must be Rollo's cloak. The two doors further along the narrow corridor led to storage rooms. The last one opened into the front hall where everyone was still drink'n and danc'n by the sounds. Their stomp'n vibrated through the floor so I didn't need to be quiet.

The storage room door opened and two men emerged. I only knew the name of one, but I'd seen both around a lot the last few days. Morrigan had hired me to follow both at times. The taller carried a long sword and a dagger. He was huge, grey-eyed, gold-skinned. Not unlike Alistair Morrigan, but broader in the shoulders.

The shorter moved smooth, like a practiced fighter. He carried a ruby-hilted sword and dagger, and smelled of ambergris, earth and arrogance. Lord Lovell.

He spoke first. 'Well done, Calain.' He shut and latched the storage room door. 'I'll set Thomas Stafford here to guard the body until we can move it. Now we need to make sure Morrigan hasn't wrecked any of my plans. Luckily, I didn't entirely trust him so he didn't know all of it. No-one does.'

He slapped Calain's shoulder. 'Come. We'll drink a mug of Rollo's appalling ginger hum to toast the death of a traitor. Then I'll take care of the blind girl.'

'My lord,' Calain said, neutrally, but the muscles in his jaw worked and his eyes glittered in the half-light.

My heart thudded so loud I thought for sure they'd hear me. But they rejoined the crowd in the front room without look'n back so I relaxed my grip on the stiletto.

Was Morrigan dead? Was that what the lord meant? God's fist! If Morrigan was dead I'd be very unhappy. I liked her. And I wouldn't get paid. For this and other things. Speak'n o which: did I still need to capture this Thomas Stafford if Morrigan was dead?

I snuck along the corridor, unlatched the door and ducked inside, leav'n it open a crack for the dim light it gave. The metallic smell o blood hit me and I clenched my teeth. Not a good sign. Under that was the smell o shit. Which either meant a body, relaxed in death, or that someone had their guts cut open. Neither was good.

My eyes adjusted to the gloom and I knelt beside the huddled form on the dirt floor. Definitely a person. Still warm. Blood, sticky on their cloth'n. A woman. The softness of a breast was unmistakable. Was it Morrigan?

The door creaked further open and I raised my crossbow. Agnes squeaked.

'Don't shoot!' She dropped to her knees beside me. 'Morrigan! Morrigan, wake up, you can't be dead, you can't be, I'm sorry, please don't be dead.'

The brighter light through the open door shone on the body. It was Morrigan.

'God's teeth! Dead. We need to get out of here, Ag.'

Agnes glared up at me. 'She's dead and it's all my fault I should have watched closer.' Tears glittered on her cheeks and I patted her shoulder awkwardly. No point in tell'n her she couldn't have saved Morrigan. People blamed themselves for stupid things and there was no sense in it that I could see. But they did it.

A soft groan interrupted Agnes's gulp'n sobs. We both froze, looked at each other, then at the body. Morrigan stirred.

'I gotta get her out.' I hooked my hands under her shoulders.

'No!' Agnes tugged at me. 'Don't move her, we have to get the surgeon and get her fixed up quick.'

'Lackwit,' I snapped. 'They're send'n a guard to watch the room. We need to get her out and lock the door again so they don't know she's gone.' No way I could capture Stafford when he came to set guard. Not and help Morrigan get to safety. I'd have to come back.

'Oh. Well, let me help, then.' She picked up Morrigan's limp arm.

'Help by gett'n out o my way,' I growled.

Wordless for once, Agnes hovered uselessly about while I dragged Morrigan out the door, into the backyard. I went back, locked the door and scuffed away the drag-marks. As I passed the alcove, I snatched up Rollo's cloak.

When I reached Agnes and Morrigan, Agnes had ripped off two more fence palings to make a hole big enough. I crunched through the vegetable patch to her side and paused. By the light o the privy lantern, the green plants were now a withered, dried mess.

Morrigan, seated with her back against the fence, lifted a hand in acknowledgement as I approached. 'My thanks, Ingaret, for your timely rescue.' Her voice was barely a whisper. Fresh blood glistened on her tunic and she shivered though the night was only cool.

I shrugged. 'You owe me money.'

She gave a breathy chuckle. 'I like you, too.'

'We'll get you to Thomasine Smith,' I said.

Morrigan grabbed my wrist so tight my fingers tingled. 'No. Take me to Eliza Parry, in Bankside.'

'You won't make it. Lost too much blood.' I wrapped the cloak about her shoulders and her shiver'n eased.

'Watch me.' Morrigan heaved herself upright, groan'n and clutch'n at her side. 'We'll pass enough gardens on the way that I'll be quite well—or at least, better—by the time we arrive.'

'That makes no sense at all. It's almost curfew. I still have to get your precious Nicola and Bella out. I can't be dragg'n a blind girl, a child, and a half-dead woman through town after curfew. The constables will throw us all in the lockup and *that* you won't survive.'

'We must,' Morrigan said. 'I'll do what I can to turn the constables' thoughts from us. But I'm weak, as you say. I'll wait with Agnes in the alley while you get Nicola and Bella. Go!'

She pressed at her temple and grimaced. 'Lord Lovell is heading toward them, now. But don't kill him. Not yet. There's too many others involved and we need to know everything before we act.'

An urge I couldn't fight turned my feet back toward the Seld. This time I entered through the kitchen door. The kitchen hall lay empty, the hearth-fires reduced to glow'n coals. The housekeeper was nowhere to be seen, which was odd, for she ran the place with an iron hand.

Music twanged from the hall, which meant Bella and Nicola were still there. How to get them out safely was the trick.

I searched the dark kitchen for ideas. Ah. That might work as a distraction. I hefted a quarter-bag o flour over one shoulder and mounted the narrow back staircase to reach the upper floor.

There, I checked the bedchambers first. All dark, but for one, at the back, in which beeswax candles burned bright. The chamber was empty. Probably Lovell's. I was tempted to leave caltrops in his bed, or a few drops o poison in his water jug, but I wasn't be'n paid to kill him and there was no time.

Hopefully Morrigan would survive and hire me for that job.

I eased up to the rail'n overlook'n the hall below. The music came from beneath the stairs, which meant the women were tucked away in that corner, somewhere. Tricky.

I hefted the bag o flour, checked the large room with its high ceil'ns, and tipped about half out onto the floor. Lucky my father had worked in a mill as a boy. I sliced open the bag.

Lovell's lean form appeared amongst the shift'n throng o merrymakers. God's fist! He would reach the women before I did.

Blackbirds Sing p339

Calain, not far behind, glanced up. I pulled back, but a small smile flitted across his lips. He moved up close behind Lovell. The lord stumbled, grabb'n at a drunken lout, but didn't fall. He spun, glar'n at the crowd.

Now I had time.

I hurled the flour into the air. A thin cloud o the fine, white powder turned the air to fog. People laughed and pointed. A few gasped, mouths wide. The smarter ones started runn'n for the door.

The flour drifted lower. Onto a candle-lantern.

I crouched behind a half-wall at the top o the stairs and plugged my ears.

The explosion punched me in the chest and shook the walls. Screams rent the air. I cast a quick look at the fireball, but I'd judged it well. The fire burned itself out before reach'n the ceil'n or walls.

In the hall, people ran, scream'n, push'n, shov'n at each other. Tables overturned. Mugs smashed on the floor. People leapt out through doors and windows, destroy'n the shutters.

I ran halfway down the stairs and vaulted over the rail'n. Bella had Nicola pushed into a corner, protect'n her. I grabbed her arm and she spun, knife drawn.

'Heya. Morrigan sent me to get you out.' I pushed her arm aside. 'Lovell's after Nicola. Let's go.'

Bella hesitated. Behind her, Nicola crouched, clutch'n her lute like a shield, her sightless eyes as pale as the flour dusting her skin and clothes.

'Nic?' Bella asked, not tak'n her attention off me.

'We should go,' Nicola whispered. 'I know what Lovell's capable of. It's not safe here. I trust Morrigan.'

Bella didn't move.

'Your choice,' I said, glanc'n over my shoulder. 'But in about two breaths Lovell's going to look around and come at you. I ain't going to be here.'

'Let's go.' Bella grabbed Nicola's wrist.

Instead o plung'n into the chaos o scream'n, runn'n people, I led the women back up the stairs. Two-thirds o the way up, Lovell spotted us. His face twisted into a snarl and he snatched out his ruby-hilted dagger. With his gaze on me, he plunged the blade into the chest of a man who blocked his way and leapt over the fallen body.

'Faster,' I urged. 'Get to the back stairs. Out through the kitchen. There's a hole in the back fence. Morrigan's in the alley outside.'

Bella passed me. 'What about you?'

'I'll buy you a little time.'

'But—'

'Go!' I pushed her and she stumbled toward the darkened back o the inn, Nicola close behind. Their light steps vanished and I strolled after them, keep'n Lovell in sight.

When he reached the top o the stairs, he drew his sword and stalked toward me. I grinned. Blood hammered in my ears and a thrill tingled from my belly to my nethers. This was more like.

I rounded a corner and dropped half a dozen small bronze caltrops to the shadowed floor. Then I retreated to the top o the kitchen stairs and waited, crossbow ready. A head appeared then vanished. Again.

I waited.

He eased around the corner, stopped and swore. One foot raised, he plucked a caltrop free and flung it aside. It *tinked* off the wall. I took careful aim. The small crossbow wasn't all that accurate, but he was close enough.

I pulled the trigger.

The bolt thwacked into his thigh, buried up to the fletch'n. Lovell let out a guttural roar.

'Stafford! Gilmore!'

Footsteps sounded, hollow on the bedchamber land'n. Someone called his name.

I chuckled. Time to retreat.

Outside in the alley, I found only Morrigan, Bella and a shiver'n Nicola.

'Heya. Where's Agnes?'

'I sent her home.' Morrigan hitched herself off the wall and peered around the corner into the main street. 'Curfew bells will ring soon. We have to go across the river and she wouldn't be safe getting back to Olivia's house.'

'Good. She'd get in the way. Let's go. Put your cloak hood up. Don't want Lovell's men recognis'n you.'

Morrigan nodded.

I inspected Nicola. 'Leave the lute.'

Nicola clutched it tighter then sighed. Bella placed the instrument carefully, high on the roof of a rickety lean-to. She leaned several planks and a torn sack over it.

'Stick close to me,' I ordered. 'Act drunk. Sing. Stagger. But move quick. We need to cover Morrigan's injury and your blindness.'

We'd made it as far as Stokfishmonger Rowe on Thames Street when the curfew bells rang. I swore and Bella echoed me. The bridge gates creaked shut with annoy'n finality. Now the only way across was by boat.

The back o my neck prickled. Someone watched us. Hardly surpris'n in this part o town. But was it one o Lovell's people, a constable, or an ordinary thief?

'This way,' I muttered. We staggered and sang our way along

Popys Alley to the nearest river steps. The air thickened with the stink o sewage, fishguts and saltwater. Underfoot, even the puddles stank o fish.

At the steps, a quick negotiation bought us passage on a dory for more than I wanted to pay, but we had little choice.

'Don't go under the bridge,' I snarled at the oarsman when he smirked and stuffed the coin into his purse. 'I'm not pay'n that much to have people shit on my head as well.'

Luckily the tide was com'n in, so the river took us toward Bankside, upriver o Southwark. I glanced back. A lamp moved steadily toward us. I swore again.

'Douse that lantern!' I pointed my stiletto at the pole-lantern at the front o the boat. The oarsman shrugged, blew it out and kept row'n, but every stroke was accompanied by a low mutter'n o choice curses against me.

'There's more coin if you shut up so I can hear,' I whispered. He shut up.

The steady splash'n o oars gained on us. Whoever followed had the faster oarsman and probably fewer passengers. This was why I worked alone. People slowed you down.

'Hey?' Bella's soft question reached me. I glanced across. She pointed at Morrigan. Even by the faint light o distant houses and street lanterns, she was paler than was healthy. Her eyes were closed. Her breath'n shallow.

The boat crunched against the muddy bank and I clambered onto the stairs that led to the tenements and the brewhouse riverside of Winchester Palace. We dragged Morrigan up and headed away from the stairs as fast as possible. But she was about dead on her feet, only half-conscious.

Nicola stumbled and tripped, measur'n her length twice on the filthy streets. She whimpered but didn't cry out. Bella hooked Nicola's fingers into her own belt, then tucked herself under Morrigan's other arm.

'Eliza Parry's place is that way two blocks,' she whispered after a while. 'Is that where we're a-going?'

'Yes.' I struggled on, but Morrigan was heavier than she looked and our steps slowed.

Footsteps scuffed on the road behind us. Runn'n.

'We're not going to make it,' I groaned. 'There's someone com'n up behind us.'

On the opposite side o the road, two nightwatchmen sauntered past, whistl'n and laugh'n. One o them glanced our way, stopped, pointed and elbowed the other. Both overweight and carry'n a basic sword and dagger.

'This just gets better,' I muttered. 'The watchmen have seen us, too. Last thing we need is them rais'n the hue and cry for us.'

I dragged all three into a shadowed alley. 'Bella, you need to get off the main street. This alley twists around behind The Hartshorn Inn and takes you to Maiden Lane. Stay on that until you get to the Queen's Garden.' I thought for a moment. Queen's Garden was a pike farm, not a real garden. 'You'll have Winchester Park on your left, so that might help.'

'Why?' Bella asked.

'Who knows? Just find Morrigan some plants,' I snapped. 'The lane next to the pike farms should take you pretty much straight to Eliza's place.'

'What are you a-going ta do?' Bella asked.

'Buy you more time. Again.' I set my jaw. 'Take my crossbow and sword. I don't want to lose them. Here's a bolt.' I loaded the crossbow for her, and handed over the stiletto, leav'n me with only a basic belt-knife and a couple o small blades tucked away close to my skin. Then I took Rollo's cloak off Morrigan, clasped it around my throat and flipped up the hood. I unlaced my tunic and half-bared my breasts.

'What are you a-planning?' Bella watched me with a frown.

I grimaced. 'Best you don't know. Keep Morrigan alive. She owes me money. If I'm not back by Matins, send someone in the morn'n to The Clink to get me.'

She grabbed my wrist. 'You canna! That place is for bawds and thieves. I've heard stories…'

I shook free. 'Believe me, I know. But it's the only way to get Lovell's man off your scent. Just go, would you?'

With several backward looks, she and Nicola half-carried Morrigan further into the dark alley. Good. *Now* I could get someth'n done.

I stepped back into the Bankend Street lamplight just as the two watchmen arrived, and I threw my arms around their shoulders.

'So glad you're here, c-con-costabbles,' I slurred. 'I was so scared! I barely gottaway from them.' I giggled and let my weight hang off their necks.

'God's teeth,' one o them grumbled, staggering under my weight. His ale-rank stink made me cough. 'Another drunken slut? Walking the streets. Dressed like a man.' He tut-tutted. 'Big fine to pay. Big fine.'

The curfew didn't apply on the southside o the river. Most business here was done at night. But the Bishop's constables preferred the stewhouse girls to work inside, where they could be charged room rent, not on the streets.

'Five whores already,' his companion said, sniff'n wetly. 'The Clink'll be full tonight. And we'll have our pick.'

'Meh,' the first said. 'I like them with a bit more meat on their bones. Let's get her back.'

I kept my head down, watch'n beneath my lashes, as they dragged me along Bankend toward The Clink. We passed a shadow, darker than the rest.

I lowered my voice and gave my best imitation o Morrigan's amused drawl. 'Gramercy goodmen. I'm Morrigan. Send a message for me, if you please?'

The watchman on my left grunted and wiped at his dripp'n nose with a filthy sleeve. 'Shut up, whore.'

Footsteps scuffed the dirt road behind me. He'd taken the bait. Bella and the others should have time to get safely to Eliza's.

The footsteps came closer.

'Gentlemen?' A deep voice startled my companions and they jumped and swore. They turned awkwardly, swing'n in a circle with me in the middle.

I kept my face in shadow. All I could see were his dark boots and dark wool hose. And a sword-sheath by his right hip. A left-hander, then. The legs were thicker and stronger than Lovell's. The voice was wrong, too. Not the big guy, Calain, either.

Who, then?

'Sir?' Snot-nose said. 'Are you lost?'

'Not at all,' he replied. 'But you have something of mine. That prisoner.'

'Now, Master—'

'*Sir* Thomas Stafford,' the newcomer replied. I hid a smile. My even'n had just improved. I gathered my feet beneath me.

Bad-breath cleared his throat. 'With respect, a gentleman like you shouldn't be out after curfew. Not in these parts. Lots of cutpurses and murderers hereabouts. And doxies like this one.'

'Of course,' the man said. 'But I think you've made an amusing mistake. I need that particular…er…doxy, you see. I am sorry to do this.'

His feet shifted. His blade slickered free from its sheath. He lunged. Bad-breath, under my right arm, gurgled a stifled cry. Snot-nose cried out.

I skipped free o both and left them to it. Snot-nose snatched at his blade, but his attacker ran him through before the steel was free.

Nicely done. He was well-taught. I palmed one o my small daggers and considered my options.

Morrigan had said capture, not kill. Stafford was older, grey'n hair and thicken'n in the middle. But he moved light on his feet. Trained fighter.

He turned to me and drew his dagger with his right hand.

'Come, Morrigan. Don't make this difficult. Lovell said you were dead. How is it you're not?'

I unclipped the cloak, held it in my left hand, and dropped into a crouch. 'Because I'm not Morrigan.'

With a flick o my wrist, I threw one blade at Stafford. He swayed aside and it clinked against the stone build'n behind. I swore and pulled out a fresh knife.

I had only two more throw'n knives and my belt-knife. Now I regretted leav'n my weapons.

'Who in God's name are you?' he snarled. 'Never mind. Tell me where Morrigan's body is, and where the blind girl went?'

'Er…no?' I flashed him a grin.

He lunged and I danced aside, slashing at his arm. He hissed and spun away. Blood blacked his sleeve. He moved slower this time. Cautious-like. I swirled the cloak, circl'n.

He closed the gap in a rush, chopping overhand. I tangled the blade in the cloak and turned aside.

He spun, tearing the cloak from my grip. The sword arced at my neck. I ducked, moved close and jammed an elbow into his gut. He grunted and turned, faster than I expected.

His sword appeared at my throat and I froze, curs'n my own arrogance.

Stafford scowled. 'Drop the knife, girl. Then tell me where the blind woman is. Or die,' he said calmly. 'I really don't care.'

'If you kill me,' I said, 'you'll never find her.'

A thin, dry smile appeared. 'You underestimate me. I have enough men to search every building in Bankside and Southwark.'

His sword tip pricked my throat. I let my blade fall to the dirt.

'And the belt-knife.'

I dropped it, grinding my teeth and think'n fast. There had to be someth'n. Some way out. He had experience, strength, reach and weapon on me. I was alone and unarmed.

My stomach churned and fluttered. He dug the blade deeper. Pain. Warmth trickl'n down my chest. Rage boiled in my belly.

'Where is the blind girl,' Stafford repeated. He dug the edge a little further into my skin and I clenched my fists against the pain.

Behind him, a small shadow moved.

God's fist! Agnes? That was the last thing I needed. She'd just get in the way or get herself killed.

And me, probably.

Then her wicked blade glinted in the dim streetlamps.

I hesitated. Well, maybe I could use some help.

Just this once.

'Heya. Look behind you, Stafford.'

'As if I'd fall for that. *Agh!*' He dropped to one knee. Blood stained the ground beneath him, his heel tendon sliced clean through.

I sidestepped, twisted his wrist, wrenched his sword free and laid the edge along his throat.

'Now it's my turn to ask the questions.'

I glanced up. Agnes grinned at me, her blade darkened by blood.

'*Our* turn,' I amended. 'Thanks, sprat.'

She bowed with a flourish. 'Told you I could help.'

'Don't push your luck.' I prodded Stafford with the sword. 'Up. There's someone who wants to talk to you.'

p350 *Aiki Flinthart*

22. And My Soul, From Out that Shadow

Philippa Bolingbroke, 49
Nun
Outside Aldgate, London,

Tuesday (early morning), 26ᵗʰ September, 1486

I found it hard to imagine never sleeping in this austere cell again.

I glanced around. Storm-grey stone walls. White linen on the straw pallet-bed. Shit-brown ewer and bowl. Shit-brown oil lantern smelling of linseed. My shit-brown habit, white wimple and faded-black veil folded neatly on the end of the bed.

The only things I kept were my rosary beads and the eyeglasses given me by the Abbess two years before, when she saw my eyesight was failing. The only thing I truly regretted leaving was my bundle of brushes and pens, for I took most pride in my illuminations—the jewel-like colours and whimsical drawings I painted in the margins of the Order's texts when I copied them.

But pride had no place in the world I was about to face. A world I knew little about, since I'd left it thirty years before. A world containing a daughter I'd thought long-lost. I'd been barely out of girlhood, at nineteen, when I had been placed in St Clare Without Aldgate. A fallen, prideful, angry young woman. A sinner. A whore, they had called me, though they knew it was a lie.

No. I pushed away the hot stirrings of old injustice and whispered a prayer for patience and humility. Now I had a chance to know my daughter. Make up for lost time. Make sure she understood our separation was not my fault; not my choice.

I straightened and threw back my shoulders.

'I'm so glad that kirtle and headdress fits you, Sister…no, it's Philippa now, I suppose.' The Abbess's gentle voice came from the doorway. 'Lucky one of the new novices is about your size.'

I turned, smoothing the kirtle's fine indigo material. 'Yes, Reverend Mother. Very lucky. Though tis strange to wear anything other than the habit after so long.' I touched a curl of short grey hair beneath the gauzy headdress. Strange to have my neck bare and hair showing.

Her wrinkled lips stretched in a brief smile that didn't reach her faded-sky eyes. She was a few years older than me. But her round face normally held a serenity I could never hope to achieve. Now she was troubled.

'You know, all of my predecessors received Royal commands,' she said.

I waited for her to continue. Would she now refuse my freedom? My fingernails dug into my palms.

She gazed around my small room. 'They were told you were not to leave the Abbey, except to minister to the poor in the houses around Aldgate once a month.'

'I know, Reverend Mother.' How I'd railed against that restriction in the first few years. How many tears had I shed at my imprisonment? A lake's worth, surely. And three attempts to escape had resulted only in a lock on my door and a guard dogging my every step.

She moved to my little oak desk, trailing the faint scent of the lavender she used for her headaches. She touched the bundle of art supplies.

'But King Henry has not sent that command. So, when that young woman came in through the window last night with Laura Kennet's message, I had no reason to deny you.' She slanted me a curious look. 'Do you suppose the king's forgotten you're here?'

I gave a wry smile. 'I think he's had a great deal else on his mind. The sweating sickness last year. His wife's pregnancy. The young Plantagenet heir locked away in his Tower. I doubt he sees me as a threat.'

'Oh,' she said, musingly, 'don't be too sure of that. But I take it as a sign from God that he never sent the command. For I am breaking no vow by releasing you. I never thought you suited to this life.' Her smile softened. 'You are far too—'

'Arrogant, Reverend Mother?' I said drily. 'Ambitious, prideful, judgemental. Pick one. They've all been thrown at me by your predecessors.'

She chuckled. 'I was going to say, talented. We have benefitted from your skills, but I would see you decorate a cathedral, if it were allowed for women to do so.'

'Forgive me, Reverend Mother.'

'You must forgive yourself, child. You've been here for thirty years and you still carry so much anger.' She searched my face. 'Whatever you did all those years ago, God has forgiven you. You have a chance at a new life. Don't waste it dwelling on past mistakes.'

I tensed. 'The mistake was not mine. I did nothing more than fall in love, marry and have a child. My only error was choosing the wrong man to marry. This…' I indicated the tiny cell '…was my punishment.'

'A life in contemplation of God's Word is not meant to be punishment, child. And God gave us free will. You made choices too, every step of the way. Although you may not care to acknowledge them. Free will doesn't, after all, guarantee good judgement.'

I said nothing. She was wrong. My choices were taken from me by the men of my family who saw me and my daughter as a threat.

The Abbess sighed and embraced me briefly, brushing her cheek against mine. Then she held me by the shoulders.

'Go, then. Find your daughter. Fill in the missing part of your life with her.' She cupped my jaw.

'But...what if she doesn't understand why I left?'

'What if it's not about you, Philippa? As Galatians 5:13 says, *Do not use your freedom as an opportunity for the flesh, but through love serve one another.*'

I clenched my teeth. She didn't understand, either.

'Here.' She pressed a groat, a penny, and three farthings into my hand and curled my fingers around them. 'It's not much—we are called the Poor Clares, after all. I believe Laura Kennet is expecting you at her house in Lyme Street.'

I stammered a thanks. I had not expected such generosity. But I pushed the coins back at her.

'I cannot in good conscience take it, Reverend Mother. Not when the poor have greater need.'

She chuckled. 'My dear Sister, your integrity is something I've always admired about you, but you *are* now one of the poor. So, take it.'

I returned her embrace wholeheartedly and turned to leave.

'Wait,' she said. 'Take these, too.' She passed over my brushes and a small, red-leather-bound book. I flipped through the pages, delighting anew in the jewel-pretty images in red and blue and gold.

She nodded. 'One of your best, I think. I saw it in the stack of prayer books made as gifts for noble families last year at Christmas. I confess I loved it too well to give it away. Keep it. Remember us.'

My throat thick, I held the illustrated prayer book to my heart and hurried from the Abbey.

My impetus carried me along Minories Street and as far as Aldgate, itself. I checked behind twice but saw only farmers and goodwives. Had the guard over me really been relaxed? When I reached the gate, I paused on the threshold of London city. It was only just past dawn, the sky still flushed pale yellows and pinks by the sun, yet the street was already teeming.

The great Roman wall embraced the buildings inside like a mother's arms. To my right another stone wall enclosed the Augustinian Holy Trinity Priory, with its towering grey cathedral and cloister house.

To my left were a rabble of stone and timber hostelries and houses, jammed up against each other. Top windows opened and the inhabitants shouted warnings as they flung warm yellow rain into the street. Painted signs in all colours, showing symbols for merchants and inns, swayed and creaked in the cool morning breeze.

'Mon Dieu!' I muttered, and pressed against the cool stone of an inn as horses clip-clopped past, hauling timber wagons piled high with hay, timber, bricks, sacks of grain and the like.

The enormity of my situation hit me and I stood still, overwhelmed by the noise and smells and choices. How would I earn a living? Where did one buy food? If my daughter rejected me, where would I live?

No. I would make her understand. She would accept me. She had to. It hadn't been my fault.

I grabbed the nearest street urchin by the arm. She yelped and tried to tug free.

Holding up a farthing, I caught her attention. Her eyes widened.

'Take me straight to the midwife, Laura Kennet, on Lyme Street, and this is yours,' I said.

She nodded and took off, darting between a gaggle of women carrying baskets and chattering, and a farmer herding half a dozen black and white goats, bells clanking around their necks.

I checked behind again, but saw no sign of anyone following.

By the time we reached Lyme street I was panting and pushing at a stitch in my side. I paid the child and stood outside Laura Kennet's neat house to catch my breath.

The limewashed door swung open and a woman maybe a decade older than me emerged. She patted her cornflower blue headscarf, fiddling with the wisps of grey hair that escaped it. Morning light fell softly on a face lined by exhaustion and laughter.

'Mistress Kennet?'

She studied me and sighed. 'Well, bless me, you did come. I've been expecting you, an all, my lady. Call me Laura.' She shut the door behind her and came down two steps to my side. She barely topped my shoulder. 'But you'd best pull that veil over your face.'

Alarmed, I glanced around, but Lyme street was quiet, with only a few goodwives hurrying to market and children playing. And a young man in a brown tunic and hose, loitering at the corner. Perhaps waiting for his lover.

'Why?' I pulled the gauzy grey silk into place.

She smiled wryly. 'Because you're very much like your daughter. And *she's* the spit of the young queen, an all. So much that tis no wonder folks have taken to calling her Queenie.'

'Mon Dieu!' I crossed myself. 'Tis a wonder she still lives, then.'

'Mmmm.' She sent me a sharp glance. 'Best keep mum if you can, my lady. Folk around here aren't fond of the French and you still have an accent. Come. Let's get a move on.'

The walk took us close to an hour, through streets crowded with people and animals, noisy with talk and braying, reeking of piss and dung. The world was a painting too busy and colourful to see all at once. So overpowering I could only cling to Laura's surcoat like a child, oblivious to direction or distance, unable to check for followers.

Blackbirds Sing p357

When we crossed the Thames, the sludgy brown river stank like a privy. We pushed our way over the narrow bridge crammed with houses and shops built cheek-by-jowl atop each other from one end to the other. The cries of fishermen and seabirds competed with hawkers of fish and apples and candles. The montage of colour and light and people dinned on my mind until I was desperate for my silent cell.

Off the bridge we passed stinking tenements, inns loud and full of drunkards even at this hour, then a blessedly-quiet priory as we headed upriver.

At last, when Laura stopped outside a three-storey house facing the river, I was able to pause and think. A long street ran alongside the Thames's south bank. The houses here were large, their fronts gaudily painted in reds and blues. Signs swayed above doors. The building on one side showed the fleur-de-lys. On the other side, a pair of keys, crossed. The sign directly in front was a beautifully-drawn cygnet.

Comprehension dawned. Even locked away in the Abbey I'd heard of the Fleur-de-Lys, the Crossed Keys, and the Cygnet.

'My daughter is in a *stewhouse?*' I took a step backward. '*Mon Dieu, mon Dieu.*'

'Hush, my lady,' Laura said, gripping my wrist so hard the bones ground together. 'Not so loud.' She directed a scowl my way. 'Your daughter's done her best to survive, an all. As we all do. Keep your judgements to yourself or this will be over before it starts. She wants to meet you. She wants to know you, an all, but you've *no right* to judge her.'

I drew myself up. 'I'm her mother. I have the right to guide her to a better life.'

Laura hesitated, then snorted a laugh. 'That will be fun to watch, an all. Well, don't say I didn't warn you.'

She knocked on the door and a slatternly maidservant opened it and let us into a large front room. Laura asked for her mistress and the girl curtseyed and bade us wait.

I gasped and clutched at my rosary. The walls. After thirty years of prayer and reading God's Word, I knew I should avert my eyes. But the paintings on the walls… Whoever had painted them was a master. But my cheeks burned at the subject matter.

Naked women, larger than life, touching themselves. Breasts and nothings exposed. Flesh rounded and soft. Silken gowns in glorious purples and greens. The other colours were just as vivid: reds, yellows, skin tones, even some gilding. The women were real; eyes half-lidded in pleasure, pink lips parted, tongues peeping out.

The maidservant returned and led us up a dark, narrow set of steps to the second floor. We entered a large room with windows facing the river. Light streamed in, reflections off the water dancing on the ceiling. To one side stood a huge bed draped with faded red velvet and scattered with threadbare embroidered cushions.

'Eliza,' Laura said. 'Philippa's here.'

I lifted my veil.

A tall, curvaceous woman rose from a desk where she'd been signing papers. Curling, bronze-gold hair cascaded down her back. Her creamy skin was free of powders and paint. But her low-cut blood-red silk surcoat left little to the imagination. It clung to her curves and showed clearly the swell of her bosom.

She swayed toward us, one corner of her mouth lifting. For a long moment we stood, staring at each other. Wide-set grey-blue eyes—so like mine—returned my gaze with shrewd intelligence.

Then she slapped me.

I gasped and staggered back, clutching my cheek. 'How *dare* you?'

She folded her arms. 'How dare I, what? Smack you for leavin me? Or for abandonin me to this life because you was too scared to stand up for me?'

'You don't understand. I had no choice.'

Eliza made a noise of disgust and strolled over to the window. 'We all got choices. But go on, anyways. Tell me why you had none. I'm all ears.' She coughed and snatched out a kerchief to cover her lips. Laura Kennet took a step toward her, but Eliza waved her off.

'You go, Laura.' Eliza's smile was wintry. 'I won't kill her, I promise. We still need her.'

'Well, if you're sure an all. I've got a babe to check on in the Fleur-de-Lys.' With an uneasy look at me, Laura left me alone with my grown daughter.

I shifted my book and brushes and wiped damp palms on my kirtle. 'What do you mean, you still need me?'

Eliza pointed at the desk. 'I have guests. One of them says she knows of you. Needs your help to copy a letter for summat. Says you're the best copyist.'

'Is that…' I eyed a letter, half un-folded, blue wax seal broken. '…is that why you sent that girl, Ingaret, to me? Because you need a copyist?'

Eliza shrugged one shoulder. 'Partly, anyways.' She rested against the window frame and folded her arms again. 'But I'm willin to give you a chance to explain as well.'

The words stuck in my throat. Words I'd rehearsed for years; gone over and over until I knew them as an actor on the stage. Now they felt awkward and stilted.

So, instead, I moved to the desk and picked up the letter. A love letter. Full of fulsome promises of future happiness. Signed by someone named Francis Lovell. But I'd been too long away from court to know which Lovell that might be. And most of my youth had been spent in France, anyway.

'Why do you need this copied? It's nothing.' I tossed the letter aside.

'Not the words, the hand,' she said. 'And the signature.'

I stepped back. 'No. I'll not be party to forging anyone's signature or falsifying a document. Tis sinful and wrong.'

'Oh?' Eliza laughed, brassy and harsh. 'Both sinful *and* wrong, is it? Nice to know there's a difference, anyways.' She placed her hands on her hips. 'So tell me, then, which of them was what you did? Sinful, or wrong?'

I sighed and sank onto the chair at the desk.

'My father was…a powerful, rich man,' I said quietly. Eliza's skirts rustled as she sat on the window seat, one silk-slippered foot tapping the floor. 'He married my mother—Anne of Clarence—without leave in 1436. When I was born, the marriage was annulled quietly and we were sent to live in France.'

'Lordy-be,' Eliza said drily. 'So you was declared a bastard. Welcome to my world.'

I opened my mouth to remonstrate her for taking the Lord's name in vain, but subsided.

'When I was eighteen, we were in Rouen, and I met a young boy of fourteen. A nobleman's son. Edward. I thought nothing of him, really.' I shrugged. 'But my mother was ambitious and angry at being set aside. She fostered his affection for me, and I came to love him. He was tall and strong and confident. My mother had us secretly married.' I pressed my lips together. 'Seems she didn't learn from past mistakes. Before long, I was with child. Edward brought us back to London and you were born.'

'And?' Eliza prompted. 'Why'd you give me up?'

I rose and paced about the room, touching things at random. A hairbrush. The drapes on her bed. A vase of wilted flowers. 'A week after your birth, they came for us. Dragged us to a hearing before the king.' Tears stung my eyes but I swallowed them. 'Edward tried. He argued for us. Twas to no avail.' My knees weakened and I sat again. 'They had our marriage annulled and made you illegitimate.'

She snorted. 'Seems three generations made the same mistake, then. For I married my George in secret, but the marriage never got recognised by his people, either. I didn't abandon my daughter, though. And nor did your mam.'

'I had no choice!' I snapped. 'They told me I could either go into a nunnery here, and you would be given to a good home where you would be raised in ignorance of your name.'

'Or?' she asked, her lip curling.

'Or we would both be executed.'

Eliza rolled her eyes. 'And you think a whore's life is better than dying?' She flung her arms wide. 'I were given to the woman who owned this stewhouse when I were a child. Her slave for a few years. Then she put me to work in the bedchambers.' Her expression hardened. 'I were ten. Mayhap you can make your prudish nun's brain imagine that. Anything you can think on, it's been done to me. And worse.'

'Stop!' I shot to my feet, dizzied and sickened. 'I told you. I had no choice. A mother will always choose to keep her child alive, if she can.'

'And did you never think on a third path?'

I frowned. 'There was no third path. I couldn't let them murder you.'

Eliza stalked over until we stood eye to eye. 'You could have run. Taken me and gone to France again. Changed your name. Remarried.'

'I...I couldn't. I had no money. No friends here. No way of

supporting us or earning money.'

Her bitter laugh echoed in the chamber and she threw me a look of deep irony. 'Mayhap it never occurred to a high and mighty noble lady to lie on her back and spread her legs to earn a livin?' She turned a shoulder and her voice grew harsh. 'Truth is, you chose to live, quiet and safe, in the nunnery because you feared to die. And because you was afraid, you condemned me to this life.'

'No,' I said quietly, regaining my poise. 'You don't understand the pressure they put on me. The threats. The day to day fear. Never knowing when the king's men would take me to the scaffold on Tower Hill.'

I turned aside, unable to continue. It had been six months imprisoned in the Tower. Six months of watching my beautiful little girl crawl amongst the mouldy straw, clamber up to the barred windows and stare out into the world, sleep on rags while I sang lullabies.

Eliza looked at me, long, cool. 'Why'd you come here today, anyways?'

'If you hated me so much, why did you send for me?' I countered. I'd been content. In a way. Believing her to be safe and loved, even if I could never be free.

She tilted her head. 'I don't think I hate you anymore. I pity you.' Her mouth twisted. 'Your mam may have been ambitious, but you're spineless. Lettin people decide your life for you until it's whittled away to nothin. I'm surprised you even left the abbey.'

'You have no idea how much strength it took to let you go.' I grimaced. 'As for leaving St Clare's? In truth I didn't think I'd be allowed. Previously there's been a guard set to watch me.'

Eliza frowned and opened her mouth.

'Mistress?' An elderly male servant poked his head into the room.

'Sorry to bother you, but Master…Mistress Morrigan is wantin' to see you. And your guest.'

'Right, then. Let her in.'

The door creaked open and a tall man about Eliza's age strolled in. His eyes were an extraordinary clear shade of grey and his skin a glorious gold hue that made me long for my paints. He wore hose and a plain brown doublet that had been patched over his stomach. He bowed, winced and pressed at the patch.

'Forgive me, ladies.' His voice was low and mellow. 'I'm not quite recovered. May I sit?'

'Course,' Eliza said, scraping a chair across the timber floor. She arranged it next to the desk, with the other. 'Mayhap you'll explain to me mam why you're dressed as a man. She's a bit prudish that way, bein a nun and all. Amsel Morrigan, Philippa.'

I inclined my head but kept my thoughts on the propriety of women wearing men's clothing to myself.

'Perhaps later,' Amsel said. 'I apologise for interrupting your tete-a-tete, but when I heard you'd called in, Philippa, I thought we could speak.' She picked up the folded letter on the desk. 'About this.'

I gathered what dignity I had left. 'I will not be part of anything nefarious, Mistress Morrigan.'

'Not even if it helped to keep your daughter safe?' Morrigan said mildly. 'And her daughter?'

'Daughter?' I looked to Eliza. 'You do have a daughter? Where is she?'

She sneered. 'Not here. She came early this mornin with that letter. Mayhap if you stay long enough this time, you might even meet her.'

'How would falsifying a document help her, or Eliza?' I glared at Morrigan. 'What would it say?'

Morrigan sighed and scraped long fingers through her collar-length, dark hair. 'Let's just say that, without this letter, we have only hearsay and the confession of a man who would recant if he saw the opportunity.' She sent a level look. 'With it, we have a chance. Without it, none. King Henry will most likely die, and his queen and the young prince with him. If the queen falls, how long do you think they'll let you, Eliza, and your granddaughter live?'

'What?' Eliza unfolded her arms and glanced back and forth between us. 'What've we got to do with the likes of them, anyways? I know I look a bit like Her Grace, but that's no reason to go about killing people.'

I strode to the window and stared out. On the glittering Thames, boats splashed and creaked their way to the docks, the sailors shouting and waving their arms, throwing ropes, unloading cargo. I gazed downriver. If only I had never left France, none of this would have happened.

Below, in the street, women of all ages, dressed in low-cut chemises, and faded kirtles strutted their wares in the shadows. Men passed over coin and lifted skirts. Across the road, a young man in brown homespuns sat on an upturned barrel, whittling and occasionally glancing up at the stewhouses.

'Mon Dieu,' I whispered. I was not free. They watched me, still. Or someone, did. My soul longed for the quiet simplicity of my cell and my paints. I could go back and leave Eliza and Morrigan to their schemes. Yet King Henry was the first to allow me even this much freedom. And I had let my daughter down once.

I swung around. 'Very well,' I said quietly. 'If it will protect Eliza, I'll help. Perhaps you were right. I was a coward. I did take the easy way out last time and we've all paid the price. You more than any. I'm sorry, Eliza. I'll try to make it right, now.'

There was a long silence and Eliza eyed me narrowly. 'Fair enough. But one question.'

I moved to the desk and sat, waiting.

She leaned over me. 'Who was your pa? And why'd they make such a fuss over your Edward?'

With a cool smile, I dipped the goosefeather pen in the inkpot and picked out a fresh sheet of vellum.

'My name is Philippa Bolingbroke. My father was Henry Bolingbroke, later Henry VI. My husband was Edward Plantagenet,' I said, scratching the first line of practice script. 'Son of Richard, Duke of York. Later Edward IV.'

I looked up into Eliza's wide eyes. 'You're the older half-sister to the current Queen. The throne is yours by birth and right, for you're both a Lancaster and a York.' I shrugged. 'Apart from being made a bastard, that is.'

Eliza snapped her jaw shut. A giggle burbled from her lips and deepened to a full-throated, roaring laugh that kept going until she was reduced to gasping coughs she buried in a kerchief.

When she recovered, she grinned at me. 'And I married George Plantagenet, Duke of Clarence.' She chuckled again. 'I can't wait to see the look on my Beatrice's face when I tell her she's the next sarding Queen of England.'

She slapped me on the shoulder and kissed my forehead.

'You'll do, Mam.'

23. That Lies Floating on the Floor

Olivia Grey, 28
Dressmaker
Hosyer Lane, London,

Tuesday (mid-afternoon), 26th September, 1486

'No, m'lord,' Joan snapped, 'and you can put that coin away for it's worthless here. Mistress Olivia is fair busy with a rush order for four surcoats and four doublets. All gotta be ready for tonight's feast. We don't have time.'

I huddled against the wall in the shadows. Joan was usually good at dealing with angry customers, but this man... I shivered. If Morrigan was right, this man was dangerous.

'That is not good enough,' Lovell's voice stabbed through the silence, sharp as a needle. 'You will tell Mistress Grey to come out now and speak to me. I need a new doublet. The only good silk one I have is stained and not even the laundress could get it out completely, damn her. I *must* have a new one for the feast tonight.'

'Sorry, m'lord,' Joan said firmly. 'That's our final answer.'

'I'll pay double,' he growled.

She was silent and I could almost hear her thinking the offer over, wondering what I would say. But I couldn't go out and tell her, for that would mean showing my face to him. I shuddered. After the fire, I'd learned to stay away from customers. My scars horrified people.

Movement caught my attention in the corridor that led to the kitchen.

'Agnes!' I whispered, gesturing her over. 'Harken.'

The young thief I'd so rashly allowed into my house hesitated then strolled over, her chin high and green eyes glittering.

'I need you to take a message in to Joan for me. She's with a customer.'

Agnes folded her arms. 'What's in it for me?'

I glared. 'By my troth, girl, if you don't do as you're told I'll lock you in your room. After last night, when you didn't come home, you're lucky to even be fed today.'

'I told you,' she hissed, 'Morrigan needed me and Ingaret needed my help and then I couldn't come back because of the curfew, so I was stuck on the Southwark side til—'

With a sharp wave, I cut her off. 'Later. Tell Joan we will *not* take the work no matter how much the customer offers.'

Lovell spoke again in the front room, his voice raised, harsh, berating Joan for stubbornness.

Agnes paled. 'Not with him out there, I won't, you tell her, yourself!' She darted away and vanished up the creaking stairs.

Unmanageable little wretch! Her brother was the most loving, adorable child. Grateful, thoughtful, helpful. But Agnes? She was disobedient, spiteful, and frustrating. If she would but do as she was told, all would be well.

Unbidden, my daughter's face swam in my memory again. The crackle of fire, the sound of her screams and mine, the heat and pain. If she had only done as she was told…

Lovell's voice rose again. I touched the hard, twisted skin on my cheek and neck. I couldn't go out there.

'I'll pay triple, damn you!'

'Sorry, m'lord,' Joan's tone was firm. 'But it's close on Nones as it is. Even if you paid fifty times its worth, we don't have the time today. Wear your old one or go naked. Don't bother me either way. Now, if you'd be so kind as to go, I have to shut the shop so we can finish.'

'By God, girl,' Lovell growled, 'I'll see you whipped for your insolence.'

'Yes, m'lord,' she replied coolly, 'I'm sure you will. Ah, Master Alfred, you're back. Would you see m'lord out?'

There was a creak and Lovell made a choking sound. I heaved a sigh of relief and sagged against the wall. My husband was a huge man, with hands the size of embroidery frames.

The shop door closed and the bolt snicked into place. Joan emerged into the corridor, dusting her hands.

'All right, now, Mistress,' she said smugly. 'Master Alfred'n me took care of him. Let's get back to the workshop.'

Alfred appeared, bussed my cheek and sauntered toward the kitchen.

I thanked Joan and led the way back to the huge workroom. My seamstress business had been going so well, that I'd bought the house next door two years before and Alfred had converted it into a workshop.

As we passed through the adjoining door, I touched the charred timber, as I always did. He'd rebuilt our house, too.

Before I entered the workshop, I checked the half-veil that covered the left side of my face. Most of my girls had seen my injuries, but the pink, burned skin made everyone uncomfortable, so it was simpler to hide from them as well.

Briskly, I strode from table to table, examining each girl's work. Alfred had knocked extra windows into the house, taken out most of the second floor and re-structured it to stand strong.

So the big space was bright and cool, even on a hot summer's day. The air tasted of the sharpness of dyes and the warmth of clean cloth. Here, I felt at home.

Silks shimmered in the afternoon light, every shade of blue, red, green, yellow. We even had a bolt of purple, set aside for someone in the royal family. And a delicious shade of burgundy wool escarlates, coloured with the horribly-expensive kermes red dye.

But the focus of all our efforts today were the four surcoats and four doublets laid out on eight of the tables. All the surcoats were the same, simple style, but in different colours and with different trims. And each one had a matching gable headdress with veil.

The doublets were also in one style, with full, slashed sleeves, brocade trims, and matching velvet caps. Hopefully the differences in colour would hide the similarity in style.

I glanced at the sun, slanting in through the window. Dust floated, sparkling like tiny gems. I chewed my lip. The timing would be close. We had to have them all delivered by Vespers.

'Mistress?' Meg called me over. She held up a completed a daffodil yellow gown. I checked the stitching and point-lacings holding the sleeves to the bodice.

'Excellent job for such quick work, Meg. Wrap it up and send that one and the bronze-brown Marianne is working on, over the river to Eliza's.' I swept a look around the room. 'Betsy, your grey doublet will go to Master Wilson's house over on Saint Marie Street. Quickly, ladies 'ere the bells toll and we fail our task.'

When I turned, Agnes stood behind me, her arms folded, her jaw sharp.

'I want to go, too,' she said. Her green eyes, lashed thick and dark, were so like my Clara's that it hurt to see them.

'You may not.' I headed for the next worktable and she stalked behind. 'Where is your brother?'

'He's fine,' she snapped. 'Playing with the boys next door but I want to be part of it tonight 'cause I'm helping, Morrigan said so. I helped last night and I deserve to be there, besides I promised Jack I'd keep an watch on Morrigan so I—'

'By my troth, no,' I said. 'Neither of us is going. Morrigan left you in my care, so you will harken to my words. We'll stay home, safe. Now go to the kitchen and help cook start supper. But keep away from the fire. We'll be done here, soon.'

'Oh!' Agnes made a noise of frustration. She stomped away a few steps then swung back. 'I *hate* you! I don't know why Morrigan brought me here when you don't even want me!' Her voice cracked and she ran from the room, still muttering abuse.

I halted, my whole body shaking. I touched the scar on my face, tracing the hard flesh, feeling the burn, hearing the screams.

The rustle of cloth and soft chatter started up again behind me. I stood there awhile longer, staring at the dark doorway into the house. No. This time she would be safe. She would obey and she would be safe.

We finished at Vespers, the last wrapped parcel handed to a well-paid messenger-boy to deliver. I stumbled into the kitchen and sank onto a bench, too tired to even think.

Alfred entered and kissed my forehead. 'Alright, love? You look done-in.'

I sighed. 'We did it, but some of the seams are barely tacked together. I hope they last the night or my reputation as a seamstress is ruined. I should never have let Morrigan talk me into this madness.'

'Where's young Agnes?' He picked up a piece of soft white bread and slapped a hunk of goat's cheese on it.

'Probably upstairs, sulking. I wouldn't let her go to help Morrigan tonight.'

He shook his head. 'She's a feisty one, for sure. Got guts, though. Never seen anyone so young be so fired up to protect other folk. Gotta admire the girl.'

'She'll get herself hurt, is what she'll do,' I snapped. 'She's too young to be carrying that dagger and gallivanting about at night.'

'Seems to me she did alright for a year or so, just her and the boy.'

'Alfred, not you, too. She's a little child. I need to keep her and Jack safe.'

Alfred squeezed my shoulder. 'People die, love. Children more than most, it seems. It wasn't your fault.'

I turned away. 'Just call her for supper.'

He returned a few minutes later, frowning. 'Not in the house. And not in the street with the other children, either. Jack's there. Do you think, maybe…?'

'Oh, God's heart,' I swore softly. 'She must have gone to the Tower. Stupid child!'

'I'll go fetch her.' He reached for his felt hat.

'You can't,' I said. 'The Tower's got extra guards tonight with the feast. They're only letting in liveried servants or tradespeople they know. People who are part of the feast preparations. It will have to be me. They know me for I've escorted Joan when she's delivered surcoats to the queen's ladies before.'

I stroked the scar then buried my face in my hands. 'But I can't. What do I do, Alfred? I can't go! Agnes'll be in the great hall, I know it. All those people!'

'Send one of the girls. You said the guards know Joan.' He draped a heavy arm over my back.

'Agnes won't listen to her.'

He chuckled. 'She won't listen to anyone, love. C'mon.' He lifted me to my feet. 'I'll escort you to the gate and wait for you. You can do this.' He held my face, his thumb stroking the numb scartissue. 'I know you're afeared of what people'll say and think, love. But there's a little girl who needs you.'

I clutched at his wrists. 'But what if I fail her, too? And what if people see me? I'm hideous. Noble women don't want to buy from a monster. I'll lose business.'

'You won't. None of that.' He kissed me. 'But think on this: maybe Agnes don't need your protection, love. Maybe she needs your trust. But I know you won't be easy til you find her, so go get dressed, now.'

I hesitated, then called my maid and threw on my best surcoat, a luxurious dark blue silk that matched my eyes. With unsteady fingers I tucked my long, dark hair into a gable headdress with a blue velvet hair net and tiny seed pearls.

I could be fined for wearing gems and silks, for that was above my station, but I was more likely to get past the guards dressed in finery than in a plain kirtle and coif. As a last touch, I arranged a wisp of gauzy blue silk to hide half my face.

'You will let me in,' I said. 'Or, perchance, you'd like to explain to Her Grace why this bolt of cloth is not delivered tonight as she asked? Her surcoat is torn and needs mending before the feast.'

The yeomen guards in their scarlet uniforms shifted uneasily and exchanged harried looks. Behind me, a grumbling lineup of minor nobles in their fluttering silks and heavy velvets began shouting for entrée through the barbican.

'Fine!' The guards stood aside, halberds lowered. 'In with ye, then, but on yer head be it if yer lyin, Mistress.'

I sailed past, leaving Alfred outside, my heart pounding and sweat staining my clothes. With the bolt of purple silk tucked in one elbow, I gathered my skirts and ran past the stinking menagerie of animals, across the long walk over the moat and into the Tower grounds.

Once inside I paused to stare in wonder. Though the sun was not yet set, the Tower's interior was awash with lanterns and torches; a diamond-studded tapestry of light and movement. All around, ladies in fine, swishing gowns of satins, silks, and brocades glittered and shimmered in the torchlight. Gems sparkled. Laughter and chatter swelled and shifted like thin material fluttering in a breeze. Perfumes hung heavy in the air, cloying; lavender, ambergris, clove, rose. And cutting through all that was a sharp, acrid scent I didn't recognise.

Then one of the red-coated yeomen of the Guards passed. He carried what must be one of the new hand-cannons. A serpentine handgonne, Alfred had called them. The glowing match that lit its explosive powder trailed the sharp smell.

The smell of death and fire. I shivered.

Child-pages darted between the adults, offering mugs of ale, cider, and wine. I inspected each child but none were Agnes. Daunted by the scale of the search, I shifted into the shadows, still clutching the heavy roll of cloth.

People seemed to be slowly making their way toward the great White Tower in the middle of the grounds. The feast must be in the large hall inside. That was where I'd find her.

In with Morrigan and the others.

I hurried that way, dodging and weaving, apologising, always turning my face away.

A great gong sounded before I reached the entrance. A servant announced that supper would be served in the upper hall and requested all ladies and gentlemen to attend forthwith to find their seats. No weapons allowed into the hall, only belt-knives.

Musicians struck up a lively tune, shawm, gittern and tabor luring people into the building. The laughter and talk waxed and I was swept along with the crowd, into Prince Arthur's christening feast.

Curious looks followed me. Whispers. Fingers pointing. Eyes sliding off my face. My cheek warmed and I resisted the urge to touch the scars, to check the half-veil, to hide.

Once we'd climbed to the upper floor hall, I retreated into the shadows so I could see the room without being seen. The smell of roasting meats drifted in and my stomach rumbled.

Huge banqueting tables stood in a great U shape, with the table furthest from the door raised on a dais. Behind it stood two gilded thrones with purple velvet cushions. The raised table was laid with at least ten ells of rich purple brocade, and set with silver candlesticks, wine goblets, and bowls of flowers and fruits.

The two long side tables were each laid with around eighteen ells of deep scarlet brocade and set with brass candlesticks and wine goblets, along with flowers and fruits.

Four musicians sauntered around the open space in the middle, with two sleek greyhounds and two wolfhounds snuffling at their heels. The two women and a man played shawm, recorder, and gittern. A child kept time on the tabor.

I stiffened. The child was Agnes. That little wretch! Her face was painted white and green, but I knew her. Oh, yes.

I studied the musicians. The women I didn't recognise, though they must be the women Agnes knew from Eliza's place and the Broken Seld, as one was clearly blind and both wore my new surcoats. The man wore the motley red-blue-green patterned hose and tunic of a jester. His face was both painted and half-masked. But I suspected it was Alistair Morrigan.

There was little I could do. As people filed in and took their seats, their attention turned to the musicians. I couldn't walk out in front of everyone and drag Agnes off the floor. Had she planned it that way? Disobedient child!

I waited, fuming, my stomach roiling and palms sweating.

A herald announced the arrival of the king and queen. Everyone rose, benches scraping on the timber floor, chatter dying to excited whispers. I craned to see around a pillar and gasped.

The queen was resplendent in a cloth-of-gold gown studded with sapphires and diamonds, sparkling in the lanternlight. She wore a matching cloth-of-gold gable headdress with a hair net made of diamonds and seedpearls. On the white skin of her breast lay a heavy sapphire and diamond chain.

King Henry wore a doublet of purple and cloth-of-gold, again stitched with pearls, sapphires and diamonds. His hose were purple, and his long, pointed shoes and purple velvet hat all glittered with more gems. He held his head high, straight dark hair neatly to his shoulders, shrewd eyes sweeping the room.

Behind the royal pair walked a young lady-in-waiting in a green brocade surcoat. She carried the baby, Prince Arthur, swaddled in cloth-of-gold, sound asleep.

The assembly bowed and curtseyed, then waited for the couple to sit before joining them. I glanced at Agnes but, instead of leaving the centre of the room, the musicians merely sat on the floor with the dogs while the king rose and made speeches.

I heard none of it, my attention fixed on Agnes. Toasts were made. Drinks quaffed. More speeches. Laughter, applause, gifts given. Would it ever end?

The musicians rose and began playing again. Servants brought course after course of food. Enough to feed everyone in London. Capons and roast quail, roast duck, swan, and goose. Soups and soft white breads. Fruits and cheeses of all kinds. Then three whole, roast boars. Sweetmeats and sugared pastries. Wines, ales, drinks of all sorts.

On a sideboard behind the long table opposite me stood a dazzling array of gifts. Swords, rolls of purple silks finer than the one I carried, wooden chests bound in gold, a strangely-prosaic ceramic jug with a red seal—like something one would store honey in.

And, all through the feasting, the music never stopped. The four musicians paused occasionally to drink or eat, but they never left the floor. I waited in the shadows, shifting, too queasy to pluck anything from the trays of food. Something was wrong. I just knew it.

At last, Morrigan whispered to Agnes, who passed her tabor to one of the girls and dashed off. I hurried around and snagged her by the arm before she reached the door.

'Where do you think you're going?'

She scowled and tugged against my grip. 'I have to deliver a message for Morrigan, and it's important so you gotta let me go, Livia. Why are you here anyway, can't you leave me be?'

'No.' I bent over her, glaring. 'Harken to me, Agnes. Morrigan left you and Jack in my care. This is dangerous. Come home now.'

Agnes wrenched her elbow free and backed away. 'You don't care about me, only about stupid clothes and about Jack, so leave me alone!' She spun and was gone before I could catch her.

I was ready to scream in frustration. All I could do was go back to my post and wait and watch. But at least Agnes seemed to be in no danger. Perhaps I had been overprotective. Perhaps my imagination had got the better of me.

She reappeared a few moments later, nodded to Morrigan, and took up the tabor again. Her gaze swept the room and narrowed when she spotted me. She showed her back.

The king rose and waved for silence. All heads turned to him, faces flushed and smeared with grease. A shout of drunken laughter was quickly stifled. One of the dogs barked.

'Lords, ladies and good folk all,' the king said, raising his goblet. 'I have one last, pleasant duty to perform this evening before our cooks bring out the final dish. We have several guests tonight who are here for a special occasion. Pray, Lord Chamberlain, read the list.'

A man stepped forward and unrolled a scroll. He rattled off several noble names and men rose from amongst the seated. Then he said the name 'Lord Francis Lovell', and I froze in the shadows. He was here.

He rose and bowed. A small man. Dark-haired, dark-eyed, sharp-featured. The set of his grey silk doublet was spoiled by the leather satchel slung over one shoulder. And the doublet bore the shadow of a dark stain on the right side. I smiled thinly.

His right hand rested on the ruby-studded hilt of a dagger. His left gripped spasmodically at the empty sword-sheath on his left hip. A red-stone ring glittered on his finger.

'All of you,' the king said calmly, 'shall be granted a full pardon for your part in the battles between ourselves and Richard, the false king.'

There were some mutterings around the hall but the king called for order.

'The pardon will, of course, be conditional on your pledge of loyalty to the crown, to myself as King of England, and to Prince Arthur as the Heir Apparent.'

A great cheer went up, but Lovell and others of those standing merely bowed, their expressions unreadable. Was it my imagination or did Lovell exchange quick looks with several of them? I put the bolt of cloth down, my stomach knotting. Something was going to happen. I could feel it.

I had to get Agnes out.

'What of our lands, Your Grace?' someone called. It could have been Lovell's voice. I wasn't certain.

The king shook his head. 'Any lands remain the property of the

Crown, held in trust by those I've appointed to administer them, until such time as those pardoned have proven themselves trustworthy and loyal. A small stipend will be given for living expenses.'

Now Lovell's scowl was unmistakable.

King Henry clapped. 'Let us celebrate! Bring in the subtlety. Musicians, play!'

Lovell's irritation lightened. He rose and sauntered toward the gift table, one hand resting on the leather satchel at his hip. He fingered the gifts, lifting and inspecting a goblet, then a glittering tray.

The musicians struck up a lively tune. Morrigan and Agnes began to wend their way around the room, encouraging people to clap along. Agnes led the way, tapping the tabor and skipping.

When they reached the gift table, she glanced away away at the wrong moment and bumped into Lovell. I took a half-step forward, wanting to call her name in warning.

Lovell turned on her, snarling. Morrigan distracted him with a flourishing bow and some words I couldn't hear. The muscians danced on, leaving the table, drawing all eyes but mine with them.

Lovell reached into his satchel and—so fast I hardly saw his hand move—he swapped over the red-sealed ceramic jar on the table for one identical. But why?

He waved a servant over and spoke into her ear. She curtseyed and he returned to his seat.

Behind him, the servant-girl opened the jar and spread what might be honey onto a piece of thick, white bread. She took the honeyed bread and the jar, placed them onto a tray and presented it to the king and queen. They exchanged looks of mild surprise then accepted.

Now nausea roiled in my stomach. What should I do? Was it merely a harmless gift, a peace offering? But why had he swapped the jars? I couldn't speak out, I was no-one. A look at my face and they would turn aside in disgust. And what could I say, anyway? Your Grace, I think you've been poisoned? What was my proof?

The royal couple nibbled on their sweetbread and spoke softly, with loving looks to each other. Lovell's smile deepened with each bite they took.

The musicians shifted to a slow, mournful song and the queen straightened. She leaned over to His Grace and murmured into his ear. He nodded, kissed her cheek, and waved for silence.

'Her Grace is indisposed. She and the prince will retire for the evening. Lord Chamberlain, send Mistress Kennet, the midwife, to check on her and the babe, pray?'

The assembled nobles rose and genuflected as the queen departed, with the lady-in-waiting and the babe right behind.

Lovell hid his delight behind a cup of wine. But I could see. Why could no-one else?

A stir at the servants' entrance rippled through the crowd, sounds of admiration and smatterings of applause. Eight male servants appeared, bearing on their shoulders an enormous timber table. On that stood a huge closed pie. The subtlety. Enough to feed five families.

The crust was crisply-golden. Perfect. I sniffed but couldn't tell whether it was savory or sweet-filled. Hard to imagine the size of oven needed for such a thing.

The men lowered the table, bowed and retreated. King Henry rose again.

'My cooks have outdone themselves.' He raised his cup. 'And, if those men I've pardoned would stand again so the servants may see them, they will get first serving of this astonishing creation.' When the pardoned men hesitated, His Grace gestured again. 'Up, if you please, gentlemen.'

They rose. Lovell's eyes narrowed. His fingers tightened around the dagger at his hip.

One of the female musicians curtseyed and spoke in a clear, strong voice.

'If Your Grace pleases, we have composed a new tune to honour this occasion.'

Henry inclined his head and sat.

The musicians played a few opening bars then launched into song, Agnes singing with them in a lilting soprano.

Sing a song for sixpence,
A pocketful of rye.
Four and twenty blackbirds,
Baked in a pie.

Lovell stilled, his attention on the singers. His mouth moved, though I couldn't hear the words. The rigid lines of his body told their own story. He was ready to fight.

And Agnes was in his sight: so small, so vulnerable.

When the pie was opened,
The birds began to sing,
Wasn't that a dainty dish,
To set before the king?

The pie crust smashed open—from the inside. Pastry scattered in all directions. Laughter and clapping gusted through the crowd. The music stopped and Alistair Morrigan handed his gittern to Agnes. She gripped it, her jaw set, determined.

I bit back a cry of warning. My head felt fuzzy, my mouth like it was muffled in velvet, my face hot.

Four people rose from inside the pie, standing tall on the high table. Four women—no, barely more than girls. Each dressed in one of my new doublets. Each wearing half-masks hiding their faces.

Each bearing a longbow or crossbow, sword and dagger.

A girl with short, dark hair and a crossbow tossed a longbow and quiver of arrows to Morrigan.

Now the crowd's chatter became gasps and cries demanding explanations. The gentry looked to the king for guidance. He rose, gesturing to his guards. They surrounded him, swords drawn.

I checked Lovell.

His face twisted into a feral grin, his gaze fixed on the women on the table. He shifted, stepping back so he stood behind the bench, free to move.

'What is the meaning of this?' The king's cry was barely audible over the ruckus.

A yeoman of the guard hurried in. 'Your Grace,' he yelled, panting. 'Your Grace, the Beauchamp Tower. It's on fire! The prisoners. We have to get them out.'

Fire? I shrank, huddled against a post. Would it spread? Were we in danger? Surely I could smell smoke. A whimper escaped me.

Henry pushed through his guards. 'God's teeth! Plantagenet is in that tower.'

Lovell gave a shout of triumph and pointed at the armed women. 'Kill the Tudor upstart!'

King Henry's lips pulled back. 'Men, take him.'

I froze, watching, waiting. Was the king to be murdered and my Agnes a part of it? She would be hung as a traitor. Had Morrigan betrayed all of us?

Five arrows flew from five bows. Women and men screamed and sheltered beneath the tables. Lovell ducked behind his dinner companion.

Four of the pardoned men cried out and fell with arrows buried deep in their bodies. Lovell's body-shield died, screaming, gurgling,

Blackbirds Sing p383

scrabbling at the shaft in his throat.

Shrill cries of terror erupted. People leapt to their feet, overturning tables and benches. Food and plates crashed to the floor.

The dogs barked, low and menacing, advancing on Lovell and the other pardoned men still standing.

Men jumped over the tables, drawing daggers.

I cried Agnes's name, but my voice was lost in the din. I had to get her out of danger.

The female archers nocked second arrows and fired again. More of Lovell's men fell, but not all.

Lovell vanished. The rest fled into the crowd, hidden by the innocent.

'Protect the king!' Morrigan cried. The four archers climbed down and ran to stand before the king.

Skirmishes broke out, men struggling against each other, throwing punches, swinging daggers. Blood spilled.

A woman plunged toward me, screaming, flailing her arms. She ploughed into me, scratched the silk from my face and recoiled in horror. Her screams grew louder and she ran toward the door, jostling with others trying to fight their way out.

Morrigan and two of the archer-women disappeared, leaving two protecting the king.

And in the midst of it all, Agnes remained, grinning fiercely.

I couldn't wait any longer. She would be killed if she stayed there. Either by a dagger or by the fire that would sweep through the tower. Only she mattered.

I sucked a steadying breath, drew my belt-knife and ran into the fray, shoving my way through to the open space in the middle.

Agnes sat calmly beneath the table, holding gittern and tabor, with the two women musicians by her side.

'Agnes!' I scrambled in beside her and snatched her into my arms. 'You're alright!' I patted her head and body, checking for injuries. 'You are alright?'

She pushed me away. 'Course I'm alright, cause I know better than to get in the middle of a fight with that many knives being waved around.' She jerked a thumb at the melee. Her eyes widened and she pointed, clutching at one of the musician's arms.

'Bella! It's Lovell! He's getting away, quick, we gotta find Morrigan and tell her.' Agnes struggled to her knees.

I gripped her wrist and held tight. 'Don't go, Agnes. Please?'

She glowered. 'I gotta. Bella hasta stay with Nic and I'm the only one who saw which way he went, so Morrigan needs me.'

'I need you, too,' I said. Grief strangled me. 'I lost Clara. It was my fault. She was playing where I'd told her not to. Her clothing caught fire. I couldn't save her.'

I brushed tears aside, covering my burnt face with one hand. 'I-I can't lose you, too, Agnes. There's a fire coming. Please? I want to protect you. I want you to be safe.'

Wonder dawned in Agnes's green eyes and she threw her arms around my neck.

'You *do* care about me?'

'More than anything.'

She kissed both my cheeks and stroked the scarred one gently. Her expression was too wise for a ten-year-old child.

But perhaps Alfred was right, and she wasn't the child I'd lost, but a strong young woman, instead. One I needed to trust, not protect.

She wasn't Clara.

I sniffed and gave a broken sigh. 'Go, then. Tell your Morrigan. But come back to me safe. Promise?'

Her blinding smile flashed and she nodded.

Then she was gone. Outside, something exploded. Then another. And fear filled me with dust and ash again.

24. Shall be Lifted…Nevermore

Laura Kennet, 56
Midwife
Lyme Street, London,

Tuesday (late afternoon), 26th September, 1486

Bless me, Oswin,' I said, sinking gratefully onto a chair, 'but there must be an easier way to earn a living. Four babies already today, and it's only just after Vespers, an all. And Goodwife Carter is due to pop.' I scrubbed at my face with hands reddened by repeated washing. Downstairs, a baby cried and I started, then relaxed. My daughter's newest. She was fine.

My husband looked over his eyeglasses. He set aside his book and folded thin fingers over his stomach. Afternoon light streamed across his lined skin and glared off the parchment maps and charts littering his worktable.

'It could be a little late to change now, dearheart,' he said. 'You've been a midwife your whole life.' He cocked his head. 'Still, you could always try gongfarming. Good money in mucking out privies—at least, based on what we pay Goodman Abbott.'

I shot him a dry look.

He patted my leg. 'You know you love helping babies into the world. Oh, a message came in for you. The queen postponed your visit to check on her and the young prince. She's getting ready for the christening feast tonight'

'Well, that's a relief. I'll go tomorrow.' I put my feet up on Oswin's lap, enjoying the peace and quiet. We'd set one of the bedchambers aside for him to use as an office for his map-making, but it had also become a place for us to spend time without the grandchildren underfoot.

'So how did the four today go, then?' he asked, rubbing my

swollen ankles.

'At least they all lived. The St Anthony's Fire took twenty in the last week.' I sighed. If only I could save them all. Each death tore away a piece of me.

'I know, dearheart. I know.'

'Maybe,' I said, staring up at the dark timber ceiling, 'there'll come a day when saving babies and mothers is easy. When keeping them alive is more important to men than killing each other over thrones an all.'

He snorted. 'Perhaps, but I wouldn't hold your breath. Men are foolish about these things.' He tapped the map in front of him. 'They never understand that people don't own the land; the land owns people. Without it, we die. Without us, it thrives.'

I stared at him a long time. 'Bless me, Oswin, that was worthy of the old-time philosophers, themselves.'

With a self-conscious chuckle, he returned to massaging my feet. 'Truth is, dearheart, there's never going to be an easy way to save all the babies or mothers. Anything worth doing, takes pain, and work, and sacrifice.'

I rose and stood at the window, looking down on the street below. Two of my dearling grandchildren played with wooden sticks as swords, shouting and chopping at each other. Half a dozen other urchins egged them on.

I'd helped birth all of them. In fact, I'd delivered most of the people under forty years old on this street.

'Haven't I sacrificed enough, Os? Worked enough? I've lost two husbands to war, three children to illness and two grandchildren to stillbirths an all. Hundreds of mothers and babies to complications I couldn't fix. How much more do I have to give before it gets easier?' My voice broke. 'Why does God punish us by killing innocents?'

The chair creaked and Oswin came to stand behind me, his arms around my thick waist.

'I wish I could answer that, dearheart,' he murmured. 'But I can't. Why don't we go downstairs and see what Ada has made for supper? You'll feel better after you eat and drink a pot of ale with me.'

I turned in his arms and hugged him close, resting on his lean chest, listening to the steady, reassuring thud of his heart.

'You're right, Os. I'll be fine. I'm just tired an all.'

He kissed my forehead, then my lips, and stroked back my wiry hair. 'I love you, Laura Kennet, you know that?'

'And I love you, you soft-hearted lug. Now get me that ale.'

Eight of us were seated, rowdy and laughing, at the kitchen table when a great banging on the front door startled us all into silence. Oswin rose.

'Don't bother,' I said, swallowing a mouthful of stew in a hurry. 'You know it'll be for me, an all. It's probably Mistress Carter's time. You lot finish up.'

I kissed Oswin's cheek and ruffled my oldest grandson's mop of hair. 'I'll be back as soon as I can, for you lot promised me a game of skittles in the front room, remember?'

Young George hugged my hips and flashed me a gap-toothed grin. The other two boys laughed and shouted in excitement until my daughter, Ada, settled them. She bounced Alice on one knee and I tickled the rounded little baby belly until I got a giggle.

The front door knocker thudded again.

'Anon!' I called, gathering up my medical bag and cloak. The evening was coming over chilly and I had no idea how long I'd be gone.

I yanked open the door and blinked at the red uniform on the panting young man standing there.

'It's the queen, Mistress Kennet,' he said. 'She's feeling poorly and the king requires you to attend her.' He pointed at the horse waiting in the street. 'We'll ride back.'

I crossed myself. 'Only if you're steering, laddie. Those beasts hate me, an all.'

I held on for dear life as we cantered through the busy streets. Barefoot children yelled and chased us. Men swept their wives out of the way and frowned after us. But the guard's scarlet coat and commanding cry for folk to make way split the crowds and we clattered through without stopping, all the way to the barbican. The guards there waved us through.

We rode to the entrance to the Queen's House. The guard helped me dismount, staggering under my weight. I groaned, holding my arse where the trotting had all but shattered my seat-bone.

'It's this way, Mistress,' the guard said, pointing up the torch-lit stairs.

I batted at his arm. 'I know, I know. Been here before, an all. Just can't walk after that rackety ride of yours. Get you gone, boy. I'll be fine from here.' I squinted over his shoulder. 'Bless me! Looks like you've got trouble.' I pointed.

He gasped. The western wall tower was ablaze, flames licking and dancing out of the narrow windows. Dirty-red smoke smudged the early stars and sank into the Tower grounds. I coughed and lifted my apron to my nose.

Screams echoed in the huge Tower courtyard. The guardsman and I froze. He drew his sword and shoved me behind him, bless the boy. More screams, shrill and deep alike, men and women. But they didn't seem to be coming from the burning tower.

People began streaming from the White Tower's first-storey

entrance, running down the wooden staircase, pushing at each other. Noblewomen lifted their skirts and ran like things possessed. Servants fled along with them, all equal in their fear. Men hesitated, forming a knot at the bottom of the stairs, staring back up at the White Tower.

Something exploded near the burning tower and everyone ducked and screamed. A flash of light and another bang. More screams.

'God's heart!' the guard swore. 'They were handgonne shots.'

I pushed him. 'You'd best go find your commander, boy. I'll attend the queen and see she's safe.'

He cast me a grateful look and hurried toward the White Tower.

I heaved myself up the stairs toward the queen's bedchamber, looking back twice.

Whatever was happening in the White Tower and the burning one, I was glad the queen and the babe were out of it. We'd have to keep a watch on the fire to make sure it didn't spread. But a bucket brigade had already formed to the well and the river. The flames were dying.

Hopefully the gonneshots had just been guards panicking in the dark. I'd treated a gonneshot wound after the last battle for the throne. They were nasty. My patient had died.

I knocked briskly on the queen's chamber door and Lady Roslyn Stanley admitted me. She glanced quickly up and down the corridor outside then closed the door behind me. She wore her finest green brocade surcoat and her mother's emerald necklace that she'd shown me last week, so she must have been to the feast already.

'Why is the queen back from the feast so soon, an all?' I asked. 'The guard said she needed me. Is her bleeding worse? Is the babe well? What's all the fuss in the White Tower about?'

Lady Roslyn cast me a harried look. 'Best ask Her Grace, Mistress. Things are quite…strange, tonight. What were those bangs I heard?'

'Hand cannons,' I said grimly. 'Vicious things. Tear great holes in flesh and leave lead balls in a body to fester and spread infection.'

She paled. Then she led the way into the royal bedchamber and curtseyed. 'Mistress Kennet…Your Grace.'

The queen sat at her desk, dressed in a shining cloth-of-gold gown, with a matching headdress, and necklace of sapphires. She nodded regally then returned to writing something. The prince seemed to be asleep in his cot, though I could only see his swaddling.

The rest of Her Grace's companions surprised me. I nodded to the two I recognised.

'Master Morrigan.'

He bowed, but his attention seemed to be elsewhere, his focus on the door behind me, or even beyond it. The remains of red and white paint showed at his ears and hairline. He wore the motley hose of a jester, but a plain grey wool tunic. He held a sword and a longbow. A quiver of arrows lay across his back.

'Flora, dear.' I addressed Lady Roslyn's young maid. 'I'm so sorry to hear about your Edmund.'

She flushed to the roots of her dark hair and dipped a quick curtsey. 'Gramercy, Mistress.'

I studied the final person. 'And who might you be, dear?' She was a tall girl, perhaps twenty years, with long, dark-blonde hair and steady grey eyes. But she carried a sword and dagger, and wore a man's grey silk doublet and hose.

'Scientia Wilson, Mistress Kennet. I'm here to protect the queen.'

'Are you, an all?' I studied them narrowly. 'Then bless you, dear. But where is she? Come on, ladies. You didn't truly think to fool me, did you? Eliza Parry what are you doing in that getup?'

Eliza laughed, rose and embraced me. 'I told you, Morrigan. Even if I kept me mouth shut she'd know me anyways. She delivered me, for Lord's sake.'

Morrigan ran a hand through his dark hair and grimaced. 'We had hoped, Mistress. For we need the disguise to be good enough to fool Francis Lovell, should he make it this far.'

'Lovell, eh?' I screwed up my nose and studied the room. 'Well, it should fool anyone who doesn't know the queen well. But you might want to hide the weapons, for we all know royalty are allergic to steel. That's what tipped me off to start with. And she doesn't swaddle the babe so tight, but I don't expect a man would know that.' I nodded at Eliza. 'Her Grace is right-handed, so you'd best swap that pen over if you're going to stay there.'

Eliza swore.

Lady Roslyn pressed her fingers to her cheeks. 'I'm so foolish! I should have realised. It's just...' She threw a fear-filled glance at the door. 'I don't quite know if I can face him.'

Flora cast her a scathing look.

'Be not afraid, Lady Roslyn,' Morrigan said. 'Flora can answer the door if he does come. You need only lend your presence to make the falsehood seem real.'

'Oh, no, Master Morrigan,' Flora said, glowering. 'If I'm to answer the door, then give me a dagger for I've a score to settle with that man.'

Morrigan gripped her shoulder. 'We cannot kill him until we know the extent of his following. No point in cutting off the snake's head if it grows another.'

'But what about that fire?' Scientia put in. 'And the shots. And the king?'

Morrigan sighed and rubbed at his forehead. 'Ladies, can we please agree that we are here for one task? To protect the queen. We must assume that Lovell or his men will come for her. He's also trying to kill the king and to liberate the young Earl of Warwick, the last Plantagenet heir. I have people protecting the king, and another protecting the Earl. So please concentrate on the here and now.'

'What else can we do?' Eliza said, hands on her hips. 'I'm not much on waitin about for things to happen.'

Morrigan's mouth twitched. 'I'd noticed. And I must leave you. If Lovell sees me here, the charade is ended before it begins.'

Eliza frowned and Lady Roslyn whimpered.

Morrigan added, 'Scientia is a fine swordswoman. A smooth transition of kingship is what Lovell wants, not outright war again. He is doing everything in his power to make the queen's seem natural, if not Henry's. He's unlikely to come storming in, sword swinging.'

'Unlikely,' Eliza said drily, 'not definitely. Not sure I'm excited by that, Morrigan. You said he ordered the girls to shoot Henry, before.' She rummaged under her skirt and came up with a wicked dagger. 'I'll be keeping this to hand, anyways.'

'Well,' I said. 'I'm no use here, since I've never used my belt-knife for more than cutting a babe's cord. Best take me to Her Grace, an all. The king sent for me, so I'd rather not disobey him and lose my head.'

'She's quite well,' Lady Roslyn assured me.

'That's as may be, dear,' I replied, 'but I'd rather be sure.'

Lady Roslyn looked to Morrigan, who nodded and said, 'She's in the Lady of the Bedchamber's private chamber.' He pointed to a wall panel in the corner. 'Through that door. Take her, Roslyn?'

The panel swung open to reveal a dark corridor. Lady Roslyn carried a candle, but her hand quaked so the light danced and quivered on the stone walls. I took it from her gently and led the way.

'Is that the door ahead?' I asked. She nodded. I passed the candle back. 'Off you go, then.' I patted her shoulder. 'Don't be afeared, dear.

Morrigan'll look after you, an all.'

She nodded again then hurried away, leaving me in darkness.

I fumbled my way to the door and knocked.

'It's Mistress Kennet, Your Grace. Morrigan and the king sent me to check on you.'

The door swept open to reveal a room about half the size of the queen's bedchamber, but with stone walls covered in tapestries, rather than the windows Her Grace's room had. The canopied bed was large enough for three people and draped with red velvet instead of purple.

The queen sat on the edge of the bed, wearing a chemise and plain grey kirtle—probably what Eliza had arrived in. The young prince lay on the bed, gurgling and waving his pudgy arms and legs.

The queen rose and hurried over. 'Oh, Laura, you've no idea how glad I am to see you.' She sent a nervous look at the other three women in the room and whispered, 'I have no idea who these women are. Master Morrigan sent them.'

'I know all of them, Your Grace. Rest easy.' I greeted the other women. 'Philippa. And young Beatrice?' Both wore elegant long surcoats of silk, Philippa's daffodil yellow and Beatrice's a shimmering dark brown to match her eyes and hair. 'What are you doing here?'

Philippa raised her silken veil and touched her cheek to mine. ''Tis simple. Master Morrigan sent us to the feast to watch over the queen. We came away with her before the screaming and banging started. Do you know what's happening?'

'Not at all,' I replied. 'A fire in the western tower which seems to be almost under control. The bangs were hand cannon shots. Maybe just guards panicking.'

The queen paled and chewed on her lip. She laid a protective hand on Arthur's stomach.

The room's final occupant had let me in and locked and barred the door behind me. She wore a man's doublet, carried a slim steel blade, and had cropped-short dark hair.

'Ingaret, dear,' I said. 'Good to see you again.'

The young assassin's deep blue eyes assessed me thoroughly and dismissed me.

'And you, Mistress Kennet. Handgonnes, you said?' She clucked her tongue. 'Nasty.' She pulled a small crossbow from her belt, cocked and loaded it. Then she stalked to the door that opened to the main corridor and stood facing it, waiting.

Leaning over to Philippa, I murmured, 'Does the queen know who you, Eliza, and Beatrice are?'

Philippa glanced across at the queen, who was cradling her baby and singing him a soft lullaby. The same lullaby I'd sung my children and my grandchildren.

Hush, pretty baby, don't say a word
Mama's going to call you a sweet blackbird.

'I don't know,' Philippa replied. 'Tis unlikely. I've given only my first name and kept my veil down.'

'Wise, I think, given how afeared she is, an all. Let's see if I can calm her while you keep watch with young Ingaret.'

I put my bag on a table and moved over to the queen. Curtseying, I held out my arms. 'May I, Your Grace?'

She flashed me a quick, worried smile and passed the princeling over. I held him in the crook of my arm and stroked his soft cheek. His little mouth opened and his head turned toward my finger. His fists thumped at my arm.

'When's he due for a feed?' I sniffed at his swaddling. 'And he could use a change, I think. Where's his wetnurse?'

'I don't know. I gave her a few hours off because we were at the feast. She was supposed to be back by now.' Her Grace's grey-blue eyes lifted to mine and she was, for once, just a frightened young mother. 'What do I do, Laura?'

I patted her wrist. 'Bless you, dear. It will all work out. First, we need to get him changed. Any fresh linens for him in here?'

She shook her head, her hands fluttering helplessly.

'Well then, let's tear up some of these sheets. That will do for now, an all.' At least it would give the queen something to do. Something to keep her occupied while Morrigan sorted out Lovell.

Once she'd learned how to change Arthur's linens, the queen seemed to steady. She rocked the boy, singing the lullaby again, smiling at him like she'd never seen him before.

'I hardly get to spend any time with him,' she murmured. 'Between the wetnurse, the ladies-in-waiting, and my mother-in-law all telling me what not to do and what to do, I've been afraid to even hold him.'

I chuckled. 'That happens in many noble houses, Your Grace. Too much help is as bad as none, sometimes. You're doing fine.'

Arthur squirmed, his face screwing up. He gave a hiccupping, thin little cry. And another.

'He must be hungry,' she said. 'But I have nothing. What do we do?' She searched round the room as though hoping the wetnurse would appear by magic.

At the door, Ingaret snorted. 'Heya, don't look at us, Your Grace.' She pointed at the others in turn. 'She's a nun, Bea's got no children, Mistress Kennet's too old, and I'll never have babies even if you pay me. You want to feed him, do it yourself.'

The queen flushed bright pink and laid a hand on her breasts. 'I cannot. He went straight to wetnursing.'

Arthur's wails grew louder, piercing in the small, enclosed space.

Ingaret's lip curled in a sneer. 'Well, find some way to shut him up or hid'n out here'll be pointless.' She stilled, scowling. 'Hist! Voices in the stairwell lead'n to the queen's bedchamber. Quiet him, now!'

'Put him to the breast, anyway,' I said. 'He may just want the comfort of it.'

I took the babe and stuck a finger in his mouth while Her Grace yanked off her kirtle and pulled open the front of her chemise. She took him back and fumbled with her breast. He cried, pummelling at her, his face beet red. Then he latched on and sucked with all his might.

We all released a sigh.

Ingaret had her ear against the keyhole. She laid a finger across her lips and frowned at us. We froze. Only the noise of Arthur's suckling broke the silence.

Male voices in the corridor outside. Someone shouting directions to the queen's bedchamber. Was that Lovell? I didn't know him. By Bea's pale face and wide eyes, though, it could well be.

The voices and footsteps faded, heading away from our hiding place.

The baby pulled away from the breast and wailed his frustration at the lack of milk, loud and shrill.

Ingaret glared.

Footsteps thudded, returning.

'Cover yourself, Your Grace,' Ingaret snapped. 'Don't give him any advantage. Stand strong.'

I held the squirming baby while she dressed again. Something thudded on the door and it rattled and creaked. The queen pulled on dignity like a cloak and took her son, holding him close, patting his back even as he squalled.

'Is there another way out?' Ingaret asked.

Her Grace shook her head, her jaw set. 'Only the corridor back to my chamber.'

Something thudded against that door, too. Muffled voices yelled, demanding entrance.

'That's me ma's voice,' Bea said, pointing at the door. 'Do we open it?'

We looked to the young queen. She nodded.

Ingaret grabbed her arm. 'What if it's a trick?'

Her Grace raised her chin. 'They'll get in soon, either way. I'd rather meet them with dignity and surrounded by friends, than be found cowering behind a bed.'

Bea rushed to the adjoining door and hauled back the bar and bolt. The panel flung open and the other women half-fell into the room. Scientia and Flora slammed the door shut and re-bolted it, panting. Then they joined Ingaret.

The main door shuddered again. Timber splintered.

'Sorry, Your Grace,' Eliza said brusquely. 'They were at our door, then we heard the baby screamin and they took off. Bastards. Goin after the babe.'

The young queen stared at her half-sister, mouth agape. 'Morrigan said you were alike me in face and form, but I had not realised how much alike. Who are you?'

Eliza grinned. 'Later, Your Grace.' She nodded at the door and hefted her dagger. 'We've got bigger things to worry about. Can't you shut that baby up?'

The queen frowned. 'No, I can't. Can you?'

'Not a chance.' Eliza looked the queen over. 'At least throw on Laura's cloak and hide your face. Maybe we can pretend you're the wetnurse and you're doin a really bad job of it.' She coughed, covering her lips with her gold-clad sleeve. Specks of blood dotted the cloth.

I hurried to throw my cloak over the queen. Her body shook and she clutched the baby tight. I patted her shoulder.

'Never mind, Your Grace. The king and Morrigan will come soon, I'm sure. We've only to hold them off a little while.'

'But what if they've lost?' she whispered. 'What if Lovell's forces are too many and the king is dead, and Morrigan with him?'

'Well,' I shrugged, 'we'll deal with it then, an all. No point in 'what-if-ing' your future away. Chin up. You're the Queen of England, remember?'

She nodded and clutched the baby close.

The door smashed open. Lady Roslyn let out a scream and shrank away. The rest of us stood firm, though my knees shook.

Half a dozen men poured into the room, steel flashing in the lantern-light, expressions grim. They brought the smell of smoke, gunpowder, and blood with them.

Ingaret's crossbow flung a bolt and a young man staggered back, screaming, scrabbling at the fletching sticking out of his eye.

The others surged closer.

Ingaret's slim blade flickered out and skewered one man in the heart. He gave a strange, gurgling sigh and collapsed, blood pulsing onto the floor in a puddle.

The others yelled and leapt over him. Scientia jumped into action. Her longsword clashed with another, loud in the small space. Her dagger slipped under his guard and into his stomach. She sliced up and blood sprayed from his lips.

I drew my tiny belt-knife, ready to defend the queen and the baby. Eliza moved forward, dagger ready, but I grabbed the gold dress and dragged her back.

'Don't you get in there,' I yelled. 'They'll kill you in a second. You're the queen, remember?'

She growled at me but stayed put.

Ingaret countered a daggerthrust with hers, spun and stabbed her stiletto up through throat and jaw, into brain. She wrenched her blade free and kicked at another man's ankles. He fell into his companions and two went down in a tangle of arms and weapons.

Scientia finished one off with a thrust to the chest. She drove an elbow into another's jaw and the crunch of bone made me want to cheer.

In the confined space, the two women had a chance of holding their own.

I began to hope.

With a cry of pain, Scientia staggered, clutching at her arm. Blood poured freely down her sleeve and dripped on the floor. Her dagger clattered to the timber. She fought grimly on, hacking a man's thigh to the bone.

More men pushed through. More blades appeared. Lady Roslyn shrieked, struggling in the arms of two men, a knife at her throat. Two more snatched Bea from my side and held her.

'Enough!' A male voice cut through the din. A small, dark-haired man appeared, shoving his way through to the front. The sword sheath at his hip was empty and he wielded only a ruby-studded dagger. His doublet bore an old, dark stain over his chest. I'd seen enough stains to know it was blood.

'Enough, I said.' He directed a glare at a man whose arm was shortened for a thrust into Ingaret's stomach.

'Lovell,' Ingaret snarled.

A chilly smile stretched his mouth. '*Lord* Lovell to you, wench.' His gaze travelled across all of us and the bodies on the floor. 'You've served your queen well. Drop your weapons and you won't be harmed.' His eye fell on Eliza. 'Most of you.'

Eliza held herself regally and looked down her nose at him. Ingaret and Scientia were swiftly disarmed and held. Someone snatched my belt-knife and Eliza's dagger as well.

Where was the king? Where was Morrigan? Was the queen right? Had we lost?

My stomach sank. That was the only answer.

Lovell glanced back over his shoulder. 'Someone keep watch in case any of the king's remaining men get any foolish ideas.'

He turned back to Eliza, covetous. 'Now, my dear Elizabeth, you can see my time has come. My men are freeing Edward Plantagenet as we speak. Your husband is either dead, or dying. England will be in York control once more.'

Eliza sniffed but said nothing. I chewed my lip. If she spoke, any chance we had was lost.

'I would like to know, though,' Lovell said circling her like a wolf, stalking, studying, 'why you aren't dead? After all, I saw you eat the poisoned honey.' He trailed a finger the length her neck and across her breasts. She curled a lip and spat at him.

He wiped the spit off his neck and laughed. 'Oh, this will be more fun than I'd hoped, even. You're a traitor to your family. Perhaps you'd prefer to die with your brat? Men?' He gestured them forward. 'Get rid of the other women. Leave only the queen and the babe.'

Lady Roslyn, Flora, and Bea were dragged, screaming and struggling, from the room. Ingaret, Philippa, and Scientia followed in silence. I stayed, folding my arms.

'You, wetnurse, give up the child.' Lovell took three impatient steps forward. He shoved me aside and yanked the queen's hood down. He gasped and took a step back, glancing between the half-sisters.

'God's balls!' He studied both women closely then pointed to Eliza. 'Eliza Parry. I had no idea how striking the resemblance was. Does she know?' He cocked his head at the young Elizabeth.

'Know what?' Elizabeth asked. She drew herself up, though her cheek was pale.

'Don't you listen to him,' I murmured.

'Sard you, Lovell,' Eliza Parry snarled. 'You men do too much thinkin with your yards and too much talkin out your arses. Just finish it.'

Lovell shrugged. 'Very well. I was hoping to make it look natural, but somehow all my plans to poison Henry and Elizabeth and their brat went amiss.' His eyes narrowed and he frowed at Elizabeth. '*Why aren't* you dead from the honey you ate, tonight?'

The queen looked down her nose. 'Because we knew about it.'

He smiled. 'If you're referring to Morrigan, I suspected he might have swapped the honey I gave the maid. I exchanged it for another jar at the table tonight. So I repeat: *why aren't you dead?*' He leaned in close to Elizabeth and she retreated a step, holding the babe tightly.

I barged in, hoping to distract him. 'Perhaps your people aren't as loyal as you thought?'

'Perhaps.' Lovell sent me a sneering look. 'But I've dealt with that. Morrigan is quite dead, I assure you, so don't expect a rescue.'

A punch in the stomach would have winded me less. I had no words left. Eliza looked at me with outright fear for the first time. Behind me, the queen choked out a denial. Arthur had cried himself into a snuffling, sobbing sleep and now his mother cried with him. For herself, for Morrigan, for all of us.

Lovell stretched a hand behind him. One of his men placed a lit serpentine matchlock hand cannon into it. Lovell coolly checked the weapon and levelled it at the queen. She glared at him. I had to admire her courage as she stared down death for herself and her child.

I'm coming. Hold him off a few more moments, Laura. We're coming.

I stiffened. That was Morrigan's voice. In my mind. But no-one else moved or spoke. Yet, somehow, I knew Morrigan was coming.

Lovell had lied. Or didn't know.

Lovell's finger curled around the trigger. His smile broadened.

But unless Morrigan was right outside the door, it was too late.

I looked at the young prince and my stomach burned. I'd brought that child into the world.

What right had a man to take a babe's life? To take a young mother's life. For the sake of a useless gold crown and the illusion of power.

True power lay in giving, not taking.

The hand cannon's gaping muzzle steadied on her heart. On the babe cradled against her breast.

Elizabeth stared Lovell in the eye. 'I hope you burn in Hell, Francis.'

'You can wait for me there, then.' He pulled the trigger.

I turned and embraced the baby and his mother.

An explosion nigh broke my eardrums. A thump in the back like someone had punched me. The queen screamed my name. The baby wailed. Voices yelled. Swords clashed. Another explosion.

I tried to breathe. The acrid smell of gunpowder.

Then came the pain. Oh, so much pain. Worse than childbirth.

I fell to my knees, coughing. Blood spattered on the queen's skirts and on the floor.

Someone called my name, over and over but the din of blood in my ears was too loud. Arms gathered me and cradled me close, like a mother holds a child. Something warm and wet slid down my back.

Each breath hurt more. Gurgled in my throat.

'Laura?' Morrigan's angular face appeared in my vision.

I whispered, 'You did come. Is the baby alright? And Elizabeth?'

He nodded, his eyes glistening with unshed tears. 'You saved them. They're fine. Lovell and his men are caught. The king lives, too.' He kissed my forehead. 'I'm sorry. I'm so sorry I was late. Lovell had snuck in more men than we thought. He almost got the king.'

'Not…your…fault,' I managed. I swallowed blood and the taste made my stomach turn.

Morrigan shook his head. 'I should have been here sooner.'

A young, red-headed woman dropped to her knees beside me. Helen O'Reilly. Maybe she could heal me? She'd saved so many of my children from St Anthony's Fire.

My chest felt heavy. She placed her hands over my breast, her brow furrowed. Morrigan looked at her with such hope and love it almost broke my heart. But her mouth drooped and she shook her head.

Morrigan swore. 'I'm sorry, Laura. We can't heal you. The lung is punctured. The heart, too. It's too much for us to heal.'

'I know. I know. It's alright.' I drew a gurgling breath. 'Just…tell my Oswin I love him? And the children.'

He bowed his head. Tears dripped on my skin.

I thought about Oswin, and my children, and theirs, and all the babies I wouldn't get to deliver.

The queen crouched beside me, tears streaming freely down her cheeks. She laid young Arthur in my arms and kissed my forehead.

'Thank you, Laura.'

I smiled and kissed his soft little cheek, leaving a smear of blood. He sighed in his sleep, lips pouting. Elizabeth gathered him up then clung to her half-sister, weeping. I glanced at Morrigan.

'Look after Her Grace and the prince for me?'

He nodded. 'I will.'

I closed my eyes.

25. Two and Twenty Blackbirds

Amsel Mór-Ríoghain, 432
Tower of London,

Blackbirds Sing p409

Tuesday (evening), 26*th* September, 1486

I lifted Laura's dying body into my arms and cradled her close. Her *enath*—her soul—slipped free of her clay with a final sigh. I travelled with her as far as I could to guide her into the *sianfath's* green warmth. Then, she was gone and the earth's binding force—the *sianfath*—brightened with the strength of her life.

I laid her empty shell on the red-canopied bed. Tears scalded my cheeks, dripping onto Laura's peaceful face. Her warm blood slicked my skin and stained the bedlinens. I raised my face to the uncaring world and roared a broken cry of loss and denial. For Laura; for Flora's Edmund; for Cecily's servant, Carter; for Thomasine's husband, Robard. For my own Cormac. For Anne de Mortimer, whose geas had set me on this path seventy years before.

For every woman who had lost a son or a husband or a father. For every innocent victim of these stupid men's games of war and power.

My hands clenched into bloodied fists on my knees and I shuddered. Such rage and despair boiled in my stomach that I could barely contain it. Had Lovell still been in the room, I might have ripped aside his mental shields and slain him with a thought.

Though that might be too quick and painless.

Standing by, Helen touched my arm. I stilled. Her strong, warm hands held my jaw, forcing me to meet her eyes.

'I'm sorry, Amsel.' Grief shadowed her again and she glanced at Laura. 'I'm so sorry.'

'This was my doing,' I whispered. 'I brought these women

together and she died because of my arrogance.'

'No.' She kissed my forehead. 'Because of you, England is not again plunged into turmoil and war. Because of you, the Tudors have a chance at a stable dynasty that can give us all time to heal.'

'But Laura…And the others who died.'

'Four, Amsel. Four instead of thousands. Remember that.'

I closed my eyes, trying to master the roiling darkness in my chest.

She gripped my shoulders and squeezed. 'But this is not yet over. We must bring Lovell before the king. Save your anger and grief. Bury it deep, for now. For we must meet these men on their own terms. Tears will not sway or move them. We must be strong.'

We carried Laura's body into the great hall and laid her out in state on one of the tables, with candles by her head and feet and flowers on her breast. I asked King Henry to admit only his privy councillors. The men he most trusted.

And the queen and her trusted ladies, of course. Henry argued, until I asked whether he really wanted the entire nobility of England to know his throne had been saved by a bunch of women and girls. He flushed and agreed.

Then I stood in the centre of the room, surrounded by twenty-one brave women, my heart breaking for the loss of one of the best. But I held back tears, for Helen was right: men don't respect them and can't understand the need for them. I would save them for later and weep with her husband and children.

Henry's guards brought in Lovell, Thomas Stafford, Richard Clinton and the dozen or so of Lovell's co-conspirators that remained alive. The vast majority lay dead, broken toy soldiers scattered about the Tower courtyards. So many deaths.

I hung my head. I should have realised how wide his reach was. How many malcontents he'd gathered to his banner. But he'd hidden that from both me and Calain.

Lovell and his men were pushed to their knees, their wrists bound, their weapons taken. He glared at me with bitter venom, but I felt nothing beyond pity and guilt. Perhaps, in time, I would look back and be satisfied with my work. But not yet.

'Now,' Henry strode in, nodding to his lords. He kissed his queen and checked his son, who suckled loudly at the nurse's breast.

Calain Gilmore followed close behind—the king's man, it seemed, though he'd not seen fit to tell me. Then again, I'd never told him my secrets, either. Perhaps we could have saved more lives if we'd been more open.

'Now.' Henry repeated, turning to me. 'Tell us. Who are you? Who is your lord?'

'I have none, Your Grace. But—'

'I requested Mistress Morrigan's presence in London, husband.' Elizabeth rose, regal even in her plain kirtle, with her hair loose like a girl's. The men around muttered, glaring. Calain looked to me, faint amusement in his grey gaze.

Elizabeth looked down her nose and the muttering died away. 'Many years ago, my mother told me that, if ever I was queen, and feared for myself or my children, I should send out a call for The Morrigan.' She waited for murmurs to run their course again. 'I heard rumours that Lovell intended to raise a rebellion against my husband.' She swept the assembled men with cool hauteur. 'Rumours no-one seemed to want to hear from the lips of a York woman. So I sent word. And Morrigan came.' She indicated me with an elegant gesture.

I bowed. 'Gramercy, Your Grace. May I explain?' I looked askance at Henry, who frowned, but nodded.

'I met Lovell in Isledon, exactly where Her Grace's message said he'd be. By chance he fell out with one of his men and I saw an opportunity. I inserted myself into his confidence.' I left out Calain's part. Twas his story to tell. Instead, I indicated two of the women around me. 'I also met Helen O'Reilly and Tilda Barrowman. Through them I discovered Lovell's plans to murder the royal family and release Edward Plantagenet from his prison here in the Tower. He had purchased certain poisons and herbs from a grain merchant. And required the merchant to sell tainted rye throughout London. He deliberately spread St Anthony's fire.' I gritted my teeth.

'Why, in God's name would he do that?' Henry asked.

'Why does any man do heinous things? Desire for power or money,' I countered, keeping my voice calm when I wanted to yell at him. At all of them. 'He wanted his lands back. The lands the crown stripped from him. Lovell had several plans in place. He hoped to make your deaths look natural—an illness—to prevent an uprising against Edward Plantagenet. The boy Earl is too young to quash a rebellion, so a clean transition would be better.'

Henry nodded and his counsellors muttered their agreement. I smiled bitterly. They all understood politics and cared little for the deaths of hundreds of innocent Londoners who'd eaten the rye.

'Once in London, I met with these other women.' I indicated them in turn. 'Each contributed her piece, her help, or her expertise to the thwarting of Lovell's plans. Under Lovell's instruction I approached Catherine Miller to bake tonight's subtlety. But, of course, I chose the people to go inside.'

Catherine bobbed a curtsey, her florid face almost purple.

I reached inside the broken pie, still in the centre of the hall, and pulled out a roll of leather. Untying it, I flattened out a folded sheet of thin vellum and walked to the high table with it. The blue-wax seal was broken. As I passed Lovell, he snarled and spat at my feet.

'What is that?' he growled. 'You have no proof of anything. I was trying to save the queen from a traitor tonight. That dead woman tried to kill Her Grace and I prevented it. You have no proof, curse you, Morrigan.'

I bowed and presented the letter to the king. 'You'll find the details of Lovell's plans here, Your Grace. Tis clear enow. The rye poisoning was only the start. He asked Thomasine Smith, the barber-surgeon, to test a quick-acting poison. Extorted from Master Wilson the location of the secret entrance into Edward Plantagenet's prison. And he threatened Emma Turner, the beekeeper, to make her give the queen poisoned honey through Flora Leon, Lady Roslyn Stanley's maid.'

Flora flushed and wiped at her eyes.

I continued, 'Lovell murdered Flora's betrothed, Edmund Moorson, in an attempt to force Flora to allow him entrance into the queen's bedchamber. Thomas Stafford wore Moorson's livery and admitted the rest of Lovell's men to the Tower grounds tonight.'

There was no point in explaining that I'd spirited Thomas away in an attempt to find out all of Lovell's plans. I had failed in that. His mind had held too little new information and was well-shielded. We had returned him to the Broken Seld—with his memory wiped clean of his kidnapping—to let this evening play out. It had been the only way? Hadn't it?

One more way in which I had failed Laura Kennet.

All I could do now was bring her murderer to justice.

I pointed at the stain on Lovell's doublet, and on Stafford's. The stains I'd asked Griselda Moor to deliberately leave in place. 'You can see young Moorson's blood still on both their doublets.'

'That isn't human blood,' Lovell said quickly. 'I ate rare roast and the blood splashed on me, that's all.'

'If I may?' I said 'We can prove the blood on Lord Lovell's

doublet is Edmund's.'

'Proceed,' Henry said.

Lovell snarled. He surged to his feet, bound hands stretched towards me. Two guards grabbed at his shoulders. One kicked at his ankles and Lovell collapsed awkwardly to the floor, yelling. The guards hauled him back to his knees and pressed their swords to his throat. He quieted, but his eyes blazed.

I nodded to Rose Griffiths. She came forward, her gaze firmly on the floor. The queen's greyhounds and the king's wolfhounds followed her. She handed me the shirt I'd given her days before.

I held it aloft. 'Tis a shirt belonging to Edmund Moorson, Your Grace. Given to us by his mother, Griselda, on the day he was murdered. Still stained with his blood.' I presented it to the dogs, who sniffed, whined and looked to Rose.

'Find,' she murmured. The dogs trotted obediently away, sniffing every person they approached. The room held its breath, and I did, too.

One after another, all four dogs touched their noses first into the stain on Stafford's then Lovell's doublets, whined and barked twice before sitting.

'Gramercy, Rose. I think that's enough.' It was a struggle to keep triumph from my voice. Every bit of evidence was another nail in Lovell's coffin and, right now, I wanted the lid immovably weighted with proof of his crimes.

Rose's smile was chill and small. 'By your leave, I'll keep the dogs where they are for the moment.'

Henry frowned, and switched his attention to the letter, reading closely. 'This says he planned to use poisoned candles as well!'

The lords present glanced uneasily at the multitude of flickering beeswax candles. Several covered their noses with their sleeves.

Blackbirds Sing p415

'Indeed, Your Grace. Luckily Dorothy Jacobson, who provides your candles, stood against Thomas Stafford's threats and refused. She substituted candles with wicks dyed to match the poison's colour. Others refused to help as well—Flora, and even Lady Roslyn Stanley, whom he tried to coerce into helping him get to Edward Plantagenet.'

Henry stroked his smooth chin thoughtfully. 'It seems we are surrounded by loyal women.' He returned to the letter. 'This is sealed with Lovell's own seal, and in his hand.'

'And you'll see, Your Grace,' I continued, sending Lovell a cool smile, 'that Lovell admits to murdering Humphrey Stafford. He brags about it, in fact. Apparently, Humphrey had second thoughts and planned to turn against him.'

'You slimy, traitorous…' Thomas Stafford scrambled to his feet and threw himself at Lovell, snarling. Henry's men held him back, barely.

'He's lying, Thomas,' Lovell snapped. 'Why would you believe him?'

Thomas stopped struggling. His dark eyes darted between me and Lovell.

'Because I witnessed the murder,' a clear voice interrupted. Nicola Willoughby stepped forward, her head high, her milk-white eyes obvious in the bright candlelight.

'She's blind!' one of the lords nearby called out, laughing. 'How can a blind girl witness anything?'

Here was the most delicate part of our evidence. Would these men—these men who valued strength and power above all—listen to a female even more helpless than they already believed women to be? Humphrey's murder would rank as a worse crime than Edmund's. They believed, after all, that a nobleman was worth more than a mere servant. I needed Henry to believe Nicola. To listen to her testimony.

I bowed to the young lord who'd laughed. 'A fair question, my lord. How can you bear witness, Nicola?'

With a scornful smile, she turned toward the young lord who'd spoken. She sniffed. 'Clove-scented is your favoured soap. You have a problem with your nose that affects your voice, and a small bell tuned to C hangs on your belt-purse. Probably so you can hear if cutpurses try to take it.'

The lord gaped and clapped a hand to his hip. Something jingled. Whispers and murmurs raced around the room. Would they hear her? If they refused, our case was weakened, for I was counting on Thomas's reaction.

Henry lifted a hand. The comments died away.

'Speak, then, girl.'

'I was outside the Broken Seld. I recognised Lovell's voice. He accused Humphrey of treachery, then he killed him. I smelled the blood. And the eau de chypre perfume he wears. And I heard the loose nail in his shoe.'

Henry nodded again and leaned over to listen to something his Lord High Constable, Lord Derby, said and murmured a reply before saying aloud, 'That seems a fair witness statement. Gramercy, Lady Nicola.'

'That's why you wanted her dead?' Thomas Stafford spat in Lovell's direction. 'Your Grace, my lords, I wish to tell you everything. All of this is true. And more.' He sent a spiteful, snarling glare at Lovell. 'Give me a pen and parchment and I'll tell you everything I know about this weakling bastard.'

Lovell wrenched at his bonds and released a scream of pure, raw frustration. The dogs bared their teeth, growling low. Talk and speculation erupted amongst the men.

Elizabeth caught my eye and jerked her chin toward the exit. She whispered in Henry's ear, rose and led the way out. I bowed one last time and withdrew, gesturing to the other women. The rest of this trial could be safely left in Henry's hands. Lovell and Stafford would not live much longer.

As I left, Lovell bared his teeth at me. I swept him a mocking bow. His curses and threats followed me out the door.

'What now, Amsel?' Helen rested her head on my shoulder. The queen and all the women had withdrawn from the great hall, leaving Henry and his counsellors to decide Lovell's fate. Now, my people were gathered in a large, airy chamber in the Queen's House, waiting.

Elizabeth entered. 'I've put Arthur to bed, but I cannot sleep until I know it all. Tell me. How did you get that letter from Francis Lovell? I find it strange that someone like him would put it all in writing so conveniently.'

'You're right, of course. He prides himself on never writing anything down. I am guilty of cheating, there. Agnes Webb stole his signet ring for me.'

The little thief left the protective circle of Olivia Grey's arm and bowed awkwardly.

'And tonight,' she piped up, 'we figured Lovell musta knew Morrigan'd changed the poisoned honey over the other day, so when he tried to put a new poison jug out, I stole it from his satchel and did a swap so he never noticed he was putting out good honey.' She beamed and I stifled a smile at the confused looks from the others.

'You did well, thank you, Agnes.'

She grinned.

I continued, 'Reina Hayward stole a harmless letter Lovell had written to his wife.' I indicated the girl, who blushed and sank into a deep curtsey. 'And she also used her father's silversmithing tools to create a copy of the signet ring. Though I'm guilty of blurring her memory of that for I feared she would inadvertently speak of it.'

Reina gaped at me, a flash of resentment in her eyes. I would need to watch her ambition and temper if my aim for these women was to work. Of all, she had the most potential for disruption and discord.

I kept speaking before she could interrupt, 'Unfortunately, Lovell's men discovered the original ring was at Cecily Hayward's Cahorsin shop, before I could retrieve it. When the Stafford brothers broke in to steal it, they murdered Cecily's beloved family servant.'

Cecily herself pushed through from the back, glowering. 'That memory-blur thing. Ya did it to me, too? Made me forget ya'd been in the shop?' She folded her arms. 'Carter died cause I couldn't recall having ya in the shop. I coulda given Lovell the ring if I'd known.'

I nodded. 'I couldn't let you remember at the time. You were terrified of Lovell and would have told him I had been there with Agnes, endangering both of us. I had to keep in mind my task: to find out Lovell's plans. I'm sorry for Carter's death. Truly.'

Sorrow wrenched at me again. Would I never escape the deaths? The loss? The guilt when it was my fault. Was this the real reason my people eschewed the company of humans? The fear of attachment and loss, over and over? Of guilt and of watching people they love suffer?

There was a long silence. Several women shuffled and looked sideways at each other and at me.

I waited. Cecily's anger and pain radiated from her. I deserved it. I had made terrible mistakes. Yes, I'd been trying to do the right thing, but that didn't make up for the hurt I'd caused. Cecily needed to lash out at me and I couldn't blame her. I bowed my head, waiting.

She heaved a sigh. And her soft arms went around me. I stiffened. She pulled me into a hug. Her tears dampened my cheek.

'Ya poor girl. You've carried this whole burden yourself for too long, haven't ya?' She patted my back then leaned away and held her palm against my cheek. 'Ya shoulda trusted me, lovey.' She kissed my forehead and stepped back.

My heart swelled. I didn't deserve such forgiveness. She was right. If I'd trusted more, we would have lost fewer.

Elizabeth's face clouded and she laid a gentle hand on my shoulder and Cecily's. 'I'm so sorry.' She looked across at Flora, who stood with Griselda Moorson. 'And I'm sorry for your loss, as well. I'll do whatever I can to make it up to you.' She turned back to me. 'Pray, continue.'

I regathered my scattered thoughts. 'There's little more, Your Grace. Philippa copied the handwriting and his signature. Rose trained her dogs to sniff out Edmund's scent. The others all did their parts to stop Lovell's attempts to poison you and your husband. Each played an important role.'

Isabella stepped up. 'But the song you had me write. What of it?'

'Do you have your lute? For that's a longer story. Sing the whole song. I'd like everyone to hear, for tis the tale of this week's events and should be passed on.'

She tuned her instrument and Nicola joined her voice in harmony.

Sing a song for sixpence
A pocketful of rye
Four and twenty blackbirds
Baked in a pie

When the pie was opened
The birds began to sing
Wasn't that a dainty dish
To set before the king?

The king was in his countinghouse
Counting out his money.
The queen was in the parlour,
Eating bread and honey.

The maid was in the garden,
Hanging out the clothes.
Along came a little dog,
And nibbled off her toes.

The dog was at the banquet,
Eating up his fill.
While his pack were waiting,
For the blood to spill.

But four and twenty blackbirds,
Forced the hounds to sing.
Wasn't that a tasty truth,
To set before the king?

There was a long pause as the women considered the words.

Elizabeth spoke, 'Lovell is the dog, is he not? They used to call him that in Richard's court.' Her smile faded. 'I never thought him so vile and ambitious. Years ago I thought he loved me. But today he was going to shoot my babe!'

Eliza Parry went to her half-sister and wrapped an arm around her shoulders. 'He had a thing for you, alright. But I think it were a bit of a dog-in-the-manger sort of thing. He couldn't have you, so no-one could. And it served him to have the last York heiress out of the way so the Earl of Warwick would be on the throne with no rivals.' She sent a warning glance at me.

I had already plucked from her thoughts the wish to keep her bloodline a secret. Twas a wise decision, for to expose her would be to endanger Beatrice and Philippa as well.

Isabella scowled. 'But I canna see how you knew who ta call on for help.' She indicated the assembled women. 'Why us? We're just ordinary women. Only a few of us can fight and that almost got us killed.'

'You believe you're ordinary?' With a smile, I encompassed all of them. 'You're not. None of you are. Men are wary of each other. Always watching, always expecting a dagger in the back. Women help each other to survive. But women are…' I laughed wryly '…invisible, if you like. Men don't realise how much you're capable of. I did. Well, my mother did. She planted the seed for an army, in case I needed one. And here you are.'

'But how?' Isabella insisted. 'How did she plant a seed? And Her Grace said she'd been told she could a-call on you. How did she know that?'

'Agnes, do you have my gittern?'

The girl started, dashed out and returned a short while later looking sheepish. 'Sorry. Left it out in the courtyard when things got mad, but it's alright, though!' She dusted it with her sleeve and passed it over.

The C strings had slipped. I tuned them. 'Dost any recognise this song?'

Hush pretty baby, don't say a word
Mama's gone and called you a sweet black bird
And when that little black bird doth come

Mama's gonna buy you a big war drum.

When that big war drum doth sound
Morrigan'll bring all the blackbirds to town
When those blackbirds they do sing
Mama mustn't worry on anything

'My mother sang it ta me,' Isabella said.

'Mine, too,' Agnes chimed in.

They all nodded and murmured assent.

I set the gittern aside. 'It goes on a little more, you'll remember. Tis a call to action. That song was written by my mother, The Morrigan. She gave it to a thousand families, to allow for some to die out, or produce only boys. Tis hard to explain, but any woman from those families, who has sung that song to her daughters, has planted a suggestion in her child's mind. A suggestion to awake when I called for help.'

My face heated as the women stared at me with wide eyes and gaping mouths.

I shrugged. 'I never thought I would need to use it. I was living quite comfortably, in Ireland.' Hoped I'd never be called on to use it, more like. So many times I'd railed against my mother's preparations for war, swearing I would never follow in her footsteps and cause death. Yet, here I was.

I nodded at Elizabeth. 'But Her Grace's message came through. I had to fulfil a promise I'd made long ago to her great grandmother, Anne de Mortimer.' I grimaced. 'I was too late to save Anne. Just after her son, Richard Plantagenet, was born, assassins slew her. On her deathbed she laid a geas on me: to help the queen and her heirs if they were in need.'

I sighed and stared out the window into darkness. 'For the next forty years I tried. Along with my husband, Cormac. But the feud between the Lancasters and Yorks took him from me and, in my pain, I hid from the world. Until now.'

Would that Cormac were here. How proud he would be of these women. For he had always told me how wise my mother was to lay the groundwork for my army in the minds of women. I had disregarded and dismissed his words—too long inured to the human way of thinking only men could effect change. How wrong I'd been.

There was a long, strained, disbelieving silence. The women exchanged uncomfortable glances. If they felt they'd been manipulated and used—which they had—then my whole plan could fall apart.

'Who's the twenty-fourth blackbird?' Agnes said. She counted heads. 'I mean, if you don't count the queen, and Laura's…gone, so who's the last one?' Trust a child's mind to find the one piece of information I preferred to withhold.

'Is it so important to know?' They nodded and I gave in. Would seeing the ruthlessness of my choices colour their decision? 'Normally the charm helps me find women of good character and strength. But I had a task that needed someone as unlike that as possible. So I chose Sarah Clark, the housekeeper at the Seld.'

'That daggletail slattern?' Isabella said, curling a lip. 'What could she do for you that no-one else could?'

'How could I ask this of any of you?' I spread my arms. 'I needed someone to kill me. Lovell had to believe me dead.'

A gasp whispered around the room. But Agnes and Ingaret nodded.

'It's true,' Agnes said.

Ingaret backed her up. 'We found Morrigan about dead in the

back room o the Seld. Took her to Eliza's and brought Thomas Stafford to her for a chat.'

I added, 'And we had to return Stafford with his memory blurred to play his part tonight and allay Lovell's suspicions around my disappearance and Nicola's.'

Ingaret folded her arms. 'Go back a bit. You were about dead. You healed. How *did* you do that? And this blurring memory thing? And how old *are* you?'

'Why must you ask such difficult questions?' I sighed. 'I was rather hoping to avoid this part of the conversation, to be honest.' I pulled out my dagger and laid it across my forearm. 'Can I trust you all not to turn me in for witchcraft?' Twas a feeble jest and none of them laughed. I sliced the flesh of my arm, wincing. Blood dripped onto the floor. Then I drew from the Tower's grove of trees and let the *sianfath* heal me, leaving the taste of cut grass and bitter regret on my tongue.

'What are you doing?' Lady Roslyn tore a strip off her chemise and reached out to bind it. 'Oh!' She retreated and crossed herself. Most of the others copied her.

'Yes,' I said, holding up my arm so they could all see. 'I'm one of the *Tuatha de Danann.* A *sidhe*. The folk of Irish lore and legend. We have the ability to draw on the Earth to heal.' There was a shuffling and the gap around me widened. Rose and Helen were the only ones who didn't move.

I gave the others a twisted smile. 'Have I hurt any of you yet? Honestly? Have I summoned any demons or stolen any children? I mean, use your intelligence, ladies. That's why I chose you. Because you're all smart women.'

Helen touched the healed cut. 'Is…is that why I can heal people? Because I'm like you?' Her blue eyes gazed at me in hope. Was there more to it than hope? I wasn't sure.

'Like me? Not quite.' I looked fondly at her. 'You're around quarter-caste, I'd say. And Rose is as well, which is why animals like her so much.' I pinned them all with a strait look. 'All of you have traces of *sidhe* blood, which is why my mother chose your families. We're still God's creatures. With souls and hearts, families and fears. You have no cause for alarm.'

Now was the moment of decision. Would they accept me? Could they set aside their ingrained fear; the fear put in them by power-hungry clergy and power-hungry men?

'Why are you tellin us this?' Eliza's eyes narrowed shrewdly. 'Makes you mighty vulnerable.'

'The truth?' I drew myself up. 'Because I hope you'll help me. I can't always be here, in London. I have other responsibilities, in Ireland.' In truth, I was tired. I needed to get away from the press of people and minds. Back to the silent green of my forest to recuperate. And I needed this to work without me. For someday, I wouldn't be here, at all.

'Tis my hope you'll come together, as a group. The Blackbirds, if you will.' I smiled at my own whimsy and an answering flicker curved Isabella's lips. Her song would go down in history. And the women would be a legacy of The Morrigan—my mother and her favourite bird-glamour. Though her crow was a harbinger of death and true blackbirds were songbirds that carolled their joy of life.

'And what would we do?' Olivia Grey asked quietly.

'Protect the queen,' I replied. 'And her heirs. And England. Train. Learn to fight so we don't lose more, like Laura, for lack of skills. Find girls to replace women who grow too old. I'll show you how to find those from the right families. How to speak the key word that calls them to your aid. But stay in the shadows. Stay invisible. Stay where men don't see you and so don't fear you. Hide til you're needed. Then strike precisely. Protect the Queen of England. That's what The Blackbirds were created for. That's what I want you to do.'

Ingaret sucked a quick breath, her eyes sparkling as she exchanged a flashing smile with Agnes.

I caught and held the gaze of each woman with as much openness and love as I could project. I could influence their minds, directly, but that would be temporary. They needed to make the decision themselves for it to stick.

Elizabeth stepped forward and laid a hand on my arm, over the top of the healed cut.

'I, for one, would be most grateful to know women like you were watching out for my children. I would provide as much support from the privy purse as I can without it raising awkward questions. I shall retire now, and leave you to consider.' She kissed me on both cheeks. 'Gramercy. If I can do anything for you, please let me know.' She swept from the room, shaking her head when Lady Roslyn would have followed.

I bowed. 'I'll be outside when you're ready.'

I stepped out into the corridor and stopped at an open window, tasting the smoke-tainted chill evening air. All evidence of the rebellion had been erased, barring a few bloodstains on the courtyard below, and the smell of smoke from the gutted tower.

No matter what the women decided, it was almost time for me to go home.

'So you told them?' Calain's deep voice cut through the silence.

'You're like a cat, you know that?' I said. 'Always sneaking up on people.' I'd felt his approach, of course, but he kept trying to surprise me, so I played along. He forgot, I was sure, how many more years I'd lived.

He chuckled and relaxed against the window frame, eyes hidden in shadow.

'Yes, I told them,' I added. 'They're thinking about it.' I listened in on the arguments inside for a moment. 'I suspect the vote may be split, but Isabella, Scientia, Agnes, and Ingaret will sway most of them. They're young and passionate.'

'And you? Will you return to Ireland to wait for their call?'

'I'll go to Ireland,' I agreed. 'But it may be in a few months' time. I have a commission for my half-brother, who's a clock-maker here in London. Then there's this…' I nodded toward the room full of women 'And if I do it right, they won't need me to come back. What of you? Staying or moving on?'

'I've given Henry my evidence against Lovell,' he said, shrugging. 'The king's offered me a place as his spy, but I'm not sure it's to my taste.'

'Yes,' I said. 'You could have told me you were working for him.'

'We both should have been more open.' His brows twitched together. 'Though it may not have made any difference. We still had no way to know the extent of Lovell's information and who his followers were. And his backers. I suspect there's a Dark *sidhe* meddling in English politics.'

'So you truly did not build those shields around his thoughts?'

'I said as much when you asked before.' Calain grimaced. 'I don't know who did that. That Dark *sidhe*, perhaps? Part of the reason I was reluctant to tell you I was the king's man. You are, after all, half Dark.'

'Ha!' I folded my arms and leaned on the wall.

He laughed and we stood in companionable silence awhile, gazing out at the new moon rising over the eastern horizon.

'You still haven't said what you'll do next,' I said.

Calain shrugged. 'I was thinking I might travel awhile. I haven't been to Italy, yet.'

I sent him a sharp look. 'It's…colourful. And the food is excellent. But…'

'But?' he prompted.

'Watch out for the Mors Ferrum.' I traced the line of an old scar on the back of my wrist. 'I'm reasonably sure they have a stronghold in Italy somewhere. Be wary.'

'Ah.' He nodded. 'I've had encounters with the Iron Death before. Unpleasant fellows. One of these days we'll have to do something about them, before they succeed in killing all the *sidhe*.'

'I'll leave protecting all of *sidhe* kind to you, I think. I have enough to do here.'

'So you do,' he murmured, glancing toward the room full of women. 'I don't think I envy you the task, either. They're a handful.'

'That's because you're a man and you think in terms of controlling women. They're not horses or dogs. They want only respect and to be heard.'

His return smile held such shadows of old pain and loss that I regretted the sharp words. I embraced him and kissed his cheek.

'You'd always be welcome in Ireland. As a friend, I mean,' I added hastily when his smile turned mischievous.

'Gramercy. I may take you up on that. But, for the moment, we'll call it fare thee well.' He kissed my cheek and vanished into the evening gloom with the ghost of a laugh.

I returned to the window and watched the stars' muted diamond-flickers for awhile.

'Amsel?' Helen's hesitant question made me turn. She gestured toward the room 'They've decided.'

'They?' I asked, fear and hope conflicting in my chest.

Her cheeks coloured and she smiled shyly. 'They'd like to be The Blackbirds. But they'll need new members to make up the twenty-four again.'

'How many?' I said, breathless. Was I willing to risk my heart again? Especially on someone who was only part-*sidhe* and wouldn't live as long as I. But I'd shut people out for so long—since Cormac's death—and it wasn't until I met Helen and these remarkable women, that I realised how much I missed companionship. The deep connection possible with another *sidhe*. The sense of being truly alive that loving someone imbued in me.

'They'll need four new people. Replacing Sarah, Laura, you…and me,' Helen said, her voice breaking. She placed trembling fingers in mine. 'I'd like to come with you, when you go. If I may?'

I held her slim hands gently. 'Are you sure? It won't be the same life you've known.' I gestured towards the vast, light-speckled darkness of London city, with its teeming madness of people.

'You forget,' she said, 'I grew up outside London. I miss the forests and the space. There are too many people here for my liking, too. It would be nice to get away…with you.' She bit her lip and stared at our entwined fingers.

I read the fear in her thoughts and voiced what she was reluctant to say. 'But you're also wondering whether you can truly trust me. Whether the Church would cast you out. Whether you would regret not having children.' I paused, images flashing in my mind. 'And you will have children, by the way.'

She started then laughed and wiped at her eyes, smearing away tears that glimmered there. 'I suppose I'll have to get used to having my thoughts read. And my future.'

I stroked a stray lock of red-gold hair from her face. 'I can teach you how to shield against it, if you prefer. But you can also learn the skill of speaking mind to mind. It saves a lot of…misunderstandings.'

Her frown deepened and I plucked the reason for it from her mind.

'I'm sorry, Helen. I couldn't tell you about my plans with Sarah Clark.'

'When Rollo told me of your disappearance…I…' She closed her lips and pushed away, scrubbing fresh tears from her cheeks. 'You could have *told* me. Warned me.'

'Helen,' I said gently, 'I had no way to reach you at the time. It happened quickly and with little time for planning. Lovell accused me of treachery. Calain could not bring himself to strike me lest the false death become real. I had no choice but to use Sarah. Lovell had to think me dead in order to believe his plans could still work. By the time I'd recovered enough to send Agnes with a message, she arrived too late. You had already visited the Broken Seld and heard from Rollo of my disappearance.'

Helen folded her arms. 'I thought you'd left. Without a farewell. Without word.'

I waited, unable to say more that would soothe her hurt, for it was fair. I had made mistakes and I could only hope she cared enough to forgive me. Her thoughts were tangled and bubbling with quick, sharp emotions, the formless ache of loss, and fears of hurt. I resisted the urge to influence her. That was no way to earn trust.

But I could speak to her, directly. *I cannot lie to you thus, Helen,* I said. *What would you know? Try it yourself, if you don't believe me.*

She started. *I…I hardly know what to say.*

Tell me how you feel about me, I replied, steeling myself. *Then you'll know the impossibility of untruths. I've made mistakes. I'm afraid of being hurt; of losing you as I lost Cormac. But…* I sucked a slow breath. *I'm willing to try.*

Helen stayed silent, searching my face for something, I knew not what. Her thoughts were too tumultuous to read what bothered her.

Finally, she threw her shoulders back. 'I can't be your Cormac, and you aren't my John. But I don't want you to be. Perhaps, though, we can find comfort in each other's company? I'm willing to try, too.'

I laughed aloud, wrapped my arms around her waist and swung her into the air. Then I looked fondly at her and wondered how I'd ever thought her plain.

'I'd like that.' I jerked my chin at the room behind her. 'Let's go get these Blackbirds started so we can go home.'

She kissed me, tentatively, sweetly, then tucked her hand into mine and smiled.

And my heart sang.

The End

If you enjoyed this novel, *please* go and leave a review.
Reviews help other people find great books.
Share the love!

For more in the Ruadhan Sidhe novels, check out *Shadows Wake, Shadows Bane,* and *Shadows Fate.*
More will be forthcoming.

Story Extras

Contents/story titles.

The story titles are based on the old nursery rhyme 'Four and Twenty Blackbirds'. But a couple of lines toward the end of it have been tweaked to fit the stories. The original reads

"The maid was in the garden, hanging out the clothes, along came a little bird, and pecked off her nose."

(or sometimes a blackbird does the deed.) But that didn't suit the premise of the women being supportive and helping each other, so I altered those lines.

The final story titles from 18 through to 24 are from the last four lines of Edgar Allen Poe's poem *"The Raven"*. Which suited the later stories as they got darker, and the underlying theme of war and the raven being seen as a harbinger of war and doom.

London Map.

This is based on the map of 1520 London (ISBN 978-0-9934698-3-1) produced by the London Topographical Society and the British Historic Towns Atlas. The cartographer, Giles Darkes, was kind enough to supply a street-outline base map of London city, itself. I then added the Southbank streets and the individual buildings named in the various stories. Plus the inset of Isledon.

When I was researching the stories, it came to light that the map was actually incorrect in two minor instances – the names of two of the wall-towers for the Tower of London were names given to them after 1520. I was able to confirm that with the Tower of London armouries librarian, Bridget Clifford, and passed the information on to Giles Darkes, who intended to update the next release of the map to reflect the correction.

Story notes.
#1
Isledon = Islington

Gittern = medieval guitar

Pottage = a thick soup made from boiling grains, vegetables and meat (if available)

Sidhe/Tuatha de Danann = Irish faery folk/gods of lore

Mór-Ríoghain or the Morrigu = Irish goddess of war and the fate of battles.

Lord Francis Lovell (Viscount Lovell). Lovell escaped the 1485 battle between Richard and Henry and went to Yorkshire to try and organise a revolt. Lovell and the Stafford brothers first conspired against Henry in early 1486. Humphrey and Thomas were captured in May 1846 and Humphrey was executed. Thomas was pardoned. Lovell disappeared and no more records exist of his whereabouts.

Fellowship of Minstrels = medieval name for the guild for Minstrels and musicians. Became the Worshipful Company of Musicians in 1500.

Tithings group and the hue-and-cry = the Anglo-Saxon tradition of community policing/justice meant everyone had to be part of a 10-man tithings group. If called on to raise the hue-and-cry, they had to chase after criminals. It was largely superceded after about 1450 by justices of the peace and constables, but it sounded great so I included it. And one assumes that old habits die hard in rural areas, so it's possible it hung on for years.

A Reeve = after the Norman conquest, a reeve was a man appointed as manager of a manor and overseer of the peasants working for the manor.

#2

Dysentery = The flux

Ergotism/St Anthony's Fire = disease caused by mould infections usually in rye grains. Causes convulsions, loss of blood circulation/gangrene, hallucinations, and death. There are two types, (one causes convulsions, the other causes gangrene) and I have joined both sets of symptoms together into one disease to make it worse.

#3

The plant Queen Anne's lace (aka Bishop's lace, wild carrot, or bird's nest) *Daucus Carota* is used as a contraception and abortifacient for centuries

Hunting of larger animals was not permitted except by nobility and royalty. Domestic pigs were allowed to forage in the royal forests.

Women often used absorbent mosses for menstruation.

Edward, 17th Earl of Warwick, was the last male of the York line. He was 11years old and was imprisoned in the Tower of London by Henry VII.

#4

Churchbells times in September.
Lauds (Dawn): 5am
Prime: 6am
Terce: 8:30am
Sext: 12:30pm
Nones: 2:30pm
Vespers: 5:00pm
Sunset: 6:00pm

Compline: 7:30pm
Matins: Midnight

Poesy ring was a gift given to show love and usually had an inscription engraved on it. Popular from the 15th to 17th centuries

A manchet was a high-quality wheat bread available only to the wealthy. Small and circular, about the size to fit in the hand.

#5

Sweating sickness = possibly influenza. Swept through London in 1485 shortly after Henry taking the throne. Thousands died quickly and many thought it was God's retribution against Henry's taking the throne from Richard.

#6

A "Seld" was a covered marketplace. No idea why it was called the "Broken Seld". It was a real tavern, though.

William Caxton brought the first printing press to England in 1476. The first printed book on it was Chaucer's Canterbury Tales. Sir Thomas Malory's *Le Morte d'Arthur* was printed in 1485

Shawm – a wind/reed instrument. An early oboe.

Prince Arthur was actually born at St Swithun's Priory, Winchester on September 19th 1486 sometime around midnight. Or possibly early on the 20th.

#7

Brothels were illegal in London, but the south bank of the Thames was outside London's boundaries, so most were situated there – along with many bath houses and taverns. The Bishop of Winchester made such good money off rents, fines and tithes from these businesses that they were tolerated.

The bath-houses were finally closed down in the mid 1500's when syphilis arrived in the UK and spread rapidly through the prostitution network.

The Clink was a prison on the south bank for both men and women. On the grounds of Winchester Palace.

There were laws in place about what a prostitute could and couldn't wear (aprons being deemed for respectable women, and material over a certain value could only be worn by noblewomen).

The Fleur de Lys was a real bawd-house or tavern, as was the Crossed Keys. The Cygnet was not.

Prostitutes were meant to rent a room, rather than working on the streets. The owners of bawd-houses who rented rooms to the girls were not allowed to sell other goods or services to the customers (for fear of price-gouging). Prostitutes were not meant to work when pregnant or sick. Women were not allowed to own bawd-houses.

It took many years for Arabic numerals to completely replace Latin ones in bookkeeping and businesses.

Marriage for common folk often took place the old way – sharing of a hearth and a bed. Or on the front stoop of a church. A marriage was considered legal if both people agreed they were married. By the late 1400s this was changing and the church was insisting on more formal exchanges of vows and recording of marriages.

George Plantagenet was a real historical figure. Eliza Parry was not.

The Bishop of Winchester was a real historical figure.

#8

Lady Roslyn Stanley is not a real historical figure.

The Lady's Bower was a room set aside for the lady of grand

houses.

Francis Lovell didn't lose his lands & titles to Thomas Stanley until 1486, when he attempted outright rebellion against Henry VII.

Margaret Beaufort—first the Countess of Richmond, then later the Countess of Derby—was Henry VII's mother. She was 13 when he was born and it was a difficult birth. He was her only child. The proper age for marriage was meant to be 14 for girls.

Yes, it's true: Henry VII preferred to be addressed as 'Your Grace' rather than 'Your Majesty.'

John De Vere, 13th Earl of Oxford, was actually invited to be Arthur's godfather. But he was late to the ceremony, so Derby had to stand in for him.

Garderobe – toilet. Usually set into the wall of a castle, with a straight drop down into a moat or place that servants would clean out.

The Queen's House wasn't actually built until Henry VIII's time, but I couldn't find a reference to where the queen's chambers were in 1486. One assumes, though, that she had chambers or a tower set aside for her personal use, as did the king.

#10

Vellum = calfskin or lambskin used for writing on instead of paper. Higher quality. The best quality was made from the skin of unborn calves or stillborn calves/lambs.

Parchment = paper substitute – made from untanned animal skin, primarily sheep, or goats, or cow – scraped thin and dried under tension to form flat sheets. Usually thicker and less smooth or polished than vellum.

Sand for drying ink was a type of clay that absorbs liquid ink to quickly dry the writing.

#13

Lord Morley (mentioned in passing) is a real historical figure whose arms had a black leopard on them.

Bishop Kempe was a real historical figure. The persecution of Jews in England was real, as well. They were banished in 1290 by Edward I and any remaining had to hide their culture to survive. The edict expelling them was overturned by Cromwell in 1657

I was unable to find details about which tower in the Tower of London functioned as young Edward Plantagenet's prison.

The modern 1520 map mentioned earlier shows the northwestern Tower in the Tower of London named "Devereaux" tower. But it was not called this until Robert Devereaux, Earl of Essex, was imprisoned there in 1601. Before that, it was "Robin-the-Devil's Tower" (referring to William The Conquerer's father, Robert "le Diable".) The SW tower shown on the modern 1520 map as Develin Tower was, in 1520, called "Tower leading to the Iron Gate".

#14

Verjuice – the juice of green/unripe grapes. Good for getting stains out of silk, apparently. Who knew? Go ahead. Try it at home. Maybe not on your best dress, though. Tell me if it works.

#15

Prince Arthur was actually baptised on September 24th at the Winchester Cathedral. He was named after King Arthur.

#17

Baron John Cheyne is a real historical figure – bodyguard to Henry VII. His son, James, is fictional.

Francis Lovell was orphaned at about the age of 8 and, in 1471 was made ward of the Duke of Suffolk.

Secret passages ran from the Robin-The-Devil's tower (now known as Devereaux Tower) to the Chapel of St Peter ad Vincula, and to the Beauchamp Tower.

#18

Nicola Willoughby is the fictional daughter of a real historical figure, Sir Christopher Willoughby, 10th Baron Willoughby de Eresby and Margaret Jenney. Their daughters Katherine and Margaret are real, but I've fudged all their ages slightly to make the whole family older than they really would have been at that time. Do you know how many families I trawled through in researching to find one I could use? I got sick of looking! Sir Christopher really was at the christening, though.

Sir Edward Sutton, 2nd Baron Dudley, was a real person. He married Cecily Willoughby, from a different branch of the Willoughby family.

In reality, Nicola would have had no legal right to sign away her dowry. Women were treated as assets and had no power over their dowries. But it's a nice fiction, so I'm keeping it.

#19

A trencher was a wooden plate – replacing the original term which described a slab or flat loaf of bread used as a plate.

#20

Lucerna pedibus meis verbum tuum, et lumen semitis meis = Psalm 119 vs 105 = Your word is a lamp to my feet and a light to my paths. (Why you need a lamp to your feet I have no idea).

#21

Yes, flour dust will explode in a naked flame. Go watch some Youtube videos. Don't try it at home.

Yes, crossbows were quite common by the 15th century. Yes, this one is small enough to cock one-handed. Meant for close-range shooting.

Caltrops are small pointy bits of metal – good for disabling horses or men by sticking into their feet.

London Bridge was jam-packed with shops and houses. Their indoor garderobes opened straight down into the Thames, making boating beneath the bridge somewhat of a hazard.

A more common personal dagger at the time was the rondel – thought to be the ancestor of the stiletto – but I figured most readers would know what a stiletto was more readily than a rondel. Personally, I like the rondel better. For some strange reason, they are illegal here in Australia.

#22

There is growing evidence that women created illuminated manuscripts, too.

The Poor Clares had a history of taking in noble women and of being supported by the Crown, which is why I chose them.

Philippa Bolingbroke is fictional. As is Eliza Parry. But Henry Bolingbroke (Henry VI), and Philippa's husband, Edward Plantagenet (Edward IV) were real. As was Eliza's husband, George Plantagenet.

#23

Purple, or gold silks were reserved for royalty. Cloth-of-gold was reserved for nobility. Expensive fabrics were, by law, only allowed to be worn by upper classes. Silk, satin, velvet, brocade, etc. What material you could wear was determined by your income and the value of the material.

A specific type of fine, woolen cloth dyed with a rare red dye was called escarlates. This particular red (aka kermes, or vermillion) made from the dried eggs of Mediterranean scale-insects. All colours that contained reds derived from this were therefore expensive – brown, perse (a blue-grey, or ash-purple), murrey (mulberry), sanguine (bluish-red). Escarlates clothes were often first dyed with blue-woad (or indigo) then redyed after fulling with the kermes/vermillion to produce the various shades. Other cloths (silk etc) dyed with vermillion/kermes were not called escarlates, but the term came to be associated with the red we call scarlet.

Hand guns / handgonne were very new at this point, and quite rare in England. Also extremely unreliable, difficult to keep lit, difficult to shoot, highly inaccurate. But such a fun addition to the story! The first matchlock hand guns appeared in the 1400s.

#24

Yes, eyeglasses were quite common.

Entry to the White Tower was, at this time, through a first-storey door, reached by external, wooden stairs – a defensive design.

Laura Kennet calls the handgonnes 'hand cannons' but the terms appeared to be fairly interchangeable for quite awhile.

END

If you enjoyed this story, please go leave a review? Thanks.

Other books by Aiki Flinthart

Discover other titles by Aiki Flinthart at: www.aikiflinthart.com
Or
The 80AD series (YA Adventure/Fantasy)
80AD Book 1: *The Jewel of Asgard*
80AD Book 2: *The Hammer of Thor*
80AD Book 3: *The Tekhen of Anuket*
80AD Book 4: *The Sudarshana*
80AD Book 5: *The Yu Dragon*

The Ruadhán *Sidhe* novels (YA Urban fantasy)
Shadows Wake (Bk1)
Shadows Bane (Bk2)
Shadows Fate (Bk 3)
Healing Heather (#4—publication 2020)

The Kalima Chronicles (YA Adventure/Fantasy)
IRON—Book One
FIRE—Book Two
STEEL—Book Three

Other Novels
Sold! (Contemporary Romance/Adventure)

Short Story Anthologies
Return
Like a Woman
Elemental

Connect with me on Facebook
Twitter: @aikiflinthart
Instagram: Aikiflinthart

Lightning Source UK Ltd.
Milton Keynes UK
UKHW041342011219
354529UK00012B/265/P